ALSO BY E.E. HO

THE WORLD OF THE GATEWAY

The Gateway Trilogy (Series 1)
Spirit Legacy: Book 1 of The Gateway Trilogy
Spirit Prophecy: Book 2 of The Gateway Trilogy
Spirit Ascendancy: Book 3 of The Gateway Trilogy

The Gateway Trackers (Series 2)
Whispers of the Walker: The Gateway Trackers Book 1
Plague of the Shattered: The Gateway Trackers Book 2
Awakening of the Seer: The Gateway Trackers Book 3
Portraits of the Forsaken: The Gateway Trackers Book 4
Heart of the Rebellion: The Gateway Trackers Book 5
Soul of the Sentinel: The Gateway Trackers Book 6
Gift of the Darkness: The Gateway Trackers Book 7

HEART OF THE REBELLION

HEART OF THE REBELLION

REBELLION

The Gateway Trackers Book 5

E.E. HOLMES

Lily Faire Publishing

Lily Faire Publishing
Townsend, MA

www.lilyfairepublishing.com

ISBN 978-0-9984762-7-8 (Print edition)

ISBN 978-0-9984762-9-2 (Barnes & Noble print edition)

ISBN 978-0-9984762-8-5 (Digital edition)

Cover design by James T. Egan of Bookfly Design LLC
Author photography by Cydney Scott Photography

For my "little" brother Eric, whose heart has always been the biggest.

i carry your heart with me(i carry it in

my heart)i am never without it(anywhere

i go you go,my dear;and whatever is done

by only me is your doing,my darling)

                    i fear

no fate(for you are my fate,my sweet)i want

no world(for beautiful you are my world,my true)

and it's you are whatever a moon has always meant

and whatever a sun will always sing is you

here is the deepest secret nobody knows

(here is the root of the root and the bud of the bud

and the sky of the sky of a tree called life;which grows

higher than soul can hope or mind can hide)

and this is the wonder that's keeping the stars apart

i carry your heart(i carry it in my heart)

-e.e. cummings

CONTENTS

SLEEPWALKING

"J ESS, DON'T MOVE and don't panic!"

My twin sister Hannah's voice reached through to me, prodding the fog of sleep so that it did not lift so much as swirl and part and swirl again.

"Jess? Can you hear me?"

"Mm-hmm," I tried to tell her, but I couldn't be sure if the response had traveled the distance from my head to my mouth. That distance felt so, so very long—a journey hardly worth taking when I could just stay comfortably asleep.

Wait a second, though. Was I comfortable?

Her voice had not yet woken me, but my senses were rousing, and what I felt wasn't comfortable at all. A sharp, biting wind made me shiver. A dampness clung to my hair. The inside of my nose tingled with night air and the mineral chill of stone. And my muscles were so taut and tense I felt as though I were being stretched on a rack.

"What the hell?" I asked myself. Again, the words lost motivation halfway to my lips and echoed inside my head instead—a head that was clearing by the second.

"Jess, whatever you do, do not move," came Hannah's voice again, and though she was working to keep it calm, there was a bite of panic in the words—a tinge of something that tasted like fear.

"Why?" I asked, and this time I heard my own voice aloud, a sort of slurred and sleepy murmur.

"Do you trust me?" she replied.

"'Course I do," I muttered.

"Then *do not move*. Just breathe."

"What...?" But the question died before I could fully formulate it. I was distracted. I had just felt something under my right hand. It was rough, jagged, and cool to the touch—stone. The moment I realized what it was, I felt it beneath my left hand, too, and—even more oddly still—pressed against my chest and the flesh of my cheek. My breath began to quicken as the cogs and wheels in my head squeaked and juddered against each other.

Another breeze lifted my hair. I was outside. The front of my body was pressed against stone. I became aware that I was upright, and that the full weight of my body was resting on my feet.

I was standing. I was outside and I was standing up and yet I was asleep.

This realization sent a jolt of electric terror zinging through my veins, waking every muscle and sense to its most heightened state. My eyes, which had been on the verge of fluttering open, now glued themselves shut in fear.

"Hannah?" The sharp note of panic was in my voice now, and Hannah heard it. When she spoke, it was with the air of an animal that was treading carefully because it had scented danger.

"Jess, listen to me, okay? Hold on to what's in front of you with your hands. Find a way to grasp on, something to steady yourself, okay? And don't move your feet."

What the fuck, what the fuck, what the fuck, became the refrain inside my head as I clawed with my fingers, trying to find a handhold. I dug the fingers of my left hand into a jagged crack in the stone and tried to grab a small outcropping of rock with my right. As I did so, I realized that I had something clutched tightly in my right hand. Without looking at it, I knew it was a writing implement—maybe a pencil? No, chalk. I fumbled it between my shaking fingers, before losing my grip on it. It hit the stone below me with a hollow snap.

I understood in that moment *what* I had been doing in my sleep, but still couldn't fathom *where* I had been doing it.

"Did you find something to hold on to? Are you secure?"

"I... yeah, I think so." I pulled first with one hand, and then the other. Both felt steady.

"Okay, now take a deep breath and open your eyes, but do not move your feet," Hannah instructed calmly.

My eyelids did not want to cooperate, but I forced them open and let out a gasp that echoed into the cold night.

I was staring out over the darkened grounds of Fairhaven from a dizzying height with my cheek pressed against a stone wall—the outer wall of the castle. Beneath my feet, a narrow ledge of rock was all that separated me from a long and deadly drop to the

2

lawns below. I was standing only a few feet from the curve of the North Tower, where the ledge disappeared smoothly into the carved stone base of a tall, arched window. No lights shone from the room behind the leaded glass. On the stretch of stone wall between myself and the tower was the beginning of a drawing—the outline of a castle and the suggestion of figures upon its battlements, already dissolving and dripping down the stones in cloudy rivulets as the first raindrops began to pelt against it.

Slowly, I turned my head, pressing my face into the wall, breathing in the damp, natural scent of the stone as it brushed against my nose before twisting my neck and resting my other cheek against it.

My eyes found Hannah, some twenty feet away, leaning her torso out of our open window. Tendrils of her long, dark hair floated around her face as though she were floating in water. Her eyes were wide with terror, staring out of her pale, pointed face like mirrors reflecting my own fear back at me.

Gently, almost tenderly, she extended her arm out into the starlit space between us and crooked her slender fingers at me. "Move slowly back toward me, now. That's it. Just kind of shuffle your feet across a little at a time."

I stared back at her, utterly unable to move. "I can't."

"You can. You got all the way out there without falling, and you can get all the way back."

"Hannah, how the hell did I—"

"I don't know. It doesn't matter. All that matters right now is getting you back inside safely, all right?"

"Yeah. Yeah, okay," I squeaked. "But, it's so dark, Hannah. I can barely see where I'm putting my feet. How am I supposed to—?"

From behind Hannah, a second face peeked out of the window, his features full of the same shock and terror that was currently flooding me.

"What in the actual...?" Milo Chang mumbled weakly. In the darkness, his form gave off a dull glow, like the gentlest, most human of lanterns.

Hannah just shook her head and he understood at once. This was not the time for questions.

"Milo, go out there and help her. Talk her through it," Hannah urged him.

Milo looked horrified at the very thought. "I... okay. But what if

I... yeah, of course." He shook off his own misgivings with a violent toss of his hair and flew out the window at once.

Oh, sure, getting on and off castle ledges was a piece of cake when you were already dead.

"Show-off," I muttered as he floated up behind me, giving me the sensation of standing with my back to an open freezer.

Milo tried to laugh in response, but the sound that escaped him was more of a hysterical squeak. "You know, if you wanted to take a walk in the night air, I hear the ground floor is really good for that sort of thing."

"I'll keep that in mind next time," I said, gritting my teeth. My fingers were starting to cramp. I tried to loosen them, but survival instinct kept them locked stubbornly in place.

Milo drifted down toward my feet, where he could get a better view of the ledge I was perched so precariously on.

"Okay," he said. "Just start sliding your feet across. There are a couple of gaps and one part that's kind of narrow, but I'll guide you across them, okay?"

"Yeah, okay," I whispered, a gust of wind lifting the words right out of my mouth and whisking them away into the sky.

For what felt like an eternity, I slid first one foot and then the other, inch by inch, across the ledge. Each time I found a new footing, I would then have to slide my hands across and find a new handhold. Some stretches of wall were so smooth that there was nothing to grip, and I simply had to spread my fingers wide and pray for balance. Milo calmly intoned his instructions. "Shift onto your toes, this bit is cracked. Pick up your right foot and shift it over about six inches to avoid the gap. A little further. Okay, now you can put it down. Good, it widens for the next few feet, so you can put your heels down."

All the while, Hannah's hand reached for me, and I turned to look at it after each movement, ensuring myself that I was getting closer, watching that distance between us shrink and shrink until at last her fingers closed around my arm just above the elbow.

"Just grab the top of the window casement. That's good. There's a ledge you can grab just underneath on the inside. Feel it?" She guided my hands as Milo guided my feet and, at long last, I collapsed into a shuddering heap onto the floor of our room.

Hannah slammed the window shut and bolted the lock upon it,

4

as though I were in danger of being yanked back through it by the malevolent hands of the night.

The three of us sat on the floor for a long time, slowly recovering from the grip of fear, prying it away from ourselves finger by icy finger, until our breathing quieted and our panicked thoughts settled into our own heads rather than thrumming unsettlingly through our shared psychic connection. That was one of the biggest challenges of being Bound to a Spirit Guide; our heads became shared spaces for each other's strongest emotions.

Finally, I sat up. "Well," I said, "that was new."

Hannah gave a shaky laugh. "You could say that, yes."

I looked over at her. Her eyes were still bright with unshed tears. "What happened?"

Hannah shrugged helplessly. "The breeze woke me up. I saw your bed empty and the window open. At first I thought..." She shuddered but did not complete the thought.

I swallowed back the memory of one of the worst nights of my life—the night I walked into our mother's room to find the window open and the curtains askew, and there below on the pavement...

Nope. Close the mental door on that one, Jess. You've got enough shit to deal with at the moment without falling headfirst down *that* rabbit hole. I refocused on Hannah, who was still talking.

"Then I looked over and saw you on the ledge with the chalk," Hannah said. "I didn't know what to do. I was afraid to wake you and I was afraid not to."

I let out a low whistle. "Yeah, that could have gone badly either way."

"I was still trying to decide what to do when the rain started and you just sort of... stopped drawing. I thought you might be coming out of it, so I started calling for you."

I nodded. "Well, I'm persistent, I'll give myself that."

Hannah dropped her head into her hand and rubbed at her temples in a weary sort of way. "I hoped... if we just locked the door..."

But doors did not stop me, it would seem. Nothing would stop this prophecy when it worked its way down to my fingertips.

It was only a few months ago that I had discovered I was a Seer, and the denial had been bone-deep. I mean, let's be honest, didn't I have enough to deal with? I was a Durupinen, which meant it was my job to guide trapped spirits between the worlds of the living and the dead. I was a Muse, which meant that spirits often used me as their own personal sketch artist when they wanted to communicate. I was a Walker, which enabled me to leave my body behind and roam the world in spirit form—a talent I had no intention of using again. And now, I was a Seer.

I couldn't decide whether the Universe was trying to tell me it loved me or it hated me, but I was more than okay with spreading the wealth around a bit. Four gifts were great on your birthday, but four gifts tying you to the spirit world was decidedly less fun.

Seeing was perhaps the least desirable gift of them all. I had come to terms with the others. In fact, I personally thought I should be congratulated for how little I whined about them. In the past few years, I had even begun to see that value in what I was able to do—the unique ways I was able to help people at a time when they were beyond other people's help. But Seeing? Seeing was nothing but trouble and I knew that all too well.

There were no two people in the history of the Durupinen who knew better the destructive power of a prophecy than Hannah and me. We had been the subject of a centuries-old prophecy that had torn apart our family, made us outcasts, and had nearly destroyed the entire spirit world. We had barely survived it, and though we had since rebuilt lives for ourselves, it was safe to say that neither of us wanted to see or hear the word "prophecy" ever again.

Then, less than a year ago, I made a prophetic drawing. And then another. I did not realize what they were at first, but my mentor Fiona, another Muse and artist, had brought me to terms with the unpleasant reality of my gift—a gift that was turning out to be far more curse than blessing. And that curse was currently on display on the side of the castle for the entire world to see.

"What are we going to do about it?" I asked, pointing to the window. "The drawing? We can't just leave it out there. Someone will see it! I'm going to have to go back out there and—"

"It's already gone," Milo assured me. "The rain took care of that for us."

I sighed. "Good. That's good." I'd once made a drawing from a creative combination of ash and my own blood while in a trance. At least I was getting better at choosing less painful media, but my choice of canvas still left something to be desired.

"So, now what?" I asked. "The locked door didn't help."

"No," Hannah agreed. "I might even argue the locked door made it worse. The hallway was exposed, but at least there was no risk of falling to your death."

Only two nights ago, Hannah had found me in the corridor outside our room, attempting to scrawl another iteration of the same prophetic image onto the wall. Luckily, I had grabbed a pastel instead of something more permanent, and a bucket of water and a sponge stolen from a supply closet had removed most of the evidence of my artwork. An tastefully arranged potted plant on a plinth had concealed the rest.

Our hope had been that, if Hannah locked the door from the inside and hid the key from me, we could at least contain my sleepwalking to the confines of our own room, and therefore have a better chance of hiding the evidence from the rest of the Durupinen in the castle.

It was now apparent that plan sucked.

"Well, the first thing we do is lock the windows," Hannah said firmly. "Although, I suppose you might just break them if you can't get them open."

"What about hiding all the pencils and art supplies?" Milo suggested. "I mean, if she doesn't have anything to draw with—"

I was already shaking my head. "If I don't have art supplies, I'll invent them, and I think we can all agree that my creativity in that regard is both impressive and dangerous."

"Oh, yeah. Right," Milo mumbled.

"I don't think we've got any choice," I said grimly. "I think you're going to have to start tying me to the bed."

Hannah looked horrified. "Jess, there must be another—"

"Hannah, I just imitated a circus high wire performer in my sleep!" I cried. "I think a little bit of rope is the least of my problems!"

Hannah didn't reply, but her face fell into resigned lines of misery.

"When is Fiona going to be back?" Milo asked, with a tinge of desperation in his voice.

"She told me the whole process would take five days," I told him.

I needed Fiona now more than ever. The compulsion to produce the drawings was getting worse by the day, and the Seer in me no longer seemed satisfied just to record the drawings on paper. It seemed bound and determined to bring this newest prophecy not just to the page, but to the eyes and attention of the entire castle.

And I could not let that happen. Not yet. Not until I understood what it meant.

No one at the castle except for Hannah, Milo, and Fiona knew that I was a Seer, and we had hidden the knowledge for good reason. Since the first Seers had recorded their predictions, they had been met with intense mistrust, scrutiny, and even outright attack. It was natural, I knew, to be afraid of the unknown, but somehow it seemed that a glimpse into the future—a glimpse without context or guarantees—inspired a kind of fear that wreaked havoc and destroyed lives. And I could not afford to let Durupinen fear cloud this prophecy. It was too important. There was too much at stake.

I would not risk him. I could not risk him.

There was another person who knew I was a Seer. Finn Carey had once been my Caomhnóir, the guardian who protected our clan's Gateway. Fiercely adversarial at first, our relationship had crossed a forbidden line when we had fallen in love with each other. But last year, our relationship had been discovered, and Finn had been sent away to the remote Isle of Skye, to guard the *príosún* there, and I had been left to pick up the shattered remains of my life without him.

But then, just a few weeks ago, I had seen Finn for a brief and heart-wrenching few minutes, during which he revealed to me that something strange was happening at the *príosún*. The Caomhnóir there were not following orders—disappearing from shifts, meeting secretly, and even their superiors seemed to be covering for their bizarre behavior. Finn had begged me to pass along this information to the Caomhnóir of Fairhaven, but a Necromancer plot had resulted in the murder of the one ally who might have been able to relay that message.

And now I was drawing that *príosún* over and over again, an army of men and spirits swarming its battlements...

"We're going to have to find a new place to hide these," Hannah said, rising and crossing the room to open the closet door. A small mountain of scrolls lay piled inside. Soon there would be no more room for any more of them amongst the clothes and suitcases. "Unless you think... I mean, I know you don't want to destroy them, and I understand why, but..."

"No," I said sharply. "No. We can't burn them. What if one of them has a clue? What if I'm missing something?"

8

"But they're all the same," Hannah said gently. "You've examined them a hundred—"

Something in my expression silenced her. She closed the closet door again.

"I just need Fiona to come back," I said, more to convince myself than anyone else. "She'll know what to do next."

"You also need to get some sleep," Milo said. "The kind that doesn't include feats of death-defying skill."

I sighed, feeling all my defiance drain away, leaving nothing but the empty suck of exhaustion in its absence.

"I know."

"But how can we go back to sleep without solving this problem?" Hannah said, twisting her fingers together in a characteristic nervous gesture. "How do we know she won't just do it all over again?"

"You're forgetting something rather important," Milo told her.

"What? What am I forgetting?"

"Ghosts don't need beauty sleep, sweetness. We are perpetually fabulous," he said. "And that means, I'm on the night shift, okay? We don't need to resort to clapping Jess in irons like an old-timey criminal. It's just going to be part of my job description from now on to watch her while she sleeps."

"Well, that sounds fascinating and not at all stalker-ish," I grumbled.

"I'd much rather watch you drool and snore for a few hours than scrape you off the pavement," Milo snapped. "I'm the Spirit Guide. This is my guidance. Heed my wisdom."

I gave him a grudging smile. "Thanks, Milo."

"No problem," he replied, then pointed imperiously in the direction of my bed. "Now both of you go back to dreamland so I can test out my creepy new hobby."

I laid back down in my bed, but I didn't think sleep would find me so easily now. Sleep and fear are uneasy bedfellows. My thoughts drifted, as they always did when they were untethered by distraction, to Finn.

"I'm trying, Finn," I whispered into the darkness. "I'm trying to figure this out. I'm going to get you out of there."

I imagined the words like balloons, floating up into the air and carried on the breeze to him—ignoring the sounds of the storm that was now whipping that breeze into a gale and lashing the rain against the windows.

Storms pass, I told myself. Storms pass, and so will this.

2

INTERPRETATIONS

DESPITE THE FEAR, despite the aching in my muscles from clinging like a mountaineer to the side of the castle, despite Milo's eyes boring into the back of my head as he watched me, sleep claimed me at last. I had hoped it would be dreamless, so that I might reclaim half a decent night's sleep, but of course, I wasn't that lucky. Instead, my exhausted brain chose to replay, in its entirety, my last meeting with Fiona. It was amazing how my mind clung so tightly to the details, replayed them so vividly, since at the time, I was so panicked that I barely knew what was happening even as I lived it.

It played like a movie on the insides of my eyelids. Fiona closed the door behind me and began shuffling around the room, turning on lamps and lighting misshapen stumps of candles. I stood and watched her, violently shaking from head to foot, the first drawing of the prophecy still draped around my shoulders like a cape on the world's most dysfunctional superhero.

Emotionally Crippled Sleep-Artist Girl, to the rescue!

When she had created enough light to see by, Fiona beckoned me over to her desk, which she cleared with a single, violent sweep of her hand. Papers, molds, paint cans, and containers of drawing implements flew across the room and disappeared into the general art-detritus that carpeted the stone floors. Then she reached out a hand for the drawing, snapping at me impatiently when I didn't move quickly enough.

I stumbled forward, pulling the thing from my shoulders and handing it to her. She took hold of it carefully, delicately pinching the corners between the very tips of her fingers and draping it over the surface of her desk, smoothing out wrinkles and picking bits of lint from its surface. She gazed down at it for a long moment, entranced, and then she looked up at me.

"Tell me how you—Jess!"

She started forward, reaching me just before I hit the ground. I hadn't even realized I was falling before she caught me. I had the strange sensation that I was under water, or else floating in space.

"Jess! Are you all right?" Fiona cried. Her face, as it looked down at me, was alive with fear.

"I... I don't know." I blinked. Her face swam out of focus and back again. "I suddenly feel so... am I crying?"

To my great surprise, my face was wet with tears, and my breath was hitching and catching over sobs that seemed to be issuing from me of their own accord.

"Yes, you're crying. You're in shock, no doubt," Fiona muttered. She threw my arm around her shoulder and swung me up from the ground with a grunt. Then she carried me across the room and deposited me on her bed.

"Don't move. Stay right there. Take some nice deep breaths. I'm going to make you a cuppa." She threw several heavy blankets over me and scurried off across the room to a table near the window, where she kept a hot plate and a kettle.

I couldn't have gotten up if I'd wanted to. I lay there under her quilts, shuddering with sobs that seemed to be attacking me from the outside rather than welling up from inside of me. I tried to catch my breath, but it felt like a new sob was always waiting to force its way out every time I tried to expand my lungs. I clenched my teeth, feeling as though I might just shake apart.

Fiona returned to my side, a chipped mug of tea in one hand and a warm, wet tea towel in the other. Kicking off her slippers, she clambered onto the bed behind me and sat with her back against the wall. She eased me up into a seated position in front of her and laid me back against her, my head against her shoulder, my back against her chest. Then she wrapped her legs around my hips, tucking all the blankets tightly around me, like a cocoon.

"Now, you just lay your head back. That's right," Fiona said, in as gentle a tone as I'd ever heard her muster. "Watch that arm now."

"I... I don't think my arm's broken anymore," I told her.

"What? But... the cast..."

"I know it sounds insane, but I can feel it in there. The drawing... it did something to my arm. It feels normal. It's the *only* thing that feels normal." My voice rose to a hysterical pitch.

Fiona pressed the warm towel to my forehead. "No more talk of arms for the moment. Take a sip of this, now, just nice and slowly. That's right, easy does it."

I slurped from the cup as she held it up to my lips. The hot tea trickled down my chin and onto my shirt, now drenched and cold with sweat. Then I leaned back against her chest. She smelled like paint and Castile soap. I tried to match the rhythm of her breathing. Long inhale, slow exhale. I began to count the beats of her heart against my shoulder blade. Gradually, my own breaths grew quieter. The tears that traced each other's tracks down my face began to slow, and then dried up altogether. The dizziness dissipated, and with it, the feeling that the walls were closing in around me. Every few seconds, Fiona pressed the tea cup to my lips again, and I would gratefully take another sip.

"There now," Fiona said quietly, when the last of the tea had disappeared from the cup. "I'm sorry. I was so caught up in your drawing that I neglected to notice that you were about to fall apart right in front of me. A mentor should be more on top of things like that, but we all know I'm utter shite at the mentor thing."

"Y-you're not sh-shite." I forced the words through my chattering teeth, which still sounded like a cartoon skeleton even though my whole body felt warm now.

"A compliment if ever I've heard one," Fiona said dryly. "Now, tell me what happened, if you think you can manage it."

I took a long, slow breath, and noted with relief that my lungs had decided to start accepting oxygen again. "I was visiting with Flavia—you know, the Traveler who—"

"I know who she is," Fiona interrupted. "Go on."

"Mrs. Mistlemoore and the Scribes think that they've been able to lift the Castings on her. She said there are hopeful signs that the effects are reversing—or at least, improving. Anyway, I sat down beside her, and it seemed like she was asleep. Much calmer and more relaxed than she was before, but not conscious. And then I started talking to her—you know, just to let her know that I was there and that everything was going to be okay. And then I reached down and took her hand and she... she woke up," I finished lamely, at a complete loss to describe what it was she had actually done.

"Woke up how?" Fiona asked in a tone that suggested she knew just how inadequate my words had been. "Opened her eyes? Talked to you?"

"Yeah, but... it was terrifying. She grabbed my hand so tightly she bruised it." I showed Fiona the bruises on my hand, as well as the puncture marks from Flavia's fingernails. "And she pulled me toward her with such force—there's no way she had that kind of strength in her, not after everything her body has been through. And then her eyes opened and..." I shuddered.

"Do her eyes still look the same as before?" Fiona asked.

"No," I replied. "The silvery color is definitely going away, but they aren't back to normal yet."

"Did she speak?"

"No. She didn't need to."

Fiona scowled. "How do you mean, then?"

"When she stared at me—when I looked into her eyes—it was like I was... falling."

"Falling?" Fiona prompted sharply.

"Yeah," I replied. "That's the only way I can describe the sensation. And then everything went dark, and when I came to..." I gestured helplessly to the drawing now draped over her desk.

"Where were you when you came to?" Fiona asked. We had moved on from encouragement to interrogation now, but I didn't mind. As the shock wore off, it felt good to get the details out, like sucking poison from a wound.

"I was sitting right there, in the same chair that I'd been sitting in before I blacked out," I told her. "But there was an inkwell and some feathers on the table next to us. I obviously must have just grabbed them and started drawing."

Fiona's brows were pulled so slightly together that it looked as though a single, fuzzy brown caterpillar had nestled into the furrow above her eyes.

"There's one thing I don't understand," I said, after a long pause.

Fiona snorted. "One thing?"

I ignored her and went on. "Every drawing I've made in the past has fallen into one of two categories. Either they were spirit-induced, or a prophecy. Either a spirit showed up and used me to express their own message, or my Seer gift brought the message to me. But this... what was this?"

Fiona didn't answer. She seemed to be absorbing my words.

I went on. "Flavia is alive. Her spirit is contained inside her body. So, it can't possibly be a spirit-induced drawing, can it? She's not a ghost."

Still Fiona did not speak. She was scratching at her cheek, eyes focused out in the middle distance. When she finally replied, her words were very measured—very cautious.

"I can't say that the normal rules apply in the case of someone like Flavia. She has... an awareness now. When that Necromancer spawn twisted her Spirit Sight, her spirit became aware of its natural state—that is to say, it likely saw itself as separate from the body and behaved as such until her Spirit Sight was restored."

I nodded. This tallied with what Mrs. Mistlemoore had explained to us, about Flavia being forced to stare at her own soul, to acknowledge it as a separate entity from her body that would long for escape once it had become cognizant of its state.

"So... do you think it's possible that, when she grabbed onto me, she used me as a Muse, just like any other ghost?"

"I... don't think so. At least, I don't think it's that simple. I think she tried to, certainly, but I think what she did instead was trigger your gift."

"Which one?" I asked dryly, to which Fiona gave me a grudging half-smile.

"Fair question. You're just so bloody talented, aren't you?" she said. "Flavia tried to use you as a Muse, but whatever it was she was trying to tell you triggered your Seer gift. Perhaps she wanted to warn you about Charlie. Perhaps she overheard something he said. Either way, her message was like a match, and your Seer gift... well, it was waiting right there like a stack of dry bloody kindling, wasn't it? Just waiting to be lit and burned to all hell."

I looked over at the drawing. "To all hell is right," I murmured. "Have... have you had a look at that drawing yet?"

Fiona grimaced. "A quick one. Enough to know it bodes no bloody good. Shall we...?" She gestured over to it, giving me a sweeping look as though trying to assess if I could join her without passing out again.

"Yeah. I think we'd better," I said, dredging up some determination from somewhere deep inside me and steeling myself with it.

"Can you sit up a bit, d'you reckon? My bloody foot has gone numb," Fiona said.

"What? Oh, yeah. Sorry about that," I said, shifting myself into a slightly more elevated position so that Fiona could slide her leg out from under me.

Fiona sat herself on the edge of the bed beside me, massaging her toes for a minute. Then she stood up, helped me to my feet, and walked me carefully across the room. My legs were a little wobbly, but the dizziness had passed, and I did not stumble. I dragged the quilt with me, clutching it around my shoulders and wrapping myself back in it as I collapsed into Fiona's desk chair, which tipped precariously. One of the wheels had long since fallen off and she had never bothered to replace it, choosing instead to nearly concuss herself every time she sat down.

Fiona approached the drawing warily, as though it might jump up and attack her if she startled it. It made me even more nervous than before, to see the awe on her face.

"You recognize that location?" I asked her after a minute or so, when I couldn't take the silence any more.

"Yeah, I sure do. Just visited the place, didn't I?" Fiona said under her breath. She looked up at me. "Do you recognize it?"

I nodded. "I do. It's the Skye Príosún, isn't it? I've never been there, but... but I knew what it was as soon as I saw it."

She placed a tentative fingertip on the fabric and traced the curve of one of the ink lines. "This triskele over the top... it looks out of place. The angles of the strokes..."

"I didn't draw the triskele. It was already there," I explained. "The Scribes drew it on the partition while they were trying to cure Flavia with a Casting."

"Ah, well, that explains that, then," Flavia said. "Could have told me that from the off."

"Sorry, I was too busy trying not to lose consciousness," I said, a bit waspishly.

"These men... many of them look like Caomhnóir. You see the boots? The staffs? And these vests... you see the way they wrap around the chest and under their arms? These are part of the Caomhnóir uniform at the *príosúns.*"

"Yes, my first thought was that some of them were Caomhnóir. But then... who are the others?"

I asked the question because I wanted her to give me a different answer than the one I knew to be true. *Please,* I begged her silently, *please, tell me something... anything except the thing I already know you're going to tell me. Just make something up.*

Fiona looked up at me as though she knew exactly what I was thinking and would not stand for it. My face crumpled and she nodded. "We both know who they are. The question is, why are they out of their cells and standing shoulder to shoulder with Caomhnóir? And then there's this fuckery," she added, waving her hand over the hordes of spirits hovering in the air above the scene. "There are many spirits at the *príosún*, of course, but they're all carefully contained within its walls. No spirit who isn't a prisoner dares hang about the place. The Castings are too strong and too unpleasant for them to tolerate for long. I just can't make heads or tails of it."

I swallowed convulsively and felt the fear that was rising up my throat slip back down into my stomach, where it roiled like the sea in a storm. "Fiona, there's... I haven't been able to tell you this yet, but... there's something going on with the Caomhnóir at the *príosún*."

Fiona's head snapped up. "And how would you know that, precisely?" she asked sharply.

"I... I saw Finn. He found me at Róisín Lightfoot's wedding. No one knows," I said quickly, for she looked as though she might revert to tradition and throw something at me. "Well, no one who's going to betray us, anyway. It was only for a moment, in secret, while he was on break. We weren't caught."

Fiona lowered herself slowly onto a stool, her expression grim but resigned. "Let's hear the worst of it then. What did he have to say?"

"He told me that the Caomhnóir at the *príosún* have been acting strangely. They are showing up late or skipping shifts. They aren't where the duty logs say they are. And he even walked in on some of them having some kind of secret meeting when they were supposed to be asleep in their quarters."

Fiona chewed a fingernail thoughtfully. "They are a rougher sort out there," she hedged. "Unruly, like. Most of them couldn't follow the code of conduct required to be a sworn clan Caomhnóir, one that protects the Gateway directly. Could be the whole operation is a bit looser than he's used to at Fairhaven."

"Yeah, Finn told me that, too. But what really disturbed him was that, when he went to report the behavior to his superiors, they blew him off. Just told him to forget about it, and not bother them with it anymore."

Fiona raised her eyebrows. "Well, now, that is odd."

"Exactly. And the superiors are the ones who have to verify and check all of the logs. So that meant that at least one of them had to be in on... whatever the hell is going on," I said.

"That's... not good," Fiona muttered, beginning to pace.

"Gee, you think?" I shot back. "And there's something else, too."

"Out with it, then," Fiona sighed. "In for a penny, in for a pound."

"Well..." I stalled, twisting my fingers through the holes in the lace edging of the quilt. Once I told her—once I said it—there would be no going back. "Charlie Wright said something disturbing when we were tied up in that basement."

"Just the one thing?" Fiona asked with a smirk.

I ignored the remark "He said that the Necromancers are rising again."

Fiona rolled her eyes. "The Necromancers are always rising. This is why they are still around. They're like a weed. We can prune them and tame them, but they're damn near impossible to kill and they always rear their ugly little heads again the next season."

"No, this was different," I said, shaking my head, which was a mistake. It swam. "It wasn't a generalization. He was being specific. He said, 'We have allies now. Allies you have lost through your neglect and your arrogance and your ingratitude.' Then he said, 'Soon your defenses shall be ours. And so shall your gifts.'"

Fiona blinked. "What the bloody hell does that mean?"

"Well, the part about the gift is obvious. He thought he was about to steal my Spirit Sight. But the other bit... about the allies and the defenses... well, it's got to mean the Caomhnóir at the *príosún*, doesn't it? It's the only thing that makes sense, especially in light of this." I gestured desperately down to the drawing.

Fiona continued to stare at me, evidently too horrorstruck to formulate a coherent response.

"Fiona?" I asked after a solid minute's silence. "What do you think?"

"A tempest in a teapot," Fiona whispered.

"Sorry?"

Fiona shook her head. "What fools we are. What bloody, bloody fools."

I frowned at her. "Do you think you could stop speaking fortune cookie and explain what the hell you're talking about?"

Fiona jumped up suddenly from her stool, which toppled over behind her and rolled away across the floor. "That *príosún* houses the most dangerous of our criminals, both living and dead. It's a fortress in the middle of nowhere, and so heavily guarded that it should be nigh impenetrable. But you don't have to penetrate it if an alliance starts from within."

"Alliance?" I repeated breathlessly. "With the Caomhnóir? But... why? Why in the world would the Caomhnóir want to join forces with the Necromancers?"

"We entrusted the neutralization of our most dangerous threats to Caomhnóir who we won't even trust to guard us in person. We should have been sending our best—our most competent and most trustworthy. What could be more important than keeping our worst enemies locked away? But, no. We were selfish and shortsighted. We didn't want to deal with the problems amongst our own Caomhnóir, so we sent them away where we could ignore them instead of addressing the issues. And now, we are reaping the dangerous harvest of what we have sown. Again."

Her horror was infecting me, coursing through me as though riding the currents of blood in my veins.

"Well, we've got one advantage here," Fiona said. "An advantage we don't deserve, but we've got it and we'd better bloody well use it before it's too late."

"What advantage?" I asked.

"You."

I blinked. "Me?"

"That's right." Fiona walked back to the desk and tapped her finger sharply on the drawing. "We've got you, and you've got this gift. It's a curse, I know it," she said quickly in response to the expression on my face. "I won't insult you by calling it a gift, but we can't pretend in this instance that it isn't a blessing."

"Blessing doesn't sound a hell of a lot better than gift, Fiona," I said through gritted teeth.

"What we call it doesn't matter," Fiona snapped. "What we do with it *does*. We've got a chance here. We've been forewarned. It's a prophecy, and it's one that we can act on and prevent, if we're smart about it."

Cold fear began stabbing at my insides. "Fiona, you promised. You promised we wouldn't tell anyone about this. You promised me we wouldn't need to tell the Council that I was a Seer."

"I know." Fiona said. "I know I said that."

"So, what, you're just... taking it back?"

Fiona didn't answer.

19

"We can't tell them!" I cried. "We can't let the Council know about this! I wouldn't have brought it to you if I thought you were going to turn around and hand it over to them!"

"No one is handing anything over to anyone," Fiona said in a tone of forced calm. "Don't get yourself all riled again, now."

"Of course I'm getting riled!" I cried, my voice rising with every word. "You promised me, Fiona!"

"Jessica, be reasonable. We have to warn them. We can't let this come to pass," Fiona said softly.

"We will warn them!" I said desperately. "We'll... we'll figure out a way."

"How?" Fiona asked, her tone infuriatingly logical. "How can we warn them about something that hasn't happened yet?"

"We... we could... I could tell them what Finn told me!" I gasped, clutching at straws.

"And how are you going to do that without getting both you and Finn in even more trouble than you're already in?" Fiona asked. "The Caomhnóir leadership will rake him over the coals for contacting you, and the Council may very well do the same to you. You'll be locked up in Skye Príosún before you can even warn anyone about what's happening there, and then you'll get caught up right in the middle of that mess!"

"And you think that's worse than what might happen if they find out I'm a Seer?" I asked in an incredulous squeak. "You know better than anyone what they do to Seers!" I shouted, and though it didn't seem possible that I had more tears to cry, they began spilling from my eyes. "Fiona, just think of your own mother, for God's sake! Look what happened to her!"

"Look what happened to her indeed," Fiona said quietly. "I realize you're feeling a bit foggy from the events of the night, but if you can shake that off, you might remember where she's currently locked up?"

For a moment I had no idea what she was talking about. Then, my heart dropped like a stone. "Oh, my God. Fiona, I forgot. I can't believe I... and she's still there? I thought you said they'd decided to release her?"

Fiona nodded, her lips pressed into the thinnest of lines. "Yeah, well, they don't seem to be in any rush to do that. Not convinced she's 'safe,' whatever the bloody hell *that* means. My sister has appealed to the Council to step in and we've put together a petition for her release."

"Oh, God, Fiona, I am so sorry," I said. "I'm such an asshole. Here I am trying to sweep this all under the rug and your mom is right in the line of fire."

Fiona shook her head. "That's not what's happening here. I'm not blaming you, and I'm certainly not throwing you under the bus to save my own mother. God knows that *príosún* could explode around her and she likely wouldn't notice. But we can't let every prisoner become a victim if the *príosún* really is going to fall into Necromancer hands. We can't sit on this information."

"So, if we aren't going to tell anyone I'm a Seer, and we aren't going to tell them that Finn and I communicated, then how the hell are we going to be able to warn anyone about what's happening?" I asked. I tried to keep my voice under control, but it rose hysterically with each word as the impossibility of the situation began to close in around me, trapping me in a little mental cage with my own panic.

Fiona began pacing again, kicking paint cans out of her path as she walked. "That's the question, isn't it?" she muttered. "That's the question."

I watched as she paced, the repetitive movement oddly soothing, like being hypnotized. Then an idea struck me.

"Could... could you just tell them that you spoke to Finn?"

Fiona stopped in her tracks and frowned at me. "Me? How in the world would I have spoken to Finn?"

"When you went to the *príosún* the first time, to see your mom!" I cried, feeling a glimmer of hope, sure the idea was a good one. "You came back and told me that you'd seen Finn there, and that he looked good. I know you didn't speak to him, but no one else does!"

Fiona furrowed her brow. "Huh. Now that is an idea."

"It makes sense," I told her eagerly. "You could just tell them that you happened to see him, and he took the opportunity of seeing a Council member he trusted, and filled you in about what he had witnessed."

"But why would I have kept that information quiet for weeks? If I really believed what he had told me, and that it was serious, why wouldn't I have alerted the rest of the Council or the Fairhaven Caomhnóir at once?"

I opened my mouth, eager to give her the perfect excuse, but nothing came out. She was right. It would make no sense for her to have sat on that information for so long.

"Unless," Fiona said, each word slow and measured, as though she were testing the validity of the idea even as she spoke it aloud. "Unless I waited until I came back this time."

"Huh?" I asked.

"I'm headed back to the *príosún*. I've just told you, my sister and I have filed a petition. Someone's got to deliver it by hand, or they won't consider it. I volunteered," Fiona said. She paused by her window and stared out into the darkness, as though she could actually see the Skye Príosún out there, looming on the horizon.

"You're... you're going back there?" I asked, my voice rising in a squeak. "When?"

"I'm meant to leave tomorrow afternoon," Fiona said. "Maybe sooner, now that I've seen this." She hitched her thumb over her shoulder to indicate the drawing.

"But you... you can't go in there!" I gasped, feeling my panic start to mount again. "You can't, now that you know what's happening!"

She turned to look at me. "But we don't know what's happening. Not yet, anyway."

"But what if something happens while you're there? What if you get stuck there, or... or something bad happens to you?" I cried, my words tumbling out over each other.

Fiona raised an eyebrow at me. "And what if I walk out that door, trip on a paint can, fall down the tower stairs and break my neck? Jess, the first thing you need to learn about prophecies—and you'd better learn it right quick—is that we can't understand if they're meant to come about, or when, or in what manner. For all we know, my going to the *príosún* could reset this timeline." She slammed her hand down upon the drawing. "One word from me, one decision from you, one syllable of one word uttered by any person involved, and this whole future could vanish from the realm of the possible."

I stared at her, trying to let her words sink in.

Fiona went on, her voice calmer now that she was sure I was listening. "Some prophecies will assert themselves. Sometimes too many forces are driving toward the same inevitable conclusion, and sooner or later, they come to be, no matter what the universe throws at them. Others will fade at the slightest shifting of the wind, never to be seen again. Your job—our job—is to test this prophecy out. Find out what it's made of, like, you see? Give it a shove, and see if it pushes back."

"You're saying we have to—what, piss the prophecy off?" I asked, shaking my head confusedly.

"If you like," Fiona said, shrugging. "If this is meant to be, it will push back. You will draw it again, maybe many times. It will reassert itself, in whatever way it can conceive of. It may stay the same, if the course has not changed, or it may twist itself into something new. We will continue to test, to interpret, to decide what we are meant to do next."

"How will we know?" I asked, trying and failing to keep the note of desperation out of my voice. "How will we know for sure what we're meant to do next?"

"Ah, Jess," Fiona said, and she shook her head pityingly at me. "We won't ever know. There is no 'for sure.' We can only just do our best in the moment with what information we have. It's like trying to find a destination with a map that only reveals one step of the path at a time."

I swallowed something painful that tasted bitter. "So, this Seer stuff is pretty much just useless bullshit then, huh?" I asked.

"Complete and utter bullshit, yes," Fiona agreed, nodding her head solemnly.

I took a deep breath. It was shaky, but I managed it. "Okay. So, if you go to the *príosún*—and I'm still not saying it's a good idea," I added quickly, giving her the kind of look my mother used to give me on the rare occasion she attempted to parent me, "what will you do when you get there? You can't let on that you know anything is happening, or they'll never let you leave."

"That's true," Fiona said. "I'll have to tread very carefully, indeed. No questions. No letting on. I likely won't be able to do much other than keep my eyes and ears open. But I'll have been there, and that will be enough."

"Enough for what?"

"Enough to give us a pretext to pass along the information from Finn," Fiona snapped, clearly annoyed that I wasn't keeping up. "If I pretend to have spoken to him, I can alert the Council and the Fairhaven Caomhnóir to the situation without you or Finn getting in trouble, and also without revealing you're a Seer... at least, not yet."

I felt a tight knot of anxiety in my chest begin to loosen. "You think that will work?" I asked.

"Yes," Fiona said. "And if it doesn't... well, we're no worse off for having tried, are we?"

"I don't know, Fiona," I hedged, still hesitating. "I still don't like the idea of you going there when we know something dangerous might be going on."

"And I don't like the idea of my half-mad mother inside those walls for the same reason," Fiona barked. "I can look after myself, but her?" Fiona shook her head grimly. "I'm going to Skye Príosún tomorrow as planned, and I'm not leaving there without my mother. If the place is about to fall under siege from within, it's more important than ever to get her out of there."

"Let me come with you!" I said, desperately, thinking only of Finn. "I can help you!"

"You're in no fit state to go anywhere," Fiona said. "I imagine that arm of yours is going to be damn painful when the shock and the drugs wear off, and there's not a nun's chance in hell Mrs. Mistlemoore will discharge you so soon. And anyway, you need a special dispensation to visit Skye Príosún. You can't just take a leisurely stroll up to the place, bang on the door, and expect someone to let you in for a bonny little tour. You need position, you need Council approval, and you need standing arrangements with the security, none of which you've got and none of which you're going to get by tomorrow."

"How long will you be gone?" I asked.

"I've requested five days off," Fiona said. "It's a complicated process," she added, seeing the incredulous look on my face.

"How can I possibly wait that long to find out if you're all safe?" I asked in a tiny voice.

"You listen to me, now. If I can fend for myself, it's nothing to what Mr. Carey can do. He's smart, wary, and highly skilled, Jess. If I can warn him, or speak to him, I will, but just know that you are wasting your worries on him. Wouldn't be surprised to get there and see that he's foiled the whole plot single-handedly, to be honest."

I gave a laugh that was half a dry sob. "If anything happens to him..."

"I know. But it won't," Fiona said. "We won't let it."

We stared into each other's eyes for what felt like a long time, until I felt some of her grim determination seep into me, filling me up where the fear had gnawed at my insides.

"No," I said finally. "We won't."

3

MARCHING ORDERS

S AVANNAH TODD LOOKED UP as I stumbled into the dining room the next morning and clicked her tongue.

"Saints alive, Jess, you look—"

"I know, I know!" I snapped. "I look awful. I'm thinking of having it printed on a shirt, just so I can save people the trouble of having to tell me every time I walk into a room in the morning."

"Sorry, mate," Savvy said, clapping me on the back, so that I knocked into a tea cup with my elbow and spilled half of its contents into the saucer. "I'll just keep me trap shut, shall I?"

"Where's Tia?" Hannah asked, sitting down and pulling a basket of muffins toward her.

"She and Frankie are off in the library already," Savvy said with a grimace of disgust. "They're helping each other study for exams. I'm glad they get on so well, but bloody hell, the things they do for fun." She shook her head, bewildered.

I was grateful that Frankie was at Fairhaven to keep Tia company, and that Tia seemed to be recovering from the shock of finding out that the boy she had been dating, Charlie Wright, was actually a Necromancer hell-bent on destroying me and the rest of the Durupinen. As was her custom, throwing herself headfirst into work seemed to be Tia's favorite form of therapy. I was just happy that she'd decided to do it here, rather than fleeing halfway around the world. I wouldn't have blamed her in the slightest if she had, and I'd told her so.

"On a scale of one to never-talk-to-me-again, how mad are you at me?" I had asked her only the day before, as we sat in the still and the warmth of the Fairhaven gardens at sunset. It had been less than forty-eight hours since Charlie had been revealed to be a criminal mastermind, and Tia had been walking around with a dazed expression, as though trying to figure out whether the entire world was a dream or not.

That dazed look turned to one of surprise as she looked at me, as though I'd said something strange instead of something totally reasonable.

"What do you mean? Why would I be mad at you?"

I raised one incredulous eyebrow. "Tia, you're supposed to be a genius. Surely you can figure this out. I encouraged you to pursue a guy who turned out to be a dangerous maniac."

"You didn't know he was a dangerous maniac," Tia said.

"I should have," I muttered.

"I should have, too," Tia said. "But he fooled both of us, and a lot of other people, too, by the looks of it. I'm not going to let him further victimize me by blaming myself or you, when I should be blaming him."

She sounded so reasonable. So rational. So healthy. What was it like, I wondered, to have a brain that worked like that—organizing and dealing appropriately with feelings instead of alternately ignoring and drowning in them?

"So, you aren't jumping a plane and heading back home to America?" I asked her.

"If you had asked me two days ago, I might have said yes," Tia said, shaking her head as though she were already ashamed to have harbored such a feeling. "I was ready to pack a suitcase and get as far away from here as possible."

"What's stopping you?" I asked. "I wouldn't blame you in the least."

"Because, if there's one thing I despise more than making a mistake, it's making the same mistake twice," Tia said firmly.

"What do you—?"

"I ran from it last time," Tia said. "I told myself I was being bold and brave and all of that, coming here, but what was I really doing? I was running away. I was hiding. I wasn't dealing with things, I was burying them."

I squirmed uncomfortably. "And you wouldn't have done any of that if I hadn't told you to."

Tia reached over and squeezed my hand. "This isn't my way of blaming you, Jess. That's not what I mean."

"But you should be blaming me!" I cried. "This was all my idea, and, just in case you needed another good reason to hate me, here's

28

one: I wanted you here for me, not for you. Well, I mean, I *told* myself that it was for you, but I'm selfish. That's something you should know about me by now. I'm selfish and I don't think things through, and then I hurt people that I love."

"You're not selfish," Tia said softly.

"Yes, I am! I am the queen of selfish. I should get a sash made. And a tiara," I replied. "I mean, listen to me right now! I started this conversation because I wanted to know how you were doing and somehow, though the power of my mystical selfishness magic, I have made the conversation about me!"

"Jess, stop," Tia said, and she looked stern now. "You didn't force me to come here. You barely had to convince me. It was my decision and I don't regret it. But I can't buy a plane ticket and leave the country every time something bad happens to me, or everything I've worked so hard for will just fall apart."

"So... you're not leaving?"

"No, I'm not leaving."

"It's not just the selfishness, Tia," I said, determined to say every terrible truth aloud. "I put you in danger."

"Charlie put me in danger," Tia corrected me.

"Charlie put you in danger because of me! Being my best friend is dangerous! I don't want anything to happen to you, and now, with all this Necromancer stuff brewing again... Maybe it would be better if you were leaving."

Tia looked at me for a moment, her face blank. "You want me to leave?"

"No, of course I don't."

"You don't want to be my best friend anymore?"

"What?! No! I will always be your best friend, but I don't want you to get hurt, and just being around me has gotten you hurt."

Tia gave me such a harsh look that I shrank back a little. It was like being in a principal's office. "Jessica Ballard, you listen to me right now! I don't care how good your intentions are! I don't care how much you are trying to protect me! If you ever try to break off this friendship, I will never speak to you again!"

I considered this. "If I try not to speak to you again, you... won't speak to me again?" I asked.

"That's right," Tia said. "And I don't care if it doesn't make any sense. You know what I mean. There's nothing those Necromancer fucks could do that would make me give up our friendship. Nothing."

I blinked. "You... you just said fuck."

Tia raised her chin defiantly. "Yes. Yes, I did. And I'll say it again, because when a guy uses me to try to kill my best friend I get to say whatever I want. Fuck, fuck, *fuck*."

I laughed incredulously. "You realize this is just more proof that I'm a terrible influence on you, right?"

Tia smiled and shrugged. "So be it."

§

"Jess? Are you even listening to me?" Savvy's voice cut straight into my thoughts with all the finesse of a blunt ax.

"What? No, sorry, I spaced out. What did you say?"

"I said Phoebe's looking better this morning. Not so restless. Her eyes still look creepy, but she sort of mumbled at me when I was visiting her and she squeezed my hand twice."

"She did? That's great! I'll stop over and visit with her when I go see Flavia later."

Flavia's recovery had progressed as well over the last few days. Although she was not yet fully conscious, her eyes had cleared of their silvery quality and she had been responding to simple requests from Mrs. Mistlemoore and her staff—squeezing their hands and wiggling her fingers on command. Mrs. Mistlemoore couldn't fully explain why it was taking Flavia and Phoebe so long to regain their abilities to communicate, but she had her theories.

"Twisting the Spirit Sight has disconnected them from their bodies," she had told me only the previous night. "My guess is that it will take them some time to accept where they are, and for their spirits and their bodies to work in tandem again."

"Is there any chance that they won't accept where they are?" I asked.

"Of course. Anything is possible. But the Durupinen blood is strong. I would not dare to underestimate it. The Necromancers have always done so, and it has always been to their detriment."

Yes, the Durupinen blood certainly was strong—strong enough to pull me from my bed and out onto a castle ledge in my sleep.

I looked down at the food on my plate. I knew I would probably feel better if I ate it, but I was so exhausted that I felt queasy just looking at it. I took a sip of coffee instead.

"Will you... you'll come with me tonight, right?" Savvy asked.

I looked over my coffee cup at her to see her face crumpled in an effort to force back tears. That evening was Bertie's funeral service. I put my cup down and rested a hand on her shoulder. "Of course, I will."

"We'll all be there," Hannah added gently. "For him and for you."

Savvy didn't answer aloud, but gave a quick nod of thanks. The corners of my own eyes began to burn, and I knocked back the rest of my coffee in one gulp, hoping to eclipse the burn in my eyes with the burn in my throat.

Bertie. Poor, loyal, hopeless Bertie. I still remembered how absurd he had looked in the line of strapping young Novitiates who had just begun their training when I first arrived as an Apprentice Durupinen at Fairhaven. He was short and chubby, his chest thrown out so that he looked like a small child playing at soldier. And he knew it. He had tried so hard to live up to his duty, and all he had ever gotten for it was unrelenting shit from all sides. No one had taken him seriously—not his superiors, not his fellow Caomhnóir, and least of all, Savvy. But he had committed himself nonetheless, determined to prove himself, charging into situations he had no business facing. None of us had ever seen a Caomhnóir funeral service, but knowing our long-standing traditions for pomp and ceremony, I was sure that it would be an impressive display.

"What about Phoebe?" Hannah was asking.

"What about her?" Savvy sniffed.

"Well, are they going to try to... I mean, she can't really go to the funeral, can she?" Hannah asked.

"I wondered that, too," Milo said. "I didn't know if maybe she had to be there? For like... ceremonial purposes?"

"Yeah, well, they can well and truly sod off with all of that," Savvy replied sharply. "I ain't been told nothin' about ceremonial anything, just when to show up, and that's going to be bloody hard enough. And I'm sure as hell not going to risk Phoebe's recovery by dragging her from her nice quiet bed to something like that. I'm not even sure if she knows that Bertie's dead."

Milo's eyes widened. "Oh, shit. I hadn't thought of that."

Neither had I. Because Phoebe was still unconscious, there was still a lot about the circumstances of Bertie's death that we didn't know. I supposed the Trackers might have been able to figure out more of the details from working over the crime scene. I supposed, too, that I might technically have access to that information, seeing as I was a Tracker myself, and personally tied to the case as another of Charlie's victims. But I was in no hurry to dig any more deeply into the terrible details of what we'd found on the other side of that hotel door. In fact, I felt like I was spending a solid part of my time trying to erase what details I had seen from my memory. On the increasingly rare occasions that I was able to sleep undisturbed, I often found myself staring at the horrific scene in that room on the second floor of the Hotel Royal, unable to look away or even blink.

I shuddered. Jesus, my mind would soon be more full of things I was trying to forget than things I wanted to remember. That couldn't be healthy. I should probably be in therapy, but then, after my last brief run-in with psychiatric help, it was clear that Durupinen and traditional therapy didn't mix. Maybe there were Durupinen therapists? I should probably look into that, but, knowing me, I'd just throw it on that giant pile of "things I should do" and forget about it.

I was so good at adulting.

"I'd better get going," Hannah said, grabbing a muffin from the basket on the table and wrapping it hastily in a napkin.

"Where are you off to this morning?" I asked blearily.

"Don't you remember?" Hannah asked, raising her eyebrows significantly. "I'm meeting with Keira this morning. She wants to discuss my proposal."

Her words felt like a slap in the face, waking me up and clearing my head. "Oh, that's right! That's today? Sorry, I'm completely out of it. So... she already read it? The whole thing?"

"Yup," Hannah replied, and drained her glass of juice in two long swigs.

"Well, did she... I mean... do you have any idea what she thought of it? Did she give you any hint?"

Hannah considered this. "She sounded... intrigued. She definitely has questions, and she said she was going to bring along the research she compiled from when she wrote her own proposals about Durupinen–Caomhnóir dynamics. I'm not convinced that she's sold one way or the other, but I won't know for sure until we meet and talk it through. She didn't laugh me off, so it's a start. I wonder if it would be a good idea to bring one of the Caomhnóir

32

on board to back the proposal," she added thoughtfully, more to herself than to me. "It seems disrespectful to consider changing all the rules without even consulting them on what they might like to see happen, if anything. But I don't even know where I would start on that front." She fell into deeper thought, pulling the napkin away from her muffin so that she could nibble at the top of it.

Hannah was using her newly won seat on the Council to introduce legislation that would overhaul the rules about how Caomhnóir and Durupinen were permitted to interact. There were a hundred good reasons to do this, but only one that really mattered to me at the moment. Romantic relationships between Durupinen and Caomhnóir were forbidden, and had been for centuries. Our own parents had briefly engaged in one such forbidden romance, and the fallout had destroyed our family before we'd ever had a chance to become one. And now, of course, that same law had torn Finn and me apart. Changing the law was the only chance Finn and I had of seeing each other again, and so, for me, this wasn't just politics as usual.

"Wait for me, I'll walk with you," I told her, jumping up from my seat.

"You haven't even eaten anything," she said, scowling at me with an expression that made her look exactly like our mother. The sight of it made me want to hug her until my arms hurt. To appease both her and our mom in her, I reached into the same basket of muffins, pulled one out without looking at it, and crammed half of it into my mouth.

"See? Eating. Let's go," I mumbled.

Hannah rolled her eyes. "I have no idea what you just said. We'll see you later, Mackie! Bye, Sav!"

Savvy waved a hand at us and returned to her breakfast. I turned and got one last look at her as we exited the double doors into the entryway. She looked forlorn, her usual sparkle dulled and diminished as she poked at her plate with her fork.

"You think she's okay?" I asked Hannah.

Hannah turned back, looking momentarily confused, then followed my gaze. "Who are you... oh, you mean Savvy? Yeah, I think she'll be okay. She's just... she needs to find a way to stop blaming herself."

"What if she can't?" I asked under my breath.

"She will," Hannah insisted, as though she could will it to be true if only her voice was confident enough. "It will take some time, and we'll all need to be there for her, to help her when she gets in her own head. But she'll be okay, Jess. Savvy's resilient."

"Yeah," I said, nodding along. "Yeah, she is. She'll be okay."

Yeah. We'd all be okay. Right?

§

"Jess! There you are!"

I'd barely taken a few steps when a sharp voice echoed down the hallway. I looked up to see Catriona marching toward me, her trademark stiletto heels clacking resoundingly on each step.

"Have you been looking for me?" I asked turning on my heel and walking back to meet her.

"Only all over this godforsaken castle," she said with a toss of her magnificent blonde hair. She came to a halt and crossed her arms, waiting for me to close the distance between us, with a look of exasperated impatience on her face.

Catriona usually looked at me this way, like I was a permanent inconvenience blundering around in her orbit. She was supposed to be my mentor in the Trackers' office, but for all the mentoring she'd actually done, you'd think she thought the definition of "mentor" was "one who rolls her eyes with great frequency."

"You might've tried the dining hall," I said dryly. "You know, that big room where people eat their breakfast every single morning right around this time? Because that's where I've been for the last forty-five minutes, along with the rest of the people who need food to live. Unlike you, we can't all subsist on snark alone."

Catriona didn't bother to dignify my sass with a response. Instead, she watched me with one eyebrow arched nearly to her hairline as I closed the last few steps between us.

"So, what is it?" I asked. "What do you want?"

"I was under the impression," Catriona said, "that you agreed to help me take a lead on this Charlie Wright case."

"And I have," I said. "It's not like I'm hiding from you. I've turned in all my paperwork, all my statements, and spoken with at least three other Trackers so far to confirm the details. If there's something else you need me to do, all you need to do is ask."

"Hence why I've been looking for you," Catriona said wryly. "I've

34

got some questioning that needs to be done, and I want you to handle it."

At her words, my heart was suddenly throwing itself against the inside of my rib cage in panic. "Questioning? Me? You... you don't mean Charlie, do you? Because I don't think I'm equipped to handle..."

"Calm down, calm down. I would never be so daft as to ask you to question Charlie Wright," Catriona said with a roll of her eyes. "No offense, but you have neither the skills nor the stamina. And I can see from your face that you would fall right to pieces anyway."

I longed to throw a barbed retort back at her, but there was no arguing with her. She was right. I couldn't handle it, and it was no good pretending that I could just to spite her. If I ever saw Charlie Wright again, it would be too damn soon. I wasn't sure if I would break down in post-traumatic tears or just beat the ever-loving shit out of him with whatever blunt object I could get my hands on, but either way, I couldn't sit and calmly ask him questions while he sat smugly across from me.

"Okay," I said, keeping my voice steady while trying to get my heart rate to do the same. "So, if it's not Charlie, then who do you need me to question?"

"Phoebe Horton. And that Traveler friend of yours who's in the hospital wing with her—Flavia, I believe her name is," Catriona said. She pulled the file folder out from underneath her arm and handed it to me. "We've got a long list of details that need filling in, and they're likely to have at least a few of the answers."

I took the folder and flipped it open. There were several pages of typed questions, along with a case report. From glancing through it, I was able to see that they were trying to cobble together a timeline of Charlie Wright's whereabouts from the time that the attacks began. There were... a lot of blanks.

"You're right," I said, closing the folder again, and looking back at Catriona. "I'm sure Flavia and Phoebe *do* have some of these answers. But how do you expect them to give them to you—or to me, for that matter—when they're both lying unconscious in the hospital ward?"

"I think I have got a vague idea how consciousness and unconsciousness work, thank you very much," Catriona said, pursing her lips together. "I rather thought that you could be responsible for checking in on them periodically, and scheduling the interview for when each of them wakes. Unless of course that's too complicated for you."

"Man, that degree from charm school is just working overtime isn't it?" I muttered under my breath.

"Sorry?" Catriona said sharply.

"Nothing, forget it," I said with a sigh. "I can handle it. I was just on my way over to the hospital ward to check on Flavia's progress, anyway. Mrs. Mistlemoore says that there are hopeful signs that she may be awake soon, and Savvy says that Phoebe is starting to show some progress as well."

"Yes, I've heard the same thing," Catriona said. "But as I'm a bit too swamped with work right now to simply wait around for that happy moment to arrive, I'm handing that task over to you. Any questions?"

"Um...."

I could think of about a hundred questions. I'd never formally interviewed anyone before, and while I was glad Flavia and Phoebe weren't hostile Necromancer prisoners, I was still kind of nervous about the idea of questioning them. What was the protocol? Was there a right or wrong way to interview someone? Did I need to write it all down word for word, or could I just take some notes? And what if there were things they couldn't remember clearly, or details that were just too painful to recall? Did I just ignore those questions? Or did I have to push Flavia and Phoebe to relive terrible things? The more I thought about it, the more nervous I became. Maybe I wasn't the person to handle this, after all.

Naturally, I said exactly none of this to Catriona. I wasn't about to give her the satisfaction.

"Nope," I said instead, trying to sound more confident than I felt. "I'm sure I can figure it out."

"Let's hope so," Catriona said. "Come and find me when you've got it all sorted."

"No problem," I said, tucking the file folder under my own arm. "So... how has the investigation been going on your end? Have you been questioning people, too?"

Catriona's eyes seemed to blaze. "Not very successfully," she said, a grudging sort of growl in her voice. "Our loquacious kidnapper is turning out to be quite a bit less charming and certainly less talkative than he was in that basement. I don't think we'll be making much headway with him, unless we can find some leverage to use against him."

"Do we have any other leads?" I asked.

"A few," Catriona said, sounding entirely unenthused. "But each of them is a bit of a longshot."

"So, then what's next?" I asked. "I mean, if Charlie won't talk?"

"I've got a few tricks up my sleeve yet," Catriona said through clenched teeth. "But we have a few acquaintances to interview, and a few witnesses to question. There may still be some details to uncover, even if Charlie Wright decides he's not going to be a good little lad and divulge them himself."

I could tell her, I thought, as I looked into Catriona's determined face. I could tell her about the drawing. I could tell her about being a Seer, right now, in this hallway. I could do that. Those details she was talking about, I might be the one who had them. It was very possible that my drawing could blow this case wide open. Was I just damning us all by keeping the secret to myself?

But even as I considered it, hot molten panic flooded up in my throat, choking me, extinguishing the words that might have risen to my lips. No. I had to wait a little bit longer. I had to at least find out what Fiona had been able to discover before I threw myself to the wolves. I wasn't sure if I was being selfish, or cautious. Perhaps it was a bit of both. But I couldn't tell her, not yet.

"Good luck," I said instead. "If anyone can break him, I'm sure it's you. I mean, I'd break, if I had to sit in a room alone with you for any significant length of time."

Something in Catriona's stern expression vanished. She threw her head back and laughed—a real, ringing laugh. "I'll take that as a compliment," she said.

I gave a yelp as my phone buzzed to life in my pocket, startling me.

"Bit jumpy there, aren't you?" Catriona asked as she watched me struggle to extract the phone from my pocket.

"Yeah, can't think of what's happened to me lately that might put me on edge," I said sarcastically. I glanced down at the screen and swore under my breath.

"What's wrong? What is it?" Catriona asked.

"It's not 'what,' it's 'who,'" I told her, grimacing. "Karen, probably wondering why she hasn't heard from me."

"Ah," Catriona said and gave a knowing nod of the head. "I see. Haven't told her about the attack yet, have you?"

"Nope, and I'm not going to right now, either," I said, sending the call to my voicemail. "Still haven't figured out how to have that conversation yet."

"Well, if I know Karen, you'd better figure out how to have it, and sharpish," Catriona advised. "She's nothing if not persistent."

I snorted. "There's a euphemism if ever I've heard one. She's going to kill me for... well, for almost getting myself killed."

Catriona laughed again. Twice in one conversation. I was pretty sure that was a record. "Good luck with that," she chuckled. "You're going to need it." She turned on her heel and began to stalk away. She'd only gone a few steps when she stopped abruptly, as though she'd only just remembered something. She turned back around, and gave me a hard, piercing look, all humor gone as suddenly as it had appeared.

"You're all right, are you?" she asked bluntly.

"I... what?" I replied, momentarily thrown off by the question.

"You know what I mean. After the attack, after the ordeal in that basement," Catriona said. She was picking at her fingernail, not quite able to meet my eyes. "I mean to say... you're holding up all right, are you?"

It took me a moment to realize that she was fighting valiantly against a show of real concern. It was almost funny to watch the struggle on her face.

Almost.

"Yeah," I said, giving her a small nod of thanks. "Yeah, I'm holding up all right. And you?"

Catriona's face gave a funny sort of twitch. "Who, me? I'm *always* all right."

And she strutted away, her body language making it perfectly clear that she would utterly destroy anyone who ever dared to suggest that she wasn't, in fact, *always* all right.

4

WIDE AWAKE

THE HOSPITAL WARD WAS QUIET and peaceful, with morning sunlight streaming in through the high windows, which had been opened to tempt in the earthy smell of the English countryside. I had only walked a few steps across the room, glancing around for Mrs. Mistlemoore, when I heard a voice call out.

"Jess! Jess, over here!"

The Tracker folder slipped out from under my arm in my surprise, and I bent to catch it before it hit the ground. My heart leapt, because I knew that voice. I straightened up and looked to the far corner of the room to see Flavia propped up in her bed with a breakfast tray set on her lap.

"Oh my God! You're awake!" I cried, closing the rest of the distance between us at a jog.

She laughed weakly. "That's what they tell me, yeah. I still feel half-asleep, but I think the food is helping."

I sat gingerly down on the edge of her bed, careful not to upset her tray, and placed the file folder carefully onto the bedside table. Flavia was still incredibly pale, her pallor all the more accentuated by the bright fuchsia tone of her hair, which was matted and tangled, and grown out at the roots to reveal an inch of jet-black natural color. Her dark-framed glasses looked too large for her face, as though she were a kid playing dress-up with her mom's glasses, and her cheeks looked sunken and hollow beneath sharply protruding cheekbones. Someone had removed her piercings—probably Mrs. Mistlemoore—and she wore a white muslin nightgown that made her look like a workhouse child from the pages of a Dickensian novel, except for the dark tattoos that peeked out around the collar. When she smiled, though, there was a wry twinkle in her eyes, which had returned at last to their rich, warm brown color.

"How are you feeling?" I asked her. I wanted to hug her, but she looked like one decent hug might snap her like a twig, so I settled instead for reaching out and squeezing her hand. She returned the squeeze gratefully.

"I'm... okay, I think?" she replied, though it sounded more like a question than anything else, like she didn't actually trust her own perceptions. "I came to around midnight last night. It was scary at first. I had no idea where I was and I started to panic. But luckily, Mrs. Mistlemoore was making her rounds, and spotted me almost at once. She was able to convince me I was safe and calm me down."

"How much... what did she tell you?" I asked hesitantly.

"I don't remember telling her it was time for visitors," came a stern voice from behind us. Both Flavia and I looked up, startled, as Mrs. Mistlemoore bustled toward us. I braced for a telling off, but as she reached the bedside table, I noticed she was smirking.

"Sorry," I said sheepishly. "I intended to ask you, I promise. But then Flavia called my name and I saw she was awake, and..." I shrugged.

Mrs. Mistlemoore's smirk bloomed into a wide smile. "Ah well, I can't say I blame you. We're all as relieved as we can be to see her awake at last. How's that tea and toast going down?" she added, turning to Flavia.

"Okay," Flavia said. "I'm taking it slowly." I looked down at her plate. She'd only managed to take a few tiny nibbles. It looked like a mouse had gotten at her toast.

"You want some eggs with that?" Mrs. Mistlemoore offered briskly.

Flavia went a shade whiter at the suggestion. "I... don't think I'm quite ready for eggs."

Mrs. Mistlemoore eyed her critically. She bent to lay her hand across Flavia's forehead, then pressed her fingers to Flavia's wrist and timed her pulse against the gold watch she wore dangling from a chain around her waist. Then she dropped a few pinches of powders from a set of little glass bottles on the bedside table into a glass of water and handed it to Flavia. "You still look peaky, and your pulse is still a bit more elevated than I'd like, seeing as you're simply lying there. I want you to drink that straight away before you try any more of the toast."

40

Flavia gave a solemn salute. "Yes, ma'am."

"And you, Miss Ballard. I'm fine with a few minutes of calm conversation, but no upsetting my patient, please," Mrs. Mistlemoore said, turning her eagle eye on me.

"Who me? When have I ever caused trouble of any kind?" I asked her, trying to look offended.

Her lips twitched, and as she walked away, I could have sworn I heard her mutter something that sounded suspiciously like, "That girl will be the death of me."

"I see your reputation precedes you," Flavia said, smiling at me.

I shrugged. "What can I say? I'm kind of a big deal around here. Okay, so... calm conversation..." I said, casting around in my brain for something to say, and then remembering the folder full of questions I was supposed to bombard her with.

"What's in the folder, then?" Flavia asked. I looked up to see that she had followed my gaze.

"Oh, don't worry about that. It's Tracker stuff," I said, and when she raised her eyebrows, I sighed. "I was instructed to ask you all of the questions in there when you woke up, but screw that. There will be plenty of time for all of that later."

"Will it help the investigation?" Flavia asked, and she seemed to be steeling herself.

"It will only hurt the investigation if you overtire yourself and set your recovery back because you had to sit through an interrogation before you even had a cup of tea," I said, sounding quite a bit like Mrs. Mistlemoore myself.

"I'd rather talk to you than a Tracker I don't know," Flavia said quietly, and I looked up to see her examining her own hands. "You can ask me about it. I know he hurt you, too."

I squeezed her hand again. "I'm so sorry, Flavia. Truly, I am, for everything you've been through. You can talk about it if you think it will make you feel better to get it off your chest, just friend to friend, but we can save the formal questions for another time, all right?"

Flavia nodded, still looking down at her hands. She sighed, shaking her head. "I still can't believe any of this. I can't believe he turned out to be such a..."

"Creep? Maniac? Sadistic wolf in sheep's clothing?" I supplied readily.

Flavia half-laughed. "Yes. All of that. I met him in the research library. I was working there, and the medical students are in and out all the time, of course, buried up to their eyeballs in assignments. He asked me for help on a few different occasions. He was nice, and I got to know him by name." She pulled in a shuddering breath. "God, I feel like such an idiot."

"Don't," I said sharply. "Don't do that. You can't blame yourself. He fooled everyone, myself included."

I watched as she tried to swallow back the self-judgement; it did not go down easily. Then she took a deep breath and continued. "He was outside the library that night. I was just locking up, and he came running up the steps, completely out of breath, saying he'd left his laptop charger plugged into one of the outlets in the quiet study room. He looked quite desperate, said he had a paper due, so what could I say? I opened back up and let him in so that he could go get it. It was dark. There was no one else there, no one around. That was his plan, I suppose. I waited by the front door for about ten minutes, and then went down to see what was taking him so long."

She paused, her face twisted with pain, and then tried to cover her moment of emotion by taking a long, deliberate draught of the herbal drink Mrs. Mistlemoore had handed her. She drained it, then scrunched her face into a grimace. "Ugh, that was disgusting," she announced, placing the empty glass down on her tray. Then she went on, her voice steadier than before. "He grabbed me from behind. I think he must have been hiding behind one of the computer bays. He... I tried to fight him off, but he was much stronger than he looked for such a lanky guy. I threw my head back as hard as I could. I don't think I quite broke his nose, but it was bleeding pretty freely all over both of us. He managed to get a piece of duct tape over my mouth, but he must have realized I wasn't going to quit struggling. That's when he hit me—hard—across the face. He knocked me cold. I don't remember anything else until I woke up in his flat."

Flavia looked up at me. I tried to smile. "At least you bloodied him up," I said.

She almost laughed. "It didn't do me much good, in the end."

I shrugged. "I didn't even get to fight him off at first. I think he learned his lesson from you, actually. He drugged me—hit me in the neck with some kind of paralytic or sedative. I got a piece of him in the end, though."

"What do you mean?"

"I bit half his ear off."

Flavia's mouth dropped open. "You did *what?!*"

"Why am I hearing raised voices?" came Mrs. Mistlemoore's stern voice, and I turned to see her frowning face poking out of her office. "Do I need to break up this visit?"

"No," Flavia and I both called back. Flavia snatched her toast up off her plate and took a bite for good measure.

"See? Eating," she said as she chewed. "Can't get loud and overexcited when I'm eating!"

Mrs. Mistlemoore narrowed her eyes at us for a moment, then pulled her head back into her office, leaving the door open this time.

Flavia turned back to me, forcing the bite of toast down with what looked like a rather pained swallow. "You bit his *ear* off?" she whispered incredulously.

"Yeah. It was stupid. And gross. But... satisfying," I admitted, keeping my voice to a whisper as well. "He probably would have killed me at that point, but luckily Tia swooped in and stuck him with his own syringe before he had a chance to retaliate."

"Tia? *Tia* did that?!" Flavia hissed, eyes wide with shock.

"Yeah, it was pretty badass. I'll tell you the whole story later. Finish telling me what happened to you, though."

"Well, he was tying me to a chair when I regained consciousness. All the other furniture in the room had been pushed back against the walls, and the curtains were drawn. I thought for sure I was going to be... be raped, or something." Her voice broke and she pulled her glasses away from her eyes so that she could dab at them with her napkin. "It didn't even occur to me that it could possibly have anything to do with me being a Durupinen. Then there was a knock on the door, and for one glorious moment I thought, thank God, I'm saved. But he just walked over, cracked the door, and then stepped back to let the visitor in. It was another guy, and at that point, I just thought, well, that's it. I'm dead."

"The other guy, can you describe him?" I asked her, sure this was information Catriona would press her for later if I didn't get it now. I flipped open the folder and grabbed a pen to jot down the details, so I wouldn't forget.

Flavia furrowed her brow, as though the memory was hard to retrieve. "Mid to late twenties. Tall—maybe two or three inches taller than Charlie. Also, very thin. Bit spotty—pock-marked, you know? Clean shaven. Blonde hair, kind of shaggy, and he wore dark-framed glasses. He looked... intellectual, I guess. Like, I wouldn't have looked at him twice if he'd walked into the library. He had a backpack with him, and I noticed it had a sticker on it from a local coffee shop: Cuppa Wonderful. I've been there a few times."

"What did he say?" I asked.

"Not a single word that I could hear. He whispered with Charlie for a few moments, then went right over to a chair in the corner and pulled it to the center of the room so that he was sitting right across from me. That was when I noticed the Summoning Circle drawn on the floor, when he was setting up the chair. He was careful about making sure that the back legs of the chair were within the boundaries of the Circle."

"What happened next?"

"Charlie took out a book. Even though I had just spotted the Summoning Circle, my brain still wouldn't accept that the whole mess was Durupinen-related. Honestly, my next thought was that he was a medical student gone crazy. Like, I was about to be the victim of some hideous medical experiment that his professors wouldn't sanction, and this newcomer was his laboratory assistant." She laughed caustically. "I guess the mind goes to strange places when you're panicking. Anyway, it took me several more minutes of spiraling down a rabbit hole of B-movie horror plots before I realized that the book Charlie was holding was the *Book of Téigh Anonn*." She suddenly froze, eyes wide and terrified again. "But I should have told that to someone straight away! Do they know? Do they know that he's got the *Book of—*"

"Calm down, it's okay," I told her, rubbing my hand soothingly on her shoulder. "They know. I told them. They've recovered it."

Flavia let out a deep breath and sagged with relief. "Oh, thank God. Do the Trackers know where he got it?"

"I'm not sure," I said truthfully. "But I'm sure they're working on it." I gave her a hard stare. She looked even more exhausted than when I first sat down. "Why don't we stop now, okay? It was stupid for me to ask you about this. You need more time to recover before we—"

"No!" Flavia cried, and her voice was strong, forceful. "I'm fine. And the faster you have all the information I can give you, the

44

better chance you'll have of catching anyone else that might be involved in this."

I considered arguing with her, but decided against it. I'd never seen someone look so fragile and so fierce all at once—well, except maybe Hannah, once upon a time, but her made-of-glass days were far behind her now.

"Okay. I'm shutting up now. Just talk. I'm listening."

Flavia nodded her thanks, adjusted herself against her pillows, and took another sip of tea. The cup had long since stopped steaming, but she didn't seem to care. "He began drawing runes everywhere—on the floor, on the walls, on... on me," she faltered, rubbing unconsciously at her arms, where the marks had been meticulously scrubbed away. "Then he began to do the same to the man sitting across from me. I kept trying to catch his eye, to plead with him to stop participating in... whatever was happening, but he either couldn't or wouldn't look at me."

"Fucking coward," I muttered under my breath. If Flavia heard me, she didn't let it disrupt her at all.

"Since no one seemed to have any interest in telling me what was happening, I fended off my panic by studying the runes, to see if I could get any kind of clue about his intentions from which ones he was using. That was a mistake," she said, and a shudder rocked her frame. "The fact that I couldn't recognize the Casting only made me panic more. I couldn't think. I couldn't breathe. I began to fight against my bindings, tipping my chair over and upsetting candles. Another mistake." She touched the shadow of a bruise that still marred her collarbone beneath several rune-shaped scars. "I'm not sure if it was necessary for him to cut the runes into my skin, but he did so after that. Then he took out the box."

She looked up at me. "Did... did you see the box?" she whispered, and I knew that she held within her more fear and horror at what that box had done to her than anything else.

"Yes," I told her. "Did Mrs. Mistlemoore explain what it was?"

Flavia shook her head. Tears tracked down her cheeks. "She just said that it twisted my Spirit Sight. I think she didn't want to upset me. But Charlie pointed it at me, like he was taking my portrait. He lit all these bright lights and told me to hold still. He even said to me..." She was rendered temporarily speechless as the disgust rose so palpably in her throat that she had to swallow it back, to choke it down. "He said to me, 'Smile pretty for the camera, now.' Then

45

there was just a blinding pain, and everything went dark, and... and that's all I can remember until I woke up last night."

"Really? You can't remember anything else?" I asked, trying to mask my disappointment.

She shook her head. "Nothing. I wish I could, but... from what Mrs. Mistlemoore has told me about what happened to my Spirit Sight, it's probably a very good thing that I can't."

I sighed. "Yes, I think that's probably true."

"That thing he pointed at me... the old camera thing... Mrs. Mistlemoore told me that it twisted my Spirit Sight, but... what *was* it? Where did it come from? What was he trying to do?" Flavia asked, her voice barely more than a whisper.

"It's called a Camera Exspiravit," I said, and the words felt like poison on my tongue. "It's a complicated process that I don't think I can properly explain, but when used correctly, it captures a Durupinen's Spirit Sight and then bestows it on a Necromancer."

Flavia's eyelids fluttered. For a moment, I thought she might faint right there in front of me. I started up out of my seat, though how the hell I thought I would help if she fainted, I had no idea. But she didn't pass out. She closed her eyes a moment and then opened them again, the horror of my words now all over her expression. "Bestow? But... that is not possible."

"It is possible. Do you remember all the Necromancers who descended on your camp four years ago? Do you remember how they controlled the spirits that came with them?"

Flavia swallowed convulsively. "The torches. They had captured their essences in the torches they used to light everything on fire."

"Yes, but did you ever wonder how it was that they could even see the spirits to command them?"

"I..." Flavia looked stunned, as though she couldn't believe she had never considered asking this question before. "I never... I just assumed, some kind of Casting. A Melding, perhaps, or..."

"Well, it was a Casting, but not one of our own. Did you ever see any of their faces?"

Flavia shook her head. "They were hooded. Masked. I never saw one of their faces, or I surely would have spit in it or else clawed their eyes out."

"Well, if you had seen any of them up close, you would have seen that their eyes were silver. It's an effect of the Casting. It's what your eyes looked like, until this morning."

Flavia looked like she might be sick. Then she set her mouth into a determined line. "How?" she asked. "How did they do it?"

"It took them years and years of cruel experiments, but they finally perfected it. They used a willing Durupinen traitor to give the Spirit Sight to all the senior members of the Necromancers, and that enabled them to carry out their siege."

Flavia blanched. "What Durupinen in her right mind would ever allow a Necromancer to put her through what I went through?"

"Well, I never said she was in her right mind," I hedged. "When done properly, the Camera Exspiravit doesn't twist the Spirit Sight. It merely lifts a copy of it from the Durupinen and bestows it on a Necromancer by means of the image itself. If the image is destroyed, so, too, is the Necromancer's borrowed Spirit Sight."

"And a Durupinen allowed that to happen?" Flavia asked in an awed and horrified whisper.

"Yes," I said. "Her name is Lucida, and she was the one who betrayed us to the Necromancers four years ago, when the Prophecy came to pass. She's still alive; she was captured and sent to the *príosún* at Skye. I imagine the Trackers will be paying her another visit soon, to answer for her part in this experiment."

"But I don't understand," Flavia said, rubbing at her temples in a weary sort of way. "If the process isn't meant to destroy the Durupinen's Spirit Sight, then what happened to me?"

"When the Necromancers fell at Fairhaven, much of the equipment and documentation of the process was destroyed in the ensuing raids. Charlie took it upon himself as one of the uncaptured Candidates to take up the mantle and try to revive the process. He thought it was the key to the Necromancers rising again."

"Well, at least that plan is dust," Flavia said, with just a hint of satisfaction in her voice. "It may have been hell for a few of us, but at least he's been caught and that... that torture device has been destroyed."

The plan may not be dust at all. The Necromancers might even be rising as we speak, turning our Caomhnóir into allies and our príosún into a fortress, I thought wildly, though I said nothing of it aloud. Instead I pressed where I knew I probably shouldn't press. And yet I had to know.

"Flavia, you said you don't remember anything from the moment that Charlie took your likeness. Is that right?"

47

Flavia seemed to freeze at my words. One corner of her mouth began to twitch repeatedly. She shook her head.

"Mrs. Mistlemoore said that might happen," I told her softly. "She said that your mind is going to protect itself, because twisting the Spirit Sight can be... very painful."

Flavia swallowed convulsively. Her eyelids fluttered. "When I think about it... when I try to recall something... it's like there's a door there, that's been slammed shut. And when I jiggle the handle, or try to peek through the keyhole..." Her whole body shuddered. "I start to feel trapped and suffocated. I can't breathe. My skin starts to crawl. And then the door just... pushes me away. Please, Jess. Please, don't ask me about it. I don't think I'm supposed to remember."

"Okay," I told her, reaching out to pat her hand, which was visibly trembling upon her blanket. "No more questions about that, I promise. What I actually wanted to ask you about happened *after* Mrs. Mistlemoore and the Scribes reversed Charlie's Casting on you."

Flavia frowned. "After?"

"Yes," I said. "So, after I ask you, if you still feel the... the door thing... then don't worry about it, okay? Don't try to answer. I'm not here to cause you any more pain."

"Okay," she said, looking mystified and still a little wary.

"The night that Mrs. Mistlemoore reversed the Casting, I was here in the hospital wing, asleep. I woke up just as they were finishing, and she gave me the good news that they believed they had succeeded in restoring your Spirit Sight to its proper state, even though they were still waiting to see if there would be any lasting damage." I paused, choosing my next words carefully. "I came to sit with you, and held your hand. When I touched you, you... you grabbed onto my hand and opened your eyes."

Flavia's eyes widened. "I did?"

"Yes. The next few minutes are a blank for me, but the next thing I knew, you were lying peacefully asleep again, and I had created a spirit drawing."

"A spirit drawing?" Flavia whispered.

"Yes. Right on the fabric of the partition that was blocking off your bed space," I said.

Flavia looked utterly bewildered. "But... how could a living person evoke a spirit drawing? I've never heard of such a thing."

48

I shook my head. "Neither have I. But then again, you were in a unique state, having your Spirit Sight twisted and then untwisted again. I don't think the normal rules apply."

Flavia gave a nervous chuckle. "No, I suppose not."

"Anyway, I... you know that I've done a bit of... of prophetic drawing," I said, not quite meeting her eye.

"I think it's fair to say I know that better than most people," Flavia said quietly. This was, of course, true. It was she who had finally correctly interpreted the prophetic drawing that enabled us to free Irina from the wrath of the Traveler Council, the drawing that I had misinterpreted as predicting Annabelle's death but that had, in fact, been revealing Annabelle's true nature as a Walker. She had promised me that she would never tell anyone that I was a Seer, and I believed her. Her promise might be moot now, as it was highly possible that I'd soon have to tell everyone myself. Still, I wasn't ready to admit to Flavia just how scared I was, or just how much could be at stake. I couldn't bring her to look any more scared or exhausted or utterly drained than she already looked.

"I... I just wanted to know if you remembered anything about that night. Do you remember seeing me? Or... or waking up at all?"

Flavia furrowed her brow. I could practically hear her gears turning as she dug through her memory for any clues or fleeting images. At last she shook her head. "I'm sorry, Jess. I just can't recall anything. It doesn't feel blocked, not like when my Spirit Sight was twisted. Just... blank."

I nodded resignedly. "Okay. Just one last thing. Would you be willing to look at the drawing, just to see if it looks... familiar?"

Flavia didn't answer right away. She seemed to be having some sort of internal struggle. At last she closed her eyes and sighed. "Okay. I know you wouldn't ask me if it wasn't really important."

"No, I definitely wouldn't," I agreed. "So, is it okay if I show it to you?"

She looked alarmed. "You... you actually have it with you?"

"No, I just took a picture of it. It's on my phone," I said, pulling my phone out of my pocket and giving it a little wave.

"Oh, okay," Flavia said, and she sounded relieved. Somehow in her mind, I supposed, an image of the drawing was less frightening than the drawing itself. "Right, then, let's see it."

I opened my gallery, found the image and handed the phone to Flavia.

Almost at once, her eyebrows drew together in confusion. She put down her teacup and used her fingers to enlarge the image on the screen, taking her time to examine every angle, every detail. I watched her very carefully for a flash of comprehension, an inkling of a memory stirred somewhere in her traumatized brain, but I saw nothing but concentration and puzzlement in her features. At last, she sighed and handed the phone back to me.

"I'm sorry I can't help you, Jess, but I've never seen that place before. It looks like some kind of Durupinen stronghold, though, with the triskele flags on top of the parapets. Maybe a seat of one of the other clans? I wish I understood it, so I could help you."

I fought to keep the disappointment out of my face. "Don't worry about it, Flavia," I told her, not bothering to mention what I'd already been able to deduce from the image. "I'll figure it out."

Flavia looked stricken. "I can't imagine why I would be the one to reveal this image to you."

"Maybe you weren't," I suggested. "Maybe it was a complete coincidence that the vision struck me while I was sitting with you."

The look Flavia gave me was almost pitying. She didn't believe that any more than I did, and we both knew it.

"Well, anyway," I said, trying to keep my tone light, "now that you've seen it, who knows? It might bring something back to you. Just think about it for me, would you?"

Flavia nodded, her lower lip trembling. "Sure."

"Hey," I said gently, taking her hand and squeezing it. "Don't feel guilty about this. And while we're on the subject, don't you dare let yourself feel guilty about any of it. Nothing that happened to you was your fault. No decision you made or action you took made you culpable in any of this, do you understand?"

Flavia nodded, refusing to look at me.

"I'm going to let you eat and get some more rest," I told her firmly, standing up from the bed. "I'll come check on you later, okay?"

Flavia just nodded again. At a loss for what I could possibly say to comfort her, I just gave her an encouraging smile, and turned to go. Her voice rang out behind me, quiet but sharp.

"Jess? Could... would you please... stay with me for a little while?"

I turned to see her looking down at her own hands twisting in her lap, as though she were ashamed to even have asked for what she needed. She looked like a child. I could have cried, but I refrained for her sake.

"Of course, I will," I told her. I walked back to the bed and tossed my folder full of interview questions onto the bedside table. I pointed to the tray on Flavia's lap. "Are you done with that?"

"Yes," she said, wrinkling her nose at the cold remains of the food on her plate.

I lifted the tray from her lap and placed it on the bedside table with my folder. "Scooch over, then. Don't be a bed hog," I told her, and she did so, giving me a tearful smile. I slid onto the bed next to her, adjusted her blankets so that she was carefully tucked in, and laid down beside her. She took my hand and held it tightly against her.

"You know what the worst part is?" she whispered after a few moments.

"What?"

"They were right. This was what our clans always warned us about," she said, and she adopted a stronger Romanian lilt to her speech as she added, as though in the voice of her Clan Elders, "The greater world cannot be trusted, and that is why we band together in blood. That is how we thrive: together but apart, isolated but protected. That is why we have survived so long."

And I could see it in her face; everything she'd fought so hard for—her independence, her education, her freedom—she was doubting that any of it had been worth it.

"You don't really believe that, do you?" I asked her.

She looked up at me, her face twitching with repressed emotion. "Maybe not forever, no. But I do today."

5

TRIBUTE

I HAD NO INTENTION of falling asleep there with Flavia, but so many nights of fractured sleep had taken their toll on me, and rather than just closing my eyes for a few moments, I woke with a start to see late afternoon sun streaming in through the high windows.

I sat up and stared anxiously all around me for some sign that the prophecy had yet again taken control of me while I slept, but I could find no trace of the familiar drawing anywhere. I heaved a sigh of relief as I extricated myself gently from Flavia, taking great care not to wake her. I tucked her hand under her blankets and pulled my phone from my pocket to check the time. It was nearly six o'clock. I had very nearly slept right through Bertie's funeral.

"Damn it!"

I ran all the way back to my room, swearing under my breath as I went. I wrenched open the closet door, forgetting all about the pile of drawings in my haste. They drifted out into the room like snow. Swearing some more, I dropped to my knees and shoved them back into the darkness and then snatched my obligatory white ceremonial clothes and my clan colors off the rack. The whole time I was dressing, I could feel the presence of the drawings, staring at me like eyes, silently begging to be released from their cage and revealed to the world.

"I'm working on it, okay?" I muttered, unsure if I was talking to the drawings, or my Seer gift, or myself. "Just... behave yourself."

We all knew how good I was at behaving myself.

"Where've you been?" Hannah asked, as I jogged into the courtyard at last. I attracted a few disapproving glares, which I chose to ignore, seeing as flipping people off would only increase the dirty looks and probably wasn't good funeral etiquette.

"I was visiting Flavia and apparently decided it would be a good use of my time to take a quick, seven-hour nap," I said.

"I'm not surprised. You've barely slept all week," Hannah said, giving me a critical look, like she was considering sending me back to bed. "I was wondering why you weren't answering through the connection. I was about to send Milo out to go look for you."

"Hello? I'm an eternal source of otherworldly guidance, not an errand boy," Milo interjected indignantly. He was sitting just behind Hannah, next to Tia, who was looking a bit frightened and out of place. Hannah had lent her a white sundress so that she could try to blend in. She had requested to be allowed to stay for the funeral, a request that Celeste had granted in light of all that Charlie Wright had recently put Tia through. Tia had never actually met Bertie, but she felt compelled to pay her respects to him, seeing as he had died at Charlie's hands.

"How is Flavia doing?" Tia whispered.

"She's awake," I told her. "She's still really weak, but she's awake and talking."

"Oh, thank goodness," Tia said, while Hannah and Milo also made exclamations of relief. "What about Phoebe?"

"No change yet, but if Flavia is on the mend, it's only a matter of time, right?" I said.

"Let's hope so, for Savvy's sake," Hannah said. "You didn't see her on the way down, did you?"

"No, I..." my voice died away. At the mention of Savvy, I looked around for her and took in the details of my surroundings for the first time, details that I had missed in my haste not to be late.

It looked as though the courtyard was playing host to a performance rather than a funeral. An enormous platform had been erected, much taller than necessary for all the gathered spectators to see what was going on. Behind it, a huge purple velvet drape had been strung between two poles like a backdrop. A table stood in the middle of the platform, but there was no sign of a casket or any other trapping that might suggest a person was about to be laid to rest.

"What's with the stage?" I asked no one in particular, but it was Hannah who answered.

She slid over to make room for me on the stone bench and patted the empty space beside her. "I don't know. Maybe there's some kind of ceremony?"

I nodded absently. The Durupinen loved their elaborate ceremonies. I took the seat and turned back to Hannah. "Sorry, I got distracted. What did you ask me?"

"I asked you if you saw Savvy on your way down. I'm starting to get worried. It's going to start in a few minutes. I thought maybe she was with you, but... you don't think she's going to miss it on purpose, do you?"

"I don't think so. I'll go look for her," I said, jumping to my feet.

"Don't take too long, Jess, or you'll be late!" Hannah hissed at me.

"I'll be quick," I assured her as I jogged back across the courtyard, being sure to greet every nasty look with an especially saccharine smile.

Halfway to the castle doors, Savvy's mentee Frankie intercepted me. Her sister, whom I had only met once or twice, lingered behind her, nodding at me shyly.

"Hi, Jess," Frankie said. She tried to smile, but the resulting expression was a grimace at best. "Have you seen Savannah?"

"No, I haven't seen her since breakfast. I've been—well, I was caught up with Tracker stuff all day," I hedged, not wanting to admit I'd been asleep for the better part of the day. "She isn't down at the service yet; I was just in the courtyard."

Frankie bit her lip. "I was supposed to meet her at her room and we were going to walk down together, but she wasn't there."

"I was just heading in to look for her. I'll find her, don't worry. She's probably just..." I shrugged, and Frankie nodded knowingly.

"Yeah. I think we all are," she replied. Then, with a nod of thanks, she and her sister headed in the direction of the courtyard.

The castle was nearly deserted as I hurried through it, passing only the occasional spirit drifting through the corridors. Everyone had already gone out to the grounds. I tried Savvy's room first, in case she'd returned to it since Frankie had stopped by, but my knocks went unanswered. I considered for a moment that Savvy might be inside, purposely ignoring all attempts to contact her, but I didn't think so, for some reason. Because of all we'd been through together, I just couldn't believe that Savvy would hear me calling for her and not answer me.

I started back down the hallway and then stopped, thinking.

Where would Savvy go? Where would she go to hide and avoid

something she didn't want to face? A flash of memory came to me, and it was almost enough to make me smile... almost.

I knew where she was.

She had drawn the shower curtain, but I could hear her sniffling. I smelled the smoke before I saw it, curling and twisting in a little serpentine plume before dissipating against the ceiling tiles.

"Knock, knock," I said softly.

I heard her swear under her breath before she replied, in a thick, tear-choked voice, "I hate those bloody jokes."

"Me, too," I said. "Can I come in?"

"I ain't stoppin' ya."

I pulled the curtain to reveal her sitting on the shower bench, knees pulled up under her chin, a cigarette dangling from one hand and a silver flask clutched in the other. Her eyes were red and bloodshot, and her hair obscured half of her face.

I sat down beside her, and she pulled her foot in to make room for me on the bench.

"How did you find me?" she asked, after a few seconds of silence.

"I tried to think of where you might go if you wanted to hide from something. This was the first place that sprang to mind."

"Really? You remembered that?"

"It's not every day a stranger busts into my shower and tells me I've got nice tits," I told her. "Let's just say you left an impression."

Savvy tried to smile, but her lips didn't have the heart to curve. They trembled a moment, then drooped back into a miserable downturn.

"So, what's going on, Sav? I know you didn't come down here just for a shower, or you would have invited me."

She looked me in the eyes and sighed. "I'm drunk," she announced.

"I can see that."

"Didn't set out to be. Told myself I'd just grit my teeth and bear it." She sighed and raised the flask. "Guess that plan's gone to shite."

"Indeed, it has," I agreed. "Don't worry about it. Plans aren't your cup of tea anyway."

"That's for bloody sure," Savvy said, draining the flask with one last swig and then tossing it onto the floor. It clattered noisily away across the tiles and came to a stop with a dull thunk against the far wall. She stared at it intently, as though she were expecting it to get up, dust itself off, and walk away.

"I came down to see if you wanted to come up to the courtyard with me," I told her quietly. "I thought maybe we could walk there together."

Savvy dragged her sleeve across her face, sniffling loudly. "I can't, Jess. I just can't bloody do it."

"Okay," I said. "Tell me why you can't do it."

"Last night, I was all right, you know? I talked myself into it, like. I knew it would be awful, but I knew I had to be there," Savvy said.

"So, what changed?" I asked her, when she didn't go on. "You seemed to be okay at breakfast."

"I went outside!" she cried. The cigarette fell from her trembling fingers and was extinguished with a soft hiss in a puddle of water on the shower floor. "I couldn't eat a damn thing, so I went outside for a fag instead, and I saw it."

"Saw what?" I asked her.

She blinked at me. "In the courtyard! In the bloody courtyard! Ain't you been out to the courtyard yet?"

"Yeah, I was just there," I said, keeping my voice calm even as I tried to understand what had her so rattled.

"Well, you saw it, then, didn't you?" Savvy asked me, eyes wide with indignation and incredulity, as though accusing me of something.

"Saw... saw what?" I asked. "I... there was a platform with a huge curtain hung behind it. I don't remember seeing anything—"

"Well, it's behind the bloody curtain, then," Savvy said, pulling a cigarette from the crumpled pack in her pocket and attempting to light it, but her hands were shaking too badly.

"What's behind the curtain?" I asked tentatively. "Is it the casket? Because I know caskets are upsetting, but..."

"No, it's not a casket!" Savvy cried, her voice rising to a shrill, hysterical screech now. "I don't care about a bloody casket, do I? Who cares about a wooden box?"

"Well, then what are you—"

"It's a fucking pyre!" Savvy shrieked, tears spilling down her cheeks. "They're not just going to drop him into a hole in the ground—as if that wouldn't be awful enough. No! No, when a Caomhnóir dies, they build a fucking bonfire and roast him in front of a crowd of people like he's a bloody Viking!"

I felt a wave of nausea at the thought. "Oh, Sav. Oh, Jesus. I had no idea."

"Nor did I, but don't you think it would have been nice of someone to warn me?! You know, just a 'Hey, Savvy, did you get some breakfast? Oh, just a heads up, we're going to light your Caomhnóir on fire and then make you watch him burn until there's nothing left but some charred bones and a pile of ash.'" Her words were tumbling out, mounting each other as though racing to get away from the unbearable image that had chased them forth. Her cigarette tumbled from her mouth as she turned and started punching the wall behind her as hard as she could.

"Oh, my God, stop! Savvy, stop it!"

I jumped to my feet and threw my arms around her, heaving her away from the wall even as she landed another blow on the tiles, leaving them smeared with blood. She twisted and struggled against me, all the while spewing forth an unintelligible stream of sobs and curses and expletives, wishing each one was another blow she could destroy something with.

She lunged for the wall again and we overbalanced, falling back into the corner of the stall. She began lashing out with her feet and I stared wildly around for a way to subdue her. Then my eyes fell on the shower faucet handle. I reached around Savvy's flailing arms and twisted it on, so that both of us were suddenly doused in icy cold water.

It worked. Savvy gasped and screamed, but her body went stiff and still in my arms as the chill of the water shocked her out of her outburst. I held on to her tightly, eyes shut against the water. I listened as her shrieks turned to sobs and her body sagged. She turned and buried her face in my neck, still crying inconsolably, and together we sank down onto the floor of the shower stall.

And the tears were hot, and the water was cold, and the pain was shattering, and all I could do was sit there and hold her while she came apart, holding all the pieces together for her because she couldn't hold them together herself.

I don't know how long we sat there, rivulets of water running over us and pooling around us, but it felt like a long time. The tears slowed and the gasps turned to shuddering breaths as Savvy finally cried herself out. At last, I felt like I could reach up behind me and shut the water off. The dripping echoed loudly in the stillness that followed.

"It's my fault, Jess. It will never not be my fault," Savvy said at last.

"I know that feels true right now. I know it does. But it's not your fault, Sav. Truly, it's not."

"It is. I know you're my mate, and you want to make me feel better, but it just ain't true, what you're saying."

I turned to her and waited for her to push the sodden curls out of her eyes so that she could look at me. "Was it my fault when Pierce died?"

Her eyes went wide. "I... that's not the same... no, of course it wasn't."

"Whose fault was it?" I asked quietly.

"It was those bloody Necromancers that killed him," she replied, almost grudgingly.

"Exactly. Don't let them do this to you, Sav. It's bad enough that they took him. Don't take the blame for them. They deserve every ounce of the hatred you're heaping on your own head right now."

"I can't help it. I can't stop thinking about how awful I was to him, Jess," Savvy whispered. "I never had a single kind word for him, and all he was trying to do was protect me. I mean, he was absolute shite at it, but he tried his best."

"I don't think that mattered. This system is so fucked up. None of the Caomhnóir and Durupinen get along. There's so much tension, and so much resentment. Look at how I treat Ambrose, for God's sake! It's not his fault that Finn is gone, but I take it out on him every chance I get. It's shitty, and I know it, but I can't help it. But Bertie never let it bother him. He took pride in it, Sav. He was proud to be your Caomhnóir," I told her.

"But I was never proud of him, and I should have been. Maybe then, he wouldn't have gone charging off to the hotel. Maybe he wouldn't have felt like he had something to prove."

"But he would have felt that way regardless," I told her. "It's the Caomhnóir mentality. He didn't charge off to that hotel because of you. He did it because that's what he's been told practically from birth that he's supposed to do—fling himself into harm's way in the name of the Northern Clans. It's messed up, but it's true. It's their culture. And it's probably why so many of them resent us so much. We're evil temptresses who will make their lives hell and yet they are forced to be around us twenty-four seven and lay down their lives without a second thought if one of us is in danger. You didn't create this system, Savvy. You're just a victim of it, and so was Bertie."

Savvy sniffed for a few moments, evidently letting these ideas sink in. Then she said, "It's got to change, then."

"I'm hoping it will," I said. "So is Hannah. She's already working on it. Maybe you can even help her."

Savvy picked her head back up off my shoulder. "Help her? You reckon? How?"

"She's drafting legislation that will totally change the Durupinen–Caomhnóir dynamic. She's doing it for me, obviously—well, for me and Finn—but we're not the only reason. The way things are right now is toxic. We could change that. That's a very real thing that we could do, for Bertie, for Finn... for everyone."

Savvy sniffed again. "It would feel good, I think. To have something to do."

"I think so too," I said, wishing at the same time that I had nothing at all to do—no mystery looming over my head, no great riddle that needed solving before our entire world was thrown into chaos again. "And there is one other thing we have to do now."

Savvy heaved a shuddery sigh. "Ah, Jess. I honestly don't know if I can do it."

"Yes, you can. He was always there for you. You can show your gratitude by being there for him this one last time. Come on. I'll be right beside you."

Savvy looked down at herself and made a sound that would have been a laugh if she'd been capable of laughing in that moment. "Look at me. I'm a disaster." She looked up at me. "And so are you."

"Do you want to run to your room to change? The ceremony starts in less than five minutes. I'm not really sure if we've got time to—"

But Savvy was already shaking her head. "If I go to my room now, you won't get me out again. Let's just go now before I lose my nerve. I don't reckon Bertie will care if I'm a bit damp."

And so, we got to our feet and walked, putting one foot in front of the other, moving relentlessly forward, all the way through the castle halls, down the stairs, out the front doors, and across the lawns. People stared at us, whispering behind their hands as we passed, pointing at our dripping clothes and sopping hair. We didn't care. I held on to Savvy's arm, steering her through the stone pillars and between the benches of solemn-faced onlookers to her seat, right in the very front row. I sat beside her, where Phoebe would have sat, if she were well enough to attend. She was gripping my hand so tightly that my fingers were starting to go numb, but I ignored it.

As we sat down, I caught Hannah's eye in the row behind us. Her voice, followed by Milo's, popped into my head through the connection.

"Oh my goodness, what happened to you two?"

"What the hell? Why are you both dripping wet?"

I shook my head. "I'll tell you later." I let my reply slip through the connection just as I closed it off. I couldn't have anyone else's emotions buzzing around in my brain like trapped bees. My own—and Savvy's—would be more than enough to deal with.

"Here," Hannah whispered this aloud, thrusting a thin white taper candle into my hand just as Frankie reached over and handed one to Savvy. All around us, Durupinen were touching the tips of their candles to each other, and tiny orange flames were springing to life at the ends of them. It took Savvy three attempts to light her candle, her hands were shaking so badly, and then she stared at the thing, trembling in her hand, as though she had never seen a candle before and was half-afraid of it. I winked at her and pulled the candle gently from her hand before she burned herself with dripping wax. "I'll handle the props," I whispered to her. "Just breathe, okay?"

We both jumped in fright as a single beat of a drum resounded through the courtyard. The whispering, murmuring crowd hushed at once. A second drum beat rolled through the space like thunder, then another, and another, the pauses between them shorter each time, until they condensed into a somber marching cadence. Then a set of bagpipes began to play in the distance, perhaps from the window of one of the towers, though it was impossible to tell, as the sound seemed to have no direction, no source, but instead to resound in the ground below our feet, or else to rise from the very air itself as a cool breeze swept through the courtyard.

The sounds of marching boots joined the beat of the drum as two long rows of Caomhnóir paraded through the central archway, Seamus in the lead. Each of their faces was stoic and grave as they processed down the aisle, eyes fixed over the head of the crowd. Celeste rose from her seat and ascended the platform, hands clasped in front of her, her head bowed respectfully as the Caomhnóir marched toward her. Beside me, Savvy was trembling violently from a combination of emotion and the chill of the wind, which was picking up now and raising goosebumps on our skin and whipping our hair around our faces. The candles in my hand sputtered and smoked, but did not go out.

The very last Caomhnóir in the procession bore an elaborately carved stretcher upon their shoulders. Long, spear-like torches had been thrust through the four corners of the stretcher, so that flames streamed above it like flags in the wind. Upon the stretcher, a long white shroud shielded Bertie's body from view, and yet drew every eye to him. The gossamer fabric clung to the shape of him, so that every detail was apparent—the turned-up tip of his nose, his hands folded upon his abdomen, the toes of his boots thrust upward toward the darkening sky.

I looked nervously over at Savvy, but she had gone oddly still. The sight of Bertie's body, rather than peaking her emotions, seemed to have quelled them. Her trembling had stopped. Her hands, which had been twisting anxiously around the hem of her top, had fallen motionless into her lap. She did not avert her eyes, but gazed directly at him, following the pale, billowing shape of him as he passed by our seats and was borne onto the platform.

I couldn't decide if this new stillness made me feel less worried about her, or more, but I did not have time to puzzle it out. The echoing notes of the bagpipes had faded away and, with a last resounding thud, the drumming and marching stopped. Several spirits hovered in the shadows nearby, watching with equal solemnity.

The Caomhnóir had assembled in two rows, stretching across the platform and down the stairs on either side. They faced not the crowd, but Bertie's body, which had been carried to the very center of the platform, still upon his Brothers' shoulders. They stood silently as Celeste walked to the center of the platform, where she met Seamus.

My only experience with funerals had involved eulogies, and so I expected Celeste to turn to us, to deliver some sort of speech, but she did not. Instead, she extended her hands toward Seamus. In them, she held a neatly folded cloth of pale purple. The firelight glinted off the golden threads that ran through it as they both laid hands upon it and began, together, to unfold it carefully. Then they stepped together back to the plinth and draped the cloth across Bertie's chest. It was a sort of stole, long and rectangular, with golden triskeles stitched onto it.

Then Seamus's voice boomed out over the crowd, reciting words in old Gaelic that I could only understand snatches of. "Spirit." "Courage." "Guardian." "Clan." It didn't matter if the details were hazy. We all knew the depth and breadth of what he was expressing, all felt it filling the courtyard as though it were riding the current of the wind. Then Seamus turned to Bertie, his expression twisted and pained, and knelt on a single knee, pressing one fist to his chest as he bowed his head.

Every Caomhnóir in the courtyard followed suit. They remained with their heads bowed as the drum in the distance beat seven times. Then they rose as one, and stood at attention again.

"Please rise," Celeste called to the assembled Durupinen, and we all complied at once.

The wide velvet curtain behind the platform dropped to the ground with a swooshing sound, revealing a tall pyre built of meticulously stacked logs. A few gasps arose from the assembly, Hannah's amongst them. Now the height of the platform made sense: the Caomhnóir could place the stretcher right on top of the plinth without so much as raising it above their shoulders. We watched as they did so, sliding it smoothly onto the topmost logs until its handles slipped into grooves that had been notched into them to hold it. The wind carried a strong scent of gasoline through the courtyard. It burned my nostrils and made me lightheaded. Then four Caomhnóir reached up and pulled the torches from the four corners of the stretcher and stood, holding them aloft, awaiting their order to set the pyre ablaze.

Seamus began to speak again. I barely listened, catching snatches of it as I stared down at the candle flames dancing in my hand. It was full of words like "duty" and "honor," words that were supposed to fill up empty, aching places with something resembling meaning and sense. The Caomhnóir echoed him, chanting words back to him, but their voices only made the words sound hollower, as though repeating them enough times drained the sense and meaning right out of them.

Then the bagpipes began to play again, and the drum began to beat. The four torch bearers stepped forward and, as one, thrust their torches into gaps in the pyre. At once the flames began to climb and lick their way up the logs, blackening the wood and sending plumes of dark smoke toward the sky, which was now deepening from the pink of sunset to the violet of twilight.

Beside me, Savvy dropped my hand and took a sudden step forward. I looked over at her to see that she had her eyes fixed on Bertie's body, as yet untouched by the flames. She took another step forward.

"Savvy?" I whispered to her. "Savvy, are you okay?"

She did not acknowledge me at all. I wasn't sure if she'd even heard me. She took another step forward.

"Savvy, what are you doing?" I hissed. I reached a hand toward her, trying to pull her fingers back into mine, but she batted it away, still staring transfixedly at the pyre. Slowly—almost dreamily, like a sleepwalker—she crossed the empty expanse of ground between our seats and the platform. She stood at the base of the steps for a moment, her still sopping clothes dripping gently onto the flagstones. Then she began to ascend the stairs.

Murmurs rippled through the onlookers, and though I could not hear their words, I knew the questions they must be asking themselves: What is she doing? Why is she soaking wet? Why is she interrupting the service like this? The Caomhnóir were all turning to stare at her as well, glancing at each other and at Seamus for instructions, but Seamus himself simply stood there, an expression of utter bewilderment on his face.

It was Celeste who stepped forward as Savvy reached the top of the steps. "Savannah?" She spoke the name carefully, as though she were afraid to startle Savvy. "Savannah? Are you all right, my dear?"

Savvy didn't answer. It was as though Celeste had not even spoken. Savvy walked straight across the platform until she was standing directly in front of the pyre, the heat from the now roiling flames blowing her hair back from her face.

My heart thudded in my chest, fear rooting me to the spot. What was she doing? What the *hell* was she doing?

For several seconds, no one moved. Then Savvy reached out a hand toward the nearest Caomhnóir and pulled a long, curved dagger from the sheath on his belt. The Caomhnóir reached out and grabbed her wrist and raised his other hand to disarm her but then stopped. He was staring into Savvy's fierce face, and whatever he saw there stayed his hand. Still looking into her eyes, he released her wrist and dropped both of his hands to his sides.

Celeste started forward, opening her mouth in some form of protestation, but it was Seamus who thrust out an arm and shook his head slowly, eyes still on Savvy. Celeste still looked fearful, but she stayed where she was, obeying the silent order that Seamus had given her.

Savvy turned back to Bertie's body, tears and sweat streaming down her face. The orange glow of the flames caught at the fiery color of her hair, which looked, for a moment, to be made of flame itself. Then Savvy reached back and gathered that flaming hair within her hand, gripping it tightly at the back of her neck. Then she raised the gleaming dagger, set the blade to the first of the fiery strands and let out a low, shuddering moan. The dagger flashed back and forth, and within a few moments, the entire length of hair came away in her hands.

The dagger clattered to the wooden floor of the platform. Savvy held the hair up and looked at it, turning it over once in her hand before tossing it, with a keening cry, right onto Bertie's clasped hands.

She stood, shoulders shaking, chest heaving, watching her hair and the boy beneath it burn. Then she turned, walked down the steps, straight out of the courtyard and into the twilit grounds. The eye of every Caomhnóir fixated on her as one by one, they knelt down and bowed their heads in acknowledgement of her tribute.

No one dared follow her.

6

MAKE-OVERS

F RANKIE CLOSED HER BOOK, sighing so deeply that the sound might've originated all the way down in her toes. "Where do you reckon Savvy is?" she asked quietly, to no one in particular.

It was nearly three o'clock in the afternoon. We were all sitting in the library at Fairhaven. Raindrops were racing each other along blurry tracks down the windowpanes. I'd promised to help Hannah gather a list of past sanctions of Durupinen–Caomhnóir relationships, to help bolster the research for her proposed legislation, which would be heard in a few weeks. I was starting to regret my decision for two reasons. First, many of the documents were in various forms of Gaelic and Old Britannic, so deciphering them was giving me a pounding headache. Second, each one was a reminder of the many hearts that had been broken and lives destroyed by a rule put in place in an effort to forestall our eventual birth. The guilt was crippling.

Hannah looked up from an ancient scroll with an equally deep sigh and replied to Frankie. "I was just wondering the same thing. No one has seen much of her since the funeral, have they?" She looked around at all of us as though hoping someone could offer a different answer.

"I don't even think she came back to her room last night," Mackie said in a whisper, as one of the Scribes shuffled by, arms full of ancient tomes. "I was waiting for her, just sort of hoping I could say something—anything—that might help. But she never turned up. I waited until close to dawn. I suppose it's just as well," she added, looking a bit sheepish. "I don't know what I would've said if she had turned up. Probably just stammered at her like a prat."

"I don't think any of us would've known what to say," I told her. "I mean, it's just a myth, isn't it—words that can actually help somebody in a situation like that? Those words just don't exist."

We were all quiet for a few seconds. I'm not sure what anyone else was thinking about, but I thought back to when I'd lost my mom, to when I'd wandered through the world aimlessly, every thought and feeling smothered under a suffocating blanket of horror. No words could have reached me in there. There was nothing that anyone could say. And honestly, I probably would've resented them for trying—for even suggesting that the pain wasn't going to end me. It would have felt minimizing—insulting, almost.

Yes, it *is* that bad. No, there is *nothing* you can do to make it better. Just let me ache until the aching is done and leave me the hell alone.

"I kept an eye out for her this morning, when Tia left for London," I said, pulling myself out of that pile of baggage. "After the cab picked Tia up, I took a walk around outside. No sign of her."

"Ah, damn. I forgot to wish Tia luck on her exam," Frankie groaned.

"That's okay," I told her. "We all had a lot going on last night. I'm just sorry she has to take an exam at all, with everything that's been going on. But that's Tia for you. Work is the best medicine for anything that's ailing her. Her classmates will walk out of that exam feeling drained. She'll walk out of there feeling like she could run a marathon. She's just weird like that."

Frankie frowned and opened her mouth, presumably to tell me that wasn't weird at all, but Hannah forestalled her by bringing the conversation back around to our original topic.

"Do you think someone should go look for Savvy?" she asked, biting her lip nervously. "I mean, I'm sure she needs space, and maybe we should give it to her, but I would hate for her to feel alone if she needs somebody to talk—"

As though Hannah's words had summoned her, Savvy barreled through the library doors like a ginger-topped tornado. The Scribe at the front desk scowled at her, and began hissing some sort of admonishment. Savvy rolled her eyes, barely looking at the woman, and continued to march across the room, flipping two fingers over her shoulder for good measure.

"Oi there, you three," she said casually, dropping into the only empty chair left at the table. "All right?"

It was only then, when she stopped her forward progress, that we noticed Milo floating along in her wake like a shadow. He had a satisfied smile on his face, which seemed odd to me, until I took a better look at Savvy.

I struggled to thread my words together. "Savvy... I... your hair!"

"Ah, yeah, I know, right?" Savvy asked running her fingers through it. "Haven't I ever told you not to let me near swords when I'm that pissed? Or microphones. Swords and microphones, big no-no's for ol' Savvy after a bender like that."

"No, it's just..." I had no way to say what I wanted to say without sounding totally rude. "Well, it's just that you... you look like you've just gotten back from the salon or something. I mean, no offense, but you sort of... chopped your hair off with a blunt dagger. And now it looks like you just had it professionally styled. I just don't think that's likely, given the way you hacked it off."

"Oh, *that*," Savvy said, grinning broadly. "Well, first of all, sorry about that. I sort of... well, flipped out last night. I don't even really know what made me do it. I just had this overwhelming need to... pay tribute, I guess. I didn't really think it through. And once I'd done it... well, I couldn't really undo it, could I? So, once I'd had a good cry and come to my senses, Milo took pity on me."

We all looked over at Milo. His wide grin now made just a bit more sense. I should have recognized it. That was a familiar look on his face: the look of someone who had just achieved the unachievable: turning a fashion disaster into something ready to strut along the catwalk.

"Milo, *you* did that?" Hannah asked, clearly incredulous. "But... how?"

Milo gave a little shrug of his shoulders. The gesture was an attempt at modesty but failed miserably at achieving it. "I couldn't let my girl walk around with a hack job like that," he said. "Even if she did do it for, like, totally honorable reasons. She deserved to smile when she looked in the mirror, after everything she's been through. So, we Habitated."

"Habitated?" I asked, looking back and forth between Savvy and Milo.

Milo saw the look on my face and winked. "Aw, come on. Don't be jealous. You know you'll always be my first."

I rolled my eyes, but didn't reply, turning back to Savvy instead.

"That's right," said Savvy. "We just got a little cozy and personal. It actually felt good, having someone else in my head, so I could listen to someone else's thoughts instead of wallowing in my own. A few snips here, a few snips there..."

"And voilà!" Milo said, and he flipped his hands toward Savvy's hair, as though we were a studio audience and she was the prize behind door number three. "And there we have it. A hairstyle befitting a woman who chops off her hair with a sword like a badass warrior goddess."

Savvy snorted. "A warrior goddess? A nutter who's lost her bloody mind, more like, but I'll take it. Cheers, mate," she added, grinning at Milo.

The haircut really was fabulous. Milo had cropped closely to Savvy's head on one side, and then sharply angled the other side into an ultra-chic angled bob that ended in a curl at her jawline. He had also done something with the color. Her hair was still red, but there were these vivid streaks of purple peeking out from underneath the top strands. They caught the light when she turned her head. Savvy's hair had been a main of ginger curls that stretched halfway down her back since I'd met her, but somehow, as I looked at her with this new style, it seemed as though it were the haircut she was always meant to have. Milo was right. It suited her perfectly.

"How did you do that with the color?" Hannah asked, still looking mystified and yet impressed.

"I have my sources," Milo said, winking. Then, he leaned in toward me, and said in a stage whisper, "By the way, you're out of purple hair dye."

"Good to know," I said, returning his wink. "In this one instance, I one-hundred-percent approve of you stealing my stuff."

Milo smirked. "I knew you would," he said.

I turned back to Savvy, and said, in a quiet voice, "We were all really worried about you. Are you sure you're okay?"

Savvy didn't quite meet my eye, and her smile faltered. "I don't rightly know," she said. "I think maybe I will be, but for now... well, I'm just going to get along as best I can. That's all any of us can do, right?"

I nodded. "Yeah. That really is the best any of us can do."

"It really is good to see you, Savvy," Hannah said, smiling gently.

"It's good to be seen, mate," Savvy said, returning the smile a bit reluctantly. "Sorry, I freaked out there for a bit."

Mackie was shaking her head. "There's no need to apologize,

mate. We've all been there. Look at me. I'm an Empath. My entire life is basically getting run over by a truckload of other people's emotions every few minutes. I try to bear up, but it doesn't always work. Sometimes I win, most times not."

"Yeah," I said. "Everyone at this table has dealt with their fair share of overwhelming situations. More than our fair share, I'd say."

"A table full of emotional wrecks," Mackie said, nodding solemnly.

"Damaged goods," Hannah said cottoning on and adopting a somber tone. "Dysfunctional beyond repair, the lot of us."

"We really should consider just turning ourselves in for scrap," Milo added cheerfully. "Between the five of us, we might be able to cobble together a single functioning human being."

Savvy looked around the table at us, and her sad smile widened as some of her pain fell away. "Cheers, you lot. Now, what are you all doing in here, anyway?"

Hannah pushed a copy of her research toward Savvy. "Trying to make a case for the abolishment of this archaic arrangement between Durupinen and Caomhnóir."

"Oh, yeah," Savvy said slowly. "I think Jess told me about this. Didn't you? When I was... less than sober last night?"

"Yup," I confirmed.

"And you think this will... will change things?" Savvy asked, looking skeptically at the stacks and stacks of books we had piled on the table.

"I think it's the best chance we have," Hannah told her solemnly.

Savvy let out a long low whistle. "If you say so, half-pint. Chuck us a book, then. Let's get to work."

§

"Hannah, why don't you take a break for a little while?" I suggested.

After a headache-inducing afternoon of research, Hannah and I found ourselves back in our room, but rather than leaving the books and reams of notes in the library, Hannah had forced me to lug them back with us to the room.

"I just have one more section to get through," she murmured, not even bothering to look up at me. She had a pencil clenched between her teeth, and she was gnawing on it thoughtfully.

"There's always one more section to get through, Hannah," I said. "You're only human. You need to step back once in a while or you're going to burn out."

Hannah sat up and rubbed at her eyes. "Okay," she sighed. "You're right, I know it."

"I hope everyone on the Council appreciates how much work you do," I said. "Honestly, Fiona can barely be bothered to keep herself conscious during Council meetings, and you've singlehandedly scoured all of Durupinen written history."

Hannah gave a wan smile. "Don't exaggerate."

"Okay, *half* of Durupinen written history," I amended.

"So, do you remember yesterday at breakfast when I mentioned the idea of getting a Caomhnóir to co-sponsor my legislation?"

"Sure," I said, having not the vaguest recollection of such a thing.

"Well, Keira gave me a suggestion for someone I might ask but... I don't know. I felt weird about it."

"Why?" I asked. "Who is it?"

"His name is Kiernan Worthington," Hannah said. "Do you know him?"

"No, but that's not surprising," I said. "I don't know most of the Caomhnóir around here."

"Well, he's a recently graduated Novitiate," Hannah said, twirling the chewed-up pencil between her fingers. "I guess, when it came time for him to be granted an assignment, he petitioned the Council to opt out of guardianship and become a Scribe."

I raised my eyebrows. "Opt out of guardianship? That's... not a thing, is it?"

"No, it's not," Hannah confirmed. "And there has never been a Caomhnóir Scribe before. The Council didn't know what to make of his request, and wound up assigning him as security for the Scribes when they travel with important documents and artifacts. It seemed to be their way of trying to accommodate his request."

"Except they kind of ignored it, didn't they?" I pointed out.

"Well, yes. Anyway, because Kiernan showed a vested interest in widening the roles and opportunities for Caomhnóir, and because reportedly he put a great deal of time and research into his request, Keira thought he would be an ideal candidate to co-sponsor my work."

I nodded, impressed. "Sounds like she's absolutely right. So, why do you look so hesitant about it?"

"Well..." Hannah let the pencil fall into her lap with a sigh. "Kiernan is Lucida's nephew."

My mouth fell open. "You're joking!"

Hannah shrugged. "I wish I were."

"Damn," I said with a long sigh. "No wonder you're hesitating."

"But that's silly, right?" Hannah asked. "I mean, I can't hold his aunt's actions against him. That would be as unfair as everyone punishing us for our mom's mistakes. I can't refuse to work with him just because of who he's related to."

"That's a good point," I agreed. "Just look at me. I spend half my life working with Catriona now, and no one was closer to Lucida than her."

"Exactly," Hannah said, sounding like she was trying to convince herself much more than she was trying to convince me. "So... so I should just find him, right? Introduce myself? Tell him about the project?"

"Yes," I said. "I think you should. And just because you talk to the guy doesn't mean you have to work with him. Just feel him out. You'll know if he's the right person for the job."

Hannah looked pensive again. She didn't commit either way, but gave me a grateful smile. "Thanks, Jess. I'll think about it."

A sudden buzzing noise made me glance around. "Is that you?" I asked Hannah.

Hannah dug around between her pillows until she found her phone hiding beneath them. "Nope," she said, checking her notifications. "Must be yours."

I searched my bed and the surrounding area until I finally found my phone, which had slipped down between the mattress and the wall. The missed call was from Tia.

"It's Tia," I told Hannah as I hurried to call her back. "I wonder how her test went."

Hannah laughed. "And why are you wondering, exactly?"

I joined in the laughter. "Touché," I told her. It was Tia. The test went great. It was the only way any of her tests ever went. Unless, I added silently, with a squirm of guilt, your best friend got you tangled up with a psychopath who destroyed all sense of normalcy in your life. Then you conceivably might see a dip in your grade point average.

"Jess!" Tia's voice squealed into the phone, causing me to have to pull it quickly away from my ear. My pulse sped up, as I was unsure how to interpret the excitement I heard in her voice.

"Hey, Ti," I replied. "Is everything okay? You sound... freaked out or something."

"No, no, I'm fine. Everything's fine," Tia said hastily. "Sorry, I should probably try to answer the phone a little more calmly, given everything that's happened recently."

"It would definitely help my heart rate," I admitted with a shaky chuckle.

"Sorry," Tia said again. "Like I said, everything is good here. In fact, everything's great!"

"So, your test went well, I take it?" I asked. My ear closest to the phone was still ringing. I massaged it with the palm of my hand.

"What test?" Tia asked blankly. Then she laughed. "Oh, my exam from this morning! Right! Oh, yeah, the exam was fine. Piece of cake."

"A piece of cake? Your med school classmates must loathe you," I said with a snort of laughter. "Well, what's so great then, if you're not talking about your test?"

"Well, when I got back to the flat, there were a bunch of messages on the machine, which, I mean, totally makes sense, because we haven't been here in days," Tia babbled, her words tumbling out over each other in her excitement, so that it was hard to decipher exactly what she was saying. "Well, anyway, the last one was from the Dean of the medical school. She said that one of my professors had submitted my paper for that conference I was telling you about—you know, the one in Paris?"

"Oh, yeah, the Paris conference. I remember you mentioning that," I said. I didn't actually remember it at all, but no need to mention that.

"Well, they don't usually accept papers from first-year students, but one of the third years had to pull out of the conference unexpectedly, so my professor submitted my paper anyway and..." I could hear the squeal building in her throat, "they accepted it! I'm actually going! I'm actually presenting my first paper at my first-ever medical conference!"

I squealed right along with her in solidarity. "Oh my God, Tia! That is so exciting! I am so damn proud of you! I mean, not that I'm even remotely surprised, because you're absolutely brilliant, but this is just... Congratulations!"

"Thank you!" Tia gushed. "I still can't believe it! I think I must've listened to the message like, I don't know, a dozen times before I let myself believe that it was real. I haven't even had a chance to get nervous yet!"

"So, when do you leave?" I asked her.

"Three days!" Tia cried. "I'm freaking out! I called the Dean back, because I was afraid that I might've missed my chance. After all, the message was from a few days ago, and I was afraid that if they hadn't heard from me, they might ask someone else instead. But luckily, they hadn't. I'll have to do a few revisions, and I'm going to want to go over the presentation with my advisor, and it feels like so much to do in just a few short days, but... I have to say yes, don't I? I mean, shouldn't I? I can't pass this up, it's such a great opportunity!"

"Of course you have to say yes! What kind of the question is that?" I exclaimed.

"I don't know," Tia said, a bit of uncertainty coloring her tone for the first time. "I guess with everything that just happened, I don't know if I'm supposed to... You think it's okay to go?"

"Tia, everything that just happened to you is exactly why you absolutely have to go," I told her incredulously. "There's no right way to handle what just happened. You're not required to sit in your bedroom inhaling pints of ice cream and engaging in armchair therapy just because somehow you got the idea that that's how women are supposed to deal with shit like this. In fact, I think the healthiest thing you can do is get right back out there and take control of your life in a major way. Don't let... *him*... overtake another single second of your life. Leave him in the dust, Tia, where he deserves to be. Thrive."

"And you're... you're okay if I go, right?" Tia asked hesitantly.

"Oh Tia," I groaned. "First of all, the fact that you're even considering me in this decision is one of the reasons why you are such a wonderful friend and why I love you so much. Second of all, stop considering me in this decision right this second. I am absolutely fine. And even if I weren't absolutely fine, that would be no reason not to take advantage of this opportunity. There is not a single thing you could do in this world that would make me happier than you getting on that plane and taking that medical conference by storm."

"And you're not just saying that, right?" Tia asked in a tiny voice.

"Of course not," I told her firmly.

"And you wouldn't tell me even if you were," Tia said shrewdly.

"Not a chance," I agreed.

"Okay," Tia said, and I was relieved to hear the decision in her voice. "Okay, that's it, then. I'm going. Thanks, Jess."

"What the hell are you thanking me for?" I asked her. "I didn't do anything."

"I needed to hear someone else say that this was the right decision," Tia said. "And you did."

"You know, someday pretty soon, you're going to have to start saying whether something is the right decision, if you want to be a doctor," I pointed out.

"I know that," Tia said. "I'll get there. Baby steps."

"Well, you'd better call your professor back and tell them to book your flight to Paris," I suggested. "And then get to work, you slacker."

"Okay, okay, I will," Tia said, laughing. "Oh, and speaking of calling people back, make sure you call Karen."

"Huh?"

"I said, make sure you call Karen back," Tia repeated. "There were, like, four messages from her on the machine, and each one sounded increasingly frantic. Have you talked to her since... well, everything?"

"Oh," I said with a groan. "Right. Yeah, I've kind of been avoiding that on purpose. You know, because I like to make problems infinitely worse by pretending they don't exist for as long as possible."

A sharp knock echoed against the door of our room. Hannah started to slide off her bed to answer it, but I was closer, and waved her away.

"Well, if I were you, I'd stop avoiding it." Tia's admonishment rang in my ear as I crossed the room. "If Karen's anything like my mom, if you ignore her long enough, she'll just jump on a plane and come over here."

"Yeah, she can get pretty feisty about things if we don't keep her in the loop," I said, as I put my hand on the doorknob. "I'll talk to Karen today, I promise."

76

I pulled the door open, and nearly dropped the phone in my surprise and alarm.

"Yes, you most certainly will talk to her today," Karen said sharply.

There she stood, on the other side of the door, a suitcase by her feet, and a storm raging in her expression.

"Jess?" Tia said into my long, shocked silence. "Jess, are you still there?"

"Sorry Tia," I said hoarsely. "I've got to call you back later. That jumping on a plane thing? Yeah, it looks like it already happened."

"Oh my!" Tia gasped. "You're kidding! You mean she's..."

"Yup," I confirmed without waiting for her to finish the sentence. "I'll call you later, if she permits me to live."

I ended the call, and slipped the phone into my back pocket before daring to look up into Karen's face. Facing that expression did nothing for my courage.

I sighed and my head drooped again. "Karen, I know you must be really angry with me. I'm so sorry, I just —"

But she didn't even give me a chance to start apologizing. The second I opened my mouth, Karen's face crumpled and she flew forward, wrapping her arms around me and burying her face in my hair, where she proceeded to cry as though she'd only just learned how and she had a lifetime of tears to shed.

I froze, completely shocked that I was not being yelled at, and it was a few seconds before I recovered enough from my surprise to wrap my arms around her in return and relax into the embrace. Before I knew what was happening, both of us were crying. Then, Hannah had crossed the room and put her arms around both of us at once, so that we became a single tangled sobbing entity, kind of like an Elemental, but snottier and in desperate need of tissues.

After several minutes of collective, soggy emotional collapse, the three of us broke apart and moved together to the chairs in front of the fireplace. Karen dropped into one of them, and I handed her a box of tissues as Hannah, still breathing in a shuddery way, walked back over to the door to lug Karen's suitcase across the threshold and pulled the door closed behind her.

"How did you find out?" I asked at last, when Karen's sobs had finally quieted.

"It wasn't easy," Karen said cynically, dabbing at her eyes. Her usually flawless make-up was now streaked and smeared all around her swollen eyes. "I got suspicious when you weren't returning my phone calls. And even more suspicious when my texts went unanswered. Finally, I decided I had to go around you if I was going to find out what was going on, so I called Celeste."

"You actually called the High Priestess?" I asked with a groan. "Wasn't there anyone lower on the food chain you could've called?"

"No one that wasn't going to patently ignore me, it seems," Karen snapped at me, with a flash of the anger I had originally been expecting. "Our clan hasn't been popular around here in recent years, as you well know, and I'd severed most of my connections to the place before you two came along. Besides, you know that Celeste and I have been friends for a long time. Her becoming the High Priestess has not changed that."

I squirmed a bit. "So, what did she tell you? How much do you know?"

"Everything," Karen sniffed, sounding on the verge of a fresh torrent of tears. "She told me about Charlie Wright and his connection to the Necromancers. She told me about that... that camera spirit-whatever thing that he created, and about the attack that you survived. She told me that you had been in the hospital wing, but that you'd been released. She told me that you'd been at Fairhaven ever since, and that you were still working on this case for the Trackers, even after everything that happened to you."

"A pretty good summary of events, actually," I said with a weak attempt at a smile that Karen did not return.

"What I can't understand—what I don't think I'll ever understand—is why you didn't tell me about any of it yourself," Karen said. The look that she gave me was still watery, but full of defiant anger.

"I'm sorry," I said to her again.

"I don't want your damn apology, Jess!" she cried. "I don't care about apologies! I don't need to hear them! I want to know why! Why don't you trust me? Why don't you feel like you can confide in me?" She heaved a sigh that shuddered through her whole body and left her looking small and deflated. "Does this all go back to when I hid the Durupinen from you? I know that that was a terrible thing to do, and I've worked so hard since to regain your trust, but it would appear that I still just don't have it! I don't know what else I can do, what else I can say to convince you how much I care about you! Both of you! My God, just tell me what else I have to say, what else I have to do, and I'll do it!"

She dissolved into a puddle of sobbing again, and I felt as though I had been punched in the gut. I dropped to my knees on the rug next to her and put my arms around her again. "Oh, Karen, I am so sorry. I know you said you don't want to hear apologies, but I have to say it, because that's not what this is about. I trust you. I swear I do. I'm not holding any kind of grudge, okay? I am not trying to hold four years ago over your head. I know that you were trying to protect me, and I know that you've been honest with me since then. I promise, I really do know that."

I looked up at Hannah, who had her hands over her mouth and was silently crying as she watched Karen break down. I cocked my head at her, so that she would come over and give me some support. She hurried over to the couch, and sat down beside Karen, placing an arm gently around her shaking shoulders.

"Then why?" Karen repeated, her muffled voice barely audible with her face still hidden in her hands. "Why are you shutting me out?"

"Because, and this is gonna sound like a terrible break up line, but in this case, it's really true: it's not you, Karen. It's me. You're not doing anything wrong. I'm just... really, really bad at letting people in. You sort of know what it was like with my mom, but she was always too busy wrestling with her own demons to really be there for me. I was always worrying about her, not the other way around. And if I did have some challenge that I was dealing with, I always hid it from her, because I couldn't bear to put one more thing on top of the pile that was already crushing her. I couldn't stand to give her one more reason to drink, one more reason to pack up the car and move somewhere else. And I know you're not my mom. I know that things are different, but old habits die hard. I've always had to take care of myself, and I've never been good at letting other people in. I've never really learned how to let people help me carry the load, even when they're begging to help me."

"It's true," Hannah said quietly. "We're twins, and I still have a hard time getting over that wall." She smiled at me and gave a little shrug. "Sorry, Jess. Not trying to add to the guilt. I'm just stating a fact."

"No, it's okay," I told her. "I get it. And it's this weird thing I have, I still feel like I need to protect people from... well, me. I hate the idea of depending on people. It makes me feel weak, like I've forgotten my own hard-won survival skills. You and Hannah and Milo—you've given me this great support system, but I just really suck at using it. It's like I'm always trying to tightrope walk, and you're standing under me with a net, and I keep saying, 'No thanks, I'm good! I'm just gonna break some shit when I hit the ground.'"

Karen let out a sound that might have been a laugh wrapped in a sob. It was hard to tell, but she looked up from her tissue for the first time and looked me in the face. It made it a little harder to keep going spilling my guts, but I knew I couldn't use that as an excuse anymore.

"I'm so sorry about that. Honestly, I've tried to get better, but clearly, I'm not doing a good job. I'm trying to keep you from being worried or hurt, but the only thing I've accomplished is to make you hurt and worry even more. That is not at all what I'm trying to do, and I'm not going to do it anymore, I promise."

"I know you're an adult," Karen said finally, her voice hitching and shuddering over the tears that she had still not managed to get under control. "I know that you need to live your own life, and make your own decisions. I missed the chance to parent you, I realize that, but I hoped that we could still manage to be friends. I know I don't have any kind of right to be one of the people you confide in. But I do want to be, Jess. I do so desperately want to be."

"You have every right," I told her. "You've been there for me... for both of us... through all of this, and shutting you out has been a really crappy way to repay you for that. And I'm not going to do it anymore, Karen."

"Thank you," Karen said, reaching out and stroking my hair. "And I'll try to make it as easy as possible for you to come to me. No judgment. Well, minimal judgment," she corrected herself, and we all laughed. She stroked my hair again, and looked me in the eyes. "And you're okay? After everything that... that bastard did to you? You're really and truly okay?"

"I really am okay," I told her. "And I'm not just saying that so that you won't worry. I really am okay."

Karen patted my cheek, her face twitching with emotions she was trying to control. "Thank God," she whispered. "Thank God for that."

"I'm sorry you had to get on a plane and come all the way over here just so you could hear me say that," I muttered.

"Oh, I didn't get on a plane just so I could hear you say that," Karen said. "Although that was a big part of it, obviously." She pointed over at her suitcase. "That's just my carry-on. The rest of my luggage has been brought to my room."

I looked at her blankly, uncomprehendingly. "The rest of your luggage?"

"That's right," Karen said, dabbing at her eyes and attempting to regain her usual composure. "I've officially requested a transfer to my firm's London office. I'm sick and tired of missing the two of you, and never knowing what the hell is going on. There was a time not long ago when I had successfully driven a wedge between myself and the Durupinen world. Thanks to you girls, those days are long gone. I'm not blaming you for that," she said quickly, realizing how her words must have sounded. "In fact, I'm grateful. The more I hear from you about the goings-on here, the more I realize that I need to find a way to become more actively involved. There need to be more voices of reason and progress around this place, and I intend to become one of them."

"Does this mean you're... you're *moving* here?" Hannah asked blankly.

"Yes," Karen said, her tone bordering on rebellious. "I used to have a life back in Boston. I had a husband, and a career that I loved. And I had the two of you, however briefly. But now I've realized that my life seems to have floated away from me in pieces. My marriage fell apart, you two girls moved away, and suddenly I realized that the only thing tethering me to Boston was a job that I was growing to resent for the very fact that it was keeping me there. So, when the news came down that one of our partners was opening a branch here in the UK, I leapt at it. I tried to call you girls to discuss it with you, but, well..." She made a helpless gesture with her hands.

"I know, I know," I said. "It would help if we answered the phone like, ever."

"So," Karen said, "here I am, like it or not. I'm not here to spy on you or micromanage your lives. I just want to be a part of them. I hope that's okay."

Karen was looking back and forth between the two of us with a somewhat anxious expression, as though she thought we were going to tell her to turn right around, get back on the plane, and go home.

Instead, I pulled myself up onto the couch beside her and gave her another hug. "Of course, that's okay," I said to her. "It's great, Karen. Seriously."

"You don't have to humor me, you know," Karen said dryly. "I'm a big girl, I can handle it."

"I'm not humoring you," I insisted. "Honestly, it will be great to have you here. Won't it, Hannah?"

Hannah nodded her head vigorously. "We need people in our corner that we can count on, especially on the same continent."

Karen laughed. "Well, all right, then. You've got one, anyway."

I caught Hannah's eye, and she was giving me a meaningful look. I didn't need the words floating through the connection to understand what she was trying to tell me.

If you were serious about letting her in and confiding in her, then you've got to tell her. Now.

I thought of Finn. I thought of the piles of prophetic drawings hidden away inside our closet, their mystery and significance permeating the room and my consciousness even now. Karen only knew a fraction of what I was hiding from her. It was time for that to change.

"Karen, if you were serious about wanting to know everything that's going on in our lives..." I began.

"Yes, of course I was serious!" Karen cried. "I just left the country, for heaven's sake!"

"Okay, then," I said. "Well then, you should probably get comfortable, because we've only scratched the surface of things I need to fill you in on."

Karen regarded me warily. "You mean there's more?" she asked weakly.

"Just a bit," I said, sharing a sarcastic smile with Hannah. "I'll start at the beginning."

7

FIREFLIES IN THE DARKNESS

I T TOOK KAREN until the next day to fully recover her powers of speech after I unloaded the full weight of all my secrets. From my relationship with Finn, to the revelation that I was a Seer, I left nothing out. She did not harbor even a scrap of disapproval over what had transpired between Finn and me. On the contrary, it was clear she viewed the law that forbade our relationship with as much disdain as I did. "That law destroyed our family," she had insisted, "and I'll do anything I can to help you get it overturned for good. I'm not sure if you've heard this before, but lawyers are really rather good at research and drafting documents." Delightedly, Hannah had handed over a massive pile of books and notes to Karen, who confidently assured her she could have it all distilled down to the finer points in a day or two.

Though she worried about what the future might hold for Finn and me, Karen was much more concerned about the present and more pressing problem of the prophetic drawings. And she was not nearly as surprised as she should have been about the revelation that I was a Seer.

"The original prophecy was made by our family, after all," she had said. "It has cropped up here and there in our family history, though never with the magnitude of consequences that Agnes Isherwood faced. My own grandmother sometimes suspected that she had a prophetic gift, but it never manifested itself in a decisive way."

One thing on which she absolutely agreed was that we should tell no one else of the gift. "It sounds as though Fiona may be able to shed some light on this situation without exposing you to exploitation by the Council. I think the safest course is to see what she has to say when she gets back."

But could I hold myself together that long? Fiona had said that it would likely take several days to sort out the issue with her mother, but each hour that ticked by felt like an eternity. Luckily, though, Savvy came barging into our bedroom the next morning with news that temporarily pushed Fiona to the back of my mind.

"She's awake!" Savvy crowed at the top of her lungs. "Phoebe's awake! Put a damn bra on and come down with me, I want to give her a proper welcoming committee when I go down to see her!" Hannah and I happily put some damn bras on and skipped right over breakfast to head down to the hospital ward. Milo, equally glad to hear the news, joined us.

Phoebe sat propped up in her bed, blinking around with the same kind of confusion as a baby who had just been born. Her expression was blank, and she stared at everyday objects as though she had no idea what they might possibly be used for. As we approached her bed, her eyes had dropped to the tray of food in front of her, as though she were trying to decide what to do with the eggs, toast, and tea that had been arranged upon it. Picking it up, putting it in her mouth, and chewing it did not seem to be the obvious course of action based on her bemused expression.

"Phoebe!" Savvy called raucously, her voice echoing around the hospital ward like a gunshot. Phoebe jumped, her fork clattering to the floor and the orange juice slopping out of her glass and into her scrambled eggs. She stared around wildly for the source of the voice, until her eyes fell on Savvy charging down the aisle between the beds. Her eyes went wide, and for a moment it didn't seem as though she even recognized her cousin, but then again, I don't think Savvy had ever grinned like that at the sight of her. Savvy's typical expression upon seeing Phoebe was one of extreme consternation, or annoyance. It was more likely, I reasoned, that Phoebe was just surprised to see her cousin with a smile on her face.

By the time we had all arrived at her bedside, Phoebe had picked up her napkin and was using it to sop up the juice from her breakfast plate. When she looked up at Savvy, she attempted a cautious smile.

"Hi, Savannah," she mumbled tentatively, before dropping her eyes back to her plate, which was still swimming in juice. She sighed, and tossed the napkin aside, apparently deciding the food was beyond salvageable. "How are you?"

"How am I?" Savvy said, and roared with laughter. "How am I?

Only someone as daft as you would wake up from a two-week coma and ask how *I* was." The words might've been harsh, but her tone was jovial, delighted even. She reached out a hand and grasped her cousin's shoulder and patted it gently, though Phoebe still flinched as though she were being punched. "Good to see you awake, mate. How are you?"

Phoebe still looked disoriented and a bit frightened, as though wondering if she had woken up in an alternate reality—a reality in which her cousin called her "mate" instead of "git" or "buggery fool." But she gave a tiny, vague smile, and replied, "Okay, I think. I just woke up, so I don't rightly know yet. I'm a bit hungry, but..." She gestured helplessly at her plate, on which her inedible breakfast still sat.

"Aw, no worries! We can take care of that for you, no problem!" Savvy said brightly. She turned over her shoulder and shouted at the top of her lungs, "Oi! Mrs. Mistlemoore! We need some new nosh out here!"

Phoebe winced at the volume of Savvy's voice, but nodded her thanks all the same once Savvy was done shouting. "Cheers," she mumbled.

"Hi, Phoebe," Hannah said, trying to keep her voice gentle in comparison to Savvy's boisterous and celebratory shouts. "It's so nice to see you awake. Are you comfortable? Are you in any pain?"

Phoebe paused and considered the question. After a few moments' contemplation, she shrugged. "Dunno," she muttered at last. "Not too bad. Bit stiff from all the lying down, I suppose. My body feels a mite... *foreign*. Like it don't belong to me no more. Best way I can describe it. And my head is bit fuzzy, like someone's gone and stuffed it with cotton balls."

"And here I thought it had always been stuffed with cotton balls," Savvy said, and chuckled good-naturedly.

"We're all relieved to see you awake and eating," I interjected quickly, before Phoebe could absorb Savvy's teasing comments. "We're so sorry you had to go through such an ordeal."

"Yeah, we are," said Milo tentatively.

Phoebe didn't look at Milo, but dropped her eyes to her plate instead, her face twitching with emotion. "I'd rather not talk about that just now," she mumbled, "if it's all the same to you."

"Of course, of course," I said quickly. "You just focus on getting well. That's all anybody wants." I made a mental note to speak to Catriona about questioning Phoebe. It was already clear that she wouldn't be quite so stalwart and determined as Flavia was to face an interview, especially if that interview dredged up painful memories.

A marching of footsteps behind us made us all turn. Mrs. Mistlemoore was plowing up the aisle between the beds, a fresh breakfast tray in her hands. "I am not accustomed to being shouted at like a servant, Ms. Todd," she snapped. "I am a medical professional, and you would do well to remember to address me as such in future."

"Sorry about that," Savvy said, grinning a bit sheepishly and adopting an appropriately contrite expression. "No offense meant, honest. Just wanted Phoebe here to have what she needed, seeing as how she's got to eat if she wants to gain her strength back."

Mrs. Mistlemoore pursed her lips but did not reply. She simply nodded her head toward the old breakfast tray. Savvy took the hint and lifted it from the bed. Mrs. Mistlemoore settled the new tray carefully in Phoebe's lap, and then snatched the old tray out of Savvy's hands. She turned to look at Phoebe. "Can I get you anything else?" she asked, her tone much kinder now.

Phoebe looked blankly around her, like the question was both unexpected and unnecessarily difficult to answer. "No, I... I think I'm all right. Can't think of nothing else."

Mrs. Mistlemoore nodded curtly, and turned on her heel, striding back up toward her open office door, muttering unintelligibly to herself.

As I turned to watch her progress, I caught sight of Milo's face. He was standing just behind me, off my shoulder. His expression was... odd. Confused. He was looking at Phoebe as though there were something not quite right about her.

"Are you okay?" I whispered to him.

Milo replied with a movement that was somewhere between a shrug and a shaking of his head. "I don't know," he said, so quietly that I barely caught the words at all. "It's... there's something different."

"What do you...?"

Before I could finish my question, Savvy had plopped herself down on the edge of Phoebe's bed, nearly upsetting her cousin's second glass of orange juice. "Oops, sorry, mate!" She steadied the glass of juice and handed her cousin her fork. "Eat up now," she said encouragingly. "You need your strength. Can't make a full recovery on an empty belly."

Phoebe nodded, still looking unsure whether this bright and cheerful version of her cousin wasn't simply a hallucination. But she heeded her words, stabbing a piece of scrambled egg and transferring it a bit shakily to her mouth.

"That's it, that's it!" Savvy exclaimed. "Can't help spirits lying about in bed like a lump, can we?"

"Suppose not," Phoebe said with her mouth full of food.

"Jess..." Milo's voice came through the connection this time, startling me.

"What is it, Milo?" I sent my reply thrumming back along the strings of our connected consciousness.

"Did Mrs. Mistlemoore mention... Is there a possibility that... that Phoebe's Spirit Sight might still be affected by Charlie's Castings?" Milo asked.

I shrugged. "I suppose so. They aren't sure what the lasting effects will be. The recovery is expected to be gradual."

Milo did not reply, but he was still staring at Phoebe as though disturbed by something.

"Milo, what's wrong?" I asked him.

"I'm... not sure. Maybe nothing," Milo replied.

Savvy, meanwhile, was chattering on about this and that, filling Phoebe in on what she had missed, but carefully leaving out all the sad and terrible details of the aftermath of her attack.

"What have you done to your hair?" Phoebe asked suddenly.

Savvy's smile faltered, and she raised a hand automatically to rub at her neck, now exposed without its thick curtain of ginger locks. "What about it?"

"You've gone and cut it all off," Phoebe said, sounding a little scandalized.

"Oh, yeah," Savvy said, with a forced casualness. "Gave it a bit of a trim, you know. It was time for a change."

A soft moan caught all our attention. I glanced over, and saw that Flavia was tossing and turning a bit in her sleep. Her strength, while improving, was nowhere near completely restored yet, and she still spent a lot of time sleeping.

"Hey, Sav, maybe keep it down a bit, huh?" I suggested, nodding in Flavia's direction.

"Oh, yeah. Sorry, mate," Savvy replied, dropping her voice just a bit, though it still seemed to carry with the force of a megaphone. She turned back to Phoebe, grateful for the interruption so that she could change the subject. "So anyway, once you're up and about, and all that, I thought maybe we could stay at Fairhaven for a bit, until you're feeling tip-top. No need to travel all the way back to the country quite yet. Besides, we're already behind on a Crossing, and I'm getting harassed."

"Harassed?" Phoebe asked, struggling to smear butter onto her toast. Her hands were still shaking rather badly, as though the knife and a piece of toast were entirely too heavy for her.

"Here, let me do that," Savvy said, snatching both the toast and the knife from her cousin's hands and slathering the bread liberally with butter before handing it back to her. "Yeah, harassed," she confirmed. "You know, by the ghosts that want to Cross. Surely, they've been hounding you, too, since you've woken up."

Phoebe shook her head, her mouth full of half-chewed toast. She gave an exaggerated swallow, and said, "No, not at all. It's just me in here. Well, and Mrs. Mistlemoore."

"Lucky you," Savvy said with a wink. "I expect this place is Warded, is it? Well, just you wait until they spring you. You won't get a moment's peace."

Hannah looked around curiously. "Is this place warded? I would imagine so. I've never thought to ask."

I shrugged. "I don't know. Maybe. I don't suppose spirits really need a hospital wing, do they? And I can't imagine Mrs. Mistlemoore wants random spirits harassing patients who are trying to get better."

"Eleanora was in here," Hannah pointed out. "During the Shattering, remember?"

"Yeah, but she was carried over the threshold as Shards inside the Hosts," I reminded her. "I don't know if she could have just drifted through the walls by herself, if she was intact."

Savvy looked up, joining the discussion. "Well, Milo can get in, can't he?"

"Well, yeah, but he's with us," I reminded her. "He can cross into any Warded spaces, as long as we're with him. That's one of the perks of being Bound."

"One of the only perks," Milo said, smirking at me.

Phoebe raised her eyebrows. "Milo can get in? Really?"

Savvy snorted. "Well obviously, you git, as he's here."

Phoebe blinked slowly. "He's here? Now? Where?"

We all looked at each other blankly.

"He's... right here," I said slowly, gesturing to the space beside me, a horrible thought beginning to dawn.

Beside me, Milo gave a feeble little wave of his hand. His eyes darted to me, and I knew from the panicked light in them that he was already thinking the same thing that I was.

Phoebe blinked again. "Where?"

Milo's voice was flat, almost morose, as he replied, "I'm right here, Phoebe. I'm right here in front of you." He floated several feet forward, until he was only a few feet in front of her face. She stared right through him, her expression blank, befuddled.

"I... I can't see him. Are you sure he's here?" she asked, her voice very small, betraying just the tiniest amount of something that could've been the beginnings of fear.

I looked at Milo again, as though not trusting my own eyes that he was actually there. He was looking solemnly into Phoebe's face, and he was nodding his head minutely, as though she had just confirmed something for him, something he had already suspected. Phoebe stared right back at the place where he sat, gazing right through him, past him, to the empty air beyond.

I turned to Savvy, and was shocked to see her smiling, looking back and forth between all of us, as though waiting for us to let her in on the ruse. "You're putting me on, right?" she asked, a trace of a laugh in her voice. "Come on now, joke's over."

She looked first at Hannah, who shook her head, eyes wide. Then her gaze fell on me, and I raised empty hands, trying to show her without words that there was no joke, and I wasn't in on anything. Her face starting to fall, she turned lastly to Milo, who looked straight up into Savvy's eyes and shook his head once, gravely.

Savvy made a choking sound in the back of her throat. She rose slowly from the edge of the bed. She looked at Phoebe with dawning horror, and backed away a step or two, before whispering, "You mean it, don't you? You really can't see him?"

Phoebe scanned all our faces. I watched her fear blossom and her eyes fill with tears. "I don't know what you're talking about," she whispered. "He can't be here. I'd be able to see him, wouldn't I? *Wouldn't I?*" she repeated, her voice rising in a slightly hysterical tone.

"I'm going to get Mrs. Mistlemoore," Hannah mumbled to me before scurrying away down the hospital ward.

Milo rose from the bed, floating backward until he came to rest right beside me. The coolness of his presence made me shiver, and I felt a lump building in my throat.

"You knew, didn't you?" I asked him silently, using the connection again, so that Phoebe and Savvy wouldn't hear. "You knew as soon as we walked into the room, didn't you? This is what you were trying to tell me a few minutes ago."

"I knew something was wrong," Milo replied. "I couldn't sense the Gateway in her. There was no pull, no lure to come closer. It was like she was just... empty."

Empty.

I wanted to be sick. Oh, God. What had he done? What had that bastard Charlie done?

Fighting for self-control, I stepped over toward Savvy and touched her arm gently. "Sav? Why don't we step out for a moment and let Mrs. Mistlemoore take a look at Phoebe, okay?"

Savvy looked over at me, like a lost child. "What?" she asked me blankly. "What did you say?"

"I said," I repeated gently, "there might be a perfectly logical explanation as to what's going on. It may not be something to worry about."

"Nothing to worry about?" Savvy asked in a strangled voice. Her chest was starting to heave, as though she could not catch her breath properly.

I leaned in to her, so that Phoebe would not hear. "She's still recovering. It might be temporary. It might be reversible. She might wake up tomorrow with her Spirit Sight completely restored. We can't know for sure, and we shouldn't cause Phoebe to panic just when she's starting to make some progress. Let Mrs. Mistlemoore work her magic, all right?"

"Yeah... yeah, all right." Savvy said dazedly, just as Hannah and Mrs. Mistlemoore came hurrying back along the row of bed spaces. "I'll... that is to say, we'll duck out for a tick, then, shall we? We'll see you in a bit, Phoebe." She hoisted her face into an attempt at a reassuring smile. Then she turned, and let me lead her up the ward and out the doors.

Behind us, I could hear Mrs. Mistlemoore speaking to Phoebe in a gentle, motherly voice. "There now, my dear. Let's have a little look-see and get you sorted, shall we?"

We trooped out into the hallway, all of us silent, our fear and horror hanging over us like a storm cloud. No one spoke a word, and no one said aloud where we were going, but we all seemed to understand, without discussing it, that Savvy should get as far away from the hospital ward as possible. We walked together down the stairs, through the entrance hall, and out onto the grounds, where the bright sunshine and the warm summer breeze seemed to mock us in its perfection. We walked and walked until we reached the gardens, and the four of us sat along the edge of the fountain and allowed what just happened to settle, to absorb.

Savvy stood up almost at once. "I need a fag. Back in a jiff."

She walked a dozen or so paces away from the fountain, stopping in a cluster of rose bushes. A few moments later, smoke started to rise from the spot in plumes.

I allowed the connection to unfold inside my head, making room there for two more anxious trains of thought that were not mine. "So, what does this mean?" I asked Hannah and Milo. I felt my question rocketing around amidst our swirling thoughts like an insect trapped in a jar.

"I don't know," Hannah replied. "How can anyone know?"

"Milo, you noticed it first," I said, turning to him. "Can you describe it some more?"

Milo sighed aloud, dropping his elbows onto his knees and his forehead into his hands. "I noticed it almost right away. Being around Durupinen is... very vivid, for a ghost. It's like... you walk through the world, and all the normal people are like shadows. You can see them, but you don't... sense them. It always feels like there's a sort of barrier. Well, I'm not sure if barrier is the right word." Milo rubbed at his head as though he could massage the correct description out. "A barrier is a solid thing, like a wall, isn't it? This is more of a film... it's not tangible except that it dulls and dims everything. It's like looking at the world through a pair of glasses with dirty lenses. Like one of those shrouds, you know, like they drape over dead people in movies, except you wake up and have to walk around the world trying to see through the damn thing all the time." He looked up. "Does that make, like, any sense at all?"

"Yeah," Hannah and I both replied. All our other thoughts had gone still and silent. I had never heard Milo talk about this aspect of his experience before. Neither, judging by the look on her face, had Hannah.

"So, imagine you're just sort of drifting through the world, and everyone around you is a dull, muted shadow behind this stupid shroud, and then, all of a sudden, you see this light. Like a firefly in the darkness. The film lifts, blown away like cobwebs or dust. And in just that moment, you feel like you're existing with someone, instead of just on a parallel plane with her. Everything is clear, like she burned the shroud away with that firefly light, and you are drawn to that person, to the sudden clarity of her. That's the Durupinen."

I let out a little breath I didn't realize I'd been holding. I'd spent a lot of time thinking about the Durupinen—about myself—in a lot of different ways. But never had I stopped to wonder what we were like from a spirit's perspective—at least, not so seriously that I'd ever stopped to ask a spirit about it. How was it possible, in all the time I'd been doing this, that I'd never asked that question? Never tried to gain a better understanding of what it must be like for those I Crossed, rather than just for myself as I Crossed them? I began to wonder what this said about me, but Hannah broke through the thought before it could drag me anywhere too dark.

"And just now, with Phoebe?" Hannah prompted, for Milo too, it seemed, had let the thought derail him a bit. "What was it like, when you saw her?"

Milo shook his head. "No light. No clarity. No firefly."

Fear restricted my throat, and I suddenly found it hard to swallow. "What do you think that means?"

Milo shrugged. "I have no idea. But not being able to sense the Gateway in her at all? That's... I mean, I don't really know what the implications of that are, but I can't imagine that it's good."

"What about Flavia?" Hannah asked suddenly. "Did you notice if she...?" Hannah did not finish the question, gesturing instead to her own chest, as though she could feel a light there, a light that radiated out like a beacon.

Milo nodded. "A firefly, just like the rest of you. I noticed it as soon as we walked in the room."

Hannah's face scrunched into a pensive frown. "Huh. But that doesn't make sense. I mean, Charlie did the same thing to both of them. Shouldn't the outcome be the same? Why would one of them show no presence of the Gateway, while the other remains intact?"

Milo shrugged. "Yeah, it's really strange."

"But Charlie didn't do the same thing to both of them," I blurted out, my memory stirred. "That is, he tried to do the same thing to both of them, but both attempts failed." Hannah and Milo both looked confused, so I pressed on in an attempt to clarify. "Okay, so Charlie kidnapped Flavia first. He wanted to bestow her Spirit Sight on someone else, but he still hadn't quite figured out how to do it, so he experimented. It didn't work, of course, so he had to try again. But he didn't try the exact same Casting twice. He already knew that whatever combination of factors he used on Flavia didn't work. They weren't right. So, he changed something. He made adjustments and tried them out on Phoebe, with a different result."

"So, whatever he changed between Flavia and Phoebe... that's what caused this?" Hannah asked.

"Not necessarily," Milo said slowly. "There's another possibility."

"What's that?" I asked.

"Well, Bertie interrupted the process, didn't he?" Milo said, tapping a slender finger thoughtfully against his lips. "Charlie may not have been able to complete his experiment on Phoebe. So maybe the real reason for Phoebe's lack of Sight is that the Casting couldn't be completed."

I nodded slowly as I let this idea sink in. "Yeah," I said at last. "Yeah, that could be it. Terrible things can happen if you interrupt a Casting. Just look at what happened to our grandfather."

Our grandfather had once burst in on Karen and our mother performing a Crossing. What he thought they were doing, we would never know, but he rushed right into the Summoning Circle and pried apart their linked hands, making himself a part of the conduit into the spirit world. Because he had no Durupinen blood and, therefore, no protection from the lure of the Aether, his spirit had been pulled partially from his body, and although he had not died, he had been driven instantly and incurably mad with longing to return to the world that he had glimpsed. Even now, he wasted away in a nursing home, constantly medicated to ease the pain of his desperation.

"But... surely there's no Casting, interrupted or not, that could actually make the presence of the Gateway just... vanish?" Hannah asked, and even though our conversation was happening silently inside the connection, her thought was a tiny whisper of horror. I had to strain to catch the meaning of it as it flitted fearfully across the surface of my brain like a well-skipped stone.

I looked over at Savvy, who was pacing between the bushes now, the cigarette dangling from her lips, her newly cropped hair swung down across her face, hiding all but the tip of her nose and the lit end of the cigarette from view. If I squinted, the tip of the cigarette might just be a firefly.

As I stared at it, she plucked if from her mouth, dropped it to the ground, and put it out with the heel of her shoe.

8

FOUND AND LOST

MRS. MISTLEMOORE COULD CONFIRM nothing conclusively that morning. She encouraged us all to come back later that day, when Phoebe had gotten a bit more rest and time to recover. Savvy refused, choosing to sit on a bench outside the hospital ward, refusing everyone's company and insisting that she didn't want to discuss any of it.

Feeling hopeless, Hannah murmured she may as well go see how Karen was getting on with the research, and Milo agreed to go with her. I shuffled back to our room, feeling like I'd aged a hundred years in a single day and longing to talk to only one person about it.

Curled up on the floor by the light of the crackling fire in our fireplace, I paused for a moment, and then put the tip of my pen to the paper.

Dear Finn,

Apologies in advance for a letter that is probably not going to make very much sense. I'm going to ramble. I'm going to rage. I'm going to say all the things that I would never allow myself to say, not out loud, not even to you if you were standing right in front of me. And all of it will probably be a big mess, but I don't care, and I know you won't either. I just need the mess to be on the outside of me, before it swallows me up.

Everything is falling apart without you, and I don't know what to do. I miss you. I used to think I understood what missing someone meant, but it's clear now that I really had no idea. I've missed other people badly—my mom, Pierce, Evan. I've missed them, but I missed them knowing that they were gone. I missed them with the knowledge that no matter where I went, or what I did, I wasn't going to have to wonder what they were doing, where they were going, or what they were thinking at any given goddamn moment. I didn't have to wonder those things. I didn't have to torture myself with those things, because those things were not the reality. I missed those people because those people were gone. There was nothing I could do to change that, and that was how I eventually made my peace with missing them.

But I don't have that peace now. Not when I'm missing you.

Missing you is like walking around with a huge, gaping hole inside me, a hole made deeper by every question I don't have an answer to. The wondering and the wishing has eaten its way clean through me, and I can't fill it. There's nothing to fill it with because every day there are just more questions. Every day of missing you feels like losing you all over again.

There's a particular kind of cruelty to your physical absence, because I know that you're present somewhere else. You're walking around, and talking, and eating, and sleeping, furrowing your brow when you consider something carefully, and you're doing all these things somewhere far away from me. Sometimes I wonder, if I do something stupid or reckless or dangerous enough, if you might actually come bursting into the room to stop me. But I don't do those things, because I know how angry you'd be that I wasn't protecting myself when you weren't here to protect me.

I'm so angry. God, it feels like I'm just so angry all the time, and I don't even know which way to focus the anger. And so, it just balls up inside me and lights me on fire. Sometimes, I'm angry that we got involved with each other in the first place. And then I'm angry that we didn't do a better job of covering it up. Then I'm angry that we didn't just leave everything behind and run away together before they could keep us apart. And then I'm angry at everyone and everything that would've forced us to make a choice like that, and then I'm right back where we started. It was impossible. It was always going to be impossible, but I can't pass up an opportunity to torture myself by wanting impossible things. It makes me wonder if I loved you more because I hate myself. Did I fall in love with you just to punish me? It feels like it.

I know that you can take care of yourself, and that you're smart and brave and careful. But none of that stops me from being terrified that something is going to happen to you inside the walls of that príosún. I'm afraid that what you've uncovered is so much bigger than us, so much more insidious than we even realize. And I'm scared you're going to try to take it on by yourself. Because I know you. I know that you won't leave it alone. I know that you'll keep tugging at all the strings, until the curtain falls away and reveals exactly what it is that's going on. It's one of the things I love about you, but it's also one of the things that makes me most afraid. Because for all the things that you're good at, protecting yourself isn't one of them. I honestly don't know if you would do it for me, even if I begged you. And I can't decide whether that's admirable or stupid. I just know that it scares me. You're reckless—at least, when it comes to yourself. I guess I am, too. Everything about this—about us—has been reckless from the start, hasn't it?

I feel like I process everything in my life through the filter of how you would respond to it if you were here, which is really weird, because it almost feels like I'm experiencing my own life secondhand. I wonder if you know about what happened to Bertie. I wonder what you would've done differently, what advice you might've given him or us, so that he might still be here. I wonder if you know about Charlie Wright, and everything that he's done. I hope not, because if you do and he's in that príosún, you've probably killed him by now. At the very least, you'll be beating the hell out of yourself for not being there to protect me from him. I hope no one's told you. I hope you're not torturing yourself worrying about me.

I wonder what you'd tell me to do about these prophetic drawings. I'm sure you'd tell me just to protect myself, but then, your sense of duty is so strong. Surely you'd be trying to find a way to let the Caomhnóir know what's going on, to alert the Council to the situation so that we could stop it before it came to pass. But how would you do that? How can I do that? Would you tell me that I'm being selfish, keeping the fact that I'm a Seer from the rest of the Council? No, of course you wouldn't. But you should. Someone should.

I want to laugh and scream at the same time when I look at what I've turned into. I'm that girl. That girl I rolled my eyes at in every book and movie and television show when she just sits there all lovesick and helpless, pining and unable to figure out what to do. I hate that girl. I hate that girl and I am that girl. Seriously, I'd like to Walk out of this body just to get away from her. And I know that if I'm ever not this girl again, I won't be able to roll my eyes at her anymore. Because I'll recognize a little bit of myself in her, and that just makes me want to light shit on fire.

I warned you that this letter was going to be a rambling disaster. But I know you'd ignore me and keep reading, so I guess I'll just keep writing until I run out of things to say or at least, the words to say them.

I want you to know that I'm trying. I haven't given up, and I haven't given in. Fiona's trying to help me. We're trying to figure out how what you witnessed and what I've drawn are connected to each other. I'm going to find a way to get you out of there. Because if there's one thing I'm not willing to risk in all of this, it's you. And there's that selfishness again, but I just don't fucking care. If I can just be sure that the two of us will come out on the other side of this together, I would let this whole Durupinen world come crashing down. You probably wouldn't. You would find a way to save it all, wouldn't you? You might even be doing it right now. You're probably coming up with a plan. Action steps. A concrete map to victory. You wouldn't be sitting on the floor of your room smearing the words you write with your own damn tears, and wasting your time pouring your heart out into the letter that you know you're never even going to be able to send.

Or maybe you would. Maybe that's what all your poems are, really. Love letters that you never send.

I hope you're still writing them. I hope you can find the inspiration, even in that place. I've barely drawn a thing since you've been gone.

So, I'm here. I'm here, and I think about you all the time, and I hope you know that. I hope it's not one of those things you have to wonder about. I doubt a lot of things. I doubt that we may see each other again. I doubt that even if we do, we'll be able to ride this thing out together. I doubt that the laws will change. But I don't doubt the way I feel about you. It's the one feeling I've never been able to bury. It's the one feeling that I've always known I'm doing right. Thank you for being the person who could make me feel so sure about something. I've waited a long time to feel that way.

I love you, Finn.

I put the pen down, having said absolutely everything that I could think to say, everything that I needed to say, but couldn't bear to say out loud to anyone else but him. I looked down at the words I'd written. I watched my handwriting, which had started out so measured and neat at the top of the page, gradually unravel into a barely legible scrawl down at the bottom of the page. It was the perfect metaphor for the way it felt to open the door a crack, just to let a few of the feelings out, and then watch the feelings break the door down and tumble over each other in their desperation to escape. I looked through the letter one last time, though I couldn't say why. Maybe I just thought that I owed myself the courtesy of making sure that somebody—some pair of eyes—read it completely from beginning to end before it no longer existed.

Sighing, I folded it up carefully and tucked it inside a stiff white envelope. I sealed it carefully, and then flipped it over and wrote Finn's name on the front. I looked at it, imagining it carried away on a breeze and fluttering down through his open window somewhere hundreds of miles away.

There, I told myself. *He knows. Somehow, some way, this was not an exercise in insanity or futility. You've put it out there into the universe, and somehow, now he knows it.*

I ran my fingers over the front of the envelope, tracing the letters of his name, and then I reached over and dropped the letter into the heart of the fire. I watched it blacken, and curl, and crumble to ash.

There was a soft knock on my door. Hastily, I scrambled to my feet and hurried over to answer it, but stopped myself from opening it too soon. I took a deep, calming breath and watched my right hand on the door handle, waiting for it to stop shaking. When I had mastered myself, I pulled the door open, just wide enough to see who had knocked.

The face I saw looking back at me sent my heart right back into overdrive.

"Celeste!" I gasped, dropping all pretense of calm and collected. "I... what are you doing here?" I probably should have addressed her in some more polite or deferential way—after all, she was the High Priestess. But my surprise at seeing her standing there left no room for inventing pleasantries.

Celeste did not seem to mind being addressed so informally, however. "Hello, Jess," she said, smiling politely at me. "May I have a word?"

My shock at seeing her was such that my usual feelings of boiling, uncontrollable anger had not yet had a chance to find their way to the surface. As they awakened, I forced them down in the interest of finding out what it was she wanted from me. After all, it was not customary for the High Priestess of the Northern Clans to make her way down to the clan dormitories and knock on somebody's door for a little chat. I knew that this had to be something a bit more serious.

"Of– of course you can," I stammered. "Would you... do you want to come in? Sorry, it's kind of messy." I gestured apologetically behind me. Clothes were strewn upon the floor where I had stepped out of them, and Hannah's Council notes were spread in piles across the floor, littered with highlighters and sticky notes.

"No, thank you," Celeste said, raising a deferential hand. "I rather hoped that you would talk with me while we walk."

"Sure, but... where are we going?" I asked. I felt jittery, and I could not help it as my eyes darted back to the crackling fire.

"I am obligated to have... well, a *difficult* conversation," said Celeste, choosing her words carefully. "I think the conversation might be just a bit easier if you are present. I would appreciate your assistance, if you will consent to give it."

For the most fleeting moment, I considered slamming the door in her face, right after telling her that I would help her when hell froze over. My curiosity got the better of me, though, and instead of shouting her down, I nodded my head rather meekly, and stepped out into the hallway, closing the door behind us.

We began walking, side-by-side, but had only gone a few steps when I blurted out, "What is this conversation you need to have? I mean, if I'm allowed to ask?"

Celeste did not look at me, but continued to keep her eyes trained out in front of us toward the end of the corridor. "If memory serves, you are rather close with Ms. Todd, are you not?"

I frowned, taken aback once again. This was definitely not the direction I thought the conversation was headed. "You mean Savannah?" I asked.

"Yes, of course," Celeste said. "I've seen you together frequently. Am I correct in my assumption that you two are close?"

"Yes," I said. "We've become pretty good friends."

Celeste smiled just a bit, the corners of her mouth curving gently upward for a moment. "I am not surprised to hear this. It is common for newcomers—that is to say, *outsiders*—to gravitate toward each other inside these castle walls." She looked up at me, her eyes sad. "I do not mean to offend you," she said quickly, "by calling you an outsider. It is far less true now than it was when you arrived."

I shrugged. "That's okay," I said. "We were outsiders. If I remember correctly, you had to personally scrub the words 'Go home, traitors' off our bedroom door on our first day here. It doesn't get much more 'outsider' than that."

"Quite so," Celeste said, frowning as though the memory pained her. "Naturally, Savannah was an outsider as well, being the very first Gateway in her clan. And of course, there were... *other* factors as well, that kept her on the outskirts of things a bit."

I smirked in spite of myself. "You mean her habit of skipping important ceremonies to go partying with her friends in London?" I suggested.

Celeste laughed. It was a nice sound, but odd somehow, as though she were out of practice these days. "That example does spring to mind, yes. I think she might've done well to stay awake once in while in her classes on occasion, too. But enough of that," Celeste added, her face growing serious again. "I'm not here to disparage your friend. She found her way, in the end."

"Yes," I agreed. "She did. So, is Savannah the one you want to talk to?"

"Yes," Celeste said. "And her cousin Phoebe as well. It is not going to be an easy conversation, and I thought that it might help her to have a friendly face in the room beside her. Are you willing to be that friendly face?"

My heart sped up, and my mind frantically raced, wondering what the content of this conversation could possibly be. "Of course," I said quickly. "I'm always willing to be there for Savvy, whenever she needs me. But... why does she need me?"

Celeste pressed her lips together, and for one frightening moment, it looked as though she might cry. But her face shivered back into lines of composure almost instantly, and I was left wondering if I had imagined that momentary sparkle in her eye. "You will see soon enough," she said. "Just make sure that you are there for her in these days ahead. She is going to need your friendship, and your guidance. This is not the only capacity in which I want to have you present, however."

Her tone became much more businesslike. The shift was jarring.

"I understand that Catriona has asked you to help take the lead on the investigation into Charlie Wright."

"Yeah. Yeah, that's right," I said.

"The information I am going to pass along to Savannah and her cousin has relevance to your case. It will need to be explained and passed along to the Trackers as well. In the interest of expedience, I would like you there so that we need only meet once to discuss it."

"Oh... right," I said, momentarily forgetting that I had anything like an official capacity. "Yeah, that sounds like a good idea. I... I don't have my case file with me, or anything."

"That's just fine," Celeste said, waving her hand dismissively. "Mrs. Mistlemoore has written up a full report that should explain everything for you. I want you to be able to focus on your friend, to offer her support."

"But why is Savvy going to need sup—"

"Here we are, just up here," Celeste interjected, and I looked around to see that we'd reached the entrance hall without my having noticed it. "We are going to meet in this room here, the small chamber right off the Grand Council Room."

My throat felt constricted as I stared at the door that was now in front of us. The last time I had been in this room had been on one of the worst days of my life. On the other side of that door, Celeste had stood calmly, waiting for her coronation as High Priestess, and informed me that Finn had been reassigned, and that I would never see him again. Ileana, the High Priestess of the Traveler Clans, had been present as well, and it had been on her evidence that Celeste had decided that Finn's and my relationship had crossed a line into illicit territory. Ileana's gloating smile still haunted me as I thought of that moment—the moment when my heart shattered more thoroughly than any spirit could ever manage. I'd brought Ileana's wrath down upon me because I had committed an unforgiveable transgression against the Traveler Clans: I had undermined their Council's prescribed justice and freed a woman who had been tormented for too long. But even as my heart ached with the absence of Finn, I couldn't regret what I'd done for Irina. And I knew that, hundreds of miles away, Finn did not regret it either. It was one of the many reasons why I loved him. For Finn, justice was always the only choice.

For just a moment, I let myself wonder if Celeste had brought me here on purpose, to torture me. But the thought died out as soon as it had sparked. Even in my anger at her, my nearly unrelenting anger, I could not believe that of her. As much as I did not want to admit it, I knew that Celeste was not a vindictive person. Ileana on the other hand... well, let's just say that I still hoped one day to be able to tell her exactly what I thought of her.

My instinct was to turn and run from that room and all the pain it held for me, but as Celeste opened the door, I saw the top of Savvy's ginger head just above the back of her chair. I knew that she needed me to cross that threshold and support her through whatever was about to happen.

As though my thought had preceded me into the room, Savvy turned and caught my eye. She shook her head at me, and I knew that she had no more idea of what this conversation would be about than I did. She looked beseechingly at me, begging for an answer I could not give her. I gave her what I hoped was a quick, reassuring smile as I crossed the room, and took the seat beside her, reaching out to squeeze her hand gently.

"You got any idea what this is about, mate?" Savvy hissed at me.

I shook my head. I didn't want to tell her what Celeste told me, about her needing a friend to get through whatever was about to happen. I couldn't bring myself to make her look any more scared than she already did.

"I'm sure everything will be fine," I said, lying through my teeth.

As I let go of Savvy's sweaty fingers and settled my hands back in my lap, the door behind us opened again, and Mrs. Mistlemoore walked in. Her face was blank—unreadable. She held a clipboard clutched tightly against her chest, and though her face was impassive, her knuckles upon the edges of the clipboard were white with tension. Behind her, one of her staff was pushing a high-backed, wooden wheelchair. Phoebe sat in it, slightly slumped, with a faded patchwork quilt tucked gently around her legs. She looked dazed, as though the trip from the hospital ward had thoroughly disoriented her. The grim-faced attendant wheeled her to a stop directly beside Savvy's chair and walked out again without saying a word. Phoebe looked over at the two of us, her expression bewildered. It was clear that she had no idea what this meeting was about either. She may not, I realized, have been told that it was a meeting at all.

Something was wrong. Something was very wrong.

Mrs. Mistlemoore nodded curtly to us as she passed, stopping only to adjust Phoebe's blanket, which was trailing down near one of the wheels of her chair. Then she took a seat in a chair right next to Celeste's desk, just as Celeste was settling herself behind it. It was nothing like the desk in the High Priestess's office—a hulking, mahogany monstrosity designed to intimidate whoever was unfortunate enough to have to sit in front of it. This desk was small and delicate, with gracefully carved wooden legs and a dainty white lace cloth draped over the top of it. It was, I realized, an official but far less foreboding place to meet with someone than Celeste's actual office or the Grand Council Room, which always gave me the uneasy feeling of facing the wrath of a hostile judge and jury. It also would have been damn near impossible to get Phoebe up to Celeste's office anyway, now that I thought about it—wheelchairs and endless spiral staircases didn't exactly mix well.

Savvy was looking indignantly at Mrs. Mistlemoore. "Begging your pardon," she said, and though the words were polite, the tone was anything but. "Are you sure she's quite well enough to be out of her bed yet?"

Mrs. Mistlemoore nodded patiently, ignoring the sharpness of Savvy's question. "I promise you, Savannah, that I would not have allowed her to leave the hospital ward unless I was quite sure that she was physically prepared to do so. The High Priestess needed privacy for this meeting, and I could not ensure that for you in the hospital ward."

Savvy nodded, but her expression was still skeptical. Beside her, Phoebe's eyelids were drooping, as though she were ready to drop back off to sleep. She might be in the room for whatever this meeting was, but it seemed unlikely that she would remember much of it. The short trip out of her bed had already exhausted her.

"I will not keep you any longer than is necessary to explain the situation," Celeste said, addressing us all for the first time since entering the room.

Savvy pulled her eyes from Phoebe and sat up a little straighter in her chair. "So, there's a situation now, is there? And what kind of situation might that be?"

"I want to discuss," Celeste said, and again, I had the sense that she was choosing her words very carefully, "the recent discovery that Phoebe's Spirit Sight has been compromised."

Savannah went rigid in her seat. Her eyes darted back-and-forth between Mrs. Mistlemoore and Celeste. "You told me that you would let me know as soon as you knew what was going on with her Spirit Sight," Savvy said to Mrs. Mistlemoore in a rather accusatory tone.

"And that is precisely what I'm doing," Mrs. Mistlemoore said. "This was information that I felt it important for the High Priestess to have as well, as the implications of it reach far beyond the people sitting in this room."

Phoebe was fighting valiantly to keep her eyes open, but it seemed to be a battle that she was destined to lose. Savvy reached over and grabbed Phoebe's hand in her lap as a sign of solidarity, it seemed. I suspected, though, that it was as much to gather strength as it was to bestow it; Savvy's face had gone starkly white.

"Go on then," Savvy said, her jaw thrust out in the very picture of the British "chin-up" mentality. "Let's have the worst of it, then. I can tell from the looks on your faces that we ain't about to hear nothing cheerful."

"No," Celeste said solemnly. "I'm sorry to say you are quite correct. It is a grave situation, I will not lie to you." She took a deep breath, and held her hand out for Mrs. Mistlemoore's clipboard. Mrs. Mistlemoore handed it to her, and as she did so, they exchanged a serious look. My heart was beginning to thunder beneath my shirt as the anticipation mounted. Savvy was looking at the clipboard like it was a loaded weapon that Celeste had just pointed at her.

"As you of course already know," Celeste began, her voice professional, but not unkind, "Phoebe awoke yesterday without the ability to see, hear, or indeed, sense any spirits at all. We cannot say whether this result of her ordeal is expected, or ordinary, for what Phoebe has gone through is extraordinary—possibly unique. Certainly, we have no record in all of our Durupinen history of any such situation occurring."

"Hang on, now. There's that other girl, Flavia," Savvy said, so defensively that it came out as nearly a shout. "That Charlie bloke's gone and done the same thing to her."

"He *attempted* to do the same thing to both of them, that's true enough," Mrs. Mistlemoore interjected quickly. "But the fact of the matter remains that he experimented upon both of them, and that each of those experiments was slightly different, producing different results. While Flavia is another victim, we cannot claim that their conditions are identical, and therefore we really cannot use one as a true predictor of the other. At least, not entirely. Mr. Wright used some different runes and positioned them slightly differently upon each of the girls. There were also traces present of different substances that were used in each attack. It is clear that he did not yet know what he was doing, and both Flavia and Phoebe have suffered differently as a result."

Savvy seemed to want to argue with this, but could not wrangle her thoughts into a rational response. She sputtered and stammered a bit, but then went silent. Phoebe did not attempt to interject. It seemed all she could handle was merely to keep her eyelids up where they were supposed to be. Everyone was basically talking about her as though she weren't really there, but it didn't seem to bother her in the least. Her eyes drifted from speaker to speaker and, based on her expression, she was only vaguely following what was happening.

"If I may continue," Celeste said, once Savvy had fallen into silence. At this point, she turned and addressed Phoebe directly. Phoebe, sensing the shift in attention, gave her head a little shake and renewed her attempts to stay conscious. "As I was saying, we cannot know, or indeed predict, what the eventual outcome will be for you, Phoebe. We can only assess what is happening now. And what is happening now is troubling in the extreme."

I recognized the look on Savvy's face, and was pretty sure she was about five seconds away from launching herself across the desk and tackling Celeste right off her seat in frustration. In order to help Savvy avoid sitting in front of the Council on charges of assault against the High Priestess, I reached my arm across her chest as a gentle reminder to stay in her seat and behave herself. She threw me a glance that was at first defiant, but quickly melted into something like shame. Her shoulders slumped, and she dropped her eyes to her lap.

When I was sure that she had regained control of herself, I looked up at Celeste and nodded my head. "Perhaps it would be best if we dispensed with the formalities and just went straight to the explanation. I think it would be best for everybody if we just get it over with. You know, kind of like ripping off a Band-Aid," I said.

Celeste nodded. "Yes, of course. I apologize. It is not my intention to make this any more painful than it needs to be." Celeste flipped the page on the clipboard, folded her hands upon it, and turned to look directly at Phoebe. "Phoebe, it is my painful obligation to inform you that Mr. Wright's experiments upon you have resulted in a severed connection with your Gateway."

Phoebe blinked. She blinked again. Her expression was utterly blank.

"Phoebe?" Celeste prompted her after a few silent moments. "Do you understand what I just told you?"

Phoebe blinked again, and then shook her head, her hair

whipping over her shoulder like a horse tail swatting at an irksome fly. "Sorry, ma'am, but no. I don't reckon I quite understand what's going on."

Celeste adjusted herself in her seat and cleared her throat again, as she tried to find the words to clarify herself. It was evident from the expression in her eyes that she found having to deliver this news terribly distressing. "It would appear," she began deliberately, "when Mr. Wright twisted your Spirit Sight, he interrupted—or somehow broke—your connection to your Gateway."

"Broke?" Phoebe asked, her voice small and hoarse. "What do you mean, broke?"

Celeste glanced rather helplessly over at Mrs. Mistlemoore, who came to her aid in that kind, yet business-like tone she always adopted at a bedside. "'Broke' is perhaps the wrong word to use, for we do not know if the connection is beyond repair or not. It may be that some Casting can be found that will repair the damage. Or else the damage may repair itself, like a creature who loses a limb, and simply grows a new one. Or..." she faltered and stopped.

"Or?" Phoebe prompted her. There was nothing sleepy about her eyes now. They had gone wide and round as coins. Where they had been dull and clouded mere moments before, they now sparkled brightly with fear.

Mrs. Mistlemoore took a deep breath, steeling herself. "Or the connection may be severed permanently."

No one spoke for a moment. The news hung over us, like a terrible storm cloud, threatening to open up at any moment and drown us all. Savvy recovered first.

"How can Phoebe's connection to the Gateway be broken?" she asked. "The Gateway is inside her, right? It's in there, in her blood. How can you become disconnected from something that's actually a part of you?"

"The Gateway exists outside of the Durupinen," Celeste replied, keeping her tone as gentle as she could while still sounding like a schoolteacher who was slightly frustrated that a student had not been paying attention. "The Durupinen are merely a conduit to it. For example, all of the spirits who choose, at the moment of their death, to cross over into the Aether, do so without the guidance of a Durupinen. Those spirits do not need Durupinen to be physically present in order for the Gateway to open and accept them, for it is always there, waiting for that very moment. It is only when that

Gateway closes that the spirits need someone to open it for them. Think of the spirit as somebody wandering around trying to get through a locked door with no key. The Durupinen have the key. But the door exists, whether the key is nearby or not."

I'd never heard anyone explain the Gateway quite in this way, but I imagined that if I had been told of my legacy as a small child, this might have been the very manner in which my mother would have explained it to me. Savvy's face was twisted in concentration, as though she were looking for a loophole. Phoebe, however, was starting to look as though she had understood something.

"So, what you're saying, ma'am, is that I've lost my key?" she asked tentatively.

Celeste nodding along encouragingly. "Yes, exactly that. And, to extend the metaphor, since it seems to be an apt one, we are not sure if that key is lost forever, or if we may in fact find it again. There is simply no way to know."

Phoebe nodded, clearly pleased that she had understood what Celeste and Mrs. Mistlemoore had been trying to convey to her, but the pleasure was short-lived. I watched as it drained from her face, to be replaced by a poignant sadness. "So... I will never see spirits again? I will never be able to help them?" she asked in barely more than a whisper.

"We cannot say for sure," Celeste answered, her lip trembling. "It is possible."

Savvy was looking at Mrs. Mistlemoore, Celeste, and Phoebe as though they had all quite lost their minds. "And what about me, then?" she blurted out suddenly, the intensity of her voice making us all jump. "What does this mean for me, then? We're the same Gateway. The same blood. Why is it that I can still see spirits, but Phoebe can't? The connection must still be there, right? Otherwise, I wouldn't be able to see them either."

"It is curious, to be sure," Mrs. Mistlemoore said, nodding thoughtfully, her face full of an academic interest. "But I think this may have something to do with your placement in the Gateway, and not just the connection itself."

"You're gonna need to explain that to me, mate," Savvy said, shaking her head. "I can barely follow what's going on here."

Mrs. Mistlemoore arched an eyebrow in response to being addressed as "mate," but otherwise let the insouciance slide. "Very well. Every Gateway has two parts—two Durupinen are required to complete the connection to the Gateway, and to allow spirits to Cross."

"Yeah, I've managed to grasp that much," Savvy said dryly.

"Well, then you no doubt also know that each Durupinen has a slightly different role to play. One of them is the Key, and the other is the Passage. Generally, it is the Key who has been seeing spirits even from her earliest memories of childhood." Mrs. Mistlemoore looked back and forth between Savvy and Phoebe, waiting for them to identify themselves.

"Yep, that would be me," Savvy said, raising a finger in the air. "Living amongst the dead since I was still in nappies, me."

"And you, Phoebe? Mrs. Mistlemoore asked, turning to Phoebe. "When did you first see a spirit?"

Phoebe shrugged. "Not all that long ago, I reckon. I was about fifteen, or maybe sixteen. Might've seen them before then, I suppose, but if I did, I didn't know they were dead."

"So, Savannah, you are the Key, and Phoebe is the Passage. Phoebe's Spirit Sight has only developed as a result of your own. As your connection to the spirit world grew stronger, hers began to develop. It's not a parasitic relationship, strictly speaking, but imagine it as the smaller creature latching onto a larger creature to nourish itself, and the growth of the one defining growth in the other."

I could tell from Savvy's face that she did not think much of this metaphor, but she allowed it to pass without her usual snark. "So, she can see spirits because I can see spirits, that it?"

"Your gift has allowed her gift to develop," Mrs. Mistlemoore said, nodding. "Now, if you had been attacked, Savannah, it is likely that neither of you would be able to sense any spirits at this time. Savannah, because your gift acts as a doorway to her gift, both of your gifts would likely be affected in that scenario. But since Phoebe was the one who sustained the attack, and since it was her Spirit Sight that was directly affected, it is only she who has lost the access to communicate with the spirit world."

"Okay," Savvy said, rubbing her temples as though trying to fend off the beginnings of a massive headache. "So, I can still see and communicate with spirits, but what can I *do* for them? It takes both of us to open the Gateway. But one of us is no longer connected to it, so what does that mean?"

It was Mrs. Mistlemoore's turn to look beseechingly at Celeste to find the words to answer Savvy's question. Celeste expelled a small sigh, and when she met Savvy's eye, her expression was full of pain. "It means that your Gateway, at least for the present, is closed."

Savvy looked blankly at Celeste. She turned to look at Phoebe. Then she turned to Mrs. Mistlemoore, her face expectant, sure that she was going to jump in with some sort of caveat, some sort of additional information that would make this blow gentler, less devastating. No one had anything to offer her. Finally, she dropped her gaze and whispered the awful truth to her own trembling hands.

"We're not Durupinen anymore."

Celeste reached across the desk and took Savvy by the hand, gripping it tightly. "Savannah Todd, you look at me, and you hear me now. Both of you hear these words and hold them in your heart. You will *always* be Durupinen. No Necromancer Casting can take that away from you, *ever*. Both of you are part of a clan now, and both of you will have an important role to play in the defending of the spirit world. We may not know what that will look like yet, but I can assure you that this man, this... *monster*... has not and cannot take that from you."

"But we won't be Crossing spirits anymore," Savvy said, still unable to meet Celeste's eye. "That's over now. That's done."

Celeste's face spasmed with repressed emotion. She squeezed Savvy's hand again. "Yes. I wish I could give you another answer, but it seems, at least for now, that that part of your journey as a Durupinen is done."

All the air seemed to have gone out of the room. I could barely breathe as I watched the force of this news hit Savvy again and again, breaking a tiny piece of her disbelief away each time it hit her. It was devastating to witness. Beside her, Phoebe was quite still, her expression blank.

My insides were writhing with pity and horror. Selfishly, I wished I was somewhere—anywhere—else. Why the hell did Celeste drag me down here, damn it? I couldn't do a goddamn thing to make this less awful! All I could do was stare and wince and avoid trying to hide my eyes like a helpless spectator of a tragic accident. I reached for Savvy's hand, but whether coincidentally or on purpose, she moved it at the same moment and tucked it firmly into her armpit as she crossed her arms over her chest in a pose that looked as though she were trying to keep her midsection from falling apart.

"So, what do we do now?" Phoebe asked in a very small voice.

"Do?" Savvy asked, her voice tight and strained. "There's nothing to do. This is the part where you tell us to pack our things and leave this castle in the rearview mirror, right? I mean, what is there for us here now? We've gone and turned our whole lives topsy-turvy for you people, and now that we're no use to you anymore, you're going to chuck us out."

"No," Celeste said sternly. "We will do no such thing."

"And even if you decided that you wanted to leave, I, for one, am forbidding it," Mrs. Mistlemoore said, folding her arms and looking suddenly quite menacing. "Phoebe has not been discharged, and I have absolutely no intention of discharging her until she is fully fit. In the meantime, there's much to be understood still about her condition, and how it may improve. It is my wish that she stay and undergo a series of tests, to be spread out over the course of her recovery. If we carefully monitor things, then we may be able to see small improvements, and maybe even a path forward, a way of mending that connection to the Gateway."

I couldn't tell if Mrs. Mistlemoore was dangling this possibility of full recovery simply to ease the severity of the blow they had just been dealt, and I didn't care. Savvy looked very skeptical, perhaps, but Phoebe gave her a small, hopeful smile, like a child who had been told that the world might just contain a tiny hint of real magic. She would cling to it, I knew, and I was just grateful that she had even this shred of hope, whether it had any basis in reality or not.

"Excellent," Celeste said briskly. "I approve of your treatment plan, Mrs. Mistlemoore. And of course, Savannah, we will need you here as well. It is crucial that we understand the progression of Phoebe's recovery as it relates to your mutual connection to the Gateway. In the meantime, however, it is imperative that you do not attempt any Crossings. I fear such an experiment could have disastrous consequences, both for you and for the spirits you would attempt to aid. Is that clear?"

"Yes," Savvy and Phoebe said dully.

"Very good. I am sure that we can find a way to keep you busy, Savannah. The Northern Clans are a complicated operation to run, and we can use all the help we can get."

Savvy pressed her lips together, as though biting back a rejection of this offer. She looked back and forth between Celeste and Mrs.

Mistlemoore, and it became clear from the determined looks on both of their faces that it was not an offer, so much as an order; an order that she would be expected to follow, until further notice.

"Just an idea, Sav," I said, clearing my throat. Savvy turned to me, her expression surprised, as though she hadn't even remembered that I was sitting there. I gave her a small, encouraging smile and went on. "You remember that Hannah was looking for some help on a new piece of legislation that she plans to propose to the Council? She thought you might be interested, and I know that she could use the help with the research and compiling her background information."

Savvy opened her mouth, but whether it was to accept or reject the proposal I never found out. Celeste clapped her hands together and answered for her.

"Excellent!" she exclaimed. "A new project to take our minds off things. That sounds like just the ticket."

"With your permission, High Priestess, I'd like to get Phoebe back to the hospital ward," Mrs. Mistlemoore said, getting to her feet and retrieving her clipboard. "She has been out of bed a bit longer than I would have liked, and rest is going to be crucial to her continued recovery."

"Of course," Celeste said, nodding her head and smiling at Phoebe, who returned the smile tentatively. "A nice rest, and a bit of time to reflect on what you've been told. And then I'll come to see you again, and we can talk further. Does that sound amenable to you?"

Phoebe's eyes widened, as though the idea of the High Priestess visiting her for a friendly chat scared the ever-loving shit out of her, but she managed to stammer out, "Y–yes, ma'am."

"Very good, then," Celeste said. Then she turned to Savvy. "Savannah, I look forward to seeing you around the castle, and speaking with you further about your role here." Her eyes glinted with authority as she added, "The spirit world and the Northern Clans are not done with you yet, Savannah Todd. You were chosen for a reason, and that reason, though it has yet to reveal itself, is stronger than ever. Search within yourself, and you will find it."

For once in her life, Savannah Todd was utterly lost for words. She did not reply or even nod, but instead stood up from her chair and looked at me helplessly, as though awaiting direction.

"Why don't you go with Phoebe," I told her. "You can make sure she gets settled, and that she's comfortable. I'll come meet you in the hospital wing in a moment, and then you and I are going for a drive."

Still, Savvy seemed unable to reply, but she did as she was told. As Mrs. Mistlemoore bustled by her, pushing Phoebe's wheelchair, Savvy turned and followed, not of her own volition, but as though an invisible string were tugging her along, and she lacked even the will to resist its pull.

Once all three of the women had disappeared through the door, I turned back to Celeste. Her face had dropped into her hands, and I could tell that she had barely held herself together until the end of the interview. A dull creeping feeling was sneaking its way up through the tangled mass of anger and frustration that I had built up against her, and it took me longer than it should have to realize that it was pity.

I was actually feeling sorry for the woman who had separated Finn and me. No wonder I usually avoided feelings. I was clearly complete shit at them.

"Are you all right?" I asked her tentatively.

Celeste rubbed her hands against her face and then ran them back through her hair, so that it was pulled tightly away from her face. She looked exhausted. "I have no choice but to be all right," she said. "And anyway, I'm not the one that anyone should be worried about. I am not the one who has just had my very life's purpose pulled out from under me."

"We'll all stick by her," I said quietly. "Me, Hannah, Milo, Mackie. She's tough, Savvy. Resilient. If anyone can bounce back from this, I know it's her." The words sounded forced, even in my own ears, because I knew I was saying them as much to convince myself as to reassure Celeste.

"I certainly hope so," Celeste said. "It took her so long to accept her destiny. So long for me, and for the others to convince her that this was her life's purpose. How cruel to tear it from her grasp the moment she decided to cling to it. How very cruel indeed."

"What do you want me to do with this information?" I asked her. "As far as the Trackers go, that is."

"Well, Catriona will need to be told, of course," Celeste sighed, shaking her head in an attempt to bring herself back into the present. "But there is one very crucial thing that you must understand."

"What's that?" I asked.

"Under no circumstances can this information ever reach the ears of Charlie Wright, or anyone who may have been in league with him," Celeste said, and her face was deadly serious.

"Why?" I asked.

"They must never know that one of their experiments, however accidentally, severed a Durupinen from her Gateway. That is a weapon that they must never know they possess, however unwittingly. The devastation that they could wreak..." Celeste suppressed a shudder. "The Durupinen would never recover. The spirit world... the Gateways... all of it could be destroyed."

She looked up at me. I met her eyes, and a silent understanding passed between us. What happened to Phoebe wasn't just unfortunate and sad. It had dangerous and far-reaching consequences for all Durupinen the world over if it were ever discovered.

"But how do we stop the word from spreading? People will realize that Phoebe and Savvy are no longer a Gateway," I pointed out.

"We will find a cover story," Celeste insisted. "But it is crucial—absolutely crucial—that this information never leave this castle."

I nodded. We would keep the secret. We would keep it because we had to.

§

I found Savvy sitting at Phoebe's bedside, staring down at her now sleeping cousin without really seeing her.

"Hey, Sav," I said, and though I spoke as gently as I could, Savvy started like I'd shouted in her ear.

"All right?" Savvy asked me, dragging the back of her hand across her face in a half-hearted attempt to wipe away the evidence of tears.

"Come on. Get up. Let's get out of here," I told her briskly.

"Huh? What are you on about?" Savvy asked me, frowning.

"We're going out," I told her firmly. I held out my hand.

"Out where?" Savvy asked me.

"I don't care. Anywhere. Anywhere you've ever wanted to go. Clubbing. Drag racing. Skydiving. I don't care. Today the answer is yes."

"I can't, mate. Not today," Savvy said, her voice hollow.

"Yes, today. Right now. Get up," I ordered, and I wiggled my hand at her. "When you think you can't, that's when you have to."

"Why?"

"Because you heard what Celeste said in there!" I cried. "Don't let him win, Savvy! Don't let him take any more from you than he already has. If you despair, he wins. If you crumble, he wins. And if there's one thing we can't ever stand for, it's letting that bastard win!" I was shouting now, but I couldn't stop myself. Any moment now I was going to wake Phoebe up and Mrs. Mistlemoore was going to swoop down upon me like a bat out of hell and throw me out into the hallway on my ass, but damn it, not before I got Savannah Todd to take my hand.

Savannah blinked, shocked that I was shouting at her. Then her mouth curved into the very slightest of smiles. "Clubbing? You?"

"Kind of weird that you think that's a more unlikely offer than plunging to the ground from a plane, but yes, I will cover myself from head to toe in glitter and dance on top of a goddamn bar if you ask me to," I told her. "Just take my hand right now. Because fuck him, Savvy. Fuck him and everything he took from you and everything he ruined. Take it back. Take my hand and take it back from him, goddamn it!"

Savvy hesitated only a moment longer, then reached out and took my hand. Without another word, she stood up and we walked out of the hospital ward, still holding hands.

As the door closed behind us, I reached out into the connection and found Milo and Hannah waiting for me. Completely silently, I conveyed the entirety of what had just happened in our meeting with Celeste. I felt first their surprise, and then their horror, and then their anger and sadness wash through the connection like lapping waves of an incoming tide. And then at last, when they had absorbed it all, I asked, "So? Are you coming?"

"Of course, we are," Hannah said without a hint of hesitation.

Milo snorted. "Girl, you don't even need to ask. You had me at glitter."

9

CONFIDANTES

"**R**ISE AND SHINE, Buttercup!"

Milo's voice cut through the veil of my sleep as subtly as a fog horn. I turned my head on my pillow and managed to pry open one eye with extreme difficulty. "Begone, evil spirit from hell," I muttered hoarsely.

"I can't begone. We're Bound for life, remember? Two peas in a happy little pod," Milo trilled.

"Ahem! Excuse me!" came Hannah's indignant voice from somewhere to my left.

"Oh right," Milo said. "So, three peas in a pod, then."

"Oh yeah? Well, get out of my pod before I pry open this Gateway single-handedly and shove you through it," I muttered. I let my eyelid drop again and tried to find my way back into unconsciousness.

"Sorry, sweetness, but it's time for you to get up," Milo said. With a flick of his hand, he used his energy to part the thick velvet curtains that had been drawn across the windows. A ray of sunlight stabbed me in the eye like a cheerful fork.

"Oh, God, why?" I moaned. "The daylight, it burns."

"Oh, stop being so dramatic," Milo said, in perhaps the most ironic statement ever to part company with his lips. "You're hungover, you're not a vampire."

True to my word, I'd spent the previous night and the wee small hours of the morning partying my way through Savvy's favorite hot spots in London. I had promised her to make it a night of "yes." That is, if she wanted to do it, my answer would be yes, regardless of the absurdity of the request. Was this a foolish decision? Undoubtedly. Would I pay for it for the next week? That seemed likely, based on the intensity of my headache. But I had been on a mission, a mission worthy of the world's worst hangover, and that was to prove to Savannah Todd that everything would be okay. This mission would obviously take more than a single night to accomplish. But from what I could remember, Savvy had spent the night laughing and smiling and having the time of her life, so that was something. A baby step in the right direction. And we would keep walking, all the way to the mythical Gates of Okayness. Well, she would keep walking. I would evidently be crawling on my hands and knees. I was going to have to find a new route to cheer her up, because I was clearly out of my league.

"Ugh," I moaned. "I am absolutely never doing that again. The next time I suggest that I can hang with Savvy on the pub scene, just do me a favor and hit me in the head with a lead pipe. It will literally be less painful than this."

Milo giggled. "I will do no such thing. That was one of the most entertaining nights of my life, and if there's ever a chance you're going to repeat it, I am here for it. I'm going to cling to that sweet memory for the rest of my afterlife."

"Cling away, because that is never happening again." I said. I may have broken my cardinal rule against excessive drinking once, but I wasn't about to do it again. I had too much experience watching from the outside, and it wasn't pretty. I lifted my head just enough to pull the pillow out from under it and then thrust it back down over my face. Somehow, the sunlight still seemed to be reaching me. "That was a one-night-only performance."

Hannah came over and sat down on the end of my bed. The slight rocking motion of the mattress made my stomach roil. "You are such a good friend," Hannah told me, in a voice barely above a whisper. "Savannah really needed you last night, and you came through in a big way."

"Ugh, don't remind me," I groaned into my pillow. I tried to focus on the details of the night, but it was a disjointed mess. "Did I... ride a mechanical bull at one point?"

Hannah let out a quickly stifled giggle. "Well, yeah, you did. Three times, actually."

"If it's any consolation, you now hold the bar record for the longest ride while seated backwards," Milo said, trying and failing to keep a straight face.

"I remain unconsoled," I said. "Please tell me that was the most embarrassing thing that I did."

Milo grinned. "I wouldn't have called it embarrassing. Actually, it was damn impressive. They gave you a blue ribbon and everything, it's around here somewhere. It was probably my favorite part of the night. Well, either that or when you stole that guy's cowboy hat and started line dancing on the bar. That was equally phenomenal."

"I don't dance. Or wear cowboy hats," I said scathingly.

Hannah cleared her throat, and pointed to the post of my bed, where a black rhinestone-studded cowboy hat was now perched. "You do now," she said fighting to keep both her voice and her face under control. "It's good to try new things."

"My God, I can't believe there are people who do this every weekend. How much do you have to hate yourself to wake up feeling like you've been hit by a truck?" I whined. When no one answered, I turned to Milo. "Now please tell me why you're waking me up so early? I mean, other than the fact that you're a sadist."

"It's not early, sweetness. It's nearly noon," Milo said dryly. "And we let you sleep as long as we possibly could, but you've got to be in Catriona's office in about an hour, and we thought you might like to shower some of the essence of mechanical bull off yourself before you headed down there."

"What? It's already noon?" I sat up quickly, which was a colossal mistake. The room spun, and the throbbing in my head felt like somebody was crashing cymbals between my ears. "Oh God, I can't have a meeting now. I'm going to have to cancel it."

"Good luck explaining that to Catriona," Milo said. "I don't think she'll accept 'part-time party girl' as an excuse for missing a Trackers meeting, do you?"

"Not a chance," I admitted. I tried to pull myself together. "Before I do anything else, I'm definitely going to need..."

Hannah thrust both her hands toward me. In one she was holding a very tall glass of water. In the other, she was holding two extra-strength pain relievers. She smiled knowingly.

"Right. Yeah. That," I said, attempting to smile at her. I popped the pills into my mouth and chugged the water until it was nearly half gone. I knew it would be a while before my headache began to fade, but at least my mouth no longer felt like a desert landscape.

"Where is Savvy by the way?" I asked, as I eased my legs out from under my blankets. I was still wearing the torn skinny jeans from the night before, and the black sparkly top. I looked up at Hannah, gesturing to the outfit.

"Sorry," she said apologetically. "We couldn't get you into your pajamas. You were asleep too fast. It was all we could do to get the boots off."

"Savvy decided to spend the night at her mom's," Milo said. "We dropped her off on the way home. You were already asleep in the car. For all the shit she gives Alice, you could tell she was really glad to see her. Sometimes you just really need your mom, you know?"

Neither Hannah nor I could respond to the question, which Milo immediately seemed to regret asking. Trying to cover the awkward moment, I yawned widely and rubbed my face with the back of my hand, which was an interesting bluish black color. For a moment, I thought it was a bruise, but then I realized that it was the smudged remnants of several stamps that had been inked onto my hand at the various stops along our epic pub crawl.

"Right," I said. "Well, I guess I better get myself cleaned up." I stood up and found myself to be steadier on my feet than I expected. Thank goodness for small blessings.

"Do you want me to run down to the dining room for you?" Hannah asked helpfully. "I could bring you up some toast. Or some coffee."

"Maybe just the coffee," I told her. "I'm not sure if I can handle the toast. Thanks, Hannah."

Hannah nodded, and slid off the bed. "Milo, you want to come with me?"

"Yeah, we'll give you some privacy," Milo told me. "We can fill you in on the rest of the shenanigans when we get back."

I didn't think I wanted to know anything else about any alleged shenanigans, so I waved them both out the door and peeled off the previous night's ensemble. I was tempted to drop it directly into the trash can but tossed it into the corner of the bathroom instead. Then I washed the worst of my hangover away in a very long, very hot shower. When I finally coaxed myself out, the bathroom looked like a sauna, and there was a steaming mug of black coffee waiting for me by my bed. Hannah and Milo had left it and gone back down to breakfast.

By the time I had finished drinking it, I was starting to feel almost like a human being again. I even felt a faint pang of hunger, and Hannah, because she was basically a saint, had anticipated this. Though I had told her I didn't need the toast, she had brought it anyway, slathered in butter and jelly and wrapped in a napkin. I nibbled on the toast while I dug through my drawers to find clothes that were both appropriate for a meeting with my pseudo-boss, but also as comfortable as I could possibly get away with. When I had finished dressing, I sat back down on my bed, opened the drawer to my nightstand, and pulled out the file folder that contained my interview notes.

I settled back on my pillows and flipped the folder open. Though my chat with Flavia had not been a formal interrogation, I had been able to get at least partial answers to most of the questions that Catriona had provided for me. I knew that I would need to fill in the blanks, but I didn't want to stress Flavia out too badly, not when she was finally making some progress on her recovery. I anticipated that Catriona would give me a fair amount of shit for the blank spaces that remained in the questionnaire, but I was willing to take it if it meant sparing Flavia a little bit of pain, at least for the present. Besides, she had answered what I considered to be all of the really important stuff: the details that might help the Trackers locate any of Charlie's associates who may have been involved in his plans. I had yet to question Phoebe, but given the sledgehammer of news that she had just been hit with, I was in no rush to do so. If Catriona was so desperate for answers that she couldn't wait another day, she could damn well question Phoebe herself. I would not be the one responsible for causing more distress than she was already experiencing right now. As much as Savvy was struggling with the loss of the connection to their Gateway, Phoebe's pain and devastation must surely be compounded by the guilt of knowing that she was the source of the broken connection. Of course, it wasn't her fault. Logically, she must know that. Nevertheless, guilt doesn't often obey a mistress such as logic. I sighed and closed the folder again, resigned to the fact that I was probably going to be told off for the amount of work I still had not accomplished. Well, I already had a pounding headache. What was a little more shouting, right?

§

The Trackers office was busier than I had ever seen it. Typically, there might be one or two Trackers hanging around, usually just breezing in and out to drop off a report, or pick up a file. Today, there were no less than six Trackers crowded into the room, and all of them looked frantically busy. I watched the flurry of activity for a few bewildered moments before Catriona looked up from the filing cabinet, and saw me standing there.

"Well, what are you waiting for, a gilded invitation? Come in already, and close the door behind you," she snapped.

"What's going on?" I asked, still staring around. The Tracker nearest me, a young woman with closely cropped blonde hair and a long scar across her left cheek, was flipping rapidly through a stack of photographs that were either head shots or mugshots. Each face that flashed past was that of a young man in his twenties. Behind her, a second Tracker, whose name I thought might be Elin, was holding slides up to the light and squinting at them.

"What do you mean, what's going on?" Catriona shot at me. "What kind of bloody question is that? We're in the middle of an investigation, remember?"

"Yeah, but... we're always in the middle of an investigation," I pointed out. "Usually more than one. I meant, has there been a development that's got everyone so... frantic?"

"Yes, well we've had a possible lead on a second Necromancer, and we're attempting to identify him and nail down his whereabouts at the time of the attacks. So, we've got a team here combing both files to see if we documented any other evidence that might link him to either scene."

"Any luck?" I asked.

"We very nearly had him in custody," Catriona said, her nostrils flaring.

Beside her, the Tracker named Elin bristled. She turned to face Catriona, a long braid of dark hair whipping back over her shoulder as she spun. "That wasn't my goddamned fault, and you know it," she growled. "If that bloody Caomhnóir security team hadn't gotten in my way, that suspect would be sitting in this office right now staring down the backside of my hand."

"It was a tactical cock-up on your watch. Spare me the sob story, Elin. The fact is that he now knows we are looking for him, and that means he's going to be much more careful and therefore much more difficult to surprise. Our job is harder now, so stop your whining and fix it," Catriona barked.

Elin gave Catriona the kind of look Catriona usually gave other people she loathed. It was strange to see it directed at her rather than the other way around. The blonde Tracker laid a warning hand on Elin's arm, and Elin, taking the hint, backed down and resumed her task of examining the slides.

"So, you're still looking for him, then?" I ventured into the loaded silence.

"Unfortunately, that is where we find ourselves," Catriona muttered. "What've you got for me? Anything that might help?"

I assumed this meant our meeting had formally begun, and so I pulled out my Tracker folder and sat down in the only chair that wasn't occupied. "I was able to get through most of your questions with Flavia," I told her. "Her answers are here. She is still pretty weak, so I'm going to have to go back a couple of times before we get everything we need from her, but we're making progress. I thought I might as well give you what I have so far."

Catriona snatched the folder from my hand and scanned about halfway down the first page. "Here," she said to the room at large. "Here, we've got something here in the statement from the first victim."

Every Tracker in the room abandoned her task in the same instant and flocked around Catriona.

"What is it then?" asked Elin, a slide still clutched in her hand.

"First victim has been able to give details about the unknown second man in the room," Catriona said excitedly. "'Mid to late twenties. Approximately six-foot-one. Thin, pock-marked from acne. Clean shaven. Shaggy blonde hair, dark-framed glasses. Carries a backpack with a sticker on it from a local coffee shop called 'Cuppa Wonderful,'" she read from the description, then yanked the page from the file and thrust it at the blonde Tracker. "Tamryn, see what you can match here with the known associates."

"I'm on it," Tamryn said stoutly, and, gathering the photographs up in her arms, she ran from the room, a second Tracker right on her heels.

"You," Catriona said, handing the rest of the questionnaire to Elin, "go through the rest of this and tell me what other leads you can generate. I don't want to see your face again until you've got something useful for me." Elin, still looking surly, snatched the papers from Catriona's hands and stalked from the room.

Catriona flipped forward to the second set of questions, which had been reserved for Phoebe. She looked up at me. "I heard Phoebe was awake. Why haven't you questioned her yet?"

123

"She just woke up yesterday," I said. "She's really not in any shape to—"

Catriona slammed her hand down on the desk. My head give a piercing throb. "Jessica, we don't have time to be a bleeding heart here. Every day that goes by is a lost opportunity to make progress on this case."

"I know that," I said, rubbing my temple. "But there's been a sort of... development with Phoebe. Can I talk to you about it alone?"

Something in my tone caught Catriona off-guard, and rather than continuing to shout at me, she turned over her shoulder and shook her head at the remaining Trackers. The last one closed the door behind her with a resounding thud.

Catriona sat behind the desk and sighed. "Okay. We are alone. Talk."

"Celeste asked me to pass this information on to you when I saw you today, and she also asked that we just keep it between us. She doesn't want anyone else to know, including the other Trackers, or the Caomhnóir, until we figure out how to contain it."

Catriona raised her eyebrows, and I knew that I had her undivided attention at last. "Let's have it then," she said seriously.

"Charlie Wright's experiments on Phoebe resulted in a severing from her Gateway. It's not just that her Spirit Sight was twisted. It seems, now that it's been untwisted, that it's been too badly damaged to use."

"Damaged?" Catriona's eyes were wide, horrified. "Permanently?"

"They don't know yet," I said, trying and failing to keep emotion out of my voice. "But Milo came with us to the hospital ward yesterday to see her, and she had no idea he was there until we clued her in."

"Bloody hell," Catriona whispered.

"It gets worse," I said. "Phoebe's severed connection has left Savvy unable to connect to the Gateway as well. She can still see spirits, but she can't Cross them."

Catriona let out a low whistle. For several seconds she didn't seem able to speak. Then at last, she said in a subdued voice, "Yeah. It doesn't get much worse than that, does it?"

"No," I said. "For Durupinen, it doesn't."

It was almost strange to hear the words come out of my mouth. I thought back on the girl I'd been only four short years ago, a girl so terrified of her new ability that she would've done anything to get rid of it. I had so resented my legacy as a Durupinen, I would gladly have thrust it from me and never looked back. But my roller coaster ride of experiences since, while difficult and sometimes heart-wrenching, taught me not only to respect my gift, but to embrace it as a part of who I was. And I knew that Catriona, raised in the Durupinen culture from birth, would be utterly incapable of imagining a life cut off from her deeply ingrained calling. Even contemplating it happening to somebody else seemed to have left her momentarily dumbstruck.

"How's she taking it?" Catriona asked at last.

I shrugged. "Phoebe? I'm not really sure. I'm not very close with her, but I don't think she's had much time to absorb it yet."

"And Savannah?"

"Honestly? Not well. I took her out last night, tried to tear up the town like she used to do, you know, to try to cheer her up and get her mind off things. That's why I'm..." I gestured to myself vaguely, sure that my pale complexion and general state of dishevelment would speak for itself.

I was sure that Catriona would take the opportunity to toss out a jab at my expense, but surprisingly, she didn't. She just nodded solemnly. "Yeah. I used to do the same for Lucida, when the pressures and prejudices of being a Caller became too much for her. I hoped that, by misbehaving a bit, I could help her cope—you know, keep her on the straight and narrow. I need hardly point out that I failed miserably."

"That wasn't your fault," I said quietly. "We can't make other people's choices for them."

Catriona shook her hair back and quickly smothered the vulnerability that had appeared on her face. "Yes, well. Ancient history, that. Thank you for filling me in. Celeste is absolutely right. We can't let anyone find out about how successful Charlie Wright's experiments were, even if the outcome is not the one he intended. I'm sure you can imagine the damage they could do with a weapon like that."

"Yeah, I can," I said. "They would never rest until they had severed us all from our Gateways."

"Too right, they would," Catriona said. "I'll keep the lid on this for as long as possible. We will have to proceed with caution. Eventually, the word will spread that Phoebe and Savannah are no longer a viable Gateway. We'll have to manufacture some kind of cover story, something to hide the true extent of the damage that has been done at the Necromancers' hands. I'll start looking into it." Catriona glanced up at me. "I think that's everything I needed from you, unless..." She stopped midsentence and looked at me with a strange expression on her face. "Are you all right?"

My head was aching again, as intensely as when I'd first woken up. "Huh? Am I... Yeah, I'm okay. Just this damn headache."

Catriona was still looking at me with concern. "You really don't look well. Do you think you need a lie-down, or...?"

Everything went dark. I didn't hear the end of her question, and though I had opened my mouth to answer it, I couldn't seem to do that either. The darkness, whatever it was, pressed in upon me, squeezing my lungs and my heart, preventing me from drawing even the slightest breath. A rushing sound filled my ears, and it seemed to be coming not from outside me, but within, as though every blood cell in my veins had decided simultaneously to race each other through my circulatory system. Just as I thought that I was surely about to suffocate, the darkness receded as quickly as it had begun. The rushing sound stopped, and though my heart was still pounding, my blood seemed to have calmed. As my vision cleared, I looked around in confusion.

"Sorry, I... I don't know what just..."

But the details around me were shimmering into view, and the rest of my sentence stuck in my throat. I was crouched on top of Catriona's desk. One of Catriona's pens was clutched in my shaking right hand. In front of me, upon the back of a manila file folder, was a very familiar image.

"Shit," I whispered. "Shit, shit, shit."

"Jessica?"

The pen slipped from my fingers and fell to the desktop with a clatter. I looked up to see Catriona standing with her back pressed against the wall, as far from me as she could possibly get. Her expression was utterly terrified, and as I looked up at her, the terror only seemed to intensify.

"Jessica?" she repeated. And as she said it, I realized that she wasn't just calling me by name to get my attention, but she was questioning whether the form crouched in front of her was actually the girl that she knew to be Jessica. My eyes filled with tears.

"I... I'm sorry, I..." My legs seemed to turn to water and I

126

collapsed onto all fours, shaking violently. "I don't know what happened," I whispered. "I don't..."

Catriona took a very measured step forward, approaching me as one might approach a rabid, feral creature. Seeing the way that she was regarding me only compounded my fear and panic about what had just happened.

"It's all right, now," she said in very soothing tones. She took another step closer, and very slowly reached out a hand toward the desk. "I'm going to take the pen away. Is that all right with you?"

I stared at her, unsure of what to make of the question, until I realized that she thought I might use the pen as a weapon. I swallowed back a hysterical sob and nodded. Catriona plucked the pen from the desk and placed it on top of the filing cabinet beside her, never taking her eyes from me.

I shivered and realized that I had broken out in a cold sweat. My stomach gave a heave, and I fought hard not to be sick all over the desk.

"I... I think I need to sit. Could you... I'm not sure I can climb down," I whispered.

Still looking intensely wary, Catriona walked around to the other side of the desk and helped me down, bearing most of my weight as together we lowered my shaking limbs into the chair.

"Do... Do you think I could have some water?" I asked. I didn't sound like myself. My voice sounded distant and trembling.

"Of course," Catriona said, and hurried to the back corner of the room where a small table contained a coffeemaker, a collection of teas, and a pitcher of water with several glasses. She filled a glass with water, carried it back to me, and held it out.

I reached out a hand to take it, but she shook her head at me. "You're shaking too badly. You're going to drop the glass, or else just spill water all over yourself. Let me hold it, all right? You just drink."

I didn't argue with her for once, but allowed her to tip the glass of water toward my face. I took several gulps, ignoring the water that dripped down my chin. Then I leaned back in the chair and took a deep breath. "Thank you," I told her. "That's better."

Catriona set the half-drunk glass of water on the desktop and then picked up the folder upon which I had drawn. "Jess, what the hell is going on here? What in blazes did I just witness?"

I couldn't think. My brain seemed to be trapped in the back

corner of my head, pinioned there by fear and panic and exhaustion. I could not muster an excuse or cover story. This was it. I may have decided not to tell anybody about the prophecy, but the prophecy had decided otherwise.

"It's a prophetic drawing," I told Catriona, my voice hollow and resigned in my own ears. "I drew it for the first time about a week ago, on the hospital ward partition the night after Charlie attacked us. And I've been drawing it almost every night since. On the walls. On tapestries. On any surface that presents itself to my touch while I'm asleep."

If Catriona had looked frightened before, it was nothing to how she looked now. She dropped the folder back on the desk as though it had bitten her but continued to stare down at it.

"Prophetic?" she whispered. "But... how?"

I didn't want to say the words, but how could I avoid it?

"I'm a Seer," I said in barely more than a whisper. "It's possible I've always been one, since the moment I came into my gifts as a Durupinen. But I didn't realize it until the weeks after the Shattering. It was then that Fiona helped me realize that the drawings I had done of Eleanora, the Shattered spirit, weren't spirit-induced. They were warnings, warnings of what was coming. But I didn't understand it at the time."

"You predicted the Shattering with your art?" Catriona asked, aghast. It was Catriona who had been the source of the Shattering, the very first Host to be affected.

"Not exactly," I said. "I predicted who the Shattered spirit was, not the Shattering itself. After we realized who was in the drawings, I assumed that Eleanora must have reached out to me somehow, the way the other spirits do, using me as a Muse. But after the Shattering had been reversed, I had the chance to ask Eleanora how she had reached out to me from the *príosún*, and she assured me that she had not. There was no way she could have. You know what the Castings are like in that place. She wasn't able to communicate with anyone. It was only through Cross-Calling with Lucida that she was able to break free. That was after I had drawn her for the first time."

Catriona closed her eyes and pressed her palms to her forehead, as though she were trying to force the information into her brain and keep it there. "Is that the only time... the only *other* time that your art has been prophetic?" she asked.

"No," I said in a tiny voice. "There have been others."

Catriona did not ask for details. It was quite possible she did not think that she could handle them. It was just too much information to absorb. "Who knows?" she asked after almost a minute's silence.

"Fiona, Hannah, Milo, and Flavia here at the castle. Finn and Annabelle also know. That's it." *So far,* I added silently in my head. Soon everyone would now, and I'd be the terrifying spectacle of Fairhaven Hall once again, a title I'd successfully avoided for a whopping several months now. It had been nice while it lasted.

Catriona took a breath and turned back to the drawing, looking at it closely for the first time. "This is Skye Príosún," she murmured, and there was wonder in her voice.

"Yeah, it is," I said.

"But I don't understand... It looks like some kind of battle. I see Caomhnóir and..." She looked up at me her eyes wide and horrified.

"Yes," I whispered. "Caomhnóir and Necromancers, standing together."

"It's not possible," Catriona whispered. "It's just not possible. They would never... they couldn't... what does it mean?"

"I don't know," I admitted. "That's what Fiona and I were trying to understand. Our family's former Caomhnóir, Finn Carey, is stationed there now. He came to find me at Róisín Lightfoot's wedding. He wanted to warn me that something strange was going on at the *príosún*, and that it seemed like the Caomhnóir there were involved in illicit activities. Missing shifts, secret meetings, lying on paperwork about where they were, and how long they've been there, that kind of thing. The leadership there told him to let it go, but he couldn't."

"Why did he tell you? Why didn't he go to Seamus, or one of the other Fairhaven Caomhnóir?" Catriona asked.

"He was scared," I told her. "He didn't know who he could trust, okay? And he wasn't sure if his word would be trusted since he had been reassigned for... for breaking protocols," I told her, tears springing to my eyes against my will.

"What protocols?" Catriona pressed. "Why did he...?"

"Because of me, all right?!" I cried out. "It was my fault! All of this is my fault!"

And the dam broke. All of it tumbled out of me, unbidden but unstoppable. I told her everything: my relationship with Finn; my prophecy at the Traveler camp that led to Irina's escape; Ileana's revenge; my illicit conversation with Finn at the wedding; how Bertie's death had prevented us from passing the information along to Seamus; all of it. And the more that I told, the more I wanted to tell, until every last poisonous drop of the secrets and the lies had drained away, leaving me feeling hollow and empty, but also free. And the last person in the world I ever would have thought to trust was sitting across from me, every one of my secrets now cradled in her hands. Catriona sat in complete silence, her face unreadable, the new keeper of my own personal Pandora's Box. I watched her, knowing that I had relinquished all control. It would be up to her to decide what would happen now, and as much as that thought terrified me, I also felt an enormous sense of relief.

"So you believe," Catriona said at last, "that what Finn was witnessing at the *príosún*, and what Charlie alluded to when he kidnapped us, and what this drawing shows, are all one and the same? That it is all leading to this eventuality?" And she picked up the paper again to stare down at my drawing.

"Yes."

"Is that why Fiona really went to Skye?"

"Yes. She wanted to contact Finn, to see if she could get a sense of what was happening, without tipping anyone off."

Catriona shook her head. "Foolish, headstrong woman. She doesn't have the training for that kind of thing and she knows it. She should have alerted me, so we could've sent a Tracker instead. And we have no way to contact her until she gets back?"

I shook my head, my throat restricted with fear. "I agreed not to try to contact her while she's there. We didn't want to raise any suspicions. She's due back late tomorrow night."

"Bollocks," Catriona swore under her breath.

Still unsteady on my feet, I stood up.

Catriona looked up at me, her eyebrows drawn together in confusion. "Where are you going?" she asked me.

"You tell me," I said to her wearily. "Celeste's office or the Grand Council Room?"

Catriona's scowl deepened. "What are you on about? Why would we be going there?"

"You're turning me in, aren't you?" I asked her. "You're going to make me show this to the Council and tell them everything that's going on, aren't you? You might as well get it over with. We're losing time here. If I'm going to be publicly excoriated, I'd like to get it over with."

Catriona snorted. "Not a chance, Jess."

"What?"

"I said, not a chance. We're not telling anyone about this."

"We're not?" I asked blankly.

"Absolutely not," Catriona asserted. "Sit back down. You still look like you're going to pass out."

Feeling completely wrongfooted, I walked back to the chair and sunk into it. "So... why aren't you going to tell anyone about this?"

"Fiona might've been a damn fool to go to that *príosún* herself, but she was right. We can't let anyone know that you're a Seer."

I reached for the glass of water and drained the rest of it while I sat and processed this turn of events. Of course, I knew why Fiona would want to keep my role as a Seer secret. Her own mother had been a Seer, and look what had happened to her. It made sense that she, as my mentor, wanted to prevent me from meeting the same fate. Catriona, on the other hand? I wasn't sure that it made any sense.

"You look like you've got something else on your chest," Catriona said, observing me through narrowed eyes. "If there's yet another bombshell in this situation I suggest you tell me now. I like to know just how deep into the shit I'm going to have to wade before I agree to get my wellies on."

"I just... I can't believe I told you all of that. But even more than that, I can't believe that you're not marching me right to the High Priestess," I said honestly.

"Look, I'm not saying that we can keep the lid on this forever, but if we parade this prophecy in front of the whole Durupinen leadership, word is going to get out. And if Mr. Carey is right, and the Caomhnóir have been breached, then we have no idea how far that breach has gone. It's important to get an idea of what's going on at the *príosún* without alerting the Caomhnóir there that we know something is afoot. And while I wish I could have gone and done it myself, I think we should wait until Fiona gets back, and see what she's found out. It's only one extra day. Then we can proceed from there. If, at that point, the best way to prevent... whatever this is," she said, and waved my drawing through the air, "is to let the Council know that you predicted it, then that's what we'll do. For now, our excuse will be that you did let the Council know what was going on. First, you told your sister. Next, Fiona. And lastly, you told me. I can take the heat for not bringing it to the wider Council, if necessary."

"I'm not asking you to take the heat for anything," I objected. "I'm not trying to get you in trouble by telling you all of this; that's not why I did it."

"I know that," Catriona said. "You're a Tracker. I'm your superior. This was information I needed to have for our investigation. You provided it. And we will act on it as we see fit. The Council has trusted my judgment in allowing me to oversee this case, and it is my judgment that we sit on this information until Fiona gets back. Is that clear?"

I just nodded my head, still slightly flabbergasted. "Yes ma'am," I said.

"That's settled then," Catriona snapped. "I'm going to make you a cup of tea, and you're going to tell me everything that you've been able to figure out about this drawing. This proves that Charlie Wright's threats were not just empty words or the narcissistic ravings of a lunatic, and that makes it even more vital that we get this case solved and solved quickly." She stood up, and turned her back to me, plugging in an electric kettle.

"Oh, and Jess?"

"Yeah?"

"If you ever call me ma'am again, I will flay you alive."

10

SOS

ESS! JESSICA!
 The voice was echoing from somewhere very far away, but even though I could not hear it clearly, I knew that it was familiar somehow.

"I'm here! I'm right here! Who is it?" I called.

Jessica! Jessica, help!

I couldn't see anything. I was almost completely sure that I was asleep, but that didn't stop me from trying to respond to the voice anyway. These days, dreams were just an extension of reality, and I'd learned to take them just as seriously as anything that happened to me while I was awake. The last thing I remembered was assuring Milo that I could stay awake until Fiona was due to get back to Fairhaven. I'd been waiting on pins and needles for her for five days, and I wasn't going to miss the chance to talk to her the second she got in the door. I'd then promptly and thoroughly passed out.

Jessica!

"I hear you!" I cried, though whether I'd said it aloud or just in my head, I couldn't tell. I seemed to be in that foggy, dim place between sleeping and waking up, when you know you're dreaming, but you don't have the power to wake yourself up. "I hear you! Who is it?"

Jessica! Help me, please! Send help!

The voice seemed to be getting further away rather than closer, harder to hear rather than more distinctive. In vain, I tried to open my eyes, but my eyelids were too heavy. I tried to move my arms and legs, but it was as though they were made of lead. All was darkness and stillness, except that voice, which continued to echo from farther and farther away as I struggled to reach it.

"Jess!"

And now it seemed as though two voices were calling for

me—one from the far-off distances of my dreams, and one from inside my own head.

"Wait!" I called to the dream voice, which was barely more than an echo now. "Wait! I want to help you!"

Jess! called the two voices at once, blending and shifting and morphing into a single voice.

And in that moment, I knew it. I knew who was calling me from across the far reaches of sleep.

"Fiona!"

My eyelids flew open, and without any concept of how I'd done it, I was standing on my bed, poised to spring off of it and leap into some still undecided upon action.

"Jess! Oh my God, what's going on? What are you doing?"

I froze mid-spring, staring around me, and my eyes fell on Milo. He was standing beside my bed with his arms upraised, as though he were going to catch me as I prepared to take a flying leap off my bed. The sight of him standing there snapped me out of whatever dream-induced panic I was in. I straightened up.

"What are you doing?" I asked him.

He stared at me. "What am *I* doing? What are *you* doing? You're the one who looks like you're about to test your ability at the high jump while unconscious."

"Yeah but..." and I started to laugh, "were you going to... to try to *catch me?*"

Milo looked at his own outstretched hands in surprise, and then dropped them to his sides, shrugging a bit sheepishly. "I don't know. Apparently, I was going to try."

"But... you don't have, like... *actual arms,*" I pointed out, stifling another giggle that came bubbling to the surface.

"It was a leftover corporeal instinct, okay?" Milo said, scowling in annoyance as I continued to laugh at him. "I panicked. I wasn't really thinking, okay? Shouldn't you just be touched that I would've at least tried to catch you instead of just standing here and watching you fall on your face?"

Finding my legs suddenly wobbly and weak, I sunk down onto my bed, still smothering this odd desire to laugh. "Yes, I'm deeply touched that, were you still in possession of a body, you would've let me flatten you where you stand."

Milo cracked a smile. "I'm stronger than I look," he insisted.

I snorted. "You most certainly are not."

Milo rolled his eyes. "Whatever. But seriously though, can we get back to the impetus for this whole exchange? What the hell were you doing?"

I rubbed my head, which was starting to ache now. "I have no idea," I admitted. "Someone was calling to me, I think. In my dream. I heard a voice, but I couldn't place who it was. And then this other voice started calling me, and the two voices sort of got mixed together..."

"That second voice was probably me," Milo said, and he drifted over to rest beside me on top of the rumpled blankets. "You started flailing around and freaking out in your sleep, so I tried to wake you up. I thought if I came through the connection that might reach you more quickly—break you out of whatever kind of trance the dream had you in. So, I guess it kind of worked, because you heard me, and a few seconds later, you were awake."

"Yeah, I did," I admitted, rubbing my head again. The throbbing was intensifying by the second. "I just wish I could remember whose voice it was. I knew for a second, and then all of a sudden, I was awake, in reality, and I was trying to jump... I kind of lost track of things." I could feel the knowledge of the voice and who it belonged to slipping through my brain, which felt like a sieve trying to hold on to the details.

"Fiona," Milo said at once.

I looked up at him, shocked. "What? How do you know that?"

"You said it," Milo told me. "You said it out loud, right before you woke up. And then you sprang out from under your covers like some sort of jungle cat, prepared to pounce on your prey. I had no idea you could move like that. It was so... coordinated."

I hoisted an eyebrow at him and said, "Yeah, well, I doubt I could pull off something so coordinated while I was actually awake. So, you heard me say Fiona's name? Are you sure?"

"Absolutely sure," Milo said, nodding his head firmly. "It was the only thing to come out of your mouth that wasn't unintelligible muttering."

Even as he said it, though, I remembered. I remembered the moment when I realized that the voice was Fiona's. My heart began to thump unaccountably loud.

"Yeah, I remember now," I said. "Yeah, it was definitely Fiona's voice."

"So, you were having a dream about her?" Milo asked.

"I'm trying to remember," I said, stifling a yawn. My legs and arms felt shaky from whatever ninja-like antics I had pulled off in order to leap to my feet so quickly. "I don't remember seeing anything, or really any other detail except for her voice. It was just her voice, calling me in the dark."

"Calling you? What was she saying?" Milo asked.

"Just my name," I said, struggling to remember. "And... I think maybe she was asking me for something...?"

"Hey, wasn't she supposed to be back tonight?" Milo asked, his face lighting up as he suddenly remembered.

"Yeah," I said slowly... "I think... yeah, what day is it?"

"Technically, it's now Thursday," he replied.

"Yeah, that must be right! She must be back!" I cried.

"You think she... contacted you in your sleep to let you know that she was back?" Milo asked, looking skeptical. "Is that a Muse thing, or whatever?"

"No," I said slowly. "No, she's never done that before. I don't think that's a thing that we can do, at least not on purpose. I must've just been remembering that she was supposed to be back, and incorporated it into my dream. Still, it was kind of weird... I think she was... asking me for something."

Milo frowned. "What was it?"

"I can't remember," I muttered, closing my eyes, and pressing the heels of my hands hard against them, so that bright white light flared behind my closed lids. "She was asking me... or trying to tell me something." I let my thoughts dive down, down, down, as deep as they could go into the depths of my own consciousness, grasping around, trying to find the last fleeting edge of my memory of the dream. Suddenly, I caught something, and when I dragged it to the surface and realized what it was, my heart sped up into overdrive.

"Help," I whispered. "She was calling for help."

Milo's eyes went wide. "Help? Are you positive?"

"Yes," I whispered. "She was calling out to me to help her."

"Do you... do you think it was real? Like, a Seer thing?"

"I don't know," I said. "I don't... was I drawing? Did I try to draw something?" I looked helplessly around myself, searching for a writing implement, or any other sign that I might've been trying to record some kind of prophecy.

"No," Milo said, looking bewildered. "No, I was watching you. You were just lying there asleep, and then you started muttering.

We cleared away all the pencils and paper and stuff before you went to sleep. The only movement you made was when you suddenly jumped to your feet."

My heartbeat was so fast now that it felt like a thrumming hum in my chest. It was incredibly uncomfortable, and I began to sweat. "I wonder if... let's just go check if she's back."

Milo looked skeptical. "It's the middle of the night, Jess. If she just got back from a long trip, and you wake her up, she might kill you."

"I'll take that risk," I said, and I swung my legs over the side of the bed. I put my feet gingerly on the floor, testing to see if my legs, which were still shaking, would take my weight. They trembled, but, to my great relief, they held. "And anyway, who am I kidding? I'm not going to be able to sleep. I'm not going be get a moment's rest unless I know she's okay. I just need to see her face, even if she's screaming and throwing things at me."

"Your funeral," Milo said, with a rueful smile. "But I'm coming with you, just in case."

I took a couple of unsteady steps across the room to grab my sweatshirt, which I had thrown over the back of my desk chair, which doubled as a hamper when I was too lazy to cross the room to the actual hamper, which was basically always. As I straightened up, ready to pull it over my head, I suddenly realized the absence of something.

"Where is Hannah?" I asked him.

Milo rolled his eyes. "Where else would she be? In the library. Again."

I looked over at my clock. It was three o'clock in the morning. "Still in the library at this hour?" I asked incredulously. "Doesn't she ever plan on getting any sleep? How is she going to make a presentation to the Council if she's too exhausted to read her own notecards?"

Milo sighed. "I know. That's what I keep telling her. But why listen to me, I'm just the Spirit Guide, the one whose destiny in the cosmic universe is to dole out epically sage advice that you two clueless mortals are supposed to be heeding, or whatever."

"That presentation is weeks away," I said. "She can't keep up this pace."

Milo nodded. "I know, but let's worry about that later. Let's go before I lose my nerve."

I pulled the sweatshirt over my head and wound my tangled hair around and around itself into a messy bun on the top of my head, securing it with one of the black elastics that lived perpetually around my wrist. "Yeah, let's go."

Milo and I hurried down the silent deserted hallway. He floated along beside me, while my feet made echoing slapping sounds against the stone in my slippers. Here and there, a ghost floated by, bringing with it a dull misty light, like so many self-propelled lanterns on an English moor. None of them acknowledged us, and we barely spared any of them a glance. We were all too accustomed to each other's presences to pay each other much mind anymore. It was strange to think that, even in a place like Fairhaven, I could've grown so used to the comings and goings of the dead. I guess we were living—and non-living—proof that a person really could get used to anything.

We passed through the entrance hall, where dying embers glowed like tiny rubies in the giant fireplace. Two Caomhnóir stood sentinel by the locked front doors, each as still as a statue and as silent as a shadow. They did not question us as we walked past, though their narrowed eyes followed our progress suspiciously.

We reached the base of the tower, but I had barely placed a single foot upon the bottom step when a voice rang out behind us, startling me.

"Who goes there?" the man's voice called sharply. I turned around to see Seamus marching toward us.

I snorted. "Who goes there? Dude, you have watched one too many old movies."

As I stepped back, taking my foot off the step, Seamus closed the distance between us, and recognized me. "Oh, it's you."

"Nice to see you too," I said dryly.

"What's wrong?" Seamus asked, ignoring my insolence. "What are you doing wandering the castle at this time of night?"

"Not that it's actually any of your business why I go anywhere, but I'm not wandering," I retorted. "I walked directly to this tower from my bedroom."

"Why?" Seamus barked the question at me like I was being interrogated. I could feel my ire rising like a tide.

"Again, not that it's any of your goddamn business, but I want to see Fiona. She just got back from the Skye Príosún."

"Fiona has not returned," Seamus told me, his eyebrows drawn together suspiciously. "Why did you think she had?"

This pulled me up short, but I wasn't about to reveal to Seamus that Fiona had been calling me in my dreams. "I... because she told me before she left that she was coming home late tonight. I just assumed that she was already here."

"Well she isn't," Seamus informed me. "She was due back several hours ago, but there has been no word from her."

"What do you mean, there's been no word from her?" I asked him, my voice coming out sharp and cracked.

"I mean that she was supposed to meet with the High Priestess when she returned, but she did not meet her car at the train station, and all attempts to reach her have failed. We have just sent word to Skye Príosún, to inquire whether she has been delayed in setting out, but no one has yet responded. Communication seems to be down temporarily."

I suddenly felt dizzy, swaying on the spot. "Communication... has gone down... at the *príosún*?"

Seamus looked slightly alarmed at whatever expression was on my face. He took a hasty step forward and half-raised his arms, as though he thought for a moment that he might need to catch me. "It's nothing you need concern yourself with. The location is remote, and it is often difficult to get messages back and forth in a timely manner. I'm sure there's a logical explanation, and I do not doubt that we will have it soon."

I could not reply. It was all I could do to bite back the horror, the nameless fear that was rising in my throat. Fiona and I were two of the only people who knew what might be happening at Skye Príosún. Now she had gone there, hadn't returned when she was supposed to, and was, quite possibly, calling me for help in my dreams. I threw a look at Milo, and saw that he, too, was looking extremely nervous.

Seamus did not miss the look that passed between us, and now his eyes narrowed as he looked first at me and then at Milo. "Do either of you have information about Fiona's whereabouts?" he asked sharply.

"No," I managed to reply hoarsely. "I just—"

A wild shriek echoed through the hallway, making us all jump and stare around for the source of the sound. A moment later, the shriek sounded again, and this time it became clear that it was echoing not down from the top of the tower, where Fiona's studio was, but up the stairs from the base of the tower.

I turned and looked at Seamus to find that he, too, was staring at the staircase that climbed down into the furthest depths of the castle.

"Moira," I whispered. "That's the Léarscáil down there, isn't it?"

"Yes," Seamus replied blankly, still staring at the dark hole of an entrance as though incapable of understanding how such a sound could arise from it.

As Milo and I shared an anxious glance, a third scream sounded, this one more urgent than the first two. Without another word, the three of us turned and ran for the staircase. Seamus got there first, shoving his way past me and turning on his heel, blocking my access to the stairs.

"Wait here," he ordered. "Let me assess the safety of the situation before you descend."

"Like hell I will!" I shouted.

Seamus looked as though he'd like to tell me off, but a fourth shriek cut him off, and he turned instead and thundered down the stairs. Predictably ignoring his instructions, Milo and I hurried after him.

Just in time, a vivid memory of the only other time I'd visited the Léarscáil flashed through my mind as I ran through the doorway, and I flung my hands out on either side of me and grabbed onto the wall as I crossed the threshold. The narrow, winding stairs that led down to the Léarscáil had no railings, nothing to stop someone from simply walking through the doorway, taking one step too far, and plunging to her death on the stone floor dozens of feet below. Trying to catch my breath at the near miss, I turned and pressed the entire left side of my body firmly against the wall and proceeded to descend the steps as quickly as I dared, while still remaining cognizant of the unevenness of the stones, and the crumbling of the ancient plaster.

I chanced a glance below me, and what I saw made my heart stutter into a violent gallop. Upon the floor below me, a map of the world had been painted in painstaking detail. The colors were brighter, more vibrant than the last time I descended into this place. I remembered that Fiona had mentioned to me that she had recently restored it. A great, golden pendulum still hung from its massive chain, and usually it swung in a slow, steady, arcing pattern over the map, tracing the gentle ebbs and flows of spirit activity, and occasionally revealing shifts and patterns that could be interpreted by Moira, the ancient, shriveled Keeper of the Léarscáil. The pendulum was not swinging slowly or gently or predictably today; it was flying over the surface of the map, spinning wildly, as though invisible and powerful forces were flinging it back-and-forth. I scanned the room quickly for Moira, and found her at last pressed against the wall beside her desk, shouting at the Léarscáil as though it were a sentient creature that would listen to her and heed her frantic commands. Her eyes were wide and terrified behind the bizarre headdress of lenses and knobs and magnifying glasses that she had strapped to her head. Around her feet, a number of scrolls and books lay scattered upon the ground, as though they had been knocked from her arms, or else flung aside in her panic.

"Bugger me!" Seamus had skidded to a halt at the bottom of the stairs, watching the progress of the Léarscáil with his mouth hanging open. "What the devil...?" he murmured as I pounded to a stop just a few steps behind him.

"Has it ever done this before?" I asked him, bending nearly in half and clutching a stitch in my side.

"I've no bloody idea," he replied, his head turning and twisting on his neck as he followed the Léarscáil's progress. "I've only ever been down here but twice, but I've never seen anything like this. This isn't how it's supposed to work, even at the most volatile of times."

I had a fleeting memory of Moira confiding to me that the most bizarre behavior the Léarscáil had ever betrayed was when the Prophecy had come to pass. Even so, she had not described anything resembling this possessed wrecking ball of a situation. The Léarscáil had gone utterly mad.

On the far side of the room, Moira was waving her arms frantically and shouting something at us, but her thick Scottish brogue and her high-pitched hysteria made it impossible to make out her words. Based on her gestures, though, it seemed that she might be instructing us to go back up the stairs and leave the place.

"We've got to get her out of here," I said to Seamus, who nodded.

"I don't know much about the inner workings of the Léarscáil," he said, "but I know a thing or two about stonework and metal craft, and that chain will not hold for long with that kind of pressure on it," he said, pointing up to the ceiling where, high above us, the chain creaked and shrieked with the strain that was being placed upon it. "If that monstrosity comes down with that kind of force behind it, it will mean death for anyone in its path."

"So, what do we do?" Milo asked.

Seamus turned, and stared at Milo as though he had forgotten that he was there. "The two of you," he said nodding his head to each of us in turn, "go for help. Find someone who can run for the barracks and call together every Caomhnóir they can find. Send them down here at once."

"No," I said sharply. "I'm not leaving. I'm not leaving her here. I want to help."

"You can help by alerting the Caomhnóir!" Seamus barked, losing his temper swiftly under pressure. "We've no time for arguments!"

"Look, no offense, but it will be much quicker if I just go by myself," Milo snapped back at him. "Having to wait for a non-floater is just going to hold me up. Just let me materialize where I need to go. Jess will be much more help to you here than she will be to me. She's not a fucking damsel in distress, Seamus. She's smart and capable. Use her."

I turned back to Seamus who was nodding grudgingly, unable to deny the logic of this. "Very well, Spirit Guide Chang, go then, and quickly."

Without another word, Milo gave me a reassuring wink and vanished from sight.

I turned back to Seamus. "Okay," I said, trying to sound brave and determined, instead of scared shitless. "Tell me what to do."

"What I want you to do," he said through his clenched teeth, "is walk up those stairs and leave this room so that you are no longer in imminent danger of being killed."

"Well, I'm not doing that, so how about you give me an alternate set of instructions, because the longer we stand here arguing about your patriarchal bullshit, the better the chance that Moira will be crushed to death."

Seamus's face went as rigid and cold as a statue's, and I thought for just a fraction of a second that he might actually reach out, grab me by my hair and haul me back up the stairs himself. He certainly seemed to be considering it. Then he blinked and, a muscle twitching in his jaw, he said to me, "I want it noted from here on out, that I asked you to vacate the space, and that you refused me.

I do not want it said that I put a Durupinen in unwarranted danger. I need that to be very clear."

"No one will ever hear any other version of that story from me," I told him calmly. "I'll make sure everyone knows that whatever happens now, it was my own stupid decision, okay?"

Seamus nodded once, and we both knew that this would have to be good enough.

"Okay," I said. "Now what do we do?"

Seamus's eyes darted around the room, taking in as many different aspects as he could. I could tell that he was thinking fast, trying to determine the best course of action while assessing how much risk would be involved for every party in the room. As much as I detested him, I couldn't help but be impressed with his clearheaded assessment in the face of disaster. All I felt capable of at the moment was arm flapping and excessive cursing.

"Right," he said at last. "No matter how quickly it's moving, or with how much force, that pendulum can't reach the outer edges of the room unless it flies off the chain. If you stick to the outer wall, and I mean keep yourself pressed flat up against it at all times, you should be able to get around to the far side of the room and reach Moira. Then you can guide her back around the perimeter to the stairs. Do you think you can do that?"

"Yes, of course I can," I said a little defiantly. The tone was less to convince him than it was to convince myself. "And what are you going to do?"

"I'm going to see if I can find something to slow the Léarscáil down," Seamus said. Even as he said it, I could see him looking hopelessly around the room, completely at a loss for how to complete this task. "There's got to be a way to slow it down," he muttered.

"It's controlled by the balance of spirit energy," I said doubtfully. "I'm not sure that any kind of physical barrier could prevent it from doing exactly what it's doing right now."

"That may be so," Seamus said. "But if we don't attempt to slow it down, it's going to destroy the room, and everything in it. And if it breaks free of the chain and crashes into the walls, the whole tower could come down."

Even as he spoke, the Léarscáil's massive pendulum swung wildly in the opposite direction, bucking every norm of gravity and momentum, and probably a dozen other physics rules I knew absolutely nothing about, and barreled over the surface of the map again, this time crashing into a small wooden cart full of scrolls and smashing it to smithereens. The scrolls flew into the air like confetti, and then rolled away across the floor in every direction.

"Bloody hell!" Seamus muttered. He was bouncing back-and-forth on the balls of his feet, and it was as though he needed to be in physical motion to keep his gears turning, to figure out what to do next. It was clear, as I watched his eyes follow the Léarscáil around on its erratic path, that he was attempting to make rhyme or reason of its movement—to detect a pattern. Perhaps he thought that if he could memorize it, if he could determine where it was going to go next, then he might be able to do something to slow it down, or else stop it. My eyes also began to follow its progress, but it soon became clear that there was no predicting where it might go next or what it might next destroy.

On the far side of the room, Moira was in preservation mode. As I watched, she scurried around like a frantic little mouse, gathering up scrolls, and tucking them into niches in the wall, hoping to protect them from the Léarscáil's pendulum, which was now basically a possessed wrecking ball. She started whistling and cawing, her little wrinkled face pointed up to the sky, and at first I thought she'd gone mad, but then I heard a flurry of wings and saw a swirling cloud of birds descending from the rafters.

I'd forgotten that Moira used birds to carry her messages and observations about our Léarscáil to other Keepers in other clans across the world. It couldn't have been a very precise or speedy method of communication, but she refused to operate under any other parameters, and none of the Council was foolish enough to attempt to argue with her. She'd once told me birds were not susceptible to Castings or gaps in internet service or other pitfalls of modern communication. They were, however, susceptible to being knocked out of the air by a wildly swinging pendulum of doom, and so she watched the birds flutter toward her with her hands pressed over her face, peeking between the spaces of her fingers. It was obvious the birds were in a panic, many of them dipping toward her before shrieking and soaring back up as the pendulum whizzed by them. Moira doggedly continued to call them down, coaxing and twittering, and raising her arms into the air as though inviting them to alight upon her fingers, promising that she would protect them.

"Come along now, my pretty little bairns," she was calling to them, wiggling her gnarled fingers in the air like so many twigs on an ancient tree. "Come now, my lovelies. Come to Moira, now."

A few intrepid birds managed to skirt the pendulum and land on her hands and shoulders. Moira scurried quickly with them over to a little door set in the wall that resembled a dumbwaiter, which I knew contained a chute that would allow the birds to fly straight up out of the top of North Tower and into the sky. Moira flung open the door and deposited the birds one by one onto a perch, frantically looking over her shoulder at the Léarscáil pendulum, making sure that it was not headed toward her. Then she hurriedly began to dash off note after note onto scraps of parchment, rolling them up into the tiniest of scrolls and affixing them to the birds' legs as quickly as her arthritic joints would allow. As each bird was armed with its communication, it took off like a bullet up into the chute and, presumably, out into the starry night sky, carrying the news of the Northern Clans' mad Léarscáil off to the other Durupinen Keepers of the world. Perhaps their pendulums had also begun swinging out of control. Perhaps the other maps had been destroyed, the records and instruments smashed. We would not know until one of the birds fluttered back, bearing the news tied to its leg.

Following Seamus's orders, I pressed my back to the stone wall and edged my way, slowly and cautiously, around the curve of the tower to where Moira stood, still trying to coax down more birds. Twice the Léarscáil blew by me, within a few inches of my face. I sucked in a sharp gasp and closed my eyes, but it seemed that Seamus had been correct; even at its greatest length, the chain could not bring the Léarscáil all the way to the walls of the tower. This observation gave me a tiny shred of relief as I inched ever closer to the tiny old woman. If I could just keep her to the edges of the room, if I could just get her to follow me, then, in all likelihood, the pendulum would not do her any harm.

At last I reached her, wedging myself up against the wall beside her battered old desk. "Moira!" I called loudly. The frantic birds were making a racket. "Follow me. We've got to get you out of here! Let me lead you over to the stairs!"

"Feck off," the old woman grumbled, and she threw a hesitant bird directly up the chute.

11

X MARKS THE SPOT

"I'M SORRY?" I ASKED, and even in my fright, I felt the incredulity creeping in. "I'm trying to help you. Did you just tell me to fuck off?"

"I cannae be leaving with ye," Moira said, turning her madly magnified eyes on me and scowling ferociously. "I must record this. I've important work to do. Begone with ye."

"But..." A note of flustered laughter escaped me. "You can't stay down here. That thing is going to kill you. There's no way that chain is going to hold," I added, pointing above us, even as the pendulum's chain gave a loud grating shriek of metal on metal.

"It'll hold as long as the spirits mean it to hold," Moira insisted stubbornly. She tipped an inkwell upside down and shook it, saw that there was no ink left in it, and swore again, chucking it away across the floor. It rolled over the surface of the map, until it was knocked with the force of a bullet across the room and into the opposite wall, where it shattered on impact, the tiny shards of glass falling to the ground like dust or snow.

"Moira, come on, now. You've got to get out of here," I repeated, starting to panic now. The old woman was tiny, but she was also feisty, and I didn't think I'd be able to carry or drag her all the way back around the tower, not if she was unwilling to go with me.

"What I've got to do is my job, lass," Moira grumbled, barely bothering to look up from her search for a new bottle of ink. She opened a desk and began to rummage through it, a steady stream of cursing issuing from her like steam from a kettle.

"Moira, you can't record the movements of the Léarscáil if you're dead!" I cried in exasperation. "Come on now, I'm serious! No one—not the Council, not the entirety of the spirit world—wants you to sacrifice your life for this job. You need to come with me right now. Just take my hand and I'll guide you across to the..."

But I couldn't complete the request, because Moira chose that moment to pick up a heavy glass paperweight off her desk and chuck it at my head. I ducked just in time, and the thing shattered against the wall behind me, just as the inkwell had done. I gasped, and turned to glare at her, but she was resolutely ignoring me, and had turned back to her small flock of birds.

Desperately, I turned back to face the middle of the room, and looked around for Seamus. He was all the way across the tower with his back pressed against the far wall. He was swaying back-and-forth, shifting his weight from foot to foot, as though he and the pendulum were involved in a deadly sort of dance. I can only assume that he was looking for paths across the room to where we were, but the pendulum was not cooperating, refusing to stick to a predictable pattern. He looked up and caught my eye.

"What are you still doing here?" he shouted at me. His voice was barely audible over the screeching and grinding of the chains that were still miraculously holding the possessed pendulum aloft.

"She won't come!" I shouted back. "She won't go until she has finished her work!"

Seamus let out a roar of frustration that echoed around the space, sending several birds fluttering up to the rafters again in fright. "Tell her she's got no choice!" he shouted at me. "If she won't come with you, you've got to drag her out! Just grab her by her bloody hair if you have to!"

"I can't! If she struggles, we'll both be killed!" I called back to him.

"She's just a bit of a thing!" Seamus called. "Just throw her over your shoulder or—"

"Throw her over my shoulder?" I practically shrieked. "Are you insane? If she struggles, and I trip, it's all over! The pendulum will crush us in a second flat!"

Seamus turned and punched the stone wall in frustration. When he pulled his hand away, his knuckles were bloodied.

"I don't think breaking your own hands is going to help us here, Seamus!" I cried, but I don't think he heard me. At that moment, the chain gave a particularly piercing shriek, and a flurry of stone dust drifted down from the ceiling. Seamus and I both looked up, frozen with fear. But miraculously, the chain continued to hold, and the pendulum continued to swing.

I turned back to Moira, who was pulling an ancient reference book off a shelf, and laying it flat upon her desk to rifle through it. I opened my mouth and then closed it again, completely out of words to try to convince her she needed to save her own life. Instead, desperate for help, I reached out into my connection to find Milo.

"Milo! Where are you? Are you on your way back yet?"

I felt Milo's anxiousness zinging into my head like a snapped rubber band. "I'm here, I'm here! I went to the barracks, but the Caomhnóir are running around like chickens with their goddamn heads cut off. They're gathering as many as they can, and are on their way to the castle now. But honestly, I don't think they have any idea what they're doing. They're all grabbing like, clubs and staffs and bows and stuff, like they're going into battle. They're totally clueless about how to stop this thing."

"Yeah, weapons are going to be totally useless down here," I told him. It should have brought comfort knowing a virtual army was now on its way, but somehow I only felt more nervous. It didn't sound like they had any kind of plan, and without a solid plan to stop the Léarscáil, it just felt like there were going to be more people in danger.

"Jess, you're not still down there, are you?" Milo asked.

"Yeah, I am!" I told him. "I can't get Moira to come with me. She's just refusing to leave until she can interpret what the Léarscáil is doing."

Milo heaved a deep sigh, and I could feel the waves of forced calm rippling across the connection, clashing with the waves of my own fear. "Jess, I do not say this lightly, and I know you're not going to like it. But you have *got* to get yourself out of there. If Moira won't come with you, you just have to leave her."

"No way, Milo! You know I can't do that! She spends all her time down here, she's not right in the head! I honestly think she'd rather let that thing crush her than miss a single opportunity to interpret what it's doing."

"Well, I'm not willing to let you get crushed for someone who is not even willing to save her own skin!" Milo cried, and the shrillness of his mounting panic made me wince. "Just let Seamus handle it, Jess, and get yourself out of there! I'm serious!"

Just as I prepared to argue with him, a third energy expanded inside my skull, and Hannah entered the connection. It only took her half a second to feel the tenseness and fear that was zooming around inside my brain like so many of Moira's hysterical birds.

"Hey, where did the two of you go? I got back to the room and... wait, what's wrong? I can feel something is not right. Where are you guys? What's happening?" Our panic was infecting her by the second, her questions becoming more and more frightened.

Knowing that I did not possibly have the words or the time to spare to describe what was going on, I instead allowed the image of the scene before me to play across the connection, so that Hannah could see what I was seeing. I listened for a few seconds as she gasped, and cried out, and swore. At last she said, "But what's causing it? Why has it suddenly gone crazy?"

"If we knew the answer to that, we might be able to stop it," I told her. "Its movements are powered by shifts in spirit energy. But it's never done anything like this before, and I can't imagine what we could do to make it stop. The Léarscáil is obviously picking up on a serious shift in the balance of spirit energy somewhere in the world, but instead of zeroing in on it, it seems to be sending it haywire."

"I'm going to find Celeste," Milo said suddenly. "And as many of the other Council members as I can track down. Someone must know enough about the Léarscáil to understand what's going on, and how to stop it."

"I really don't think so, Milo," I said skeptically. "If Moira hasn't figured it out, and she spent her entire life down here studying this thing, then I don't know how anyone else would—"

"I don't care," Milo snapped. "It's worth a shot. I'm not just going to sit around and wait for that thing to fly off the chain and kill someone. I'll be right back. Just... don't die, okay? It's complicated enough around here with one of us dead." And with that, he pulled out of the connection with the sharp crackle of evaporating energy and was gone.

"That's it. I'm coming down there," Hannah said. "I'm coming down to help."

"No!" The thought was so forceful inside my head that it echoed like a bass drum and made me wince. I tried again, attempting to keep my emotions under control. "Hannah, stay away from here! We don't need anybody else in danger, and there's nothing you can do to—"

But there was no time to complete the thought. A sudden, thunderous rumbling noise made me gasp and look up. For one heart-stopping moment, I was sure that the ceiling of the tower was going to fall in, crushing us beneath it, but a moment later, the door at the top of the stairs flew open, and the rumbling sound revealed itself to be the pounding of dozens of pairs of Caomhnóir boots. At least thirty Caomhnóir came crashing downstairs one after the other, their weapons drawn and their faces set. They lined themselves up along the entire length of the winding staircase. All of their eyes, which were watching the progress of the pendulum, widened in shock. They looked like jackasses standing there clutching their flimsy wooden weapons, which would surely be smashed to splinters if they so much as brushed against the Léarscáil pendulum traveling at such speeds. I could tell from the looks on their faces that they had no more idea of what to do than I did. Seamus edged his way around the base of the tower until he reached the bottom of the stairs, and started consulting with the Caomhnóir that was standing at the bottom. Within moments, they seemed to be arguing. Both of them were gesticulating wildly, and though I could not hear their words, I could tell that they sure as hell weren't agreeing on a plan of action.

Unable to think of anything else to try, I turned back to Moira, determined to convince her to come with me. If the Caomhnóir couldn't stop the Léarscáil, we could at least bring her out of harm's way. I inched closer to where she stood, now working furiously over a map with a tool that looked like a many-legged compass. She was twitching the thing back-and-forth over the map marking the points where the tiny sharp legs met the parchment. She was also muttering to herself, though between the noise and her accent, I had absolutely no idea what she was saying.

I slid carefully along the wall until I was standing directly behind her and looked over her shoulder. The map she was working from was an exact replica of the map on the floor of the tower. She had drawn so many lines and marks across it that it looked as though an overexcited toddler had been let loose upon it with a pencil she knew she wasn't supposed to use. As I leaned around her to try to get a better look, the pendulum swooped past again, whipping my hair around my face and causing me to gasp and retreat to the wall again.

"Moira, please," I begged her once more. "This isn't about work anymore. This is about life and death. We have to go. We have to get out of here before someone is killed!"

Moira completely ignored me, still immersed in her work.

Desperately, I changed tactics. Maybe if I tried to help her, if I showed her I understood that what she was doing was important, she would stop rebuffing me and actually listen? It was worth a shot. Almost *anything* was worth a shot at this point. I cleared my throat and called over the sounds of the pendulum's whooshing and shrieking. "What have you found out?" I asked her. "Have you figured out what's causing it? What do all those lines mean?"

Moira turned her mad, magnified eyes on me. The wild, unhinged gleam in them made me take an involuntary step back, so that I scraped the back of my head against the wall. "This is the path!" she shouted, tapping a gnarled finger on the parchment. "That's the path that it's taken. And I dinnae think it made sense, until I saw it here, laid out before me."

I stared down at the tangled web of pencil lines, incredulous that anyone could make even a modicum of sense out of it. "How does it make sense?" I asked her, trying to keep my voice even as the pendulum swung within inches of us again. "What does it mean? Why is the Léarscáil doing this?"

"It keeps trying, more and more violently, to make contact with a single point," Moira said. Her fingers scuttled over the surface of the map like spiders, following the lines around and around. "But each time it tries to make contact, the spirit energy sends it sailing away again. It's too strong, too concentrated. It's disrupted the balances, throwing it all off kilter. And it all comes back to this. This is the place." She snatched a red wax crayon from a cup on the desk, and scribbled an "X" on the parchment, like a mad old pirate marking the place where we ought to dig for treasure. "Something is happening here," she whispered, her face now barely an inch from mine. Something is terribly wrong here, and it cannot be ignored. The Léarscáil is warning us. This be where the danger lies."

"Danger?" I repeated blankly, hoping I had misheard her, but knowing that I had not.

"Danger!" she confirmed, nodding her head of mad cotton candy wisps of hair.

She turned away from me, the parchment now clutched in her hand, and stepped forward to call another bird. She lost her balance and faltered forward just a bit.

"No! Moira, be care—"

It happened in the blink of an eye. One moment, she was standing there, one hand pressed to the side of her mouth as she opened it to call for her birds. The next, she was gone, swept up from the ground by the violent swing of the pendulum. Shock paralyzed me safely against the wall and I could not even scream as I watched her fly through the air, a tiny, bent, and wrinkled thing, like a child's doll that had all its stuffing loved out of it. Her limp body tumbled through the air and collided with a terrible, muffled thud against the rough stones of the far wall. Then she slid to the floor and crumpled into a heap of robes and tangled limbs. She did not stir.

I felt as though all the air had been sucked from my lungs, as though the Léarscáil pendulum had hit me too, knocking all the wind out of me. I couldn't think, couldn't move. I just stood there, staring at the broken little body, letting the horror seep like poison through my veins, paralyzing me where I stood.

There was shouting and a flurry of activity around me, but I barely registered it. Figures were moving on the outskirts of my vision, which seemed to have turned into a dark and narrow tunnel. I could not see anything around me, just Moira lying on the ground, the sole object in my line of vision, which had become a small circle, like a spotlight in the gathering darkness. My legs were turning to water. Any moment, they would spill out from under me.

A pair of calloused hands seized me by the shoulders, shaking me from my stupor. I turned to see a dark-complexioned Caomhnóir, his face an unfocused blur of stubble and scowling brows and bared teeth. He was shouting something at me, but my blood was roaring in my ears, and I could not make sense of his words. When he started pulling me toward the staircase, I obeyed the pull at first, letting him take me where he would, my brain completely disengaged. I probably would have let him drag me right up the stairs, through the door, and clear out onto the castle grounds without a shred of resistance, if it weren't for the parchment.

A little flutter, like the wings of the frightened birds, caught my eye, and I recognized it: the map that Moira had been holding in her hand when the pendulum had collided with her. It was skittering around the tower floor, blown here and there by the breeze that the swinging pendulum was generating. As I watched it numbly, it fluttered past me like a wayward bird, and I saw the little red "X" that Moira had scrawled upon its surface just before she'd been hit. I followed it with my gaze as it tumbled back-and-forth across the surface of the map, as though it were hypnotizing me, and then, just as my heels hit the bottom of the staircase, a thought occurred to me. I had to get that map. It was the only way to understand what was causing the Léarscáil to go out of control.

Looking back on it, I was pretty sure I'd gone temporarily insane, but in the moment, it made sense to do quite possibly the stupidest thing I'd ever done.

I turned toward the stairs, and the Caomhnóir loosened his grip on my arm, evidently convinced that I was going to willingly follow him up the steps. As his fingers slackened, I shook my arm free of him and bolted across the room. I could hear shouts and cries echoing and bouncing all around the room, and I knew they were directed at me, but I did not care. I had to get that map. Moira had figured something out, and we would never know what it was unless we rescued that damn paper. I hadn't been able to save her, but dammit, I would save the work that she died doing rather than abandon it.

After only taking four or five steps across the room, I had to drop to the ground and roll to my left to avoid the pendulum as it whizzed by me. I crawled a few more feet before I had to jump up and leap to the side to avoid it once again. Each time the pendulum flew by, the map fluttered away in an unlikely direction, and I had to keep changing my path across the room in order to follow it. At last, when I made it nearly to the center of the room, I saw it flap up against Moira's still body, seeming to wedge itself beneath her arm. And though it continued to flutter and flap, it no longer floated away as the pendulum swung by it.

Desperate to reach it before it freed itself and flew away again, I made a mad dash the rest of the way across the room. A few feet from Moira, I wasn't quite quick enough, and the pendulum caught me on my outstretched elbow. I was knocked to the ground, and landed with a thud beside her. Ignoring the throbbing pain in my arm, I looked down and heaved a sigh of relief to see the map a mere foot from where I lay. I reached out and snatched it from under Moira's robe, and then slid myself across the floor so that I was pressed safely against the wall beside her. Though it was the very last thing I wanted to do, I could not stop myself from looking at her.

The bizarre headdress of binoculars and lenses, like something out of a steampunk fantasy, had been knocked from her head and lay battered and bent on the ground beside her. Her neck was turned at the strangest angle. Just the sight of it sent a shiver of horror up my spine and into the roots of my hair. I didn't need to reach my hand out and feel for her pulse, but I did anyway. The Durupinen blood had fallen still inside her veins.

"I'm sorry," I whispered to her, and I couldn't even hear my own voice in the tumult that surrounded us. "Oh, Moira, I am so, so sorry."

The apologies just kept coming out of my mouth, over and over again. I couldn't seem to stop them, and I was still babbling hysterically about how sorry I was when Seamus appeared at my side. I didn't hear him approach, and I didn't even realize he was there until he took my face in both hands and wrenched it around so that I had no choice but to look at him. It was only then, without the awful sight of Moira's broken body filling my vision, that the apologies died in my throat and the tears found their way through my shock and into my eyes.

"It's all right," Seamus was saying, still clutching my face. "It's all right, now. You've nothing to be sorry for, do you understand me? You tried to get her out of here. You did everything you could."

He thought I was apologizing to him, but I didn't bother to correct him. I was too busy fighting against a tidal wave of sobbing that was threatening to push its way out of me.

"Come now," Seamus said, and despite the fire blazing in his eyes, his voice was not unkind. I even thought I detected a tremor of emotion in it. "There's nothing more you can do for her. There's nothing more that any of us can do for her. It's time to get you out of here before the same can be said of you."

My throat was too choked with repressed tears, so I just nodded, and trusted that he understood that to mean that I would follow his orders and do what I needed to do to get out of there.

Seamus reached down for my hand to help pull me to my feet, and then looked down in surprise. "What is that?" he asked, pulling at the corner of the parchment still clutched in my hand.

"It's Moira's. She was trying to—"

An uptick in the shouting made us both look around, and we saw that the door at the top of the stairs was open once more, this time revealing Catriona, Hannah, Milo, and several other Council members gathered behind them. They were all staring down at the pandemonium below, and not one of them looked as though they had the slightest idea of what to do.

"Christ," Seamus cursed under his breath. "Why won't anyone in this bloody castle listen to me? This is just what we need, half of the damn Council in danger now as well!" He cupped his hands to either side of his mouth and shouted up toward the staircase, "Stay where you are! Please, we can't keep anyone safe down here."

Catriona nodded her head once, to show that she had heard him, and turned back over her shoulder, presumably ordering the rest of the Council members to stay where they were. Satisfied that he was not going to have to rescue the newly arrived crop of Durupinen as well, Seamus turned back to me. "I saw it hit you—the pendulum. You're lucky you weren't killed. Are you hurt? Do you think you can walk?"

I attempted to assess my own physical condition for the first time. My elbow was aching, but it seemed bruised at worst, not broken, and the rest of me seemed unharmed. "I think so," I said.

"Right then," Seamus said. "I want you to keep close to me and keep your back against the wall. We'll work our way around as quickly as we can until we get to the staircase. Stay on your toes and do what I tell you to do. No more heroics, you understand me?"

I nodded. I didn't feel capable of any more heroics. I barely felt capable of putting one foot in front of the other. Seamus helped me to my feet, careful to avoid touching my injured elbow. With both of our backs to the wall and our eyes fixed carefully on the pendulum, we began to shuffle around the perimeter of the room. We'd only made it a few feet when a deafening noise caused us to throw our hands up over our ears.

The cacophony came from high above our heads. Every eye was drawn upward as the trickles of stone dust turned to an avalanche of stone. It was happening at last. The chain was going to give way, and the ceiling was going to cave in. And once that pendulum was free of its chain, there would be no stopping it from barreling right into the walls and killing everyone in the tower.

The Caomhnóir were panicking. They were raising their weapons, and spreading out around the room, as though taking positions for a battle that there was no chance they could possibly win. The links of the chain shrieked, and the pendulum seemed to drop another half a foot closer to the ground, so that the point of it was scraping with a spine-tingling grating sound across the surface of the map. Still, it continued to swing wildly back and forth, only now there was almost nowhere left to hide from it.

"Run," Seamus ordered. "We must run. Now."

My brain was freaking out, but thank God the muscles in my legs knew what to do. They took off at a sprint, following Seamus around the outside of the room. A few seconds later, we had to stop as the pendulum whizzed by in front of us, heading straight for Moira's workstation. With a deafening crash, it slammed into the desk, sending lethal shards of wood flying everywhere. Without hesitation, Seamus turned and pinned me against the wall with his body, shielding me from the debris. I heard him grunt as several pieces of the wood struck him. When the pendulum had veered off in another direction, he leapt aside, grabbed me by the hand, and continued pulling me around the tower walls toward the staircase, which still felt a mile away.

I glanced down at Seamus's torso and saw a sharp, splintered shard of wood protruding from his side. Blood was seeping through the ragged hole in his shirt. "Seamus! Oh, my God, you're hurt!" I pulled back instinctively, wanting to stop to examine how badly he'd been injured, but he just tugged on me harder.

"I've noticed. And I'll deal with it when we're safely out of here," he growled, his teeth gritted against the pain.

We took off again, Seamus grunting with every step. *We're never going to make it in time,* said a small terrified voice in my head. *We're never going to make it. It's too far.* I spared just enough energy from running to tell myself to shut the hell up, and then a shout from the middle of the room caught our attention. Two Caomhnóir had run up behind the pendulum as it swung past them and attempted to grab onto it. I think they may have been trying to slow it down with the weight of their bodies, but it didn't make the slightest difference. The first Caomhnóir merely stumbled a few feet behind it before he lost his grip and fell on his face, sliding across the surface of the map. The second Caomhnóir, whether out of stubbornness or panic, continued to hold onto the pendulum even as it arced high toward the side of the room, lifting him off his feet and taking him with it. A few seconds later, the force of the motion flung him off, and he crashed into the wall just as Moira had done. But even as I screamed, he leapt to his feet, evidently uninjured, or at least, uninjured enough to get the hell out of the way as the pendulum swung back toward him yet again.

"It's no good!" Seamus was shouting. "It's no good! Just get out of the way. There's nothing we can do to stop it!"

Another deafening bang, and two huge chunks of stone fell to the ground, with such force that the ground beneath us trembled. With a final, earsplitting shriek, the massive chain finally let go. The pendulum hit the ground, and began to roll across the room, aiming for the Caomhnóir like bowling pins until it crashed into the wall. The entire tower shook with the force of the impact, and screams and cries rose into a chorus of terror from Caomhnóir and Durupinen alike. The Caomhnóir started running for the stairs. Catriona started pushing the crowd of Council members back through the doorway up above us. Only Hannah remained where she was, a strange blank look upon her face.

The expression was so odd, so inexplicably calm in that moment, that it drew my eye, and even with the massive pendulum barreling around, placing us all in imminent danger, I could not look away from her. Was she in shock? Why was she just standing there? I reached into our connection, calling out to her, absurdly concerned about her when I was the one who was likely about to be crushed to death.

The connection was blank. Empty. All I could hear was a great rushing sound, and a tug on something that was deep within me. Then I realized what was happening and I gasped aloud.

Calling. Hannah was Calling.

Even as the realization hit me, the temperature in the tower dropped so significantly that my panicked breaths turned to puffs of steam instantaneously. From all around the walls, from above and below us, spirits were flocking to the tower. They flooded in, the power of their energy pressing in upon us so forcefully that I could barely get breath into my lungs. Beside me, Seamus had a hand pressed to his chest as though he were being suffocated by the sheer pressure of spirit energy. He stared around us, his mouth agape as he took in the hundreds upon hundreds of spirits that were crowding themselves into the space.

Above us, Hannah's hair was floating gently around her face, buffeted here and there in the waves of ghostly presence that were crashing down upon us, waves that she was commanding. Beside her, Milo looked both thrilled and wary, in awe of her power and yet terrified by it. Behind her, blocking the doorway with her body so that the other Council members were safely contained in the corridor, Catriona's fascinated fear had turned her to stone. It was clear from her expression that Hannah had not told her what she was about to do, and that she did not dare try to intervene now that she had begun.

As the spirits flooded in, something was happening to the Léarscáil. The pendulum's seemingly endless momentum was slowing, as though it were suddenly trying to push its way through water, instead of air. When it next made contact with the wall, it bumped against it, making a grating sound, but it did not send tremors through the stones, and no pieces of rock broke away. It pitched drunkenly back from the wall, but it no longer seemed to have a clear direction in which it wanted to move. It was almost as though the pendulum itself were confused and disoriented. It rolled a few feet in one direction, and then stopped and veered off in another, before stopping again and rolling in a slow circle. At last the pendulum came to a stop, rolling back-and-forth just a few inches in each direction as though it were being pulled between two points in a well-matched game of tug-of-war. It was shaking with the tension of being pulled so strongly in two opposite directions at once. I stole a glance down at the map, and saw that the point of the pendulum was hovering over the craggy island mass of the United Kingdom.

I looked back up at Hannah, and saw her face transformed, lit from within by her uncanny power. It was a look that I had hoped never to see on her face again, a look that she was frightened she could not control. And I knew that she was doing it to save me.

"Move," I said to Seamus. "To the stairs, now. I don't know how long she'll be able to hold it."

If Seamus was put off by the fact that I was now giving the orders, he did not let on. Without a word of discussion, he turned and pelted for the stairs, with me right on his heels. Taking a cue from him, all of the Caomhnóir seemed to snap themselves out of a trance as one and began to run as quickly as they could. We all thundered up the staircase, crowding two and three to a stair to be sure that everyone was high enough off the ground and out of reach of the pendulum in case it began rolling again. When at last not a single person remained in harm's way, we turned as one to watch the pendulum. It gave a long, groaning shiver and shattered as though it were made of ice, tiny bits of metal falling to the floor like a deluge of raindrops, until the last of the tinkling sounds died away, and we were left to stare down on the sea of glittering golden debris that had once been the Fairhaven Léarscáil.

I was the first to break the spell the Léarscáil's destruction seemed to cast over us all. I turned and scaled the last two steps, until I was standing beside Hannah. Slowly, I reached out a hand and slid it gently into hers, which was hanging loosely at her side. Her hand was shockingly cold, and I could feel a pulsing current of incredible power flowing through it beneath the surface. She seemed completely oblivious to my presence, but I expected that. There was little that could contend with the all-consuming nature of such control as she was channeling now.

On Hannah's other side, Milo was watching her with a rapt and terrified expression. He tore his eyes from her just long enough to give me a pleading look. "You have to help her," he whispered to me. "I'm not sure she can let go by herself."

I nodded my head. Yes, the compulsion to Call was strong, but I knew one thing that was stronger, and it was flowing back-and-forth between my sister and me, flowing freely between our two clasped hands like the blood that bound us from our very conception. It had led me back from the other side of the Aether, and it would lead her back to me right now.

"Hannah," I said quietly, and as I said her name, I squeezed that hand I knew so well, that hand that I felt for the first time in a dream, so familiar that it felt like holding my own hand. "Hannah, it's time to let them go now. You've saved everyone. You can let them go. Just let go."

Beneath my fingers, Hannah's hand twitched ever so slightly, and from that tiny movement, I knew that she heard me, knew that she was struggling against the pull and lure of her own power. I gave a small encouraging smile, knowing that she could not see it, but hoping that she could feel it: my confidence in her, my surety of her control.

"Go on, now," I told her again. "You can do it, you control this gift. This gift does not control you. Let go now."

All around us, a legion of spirits, hundreds deep, was crowding the tower and expanding out into the air around it, waiting like soldiers for her slightest command. I could feel their eyes upon her, but I could also feel all the living eyes upon us too, the Council members and the ranks of the Caomhnóir, all holding their breath in anticipation of what Hannah would do next. Beside her, Milo gave a nervous twitch, but I held up a hand to still him. "Give her a chance," I said. "She's right there. She's fighting it. She can do it on her own, I know she can."

As though my words of confidence in her was the key to finding her own confidence, Hannah's body language began to change. Her fingers stopped trembling, and instead closed around my own, returning their gentle pressure. The wild, faraway expression in her eyes shrank away, retreating far into the recesses of her mind. The sparkle that I associated with her, that I knew so well, lit again within her eyes. She gave her head a gentle shake, and her eyelids fluttered before they closed. When she opened them again, I could see that she had fully pried herself loose from the grip of the Calling.

"My deepest thanks to you all for answering my Call," she said in a soft, but wholly commanding voice. A shocking burst of cold swept through the tower, making everyone gasp, as every spirit pressed in closer to raptly follow her words. "I am grateful for your help," Hannah continued. "All of our clans are grateful for your help. You are free to go, with our abiding gratitude."

With an audible *whoosh*, as though a great psychic blade were cutting the strings on thousands of balloons, the spirits found themselves suddenly untethered from my sister, and began to float and fly away, drifting further and further through the walls of the tower out into the night, free to roam the world again.

Hannah turned and took me in from head to foot as though checking to see if I were injured, and then pulling me into the fiercest of hugs. Her entire body was shaking and cold, but the tears against my cheek were hot. Her hands dug painfully into my back.

"Oh, thank God," Hannah sobbed against my cheek. "Thank God you're all right. You are all right, aren't you?" She pulled back from me and stared into my face. "I am so *mad* at you!" she cried, her face crumpling into a fierce scowl. "Why didn't you get out of there? What do you think I would do if I lost you?" She pushed me away from her with an angry little shove but then immediately caught at my shirt again and pulled me back toward her and crushed me against her again in a hug even fiercer than the last.

"I'm sorry," I whispered to her. "I'm really sorry. I didn't mean to scare you. Thank you for doing that for me."

"You're one of the only people I would do that for," Hannah hissed. "I shouldn't have. I almost lost control. It was reckless, it was—"

"No, *I* was reckless," I cut her off. "You were incredible. I could feel you. I could feel your control. You have better command of that gift than you would ever believe."

Hannah narrowed her eyes at me, and I could tell that she was trying to decide whether or not to believe me, but then seemed to decide that she didn't care. She pulled me into one last hug, a hug that went from warm to bitingly cold as Milo threw himself on top of us, sobbing uncontrollably. He was mumbling something through his tears. I could make out the word "sweetness," and the words "heart attack," and then at least six or seven curse words, but that was all the sense that I could get out of it. But it was enough to know that I heartily agreed with the sentiment.

I felt a hand on my shoulder and pulled myself out of the embrace just enough to turn around and see Catriona looking at me. A hundred questions flashed across her face, but there was no time to answer any of them.

"I need your help," I whispered to her.

"My office," she muttered back. "Now."

12

GAME PLAN

THE DOOR HAD BARELY CLOSED behind us when Catriona whirled around and fixed the full intensity of her gaze upon me. It wasn't a glare, necessarily, but she wasn't exactly capable of a truly sympathetic look, not in her current state of agitation. Or maybe ever.

"Okay," she said bluntly. "What the hell happened down there?"

I tried to marshall my racing thoughts. The moments following the destruction of the Léarscáil had passed in a frantic blur. Because she was the most senior member of the Council present, Catriona had been able to issue the orders that sent everyone flying off in different directions. She sent the other Council members to round up their sisters and gather in the Council room for a briefing. She sent the majority of the Caomhnóir back to the barracks to wait for orders. She sent Seamus to the top of the North Tower to report to Celeste and inform her of what had happened. And finally, she asked Hannah and Milo to go to the hospital wing and wait for me there. Only two Caomhnóir had remained behind to remove Moira's broken and battered body from the tower and whisk it off to the hospital ward. What would become of it there, I did not know, and I did not ask. I couldn't even bear to look back at her as Catriona pulled me by my uninjured arm out of the tower room and dragged me off to the Tracker office.

"It's this," I told her, and I pulled Moira's crumpled piece of parchment from the back pocket of my jeans and spread it on the desk in front of us. Catriona squinted down at it, then cursed, and pulled a pair of cat's eye reading glasses from an inside pocket of her leather jacket. She thrust them onto her nose and examined the paper.

"What is this?" she asked me sharply. "What am I looking at here? Am I supposed to be able to make sense of this?"

"This is what Moira was working on when she was killed," I said, barely able to say the last word without emotion swallowing up my voice entirely. "It's the Léarscáil map, and the pencil marks are showing the path of the pendulum just now when it was crazy."

Catriona's eyes widened. "Are you telling me she actually made sense of this?" she asked, waving a hand over the utter chaos of lines and numbers and markings that crowded the page.

"Yes," I told her. "I know it seems like the pendulum was just completely out of control, but Moira said that it was a shift in spirit energy that caused it, and this is the paper she used to figure out what that was. She said the source of the chaos was here." And I tapped my finger on the big red X she had scrawled in the center of the page.

"It's... Scotland, isn't it?" Catriona asked, leaning closer to the page so that she could make out the details of the map beneath all the scribbling. "You say that something in Scotland is causing all of this chaos?"

"Not just anywhere in Scotland," I said, my heart beginning to thunder in my chest. "She narrowed it down to one particular place in Scotland. The Isle of Skye."

Catriona's face jerked up and she stared at me over the top of her glasses. "The Isle of Skye?" she repeated in a whisper.

"Yes," I whispered back. "And you and I both know there's only one place in the Isle of Skye that could attract such a chaotic spiritual event."

"The *príosún*," Catriona mouthed, no sound escaping her lips.

I nodded. "The *príosún*."

If there was one other person in Fairhaven Hall that could truly comprehend the dangers and implications of trouble at a place like the Skye Príosún, it was the woman now standing next to me, her face awash in horror. Not only did she have to travel back-and-forth to the place for her work, but her own cousin Lucida had been imprisoned there since she had betrayed the Durupinen and helped the Necromancers bring about the Prophecy.

"What about Fiona? She's meant to be back already. Have you seen her yet? What did she say?" Catriona cried.

"She isn't back," I said. "Seamus told me that communication from the *príosún* has gone dark, and that Fiona missed her escort back to the castle. He was explaining to me that they were looking into it, but that was the moment that all hell broke loose down at the Léarscáil, and we didn't have a chance to talk about it any further."

What little color there was in Catriona's face drained away, leaving her complexion milky, her features looking remarkably younger in the grip of fear. "This is it, then," she said softly. "This is your prophecy, isn't it? It's begun."

I took a deep breath, and then nodded my head. "It has to be," I said. "It's too much of a coincidence. A spiritual shift at the *príosún* so big that it tears a centuries-old Léarscáil from its path and destroys it? This has to be what my drawings have been warning me about. There's just no other explanation."

Catriona stared at me, and I knew we were both thinking the same thing. We were out of time.

Catriona blinked, pulling her gaze away from mine, and then ran her fingers frantically through her mane of golden hair. "Okay," she muttered to herself. "Okay, okay, okay." Her head snapped up suddenly, startling me as she locked eyes with me again fiercely. "Who else has seen this? This map, have you shown it to anyone else?"

"Seamus has seen it. He knows that Moira had it in her hand right before the pendulum..." I swallowed the rest of the image along with a strong desire to be ill.

"But does he know what it means?" Catriona continued sharply. "Did you explain it to him?"

"No," I said. "He knows I grabbed the paper, and he knows that Moira was using it to figure out what was happening with the Léarscáil, but he doesn't know what her work means, or that it has anything to do with the *príosún*."

Catriona expelled a relieved breath and began pacing like a caged animal. "Okay," she said again. "Okay, well that's something. We can't let anyone know what it means. That's crucial."

"But..." I cast desperately around for a different conclusion, but could find none. "This is it, isn't it? I can't conceal the prophecy anymore. I have to tell them. I have to tell them that I'm a Seer. There's no other way."

"No," Catriona said, shaking her head fiercely. "No, not yet. Not if we can avoid it."

"But how *can* we avoid it?" I went on. "Look, I have no desire to tell them that I've been hiding this prophecy from them, but what choice do we have? Something really dangerous is happening right now at the *príosún*, and if we don't warn them, then we are as good as aiding and abetting the enemy, aren't we?"

"We are not handing your Seer abilities over to that Council!" Catriona practically shouted. She closed her eyes to gather herself, and continued in a hushed but intense tone. "For all our expertise in the spirit world, for all we take our calling extremely seriously, we have never learned to deal with the powerful outliers in our sisterhood. Over and over again, we have punished our own for daring to be born with powerful gifts. Just look at what they did to you, to your sister. Look at what they've done to Fiona's mother, and to Lucida. Now, I'm not saying that Lucida isn't partly to blame for what's become of her. She gave in to temptation, and she made poor choices, and she has to live with the consequences of those choices. I accept that, and I think she does now, too. But the fact remains that if the Northern Clans had not treated Lucida like a science experiment rather than one of their own beloved sisters, she never would've been tempted in the first place, and those choices would never have presented themselves to her. Why, even your own ancestor, Agnes Isherwood, who made the most terrible prophecy of our very long history, was tortured by the responsibility of her power. She was forced to step down from her High Priesthood because of the pressure that the rest of the Durupinen thrust upon her to see more clearly, to provide more details, to save them from a fate that was hundreds and hundreds of years away. Just look at the way they *still* treat your sister! Even though the prophecy has passed, even though the threat of a Caller died when the Prophecy was thwarted, they are still half-terrified of your sister and what she can do. Hell, I'm *still* half-terrified of her, and I grew up with a Caller for the other half of my Gateway! The fact is, that if we tell them you are a Seer, you will never know another moment's peace. No. There's got to be another way to warn them."

There was a soft knock on the door, and Catriona and I both whirled around, hearts hammering. With a flick of her wrist, Catriona flipped Moira's parchment upside down, hiding the markings upon it, and slid a book on top of it to obscure it.

"Who is it?" she barked.

"It's Hannah," came my sister's frightened voice. "Can I come in?"

"Are you alone?" Catriona asked.

"I have Milo with me," Hannah said. "But no one else."

"Come in, then, and be quick about it," Catriona said.

Hannah slipped quickly through the door, Milo right on her heels, and closed it behind her. Her complexion was pale and clammy, and there were deep circles under her eyes. The Calling had left her weak and exhausted.

"Are you okay?" Hannah and I asked each other at exactly the same time. Hannah's mouth curved into a little smile. "I'm fine," she assured me. "Just a little tired."

"Mrs. Mistlemoore just checked her out," Milo told me. "Hannah thought I was overreacting, but I insisted. I can be pretty persuasive when I need to be."

"Persuasive and annoying are not the same thing," Hannah muttered to him, rolling her eyes. "I told you I was fine."

Milo shrugged unconcernedly. "Whine at me all you want, sweetness, but it's my job to make sure that you're taken care of. I did my job. End of discussion."

"Anyway," Hannah said quellingly, "once Mrs. Mistlemoore had finished with me, she started patching up the other Caomhnóir who were down in the tower. But Celeste is going to want to see everyone in the Grand Council Room as soon as she's finished, so that doesn't leave us much time to figure out what to tell them."

Hannah gave me a knowing look, and I waved her off. "It's okay," I told her. "Catriona knows about the prophetic drawings. I've already told her."

Hannah's mouth fell open. "You... you told her? But... now the whole Council will know!"

"I can keep a secret, thank you very much," Catriona said dryly. "The Council won't be hearing a bloody thing from me."

"Our bigger problem is this," I said, taking Moira's paper from the desk and showing it to Hannah and Milo. "Moira tracked the source of the spiritual disturbance. It's at the Skye Príosún, and it's happening right now."

"But then..." Hannah looked back and forth between Catriona and me, still trying to process this new development. "What do we do?"

A second knock sounded against the door, this one much more authoritative.

"Who is it?" Catriona asked again.

"It's Seamus," came a deep bark of a voice.

Catriona gestured for me to hide the paper again, which I quickly did. "Come in, Seamus."

Seamus entered, moving gingerly to accommodate the fresh dressing of bandages wound around his middle.

"I've come to let you know that the High Priestess wants to see you all in the Grand Council Room so that we can discuss what happened down in the Léarscáil," he said.

Catriona inclined her head. "Thank you. We'll be right down. Are you all right?" she added, pointing to the dressings.

"I'll live," Seamus said shortly. "But I'm going to need some stitching up. Would you be so kind as to pass this along to the High Priestess for me." He pulled an envelope from his pocket and held it out to her.

"What is it?" Catriona asked, taking the envelope curiously.

"It's a message from Fiona," Seamus said. "She has sent word that she will not be returning as previously discussed. She wished to see her mother safely settled at home, and to spend some time with her there. She expects to be back at Fairhaven in a week or so."

Catriona's eyes darted quickly to me, and then back again. "Jessica told me that communication was down with Skye Príosún. Isn't that where she was?"

"Yes, but communication is back up now. Eamon has been in touch to say that they had some inclement weather, which knocked the power out, but they are up and running once again," Seamus explained. "He was able to confirm that they arranged transportation for Fiona to her family home instead of back to Fairhaven, so all seems to be in order."

"Thank you, Seamus," Catriona said, pressing her lips into a smile. "Go see to your injuries. And thank you for your bravery down in the Léarscáil."

Seamus gave a cursory bow and slipped out of the room, closing the door behind him.

I rounded on Catriona at once. "That's bullshit!" I cried.

Catriona shushed me angrily. "Keep your voice down!"

"There's no way that Fiona went home! She would never leave me hanging when I'm expecting her back, especially for something as important as this! And I dreamed that she was calling for me. I heard her voice. I don't know if it was a premonition or if she's reaching out somehow, or what, but something's up!"

"It's too much of a coincidence," Hannah agreed. "An event at the *príosún* causes the Léarscáil to self-destruct, communication goes down, and suddenly Fiona is making excuses and disappearing off to Scotland?"

"Agreed," Milo chimed in. "It sounds like the Caomhnóir at the *príosún* are covering something up—something they don't want the Council to know about."

Catriona had begun pacing again. "We need to consider," she said very carefully, "that the Caomhnóir at the *príosún* aren't the only ones covering it up."

A stunned silence greeted these words. I was the first to break it.

"You think some of the Fairhaven Caomhnóir are in on it," I said quietly.

Catriona gave a grim nod. "We cannot rule out that possibility. It may be too dangerous to let anyone here at the castle know what we suspect about the *príosún*."

"But... that's just... Seamus? No way," Milo stammered.

"Not just Seamus. But yes, I think we must consider him under suspicion," Catriona said.

"Is... is that a likely possibility?" Hannah asked, her voice rising to a squeak.

"Your former Caomhnóir obviously thought it was a possibility," Catriona pointed out. She turned to me. "That's why he sought you out, to warn you, isn't it? Instead of simply confiding in another of his brothers from Fairhaven?"

I swallowed, barely able to meet her eyes. "Partly," I admitted. "I don't think he ever considered that Seamus himself might be compromised, but he did tell me he wasn't sure who he could trust."

"And that's a remarkable statement for a Caomhnóir," Catriona said. "Trust amongst the Caomhnóir Brotherhood is traditionally absolute."

"Well, I think we can agree that tradition is out the fucking window at this point," Milo said, a hysterical edge to his voice. "We're in uncharted territory here. The normal rules do not apply."

"Yes, there I agree with you," Catriona said. "The normal rules do not apply. Normally, for example, I'd have no choice but to bring Jess' prophetic drawings to the Council. But we're not going to do that. We're not going to say a word about them, because if the word gets out that you know so many details of the potential coup at Skye Príosún, the panic will be absolute, and word will almost certainly reach the Caomhnóir at the *priosún*. And if that happens, we have no chance of foiling their plans."

"But we don't know their plans!" I cried. "I've got one image of one moment in time! We have no idea how far away that moment might be, or how events are going to unfold to get us there!"

"Yes, that's true. But if we let on what we know, then we've lost the element of surprise," Catriona said, fighting against an urge to lose her patience with us. "You've never seen the Isle of Skye in person. You've never experienced the sheer magnitude of the place. It's a fortress by design, meant to be unassailable. If the Necromancers take it from the inside, we will have absolutely no chance to take it back."

"But, what will the Necromancers want the *priosún* for?" Milo asked. "Like, what can they do with it? It's a building. Even if they take control of the physical location, what kind of advantage does that give them? They still don't have control of the Gateways. They're just... trapped, aren't they?"

Catriona shook her head. "That's where you're wrong. The *priosún* is home to a wealth of weapons that the Necromancers can never be allowed to wield."

"Like what?" I asked.

"The first and most obvious is the release of all our most dangerous enemies. The Skye Priosún holds at bay every person, alive or dead, that ever posed a true threat to us. Every Necromancer, every Durupinen traitor, every spirit who railed against our control—all of them, free of their bonds and willing to serve the Necromancers in pursuit of our destruction."

Hannah made a small sound like a wounded animal and dropped into the nearest chair.

Catriona looked satisfied. "I'm glad you understand the magnitude of the problem. The second danger is the catacomb archives," she went on.

"What's the catacomb archives, besides the title of a hypothetical horror movie I kind of want to see?" Milo asked. Hannah made a motion to smack him, which went straight through the specter of his torso.

"In essence, it's a library of crime records deep within the bowels of the *priosún*. Every criminal who has ever been housed at the *priosún* has a file there, detailing everything related to their offenses against the Durupinen. There are also many artifacts down there—important evidence and exhibits from criminal trials that have been preserved for archival purposes. I can't even begin to imagine what the Necromancers could have at their fingertips should they breach it."

"You... keep a library of weapons and dangerous information in the same place you house the criminals who would love to get their hands on it?" I asked weakly.

Catriona glared at me. "Those catacombs have remained unbreachable in the thousand years the fortress has stood on that site. The protections of the Caomhnóir have never been penetrated!" she snapped.

"The protections of the Caomhnóir won't matter if the Caomhnóir are the ones doing the penetrating," Hannah said quietly.

Catriona looked as though she would dearly have loved to shut Hannah's observation down with a cutting retort, but she couldn't. Her point, in all its terrifying reality, was too true to be brushed off.

We all sat in silence, letting the horror wash over us. Finally, when I thought I might scream aloud from the weight of the dread, I said, "So. What do we do? Because we can't just sit back and do nothing. We've already wasted enough time as it is, trying to be cautious. If we are not going to tell the Council about my prophetic drawings, then what are we going to do? Because Finn is at that *príosún*, and so is Fiona, most likely, and there's no way in hell that I'm abandoning them there, so give me an alternative plan, or I'm marching up to Celeste's office right now and telling her everything."

"No, you're right," Catriona said. "The time has passed to wait and see."

Catriona paced in silence for what felt like a long time, and I could see her wheels turning furiously. Finally, she planted her foot and turned on her heel so sharply that she looked like she was doing a military exercise.

"We need to get a Tracker inside the *príosún*, and we need to do it without alerting the Caomhnóir that we know something is going on."

"What will it matter if we get a Tracker in there?" I asked. "Whatever is happening is still... happening. It's not like one Tracker inside the walls is going to stop it."

"Yes, but if that Tracker has the ability to communicate with those of us on the outside, then we would have a window into what's happening, and be able to prepare for it. You see, we don't want to face the eventuality that your drawing portrays. Once that fortress is fortified for battle, it's already too late. We're done for. If our warriors are turned against us and holed up in the strongest defensive position we possess, we might as well just hand the Gateways over to the Necromancers now. I don't see how we could possibly win."

Beside me, Milo was muttering a monologue of profanity under his breath. Hannah, on the other hand seemed to have stopped breathing entirely.

"Okay," I said slowly, "let's say that I agree with you. If we were able to somehow get a Tracker into the *príosún* unobtrusively without any of the Caomhnóir or the Necromancers getting suspicious, and that Tracker could act as a spy and relay information to us, that would be incredibly useful. The fact remains that they would never allow a Tracker to just walk in there in the midst of their plans!"

"I think they just might, in fact," Catriona said pensively. "I've just had an idea, you see. It's mad, quite frankly, but it just might work. I just need to know one thing: Do you trust me?"

I was surprised how easily the words sprang to my lips. "I do."

"Excellent," Catriona said, and her face broke into the kind of smile that only a ludicrously dangerous plan could've brought to her features. "Let's get to work, then."

13

CAPTIVE

B ANG. BANG. BANG.

For once, I was being woken out of a dead sleep by a disturbance that I had not personally made—some of the only sleep I'd managed to get in the two days since Moira's death. My heart was in my throat as I stared around in the darkness. To my left, Hannah had also sat up in her bed, gasping with surprise.

"What?" she cried, her voice still slurred with sleep. "What is that? Jess, what's going on? You don't think... ?"

"I don't know," I replied, attempting to master my own breathing. I cleared my throat. "Who is it?" I called, trying to sound authoritative rather than scared shitless.

"It's Seamus," said the familiar bark of a voice. "It's urgent. Open the door, please."

The "please" was perfunctory, I noted. His tone left me in no doubt that this was not a request that could be ignored if I wanted the door to remain on its hinges.

I rubbed the sleep from my eyes and scrambled out from under my blanket. I slid my feet into my slippers and shuffled over to the door.

"Wait!" Hannah hissed. I turned to look at her, but my eyes had still not adjusted to the darkness, and all I could see was the slight glint of her frightened eyes.

"What?" I hissed back.

"I just... what if it's... do you think we have to open it?" she whispered.

"I guess we don't have to open it, but it sounds like he's going to break it down if we don't," I replied quietly.

Hannah whimpered, but couldn't argue with me, and so I closed the rest of the distance between myself and the door, pulled back the deadbolt, and wrenched it open just wide enough to see who was standing on the other side of it. I tried to stifle a gasp of shock, but failed.

Waiting in the hallway, standing shoulder to shoulder like comrades-in-arms, were Seamus and Ambrose. Just behind them stood Catriona, looking particularly solemn.

"Good evening, Jessica," she said.

"It's…" I squinted at the clock by my bed, "two o'clock in the morning! This isn't evening. What the hell is going on?"

"We'll explain everything when we get downstairs," Catriona said, glancing up and down the hallway. "Will you just come with us please, Jess?"

"No, I won't," I said, crossing my arms over my chest protectively. "And you will explain now."

Hannah had slid down off of her bed and walked over to stand beside me by the door. Milo had appeared beside her—evidently, she had used the connection to silently contact him while I was talking to Catriona—and his face was wary when he caught sight of who was standing on the other side and struggled to catch up with what was happening.

"What's going on here?" he asked the group at large.

"Catriona was just about to explain that, actually," I told him. I turned back to Catriona. "So, let's have it. We all know this isn't a pleasant little social call."

"Are you really going to make me do this here, where anybody could hear me?" Catriona asked. She was keeping her voice hushed, but Seamus' loud knocking and shouted demands had already woken several people along the hallway. Up and down the corridor, doors were opening, and sleepy faces were peering out, searching for the source of the commotion.

"Yes, I am," I said, ignoring the eager stares.

Catriona rolled her eyes, and then shrugged off-handedly. "Very well, then," she said. "I was going to try to make this easier on you, but if you want to be a public spectacle, then be my guest."

She turned to Seamus, who pulled out an official-looking piece of parchment. "Jessica Ballard of the Clan Sassanaigh, you are being placed under arrest and charged with conspiracy to undermine the will of a foreign Durupinen Council."

"What?!" I cried, but I could hardly hear myself over Hannah and Milo's shouted protestations.

"This is insanity!" Hannah cried, and her voice was shaking violently. "Jess hasn't done anything wrong!"

"As it turns out, she has," Catriona said evenly. "The Traveler Council has filed formal charges, and it is our duty to enforce them."

"The Traveler laws are antiquated bullshit, and you know it!" Milo shouted.

"The events at the Traveler camp happened months ago," I pointed out, trying to keep my voice calm. "If the Traveler Council was unhappy with my actions, why didn't they file a complaint then?"

"New information has come to light about your actions surrounding the trial of Irina Faa because a corroborating witness has come forward," Catriona said.

"What witness?" I challenged her.

"Flavia," Catriona said quietly. "I've spoken to her myself about the matter."

I just stared at her. Hannah and Milo also went quiet in their shock. Catriona took advantage of the silence to continue.

"Now, would you like to continue to do this here, or shall we take this conversation elsewhere?" She looked pointedly down the hallway where more and more faces were poking out of doorways and whispering to each other. I could feel the flush of humiliation rising in my face.

"Fine," I spat at them, keeping my voice down as the gathering crowd craned their necks to get a better view. "Hannah, toss me my sweater," I said, turning over my shoulder. "And my sneakers."

Hannah stayed exactly where she was, her wide and terrified eyes fixed incredulously on my face. "You're not seriously going to go with them, are you? They can't arrest you like some criminal."

"Actually, I think they can," I said. "Just hand me my stuff, Hannah. We'll sort this out downstairs. I'm sure it's just a misunderstanding."

Hannah still looked like she wanted to argue, but she hurried over and grabbed my sneakers and a sweater from the back of my chair and handed them to me. I kicked the slippers off, slid my feet into the sneakers, and pulled the sweater on over my T-shirt and ratty sweatpants.

"All right then," I said to Catriona. "Let's go. The quicker we figure this out, the quicker I can go back to bed."

At my words, Seamus half-lifted his hands toward me, and I saw that he was carrying a pair of handcuffs.

"Oh, hell no!" Milo growled. "If you so much as touch her with those..."

But Catriona was already putting up an admonitory hand. "Those aren't necessary, Seamus, as long as Jess agrees to come with us willingly. You do, don't you?" she asked me.

I threw Milo a warning look and then replied, "Yes. I'm not resisting, so hard pass on the fancy convict accessories, okay? Just tell me where to go so we can sort this out. This has to be some kind of mistake."

"I'm resisting!" Milo cried. "I'm fucking resisting, okay? Does Celeste know about this? Or the rest of the Council? There's no way they would stand for this kind of—"

"The High Priestess has been notified," Catriona said in an almost bored voice. "She has countersigned the arrest warrant. Would you care to analyze her handwriting?"

Milo opened his mouth again, but I forestalled him. "This is just making it worse, Milo. Let's just go, okay?"

Milo looked mutinous, but he fell silent. I stepped through the doorway, and a voice rang out.

"Jess! What in bloody blazes is going on here?"

Savvy had emerged from her room, tousle-haired and wearing nothing but an oversized t-shirt. She squinted at the scene, understanding dawning in her still-drowsy face.

"Nothing, Savvy. Just a misunderstanding. Everything's fine," I told her in the most soothing voice I could manage. Her face looked so distraught that I took an unintentional step toward her and away from the Caomhnóir.

Instantly, Seamus and Ambrose were flanking me on either side, each of them with a warning hand resting just behind my elbow.

"Oi! Get your bloody hands off her!" Savvy shouted, stumbling forward. Frankie reached out a hand and pulled her back.

"Savvy, it's okay. Hannah will explain. I can handle myself. Everything's fine," I reiterated. When I was sure that Savvy wasn't going to come barreling down the hallway, I faced my captors again. Seamus was stony-faced, but as I glanced at Ambrose, I caught a fleeting glimpse of a smirk on his face before he composed his features.

"Enjoying this, are you?" I muttered at him.

He did not reply. The smirk disappeared, but I knew I had not imagined it. I guess I wasn't all that surprised. He probably resented and disliked me as much as I resented and disliked him. I couldn't pretend that I wouldn't have cracked a smile if I thought he was being carted off to prison.

I turned back to Seamus. "I assure you, I do, in fact, know how to walk without assistance," I told him. He did not so much as blink. He kept his eyes facing stubbornly forward, and his hand in exactly the same place upon my elbow.

Deciding that physically pulling away from them would probably just result in me being clapped in irons, I grudgingly accepted being led by the elbows down the hallway with spectators now gathered eagerly on every side. I felt like the proverbial woman being dragged through the streets, the only difference is that I was being bombarded with stony glares instead of actual stones. I suppose I should've been grateful for that, but I was finding it hard to muster that particular emotion at the moment. The chilly stares of ghosts joined those of living people as news of my perp walk spread rapidly through the castle.

We reached the main staircase, and I turned automatically to head down the corridor that led to the Tracker office, but both Seamus and Ambrose tightened their grip on my elbows, halting my progress, and making me stumble.

I turned to Seamus. "What are you doing?" I asked him. "The Tracker office is this way."

"I'm aware of that," Seamus replied, still refusing to look at me. "We are not going to the Tracker office."

I looked from him to Ambrose, and then at Catriona. "So, where are we going, then?" I asked them.

Catriona hesitated before she replied, "Out the front doors. To a waiting car."

"And where exactly is that waiting car going to take me?" I asked, my voice rising with badly suppressed hysteria.

"To be held at the Skye Príosún until such time as the hearing can be scheduled," Catriona said at last.

Hannah and Milo burst into a fierce stream of protestations, and I had to shout to be heard over them. "You're sending me to jail?"

"Yes," Catriona said, almost automatically.

"You can't do that!" Hannah cried, her voice breaking in a sob.

"You can't just throw someone in jail when they haven't even had a trial or anything!"

"Jessica will have her chance to defend herself against the charges," Catriona said with an almost robotic calmness, as though her brain had completely disengaged and she was simply reading from a prepared script. "But until that time, the Traveler Council has requested that she be held. They believe she is a flight risk, and she has sufficiently confirmed their fears on that point."

"But..." Hannah looked in serious danger of completely breaking down. "Why can't you keep her here? Like, Durupinen house arrest. Isn't that a thing?"

"No," Catriona said. "I'm afraid that's not 'a thing.' We have protocols, and we must follow them. Jessica will have her due process, but she has to follow the rules like everyone else."

"Seriously? Due process? Are you even listening to yourself?" Milo raged. "Dragging someone out of their bed at two o'clock in the morning instead of just summoning them to your office during daylight hours? Locking her up in that... that hellhole with Necromancer scum? Does that seriously sound like due process to you? Are we supposed to believe that she's being treated like an innocent person right now? Because I think we can conclusively say that's bullshit."

"Are you quite finished with your dramatic monologue, Spirit Guide Chang? Or would you like me to write you up for insubordination? They have cells that hold spirits in Skye Príosún, you know."

Milo was sputtering incoherently. Seamus and Ambrose were so still and impassive on either side of me that it seemed they had turned to stone. Catriona's face was set, even as Hannah broke down in a storm of crying. What else was there to say?

"Fine, then," I said, endeavoring to keep my voice steady and fortified with the bravery I did not feel. "Let's get this over with."

I turned to Hannah and Milo. "It's going to be okay," I told them, and the words rang hollow as they echoed around the entrance hall. "Everything is going to be fine. I didn't do anything wrong. This will all blow over, okay? Go wake Karen up and tell her what's happened. Evidently, I'm going to need a good lawyer." Then, because the looks on both of their faces were going to cause me to lose it, I turned back to Catriona. "I concede that I don't have a choice here. Let's go."

Catriona nodded solemnly, not a spark of her usual sarcasm evident in her face, and turned on her heel to march toward the front doors. My two captors and I followed.

I didn't look back at Hannah or Milo, even though I could feel both sets of their eyes boring into the back of my head, even though I could hear Hannah's barely stifled sobs echoing through the entrance hall. Even though I could feel both of them knocking hard against the connection for me to let them into my head, I couldn't do it. Not now. If I tried to talk to either of them, their fear and anxiety would infect me, and then how could I ever do what I needed to do? No, I needed to keep them shut out, at least for the moment. There would be time to put their fear to rest later. There was plenty of time to sit around and chat when the only thing on your agenda was wasting away in a jail cell for the foreseeable future.

Seamus opened the door of the car and stood there until I had slid into the backseat. Then he slammed the door shut, and walked around to the front of the car to speak with Catriona. Through the tint of the car window, I could see Ambrose still standing there looking at me. The expression on his face was undeniably smug. He gave me a nod of satisfaction, and then turned and walked back to the castle. I was fighting the impulse to roll the window down and shout after him, but a different raised voice caught my attention instead.

"... really think you ought to let me find a Caomhnóir to drive you there," Seamus was saying, his voice tense with badly suppressed anger.

"Oh, Seamus, talk sense, would you? Who can you possibly spare at the moment?" Catriona asked. "Half a dozen of your men were injured in the Léarscáil incident, and you're shorthanded as it is, just for regular security details on the castle grounds. You can't safely spare anyone, and you know it. I know it irks you to admit it, but I am more than capable of making the drive and handling a prisoner on my own. You ought to know, you helped train me."

"I am not doubting your capabilities," Seamus said through gritted teeth, "but it does not feel prudent for a single Tracker to undertake a prisoner transport without adequate support."

"I'm not carrying her through the wilderness on my back, Seamus," Catriona cried. "I'm driving her twenty miles to an airport. Another Tracker and a Caomhnóir pilot will be meeting me there. I assure you, I have arranged for adequate support."

Seamus appeared to be chewing his tongue in an effort to bite back whatever it was he wanted to say. Finally, the tenseness in his shoulders seemed to relax. "I would be more comfortable," he said evenly, "if you would allow me to put the handcuffs on her. You may feel it is an unnecessary precaution, but my experience has taught me otherwise. If you would indulge me in this small detail, I will let the rest of this go."

Catriona rolled her eyes and then threw up her hands in exasperation. "Fine. For heaven's sake, just cuff her, then. Anything to get you off my back and me on the road. We're on a tight schedule to beat an incoming storm. I don't want to be stranded on the helipad for hours because you couldn't stop mollycoddling me."

"Very well, then," Seamus said. He walked around the side of the car, opened the door, and leaned in. "Hold out your hands," he ordered.

Recognizing a hopeless situation when I saw one, I did as I was told, and threw Catriona a filthy look while I was at it. I waited while Seamus secured the handcuffs a bit tighter than was absolutely necessary. He checked them several times, pulling on various parts of the cuffs to make sure that they were secure, and then stood up. I looked up at him and he caught my eye for the first time since he had pounded on my bedroom door. There was something very strange in his expression. Almost... triumphant.

Was the contempt amongst Caomhnóir for Durupinen so widespread that just the sight of a Durupinen humbled in this manner could make a Caomhnóir smile? Was something else at play here? I didn't know. But one thing I was sure of: the deeper we dug into the situation, the clearer it was that the toxicity that had long poisoned Durupinen–Caomhnóir relationships was reaching a critical mass. With each passing day, with each successive interaction, I was less and less surprised that our system was falling apart at the seams.

The slamming of the car door broke into my thoughts and made me jump. Catriona slid into the driver's seat and pulled her seatbelt across her chest. She rolled down her window. "I'll check in with you when we arrive at the helipad," she told Seamus.

Seamus did not reply, but merely inclined his head, stony-faced.

Catriona threw the car into drive and peeled away with a screeching of tires.

I watched her through the tinted glass of the partition as she raised her phone to her ear and mumbled a few incoherent sentences. Then she tossed the phone aside and drove in silence until we had safely passed through the gates of the outer grounds and onto the main road.

"The car?" I asked quietly.

"It's clean," Catriona said. "Searched it myself. No bugs, no cameras."

I let out a sigh of relief, allowing my body to relax for the first time since Seamus had pounded on my door. Then I looked up and glared at Catriona in the rearview mirror.

"Seriously, though? At two o'clock in the morning? Was that really necessary? You scared the shit out of us."

"I meant to scare the shit out of you," Catriona said pleasantly. "We've learned from your time as a Tracker that you're absolute rubbish at acting. So is your sister. It was necessary to catch you both by surprise, so that you might have a chance at a genuine reaction that wouldn't raise suspicion. And I'm pleased to say that we might have managed to pull it off."

"You could have warned me," I grumbled.

"That would have defeated the purpose," Catriona said. "Even so, I'm impressed that your sister was able to whip up those tears."

"She wasn't pretending," I told her quietly. "She's genuinely terrified. She hates this plan, and she's angry at me for agreeing to it. I think she would've been a wreck no matter how or when I left."

"Well, regardless, her emotional outburst played into the scenario quite nicely." Catriona caught sight of my disgusted glare in the rearview mirror and snorted. "Don't be so naïve, Jessica. You know how important it was for us to sell this to the Fairhaven Caomhnóir. You know how crucial it was for them to really believe that you're being arrested. Your sister's fear was useful. It helped. And in the long run, it will be worth having put her through it."

I shook my head and looked out the window. There were some parts of this job Catriona and I were never going to agree on, and I just had to accept that.

"So how much of that was actually true?" I asked after my anger had subsided. "The story you told Seamus and Ambrose, how much of it is true?"

"What do you mean?" Catriona asked impatiently. She floored the gas pedal and zoomed around a small sputtering car that had been trundling along in front of us ten miles under the speed limit.

"I mean, did you actually draw up a formal charge? Did you really talk to Flavia? What about Celeste? How many people are in on this?"

"No. So far, we're the only ones involved," Catriona said. "Well, that's not exactly true. The Trackers waiting for us at the helipad are also in on the plan. I've had to forge Celeste's signature on the warrant, and I had to invent a few teensy pages of testimony from your friend Flavia, but I'm quite sure I've done it all convincingly."

"Aren't you going to get in a shitload of trouble for that?" I asked her. "Forging the High Priestess's signature? Couldn't that land you in the *príosún* yourself?"

Catriona shrugged. "I don't think Celeste will give a good goddamn what I've forged or what I've lied about when she realizes the enormity of what it is we're trying to foil here. We had to get you in without the Caomhnóir knowing that you're a plant. It's that simple. Whatever measures we had to take in order to pull that off are therefore justified. I'll have no problem defending myself, if anyone chooses to challenge me on this."

"If you say so," I muttered. Personally, I could see a lot of people on the Council disapproving of what Catriona had done. Then again, Catriona had never been a person who cared what people disapproved of. It was probably one of the reasons why she was so good at her job. Then again, it was also one of the reasons that it took me so long to trust her.

"I was afraid Seamus wasn't going to let us leave without an escort," I said.

Catriona pressed her lips together into a thin line. "So was I," she said at last. "For all the benefits of their protection, trying to get anything done with Caomhnóir around can be nearly bloody impossible."

"Both of them seemed kind of... well, *glad* to see me in cuffs, actually," I admitted.

"That did not escape my notice," Catriona said, nodding thoughtfully with her eyes trained on the dark road ahead. "I've launched an internal investigation of the Caomhnóir, trying to uncover if there might be a connection between what's happening at the *príosún* and the Caomhnóir population at Fairhaven. It made the most sense to start at the top, given Seamus's close ties with the *príosún*. As the head of the Caomhnóir here, he's responsible for any and all assignments—and reassignments—in and out of the *príosún*. Communications to and from the *príosún* are handled through his office, and only a small number of Caomhnóir working directly beneath him are authorized to see such communications."

"Do you really think that Seamus is in on it?" I asked her quietly.

"I don't know what to think," Catriona said. "If you'd asked me a week ago, I would've said not a chance in hell. But a week ago I also would've bet my life that nobody could infiltrate the protections of the *príosún*, and here we are. I will say that Seamus has only shown unwavering loyalty to the Council. But he's not immune to the disdain that has spread through the Durupinen ranks. You saw it just now. He can't stand it when a Durupinen takes control of any situation that he considers to be Caomhnóir territory."

"He looked a little too happy to see me wearing handcuffs, if you ask me," I grumbled.

Catriona chuckled. "You're a special case," she said.

"A special case?" I repeated. "What the hell is that supposed to mean?"

"Jessica, I'm not quite sure how this could have escaped your notice, but you've got a reputation for being a right pain in the ass around here," Catriona said. "You spit on tradition. You don't follow rules. Your relationship with one of Seamus's best Caomhnóir reflected poorly on Seamus's ability to judge the behavior of his own Novitiate. And, as recently as two days ago, you patently ignored every single order that Seamus gave you, putting yourself and many Caomhnóir in danger when you tried to rescue Moira from the Léarscáil. In a great many ways, you are a Caomhnóir's worst nightmare."

"I... oh. Right." I mean seriously, what was there even to argue with there?

"So," Catriona went on, smirking at the resigned look on my face, "what I'm getting at is, Seamus might just be happy to have you out of his hair. It's not necessarily a reflection on his commitment to protecting the Durupinen. He probably just can't bloody stand you."

"Fair enough," I said, shrugging.

"Anyway, we'll find out one way or the other," Catriona said confidently. "To my knowledge, the Trackers have never launched an investigation into the Caomhnóir as a whole. It won't be easy, but it should certainly be interesting, and one thing is for sure: the Caomhnóir will not be expecting it. I anticipate it will raise some hackles, but we don't have a choice. We've got to find out how widespread this conspiracy is."

"Okay, well, speaking of the conspiracy, can we talk a little more about what's happening when we get to the *príosún?*" I asked, feeling a renewed gnawing of fear in the pit of my stomach.

"Yes," Catriona said, adopting a businesslike tone. "Yes, we need to be sure that you're prepared. Well, at least, as prepared as you can be given that we have very little idea of what it is you'll be facing once you're inside."

"Maybe we could talk about it without simultaneously trying to scare the living daylights out of me?" I requested. "Seriously, Catriona, this is hard enough as it is."

"Right," Catriona said, catching my eye in the rearview mirror. "Sorry. Just the facts."

"Thanks," I said.

"When we arrive, I'll escort you in and bring you to your cell. Don't look at me like that," Catriona said. "They're not going to chain you to the wall or anything like that. Your bonds will be Castings, not chains. And, as I will be the one overseeing and double-checking all of your Castings, I'll be able to tamper with the most important one."

"The one that would prevent me from Walking out of the cell," I said at once.

"Yes," Catriona said, nodding her head. "With that Casting disabled, you should be able to move about the fortress freely. You will still need to be extremely cautious. If at all possible, you must restrict your Walking to nighttime hours, so that the sight of your body lying still in your cell will not arouse suspicion. The security is slightly lessened on the living floors at night, but not by much. There will still be plenty of Caomhnóir around, and so it will be crucial for you to keep yourself as hidden as possible."

"But," I reminded her, "the Caomhnóir shouldn't be able to see me, should they? Finn couldn't see me or hear me, when I first Walked in the Traveler camp. The Necromancers couldn't see me, either."

"No, but there are Durupinen locked in the cells of the *príosún*, and they will be able to see you, as will the many spirits who inhabit the place. It's likely that most of them will not recognize you for what you are. Hardly anyone, living or dead, has ever been exposed to a Walker before."

This was certainly true. I remembered when I used my Walking abilities to enter Fairhaven, when it was under siege from the Necromancers. I had found Finvarra imprisoned in a cell, and when she laid eyes on me, she immediately assumed that I had been killed, and was now a ghost. And her Caomhnóir Carrick, who happened to be both a ghost and also my father, had jumped to the very same conclusion, breaking down at the sight of me, convinced that he had failed in his efforts to protect me, and that the Necromancers had killed me. It took a good deal of convincing before he believed that I was, in fact, still alive.

I rarely used my Walking ability to leave my body behind, to stretch the bonds that tethered body to soul, and walk free of my physical form. But it was this unique skill, above all else, that made Catriona sure I was the right Tracker for this job. There were dozens of Trackers more experienced and more skilled than I was, but I was the only one with a prayer of slipping through the halls of the *príosún* unnoticed.

"Even so," Catriona said, breaking into my thoughts, "we cannot assume that one or more of them will not recognize you for what you are if they spot you. So, when you are Walking, you will need to conceal yourself when possible, and move quickly. Do you have the soul catchers?" she added sharply.

Awkwardly, because my hands were cuffed in front of me, I lifted the great curly mass of my hair to reveal a row of thin braids along the nape of my neck. Flavia had taught me how to make them, back when I was first learning how to Walk in the Traveler camp. In order for my soul to part company with my body safely, I had to say an incantation, and then slice through one of the soul catchers while it was tied around my wrist. Cutting through the soul catcher was like cutting through the bonds between my body and my soul, and enabled the Walking to begin. Without them, I was trapped inside my own body like any other normal person. In the days since Catriona and I had formulated this plan, Hannah and I had been working to create as many as possible to bring with me to the *príosún*. Knowing I would never be allowed to bring them with me in bracelet form, Hannah had braided them into my hair instead as a way to conceal them.

"Let's hope I don't have to Walk more than fifteen times," I said, lowering my hair again. "Otherwise, I'll be out of soul catchers, and out of luck."

"We won't let it come to that," Catriona said firmly. "In and out as quickly as possible, that's the plan."

I didn't bother to voice aloud my concern about how frequently the plans that I was involved in rapidly went to hell in a handbasket. There was no need to. We both knew it.

"And you're sure that I'll be able to communicate with Hannah and Milo?" I asked.

"Absolutely," Catriona said. "There's not a Casting in that fortress that could contend with the bond that you and your sister and your Spirit Guide possess. The only way that you wouldn't be able to communicate with them is if one of you purposely closed the connection, and Hannah and Milo know the importance of keeping it wide open at all times, in case of emergencies. Use the connection to get instructions from me, and to relay any and all information that you can find out about what's happening at the *príosún*."

"It's like I'm going undercover to spy on the mob or something, wearing a wire, and reporting back to a bunch of guys crouched in a surveillance van," I said, with a slightly hysterical chuckle. The chuckle died quickly. "You'd think that I would feel more excited, but I'd say the dominant feeling is nausea at this point."

"Nervousness is a good thing," Catriona declared. "It will keep you on your toes. Just keep your mind focused on the goal, and don't let your emotions get the better of you. If you fall apart, so does the plan, and so, likely, will the world of the Durupinen as we know it."

"Yeah, no pressure, right?" I muttered. One of my legs was bouncing up and down uncontrollably. I placed both of my handcuffed hands on top of it to stop the shaking. "So, when I'm Walking, what's the priority?" I asked Catriona. "What should I try to find out first?"

"I'd say the first thing to assess," Catriona said thoughtfully, "is the state of the Necromancers within the prison. If they really are forming some kind of alliance with the Caomhnóir, there should be evidence of it. You need to find out if they're being allowed out of their cells, or if any of the Caomhnóir are meeting with or speaking with them in a way that seems inappropriate."

"And how do I do that?"

"I can lead you to where they're being held," Catriona said. "Necromancer prisoners have their own block within the *príosún*." She looked in the rearview mirror again, and saw the fear in my face. "They aren't being held anywhere near the Durupinen prisoners. The security for the *príosún* designed it that way. It would have been too dangerous to have Durupinen and Necromancers in close proximity. Well, with one notable exception."

"What exception?" I asked, hearing a strange bitter note in her voice.

"My dear cousin," Catriona said. "When you align yourself with Necromancers, you get incarcerated with them. It's a simple matter of making sure the punishment fits the crime."

I had no idea how to respond to this information, so I decided to change the subject. "What else should I be on the lookout for?"

"We'll need to try to confirm what Finn told you, about the Caomhnóir slipping away and disappearing when they're supposed to be on duty. You need to try to find out where they're going, and why they're going there."

The mention of Finn's name sent a thrill of a dozen discordant emotions rushing through my body. Excitement at the thought that I might see him again. Crippling fear that something might've happened to him. Aching loneliness, knowing that even if I did see him, it would likely be impossible for us to speak together even for a moment. And anger, anger that we had been torn asunder like this, anger that pointless and antiquated laws had kept us apart.

"Hey," Catriona said sharply. "Don't start doubting yourself, now. You can handle this. I wouldn't be sending you in if you couldn't, understand?"

She had misread the feelings that were playing across my face, but I didn't bother to correct her, just nodding instead and trying to muster a small smile of confidence.

"If, and only if, you're able to detect some sort of cooperation between the Caomhnóir and the Necromancers, will we continue with the next part of the plan," Catriona said.

"Which is?" I asked.

"Which is to determine how far the corruption has spread into our own Caomhnóir and retake the *príosún* before the Necromancers can claim it," Catriona said.

"And how do we do that?" I prompted.

"We'll cross that bridge if and when we get to it," Catriona replied.

"Which is a pretty, metaphorical way of saying that you have absolutely no freaking clue, right?" I asked her.

The corner of her mouth twitched into a sardonic smirk. "Could be," she admitted. "Any and all of this plan could change at the drop of a hat. We're going to have to think on our feet and be willing to adjust the goals of this mission. And I need to make one thing absolutely clear to you."

I looked up and caught her eye in the rearview mirror.

"I don't let my Trackers sacrifice themselves in the line of duty, not for Gateways, not for victory over Necromancers, and certainly not for ephemeral rubbish like love," Catriona said. "If I tell you it's time to get out of there, if I turn up to get you out, you follow me without a single glance over your shoulder, is that clear?"

"Yes," I said.

"Don't you dare say it just to placate me," Catriona said. "Finn can look after himself, and he does not require your jeopardizing of a Tracker mission because you fancy yourself his knight in shining armor. And so, I repeat: is that clear?"

"Crystal-clear," I replied.

14

FIGHT AND FLIGHT

C ATRIONA CONTINUED TO GIVE ME a suspicious look, but she had no choice. She had to accept my word and move on. We were running out of time to talk. It was only a few short miles until we reached the helipad where the other Tracker and the Caomhnóir pilot would be waiting for us. Once we arrived, there could be no more talk that would suggest we were anything other than captor and captive.

"Look, I don't want you to get hung up on the details now, okay?" Catriona said. "There are too many variables, and we can't plan for everything. We're going to have to figure this out as we go, and I know that's probably not very reassuring, but it's the best we can do. We will be in contact, and I'll be able to walk you through a lot of what you need to accomplish. If things seem to be going south, we will get you out of there quickly. I have all the necessary paperwork drawn up and ready to go. I can walk in that *príosún* at any time, slap the form down on the desk, and take you with me."

"Unless, of course, the place goes into lockdown before that can happen," I pointed out.

"We're going to hope that it doesn't come to that." Catriona shook her hair back and jutted out her chin, as though the sheer force of her determination could control the situation. "Whatever is happening secretly at the *príosún*, the Caomhnóir there are still trying to carry on as though everything is running normally. They're still communicating with Seamus's office after that brief hiatus. And they're still accepting and transferring prisoners like normal. So, whatever may be going on, they are certainly trying to function as though it's not. We're going to take advantage of that charade to get you inside the walls. After that, it's a crapshoot."

"I hope you have better luck with gambling than I do," I muttered.

Catriona turned around, taking her eyes off the road to look me right in the eye. "I have excellent luck with gambling. I know exactly where to lay my bets. I may just have a little flutter on you foiling this entire plot. And I look very much forward to doubling my money, so don't let me down."

"I'll do my best," I told her. We very nearly smiled at each other. Nearly.

"Look, you're just being held in the lowest security area of the prison. You're not a dangerous criminal, at least, not on paper. If they knew what a nightmare you were to deal with, they might lock you up somewhere a bit more secure. In any case, when you're simply awaiting a hearing, and haven't yet been convicted of anything, the accommodations are a bit more relaxed. Your corridor will be patrolled periodically, not constantly. I mean, you're not going to have armed guards standing outside your door staring at your every move. They save that kind of thing for people like Lucida."

It would be easy, if you listened to the careless way that Catriona tossed her cousin's name around, to believe that she wasn't carrying the weight of Lucida's betrayal around everywhere she went, but I knew better. I knew that she worked harder, fought more fiercely, and found ways to prove her own loyalty every single day. I was sure there were those who thought it impossible that Catriona didn't know that Lucida had been a double agent. At first, I would've counted myself among those people. But in the time I'd gotten to know her, I realized that Catriona truly believed that her role as a Durupinen was the most defining characteristic of who she was, and what she was meant to do with her time on Earth. Her entire life was consumed with Council business, Tracker missions, and Fairhaven politics. She had, to my knowledge, no social or romantic life to speak of outside the walls of the castle. And especially now, with her clan thrown into such disgrace over Lucida's actions, she seemed more determined than ever to devote every ounce of energy to fixing what was broken in the Durupinen world, whether it was Lucida who had broken it or not. It would be easy to pity her, if Catriona had allowed such a feeling to be directed toward her. Catriona was the kind of woman who resented even the slightest insinuation that she was anything less than a rock: steady, and strong, and impervious to weakness, especially of the emotional variety. I was sure that would catch up with her eventually, but honestly, who was I to judge? The inside of my head was a graveyard of emotions that I had chosen to bury deeply rather than deal with. I knew they'd dig their way out of those graves eventually, and then I'd be unable to escape them. They were like feeling zombies, moving doggedly and inexorably toward me, until eventually they destroyed me and ate my brain. It was inevitable, really. And I had a feeling that Catriona, too, would likewise be a victim of her own emotional zombie apocalypse.

It's not that I wanted to add another fresh grave to Catriona's mental graveyard situation, but I couldn't suppress the question that I asked her next.

"Do you think that Lucida might be involved with what's going on?" I asked quietly. And then I braced myself, not sure if Catriona was going to explode in a tirade, or else just ignore me completely.

Catriona didn't ignore me, and she didn't explode. I watched her face carefully as she drew her eyebrows together and seemed to really consider the question. I held my breath in anticipation of a response I had not really expected to get.

"I'm not sure," Catriona said at last, her voice very quiet, almost small. "She doesn't talk to me the way that she used to. I always hope that, when we do talk, I can sense a kind of remorse, even if she's too proud to acknowledge it. I'd like to think that if she had the chance, she would make a different decision about getting involved with the Necromancers. And I'd like to think that she would avoid the temptation this time around, if they tried to involve her in whatever they're planning. But I can't honestly say I know for sure. She was badly used, first by the Durupinen, and then by the Necromancers. It doesn't excuse what she did, but I'm not sure what was left of her, the girl she used to be, when she finally made the choice that she did. It's been a very, very long time since my cousin let me see exactly who it is that she has truly become. I'm not sure I would recognize her if she did."

I didn't reply. It would've been all too easy for my very own sister to have ended up exactly the same way. I think I had tried to forget that, because it was an uncomfortable truth to sit with.

Catriona cleared her throat and shook her head back again, attempting to compose her features into her usual mask. "So anyway," she said briskly, "I guess what I'm saying is, I wouldn't trust her while you're in there. Hopefully, you won't find yourself in a situation where you need to make that decision."

I nodded. I, too, hoped I wouldn't find myself in that situation.

"This is the exit just up here," Catriona said, pointing. "We'll be at the helipad in just a couple of minutes. I suggest you take a moment to settle yourself back into our cover story. I won't be able to speak to you anymore about what to do once you get inside the *príosún.*"

I sighed and laid my head back against the seat of the car. I tried to close my eyes and take a few deep breaths to calm the nerves that were starting to mount again. This plan was insane, and reckless, and the only chance we had. I focused my energy on not fucking it up.

Catriona pulled the car off the motorway and followed a dark, winding, increasingly narrow road out to the edge of a huge open field. Ahead of us, I could see a large rectangular building looming up out of the darkness and several large shapes sprouting up around it like massive toadstools, which revealed themselves, upon closer inspection, to be a number of helicopters and small airplanes in various states of disrepair.

We pulled up to a gate. Catriona rolled down her window and punched a code into the keypad. A few seconds later, with a loud buzzing sound, the gate lifted, and we pulled onto a long gravel drive. As we approached the building, the narrow beams of our headlights jittering and shaking, a great metal garage door began to lift and open. Light flooded from the interior of the hanger, and two figures stood silhouetted in the opening, both of them with their arms crossed, waiting for our arrival.

Catriona pulled the car directly into the hangar and killed the engine. I recognized the Tracker waiting for us: it was Elin. She avoided looking at me, betraying no hints that she knew anything unusual was going on. She watched in silence as Catriona slid out of the car, opened my door, and pulled me from the back seat. I tugged a little against her grip in a show of defiance, but I tried not to overdo it. I was counting on my evident terror and nervousness to carry me through this exchange convincingly.

"Have you brought the paperwork?" Elin asked, keeping her eyes fixed carefully on Catriona.

"No, I left it back on the desk along with my competence and twenty years of experience," Catriona sneered. She pulled a packet from the inside pocket of her jacket and handed it to Elin. "That's the copy for the crew in the booking area. We'll need a copy of the sealed and signed version once they've signed off. For our records."

"Of course," Elin said. "No problem."

"Is the helicopter ready to go?" Catriona asked. "We're going to have to leave soon. I've been checking the radar, and that front is moving in pretty quickly."

"Just waiting for you," Elin said. "We can leave whenever you're ready."

"Off we go, then," Catriona said. She adjusted her grip on my arm and jerked her head at Elin, who placed a restraining hand on my other arm. I couldn't be positive, as she was still refusing to look at me, but I thought that the gentle squeeze she gave my arm might have been meant to reassure me. I chose to believe that was the case. I was grasping at any small comfort I could find.

Together, Catriona and Elin marched me through the tall, echoing hanger to the spiral staircase in the back corner. The room was full of cold, flickering fluorescent light, as well as endless shelves full of airplane parts and two small prop planes, each clearly in the process of being repaired or restored. A scruffy-faced, elderly man in oil-spattered overalls stood at the base of the staircase that led up to the roof. He yawned and then leered at me as we passed, revealing several missing teeth.

"Be sure to lock it up once we've taken off, Bill," Catriona commanded him. "We won't be back until you're open for the morning."

"Yes'm," Bill mumbled, inclining his head and doffing a filthy blue and white striped engineer cap.

We took the narrow staircase single file and emerged onto the roof of the building. A helicopter was waiting for us there, parked in the center of a huge landing pad. I'd never been in a helicopter before, nor even seen one up close, but it predictably filled me with the same dread as the sight of an airplane. I'd been terrified of flying for as long as I could remember, and I was sure that being in a helicopter would be no different. The moment Elin closed the door behind us, the helicopter roared to life, headlights blazing and great blades whirring above our heads, creating a powerful wind, whipping dust and debris toward us. I scrunched my eyes closed and turned my head to the side, coughing. The Trackers must've been used to the helicopter, however, for they barely broke their stride as they hurried forward. I hunched myself over as we approached the helicopter. Even though the blades were several feet safely above my head, I could not shake the feeling that if I stood up straight, I'd be instantly decapitated. Catriona climbed up into the helicopter first and then turned around and reached out a hand to help me inside. I fell sideways into one of the two seats in the back of the helicopter, and Elin closed the door behind me. I struggled to sit myself up straight and looked around.

The helicopter seated four people, two in the front, and two in the back. A short, broad-shouldered Caomhnóir sat in the pilot's seat, focused entirely on twisting and turning and pressing a dizzying array of buttons, knobs, gauges, and levers. Elin pulled herself up into the other bucket seat in the front and began securing herself with the many straps of her harness. A large console separated Elin from the pilot, and this, too, was covered with an impossible number of gadgets. Elin placed a massive set of headphones over her ears, adjusted the attached microphone so that it rested right in front of her mouth, and then began to converse with the pilot. Beside me, Catriona began pulling and tugging on the various straps of my safety harness, making sure that I was secure in my seat, since I was unable to do so myself thanks to the handcuffs still fixed around my wrists. She gave me a swift, apologetic look before reaching down and placing my ankles into manacles that seemed to be attached to the bottom part of my seat. I gritted my teeth and allowed her to fasten them. She straightened up and glanced over at the pilot, to make sure he was otherwise engaged before turning back to me and leaning close enough so that I could hear her voice over the deafening sounds of the helicopter.

"Bloody hell, Jessica," she said. "Are you quite well? You look like you're going to be sick."

"I probably should have mentioned my crippling fear of flying," I said faintly.

Catriona barely refrained from rolling her eyes. "Yes, you probably should have. I could've brought you something for that."

"What, like drugs? Not a chance. There's no way I'm walking through the doors of Skye Príosún doped up out of my mind. I need to be clearheaded. I'll be fine; just... don't make me open my eyes once we take off."

The back of the pilot seat was only a couple of feet in front of my face, and my shoulders were bumping against Catriona on my right side and the interior wall of the helicopter on my left. The whole experience would have been incredibly claustrophobic, were it not for the fact that the bulbous front end of the helicopter was made almost entirely of glass.

I could feel the full-blown panic starting to set in as Catriona gave the straps of my harness one last, sharp tug and I felt my back press into the rough fabric of my seat.

"Can... Can a helicopter even get all the way to the Isle of Skye from here?" I asked in a high, trembling voice. "I thought helicopters were just for short trips."

Catriona glanced at me, and her expression softened when she saw whatever was on my face. I watched the sarcasm drain out of her reply as she said, "This helicopter can. Based on the military design. It's less than five hundred miles to Skye, and this darling can do close to six. We've made the trip many times, I promise you."

I nodded my head for an abnormally long time, as though I were trying to shake the reassurance from Catriona's words into my brain. It refused to stick.

"Here," Catriona said, and plunked a huge pair of noise-canceling headphones over my ears. Instantly, the deafening sounds of the helicopter were reduced to a gentle hum. I looked over at her and mouthed my thanks before putting my head back against my seat again and closing my eyes. I didn't open them again for several long, terrifying hours, feeling oddly grateful for the current fear that was so successfully distracting me from the fear of what I would face when we arrived at our destination.

I didn't know how long the journey was supposed to last, and I didn't ask. There was no clock visible from where I was sitting, even if I had decided to open my eyes and mark the passage of time. Logically, I knew that it was probably only a few hours or so, but sitting there aloft in a helicopter with my back pressed to the seat, my eyes squeezed shut, and my fingers white-knuckled upon my knees, those several hours felt roughly like eternity. I breathed in slowly through my nose and expelled the air out through my mouth over and over again until I felt quite dizzy from the regularity of it, as though my brain were not used to getting flooded with this much oxygen. I thought breathing was supposed to be good for you, but my body's reaction was suggesting otherwise.

Casting around for a distraction, I became aware again of the connection that I had snapped shut when we were leaving

Fairhaven. I hadn't wanted to be distracted then, but now, I was desperate for someone else's thoughts inside my head. I gave up on the breathing bullshit and focused instead on that place in my brain where I could feel the steady pulsing of energy trying to get through the barrier. Hannah and Milo were both clamoring to communicate with me. I glanced first at Catriona, absorbed in her paperwork, and then toward the cockpit, where Elin and the pilot were focused on the sky in front of us. With everyone else in the helicopter otherwise engaged, it seemed like it was finally a safe time to open the connection and update them.

The voices and emotions gushed into my head like water tumbling down over a waterfall, and I actually gasped out loud from the sensation of it. Luckily, nobody could hear me over the steady droning roar of the helicopter.

"Jess!"

"Oh, thank God!"

"Why the hell did you close that off for so long? We've been worried out of our minds!"

"Oh God, what's wrong? There's so much fear in here, it's making me nauseous!"

"What's going on? What are they doing to you? Are you okay?"

"Calm down, both of you, before I close this connection right back up again!" I replied. "Seriously, I'm freaking out badly enough as it is. Can you please take it down a notch before we're all drowned in a sea of our collective neuroses? I know you're both nervous," I said, in my best impersonation of a Zen master. "But I'm not going to be able to keep this connection open if you're going to compound things, okay?"

"Sorry, Jess," Hannah mumbled at once.

"Ugh. Okay, you're right. Sorry. Attempting to locate my chill," Milo added.

A tangible calmness began to smooth the choppy emotional waters as both of them made a concerted effort to rein in their emotions, continuing all the while to mumble apologies back to me. I took another deep breath, and then remembered how too much breathing seemed to be making things worse rather than better.

"Good," I said at last. "Let's try to keep it this way, okay? For all our sakes."

"Okay," came both of their replies.

"But... can you just... are you okay?" Hannah added.

"I'm fine," I assured them both in the expectant silence that followed. "We're not there yet, obviously. But we are in a helicopter, so hence, the crippling levels of fear you were just feeling from my end."

Hannah groaned. "Oh, shit. I thought they'd probably be flying you there, but didn't want to say anything, because I didn't want to make it worse."

"That was a good call, and I appreciate it," I said grudgingly. "The anticipation of the flying definitely would've made it worse."

"Helicopter?" I could feel the longing in Milo's voice. "That's... I mean, come on, that's pretty cool. The views must be incredible!"

"I wouldn't know, I've got my eyes closed. But you can ask Catriona all about it," I told him.

"Oh, right," Milo said sheepishly.

"So, you're on your way, then," Hannah said firmly, as though forcing herself to accept the fact. "We were watching from the window. I can't believe Seamus let you go without a Caomhnóir."

"Yup. He wasn't happy about it, but Catriona prevailed in the end, like she usually does."

"You didn't run into any other problems?" Milo asked. "No other awkward questions? No one suspicious about what was going on?"

"Nope, not yet at least," I told them. "We've only seen Elin and the pilot since we left, and Elin's in on it. The real test will be when we arrive at the *príosún*, I guess. If anyone is going to get suspicious, it will be the Caomhnóir there."

"So, you and Catriona had a chance to talk a little bit more?" Hannah asked. "Do you... do you know what you're going to do, once you get in there?"

"Yes and no," I said truthfully. "Obviously, we don't know the state of things inside, so we're going to have to wait and see. But it's going to be really, really important for Catriona to have access to you guys while I'm inside. The connection is the only way I'm going to be able to communicate with her, and the only way she's going to be able to give me instructions."

"No problem," Hannah said at once. "We'll make sure she always knows where we are. And obviously, we won't be leaving the castle until you're back here, safe and sound."

"You don't have to stay under house arrest or anything," I said. "Just make sure Catriona can get in touch with you, that's all."

"Of course," Hannah said.

"Look, I know you want to figure this out, but don't think you have to turn into some kind of action hero, okay?" Milo said, and although he was attempting to keep his voice light and sardonic, I could feel the current of fear that was humming beneath it. "You don't have to do everything that Catriona tells you to do. She's a lot... I mean, she's been a Tracker a lot longer than you, and she's got skills that you don't have. Just... don't put yourself in harm's way just because she tells you to, okay? Be smart about it. None of this risk will be worth it if you don't come out of there alive."

Hannah made a sound like a strangled sob, and Milo sighed contritely. "Look, I'm sorry if that was a little too much realness, but somebody had to say it. We're not doing Jess or ourselves any favors by pretending this whole plan isn't stupidly dangerous. So, in the interest of getting her back here safely, I think she should go by the rule of Finn."

Finn's name sent a jolt of messy emotions coursing through me, which I knew the others would feel. "What's the rule of Finn?" I asked him quickly, in a totally transparent attempt to mask my vulnerability.

"Just ask yourself, would Finn think this was a good idea? If he would, then go for it. If he wouldn't, then find another way to do what you need to do," Milo explained.

I nearly laughed out loud, but managed to stifle the sound. "If I went by the rule of Finn I wouldn't even be on this helicopter right now," I reminded him. "I'm pretty sure Finn would rather burn the *príosún* to the ground than let me set so much as a foot inside it."

"I know," Milo said. "But Finn hasn't seen what you've seen. If he knew what was in that prophecy, he might change his mind."

"No, he wouldn't," Hannah and I said together.

Milo sighed impatiently. "Whatever. My point is that Finn always makes the choice that keeps you safest. So just... ask yourself, WWFD—what would Finn do, and then do that, okay?

"Fine," I said. "I promise to abide by the rule of Finn, but you have to make me a promise in return, Milo."

"What's that?" Milo asked.

"Don't ever tell Finn about the rule of Finn, okay?"

It was Milo's turn to laugh. "Yeah, okay. I see your point. That would undoubtedly go straight to his head."

"Exactly. So, speaking of what's going to happen when I get in there, remember that I'll have to shut you both out for a bit right when I arrive, just so I can focus on what's going on. But once I get settled in my..." I stopped myself, not wanting to think the word "cell," "... wherever it is that I'm staying, then I'll reach out again when I'm alone, when it's safe. Then we'll go from there."

Hannah was having trouble keeping her panic under control again. "Okay," she said, bravely nonetheless. "Yeah, just... just let us know when you're in."

"It'll be a piece of cake," Milo said with an almost defiant surety. "Catriona books prisoners in and out of the *príosún* all the time. She knows exactly what to do. Just keep your head down."

"I will," I said. "And you two take care of each other, and try to stay out of trouble while I'm gone."

They didn't laugh at my feeble attempt at humor. I couldn't say I blamed them.

"Try to get some sleep, Hannah, okay?" I told her. "Milo, make sure she at least lies down."

"Cross my heart," Milo said solemnly.

"I have about as much chance of falling asleep tonight as you have of taking a nap on that helicopter," Hannah said acidly.

"I don't know what you're talking about," I said. "I'm about ready to doze off right now. So relaxing, this whole hovering thousands of feet above the earth, one brisk gust of wind away from plunging to our deaths. Gotta go, my eyes are closing."

"Remember!" Milo reminded me one last time. "The rule of Finn!"

"I promise," I said. "I'll talk to you both later. Don't forget to keep up the charade about my arrest at Fairhaven. Make a big stink about it. Make sure everyone knows what happened—it will provide us with better cover and keep the Caomhnóir from getting suspicious. I will now return to my regularly scheduled panic attack."

And with that, I closed the connection again, feeling their absence expanding inside my head once more, making room again for all the fear to filter back in. With a gasp and a lurch, I felt the helicopter take off, leaving the last of my courage on the ground far below us.

15

SOLITARY

A FEW MINUTES LATER, or maybe several hours, or maybe an entire lifetime, Catriona put her hand on my shoulder and shook it gently. When I didn't open my eyes, or acknowledge her in any way, she lifted one side of my headphones and said into my ear, "Look, I know heights really aren't your cup of tea, but you're going to regret it for the rest of your life if you don't take in this view that we're about to fly over."

To my very great surprise, a surge of curiosity triumphed over my fear, and I pried one eyelid partially open, taking in, for the first time, the view through the front of the helicopter. As I registered the magnificence of the sight, both eyes sprang wide open, and I strained forward against my harness, my whole body aching to get closer to the expansive beauty that stretched out before us.

The sun was rising over the jagged, rocky cliffs of the Isle of Skye. And the island was waking up, inch by newly sunlit inch, revealing something out of a Celtic dream. Far below us, a rough and white-crested sea was aglow with flecks of gold and rose and diamond. The waves flung themselves against the base of the towering rocky cliffs, as though they longed, too, to take flight, desperate to splash upward for a glimpse of that same view that I had now. The cliff tops were capped in the purest, deepest of greens I had ever seen, blanketing the rugged, mountainous landscape. There was not a single man-made structure as far as the eye could see. Only an untarnished, unfettered landscape, regal in its solitude, wearing its remoteness like a wild, thorny crown. The victor in a great battle against the encroachment of the outside world, it commanded its place by the sea with the pride of a monarch.

I could barely breathe as something ancient and ineffable and akin to magic shivered through me like a discovery. The enchantment of it settled over me, sunk right down into my bones, and seeped into the rushing current of my blood. I had felt this once before—this connection to something deep within my past—an almost mystic connection to the generations of women of the Clan Sassanaigh that had come before me, and with it, a deep and abiding knowledge that here was a place where my roots had taken hold.

Beside me, Catriona was watching me carefully. "There now," she said quietly. "Whatever happens next, that was worth it, wasn't it?"

"Yes," I breathed.

The helicopter continued to follow the shoreline, and as it rounded the great crest of the highest point of the cliff, I gasped involuntarily yet again. The *príosún* came into view at last, perched upon a lethal-looking outcropping, surrounded on three sides by violently thrashing waves, and the sheer, unscalable cliff face. Weeks of regular premonitions had prepared me for what it would look like, and yet the sight of it in reality still snatched the air straight out of my lungs and replaced it with a strange feeling of déjà vu that was the fulfillment of a dream... or, more specifically, a nightmare.

The walls of the *príosún* were high and rounded, worn to an unnatural smoothness by age and the erosive power of wind and salty spray. Set impossibly high up in their face were thin slits of windows that could scarcely be expected to let in much light but from which weapons could surely be launched with maximum cover. The crenellated ramparts were topped with fluttering flags: deep purple triskeles on fields of purest white. The sight of that symbol ought to have left me feeling fortified, even proud, but in that moment, it only filled me with dread. For I was one of the few who knew now that the flying of that flag over that fortress was mere artifice, and that the inner workings within the walls beneath it were threatening to supplant those flags even as they stood proudly flapping in the cold, salty dawn.

I threw a nervous glance at Catriona, but she was either purposely avoiding looking at me, or too distracted by the long-awaited sight of the *príosún* to notice my attempts to get her attention. Her eyes seemed fixed, like mine, on those flags, and wondering whether the people in the fortress below them would still defend them as they had once sworn to do.

The helicopter took a wide, arcing turn as it made its approach to the field that had been marked out for its landing. The pilot was saying something about the wind speed and its direction in relation to the shoreline, but I was no longer listening. My stomach had given a nasty, nervous lurch as we buffeted against the breeze, and I had shut my eyes again in a vain attempt to pretend that it wasn't happening. I didn't open them again, or even take a breath, until Catriona shook my shoulder to let me know that we had landed at last. The pilot killed the engine, and the deafening roars died away.

Despite the knowledge that we were finally on the ground, my body still felt frozen against the back of my seat, my fingers clenched tight, and my legs locked in place. My ankles felt numb where Catriona had fastened them into the restraints, and they were slow to regain sensation as she released them at last. It was only with both Catriona's and Elin's help that I was able to coax my joints into moving and successfully exit the helicopter. Once I found myself standing in the grass, my limbs, which had felt like they were made of steel only moments before, suddenly seemed to be composed of Jell-O. I barely managed to stop myself from sinking to my knees before Elin and Catriona took hold of both of my arms and marched me forward. I leaned my weight gratefully into the two of them and let them guide me toward the imposing façade of the *príosún*.

I could not shake the feeling, as we approached the great hulking front doors, that I was being led to a medieval gallows, or perhaps the stocks, where instead of taking a goofy tourist photo, I would actually be pelted with stones for some outdated crime, like gossiping in the street, or exposing an ankle to the general view.

As we moved into the deep shadow that the *príosún* cast like a dark, forbidding net over the ground before it, a deafening creaking and grinding sound began to reverberate in the air around us. It sounded like mountains moving, or the very cliffs under our feet shifting against each other, but a few moments later I saw that the massive front doors were being lowered open on chains, like a drawbridge with no moat.

"You've got to be kidding me," I muttered weakly. Entering your standard, modern-day prison would have been frightening enough, but *this?* I found myself half-wishing to dive back into the helicopter.

The ancient timbers protested loudly, and the links of the great chains now visible on either side groaned and shrieked with each turn of the great wooden wheels on the far side of the walls.

Catriona placed a hand upon my shoulder, an unspoken order to stop and wait until the doors had at last reached the ground. I assumed we were waiting for some kind of signal to be allowed to enter the building—a trumpet fanfare, or a processional drumbeat, or something equally old-timey—but Catriona and Elin seemed to be waiting for nothing of the kind. We had not seen a single person in our approach to the *príosún*, and still not a single Caomhnóir was visible from where we stood, and yet Elin and Catriona seemed sure that we now had permission to enter the *príosún* by virtue of the lowered doors. They marched confidently forward, taking care to help me as I stepped up onto the battered and time-worn timbers, and began to walk across them and over the threshold into the inner sanctum of the *príosún*.

It wasn't until we had cleared the massive stone archway that the first signs of life began to emerge within the castle. To my right and left, four hulking Caomhnóir were grunting and straining as they shoved and pulled at the great crank that was now raising the front doors back up into their original and closed position.

I had assumed that the outer wall of the *príosún* was simply the outer wall of the building itself, and that once we were inside, we would be under its roof. But I was wrong. We stepped into a courtyard that held a second tower within the first, like a nesting doll of medieval architecture. What had appeared to be a great deserted barrier was swarming on the inside with all manner of protection, like a rock on the ground that had been turned over to reveal teeming hordes of life beneath. Caomhnóir were patrolling the top walls, stationed at the narrow windows, engaging in training exercises, and marching in formation all over the interior courtyard. The sight was alarming to me, because it looked very much like an army preparing for battle. But when I turned to Catriona to gauge her response, again her face was completely impassive. It seemed that the sight before us was exactly what she expected to see when she walked through the doors of the Skye Príosún, and she betrayed not a hint to the contrary. My overwrought brain was still trying to process all of this when four more Caomhnóir began marching toward us, all of them armed, one with a clipboard in his hand.

I looked at this Caomhnóir holding the clipboard with something akin to shock. It was jarring to see a man so far removed from my admittedly limited experience with what a Caomhnóir was supposed to be. This man had to be close to seventy years old, and though his figure gave the suggestion of faded strength and proud bearing, it was strange nonetheless to see a Caomhnóir look so old and stooped and battered. One side of his face was badly scarred, as though it had been exposed to something corrosive, like acid. He wore a brown leather patch tied over one eye, and his visible eye was a piercing, ice cold blue. His hair, or what was left of it, was white and had been shorn close to his scalp. He walked with a distinct limp, but rather than making him seem weak or compromised, this imperfection of his gait gave the impression of a wounded beast, all the fiercer and more dangerous because of the injury he had sustained. He limped to a halt in front of us, and the accompanying Caomhnóir quickly fell into formation behind him. He barely spared a cursory glance for me, before turning an expectant gaze upon Catriona.

"Good morning, Catriona," he said, with the barest inclination of his head.

"Eamon," Catriona replied, exquisitely careful to give no more deference to him then he had given to her.

"You've arrived awfully early," Eamon said, pulling a battered gold pocket watch from a pouch on his hip and checking the time carefully before recording it upon the clipboard in his hand.

"You have no objection, I hope?" Catriona said dryly.

"Not at all," Eamon countered. He gave a vague gesture over his shoulder at the flurry of Caomhnóir activity behind him. "There is no hour of the day or night that you would find us unprepared for your arrival. Surely you know that by now."

"Of course," Catriona agreed.

"I mention the time only to acknowledge the length of your journey," Eamon said. "Undoubtedly, you have been flying a good part of the night."

"Yes," Catriona said. "But certain matters of a more... um... *delicate* nature are best handled when the vast majority of prying eyes and flapping tongues are well asleep, wouldn't you say?"

The craggy folds of the man's face lifted slightly on one side in the suggestion of a smirk. "Oh, indeed. There can be no doubt about that. I appreciate the forewarning, nevertheless. Is everything in order?"

"Naturally," Catriona said. She nodded at Elin, who produced a wax-sealed envelope of paperwork from an inner pocket of her jacket and held it out for Eamon to take. He barely glanced at it, but instead handed it straight back over his shoulder for the Caomhnóir behind him to open and examine. After a few moments of scanning the documents, the second Caomhnóir nodded briskly, and Eamon made a small check upon his clipboard.

"Very well, then," he said, tucking the clipboard under his arm. "The cell has been prepared to your specifications, and all Castings have been completed."

"You'll understand, of course, if I double-check all of that?" Catriona said with a somewhat condescending half-smile. "Just procedure, as you know."

Eamon's mouth might've been returning Catriona's smile, but his eyes were full of frosty indignation. "Oh yes," he said. "Procedure. Trackers' privilege. We are well used to it by now." With a sharp flicking motion of his finger over his shoulder, Eamon summoned one of the other Caomhnóir forward. "Please escort the Trackers and the prisoner to the appropriate block. See that everything has been done to their satisfaction. I must say," Eamon added, looking at me for the first time with nothing short of contempt, "I'm rather surprised that the Travelers did not wish to deal with this one themselves. It is rare for them to outsource their means of justice, is it not?"

"It is," Catriona agreed. "But the High Priestess claimed jurisdiction, at least for the present." She leaned forward just a bit, conspiratorially. "You know how crude their infrastructure is," she said scathingly. "Nothing at all like the sophisticated system we have here. Why, their leadership can barely keep their own Caomhnóir in line, and as to their Trackers…" Catriona used only a roll of her eyes to complete the sentence, but Eamon clearly got the point. "You run a much tighter ship here, Eamon," she added, and put two fingers gently to the side of her forehead, in the suggestion of a respectful salute. "We know she'll be in good hands here."

"Yes, indeed," he said, looking a touch surprised, but gratified by the implied compliment. "We will ensure that proper procedure is followed down to the very last letter."

To our left, a peal of raucous laughter had broken out amongst some of the Caomhnóir who were sparring. They started to shove each other back-and-forth like undisciplined schoolboys. One of the elder Caomhnóir, who had been overseeing the exercise, stepped forward and brought his staff down across the shoulders of one of the men with a sharp, resounding crack. The man dropped to one knee, swearing, while the other leapt to attention, eager to avoid the same punishment.

Eamon, whose eyes had also been drawn to the scuffle, turned back to us with a satisfied expression. "You see? It is as you say. We've no tolerance for stepping out of line here."

This entire exchange occurred on the periphery of my attention. I used the distraction of the fight to search the entirety of the inner courtyard, scanning face after face, desperate to find the one familiar one. But I did not see Finn anywhere. My nerves, already frayed at the edges, began to feel like live wires. We were coming closer and closer to the moment that Catriona would turn around and walk out of this place, leaving me completely alone. And I was starting to think I might not be able to stop myself from screaming after her to please not leave me behind. My fear was sharpening, and it tasted like acid on my tongue.

Eamon swept aside and gestured for us to follow two of the Caomhnóir who had been standing behind him. Catriona thanked him and pulled me along, perhaps a bit more forcefully than she needed to, but I knew it was all for show.

Not wanting to draw any more attention to myself, I dropped my head and concentrated on my feet, trying to put myself into Tracker mode. Now was not the moment to give in to my terror. Now was the moment to focus on why I was here, and what I needed to do. I began casting covert looks around to try to get my bearings in these new surroundings. I tried to memorize as many details as I could; the placement of the doors, the number of staircases, the arrangement of the Caomhnóir who were stationed on patrol. All of this information could be useful to me once I began Walking within the confines of the *príosún*. One thing was certain at once from my observations: there were far more Caomhnóir here than there were within the walls of Fairhaven. The place was absolutely swarming with them, like an oversized ant farm. It was much clearer now why Catriona had been convinced that only a Walker could traverse the place unseen. My teeth began to chatter with the tension, and beside me, without looking at me, Catriona gave my arm a gentle squeeze of encouragement. It was all she could do to reassure me in the present company. It was a small thing, but I was grateful for it just the same.

Just as we reached the interior wall and the second set of doors, these ones much smaller and less imposing, a line of Caomhnóir trooped out into the courtyard, each carrying a long length of rope and a grappling hook. The last of them looked up as he passed me and his eyes popped with shock.

My breath caught in my throat. It was Finn.

He looked thinner than when I had last seen him, the muscles beneath his skin more pronounced, and his eyes rather sunken. His hair was tied back in a braid, and his face was covered in a shadow of stubble and dust. He broke formation with his fellow Caomhnóir, staring wildly first at me, and then at Catriona, who had also spotted him.

Whether she interpreted his desperate expression as I had, I could not tell, but she had certainly recognized him, and she knew something was wrong. She locked eyes with him and jerked her head sharply over her shoulder, as though silently ordering him to resume his marching. He looked once more at me, his eyes blazing with questions that I could not answer. I gave him a tiny wink and a ghost of a smile, hoping that this would somehow signal to him that everything was okay. He took a single step toward me, opening his mouth to speak, but Catriona yanked on my arm, pulling me away from him and steering me forcefully toward the inner doors. I did not dare look over my shoulder for fear of drawing the attention of the surrounding Caomhnóir.

Feeling lightheaded and shaken from my brief encounter with Finn, I followed the two younger Caomhnóir into the inner tower. Neither of them had a single glance or word to waste upon us, it seemed, which was lucky, because neither of them seemed to have taken the slightest notice of the silent exchange with Finn. Catriona and Elin, too, were behaving as though nothing had happened, and followed in equal silence. Every impulse I had was screaming at me to run back to Finn; only fear kept me shuffling forward with my captors.

We entered the interior tower, and I was unable to stifle a gasp. The front of this inner sanctum followed the curve of the outer wall, and stood six towering stories high. Staircases zigzagged the walls connecting six floors worth of galleries lined with iron railings. Each gallery walkway provided access to dozens of doors, each of them of heavy iron, and studded with ancient and rusty hardware, each with a tiny, barred window set high in its face. At the base of each door was a guillotine-looking contraption, which

I could only assume was meant to be lifted to allow for trays of food and other necessities to be passed into the prisoners. And of course, carved into the stones surrounding each door, and branded into the metal itself were a set of permanent and binding Castings, meant to subdue and ensure the incarceration of each inhabitant. Corridors branched off at each end of every floor, leading to other wings of the fortress, other chambers and facilities that could not be seen from where we stood. A broad stone staircase descended through the floor at either side of the ground floor cellblock, which could only mean that more chambers existed beneath the ground on which we stood. The scale and bleakness of it all made me feel momentarily faint. How was I going to navigate a hellscape like this? My hands, clasped together, were now clammy and slippery with cold sweat.

To my slight relief, the Caomhnóir did not descend into the underground bowels of the castle, but turned to the left and began climbing the nearest staircase. We followed, climbing three sets of stairs, until we had reached the fourth floor cellblock. I could hear and see nothing that gave any sort of indication about who might be in any of the other cells on the floor, but based upon what Catriona had already told me, it was certain that they were all living people, and not spirits who had been incarcerated. It was also certain that none of them were Necromancers. She had assured me that prisoners such as those were kept in much more high-security areas of the *príosún*. Both of these pieces of information did little to calm me as we stopped five doors along, and waited for the Caomhnóir to work their way through the several locks on the outside of the door.

"Thank you, gentlemen," Catriona said to the two Caomhnóir. "I'm glad to take it from here. If you would be so kind, Tracker Ford here has paperwork that needs signatures from a second prisoner."

The taller of the Caomhnóir frowned. "A second prisoner? Eamon said nothing about a second prisoner."

"Well that's why I'm informing you now, isn't it?" Catriona said coolly. "Elin, the paperwork?"

Elin produced a packet of papers and handed them to the taller Caomhnóir, who looked them over quickly, and then nodded, evidently satisfied. "That's cell block six," he said, handing the papers back to Elin. "Follow me please." Then he turned to Catriona and grunted, "We'll be right back to lock up."

"I'll be waiting with bated breath," Catriona replied dryly. Then she watched for a few moments until Elin and the two Caomhnóir began to ascend the next staircase.

"Who is the second prisoner?" I asked her shakily when they had gone.

"Don't worry about that," Catriona said. "We just needed to make sure that you and I had a few moments alone." She pulled the cell door open.

I'm not sure what I had been expecting. A pile of straw on the ground upon which to curl up and sleep? Manacles hammered into the wall? A metal bowl of food scraps, the kind of thing you might feed to a dog? Whatever nightmare I had conjured for myself, the inside of the cell came as a welcome surprise. It was clean and dry inside, with a small metal bed frame, a desk and chair built into the wall, two small bare shelves, where I might've put some personal belongings, had I brought any with me, and a small window covered with a metal grate that looked out over the outer courtyard. A pile of linens, towels, and clothing that looked not unlike a beige set of hospital scrubs sat folded neatly on the end of the mattress. A metal toilet gleamed in the corner, alongside a sink, a stool, and a silver cup containing a toothbrush.

"Home sweet home... for a few days, anyway," Catriona said as she produced a key from the pocket of her jeans and swiftly released my wrists from the handcuffs.

"Thank you," I murmured gratefully, rubbing at the places where the metal had begun to chafe.

"You'll need to put those on," Catriona said, pointing to the clothes on the end of my bed. She stepped over to the door and pulled it nearly shut. "First things first, however," she said. "While you're doing that, I've got one important detail to take care of." She walked slowly around the room, taking in every rune and every Casting. At last, she came to a stop at a set of runes near the window. "Here we are," she murmured under her breath, and pulled a Casting bag from her back pocket. By the time I had slipped out of my clothes and tightened the drawstrings on my overly large cotton pants, Catriona had made the necessary adjustments to the Casting.

"There you are," she said with a grim smile. "You're free to shift that mortal coil whenever you need to."

"You're absolutely sure?" I asked as I emerged from the head hole of my drab new uniform.

"Dead sure," Catriona said. "As long as you don't lose those soul catchers, everything is ready for you."

I reached up under my hair and felt each of the braided sections with my fingers, taking stock and counting each of them again, as though they somehow could have magically disappeared from my head during the flight. "All set," I said meaning to reassure her, but reassuring myself at the same time. "Fifteen soul catchers, ready to be yanked from my scalp as needed."

"Excellent," Catriona said. She reached out her hand. "Give me the clothing. And any jewelry, too. There are socks and shoes for you tucked under the bed there."

I pulled out my earrings and all the rest of my jewelry. I hesitated, though, upon placing my locket into the bag.

"I can't let anything happen to this," I told her quietly. "It's... Fiona painted it... my mother's portrait..."

Catriona's face tightened, and she reached out a hand. "I'll hold onto it for you," she said stiffly. "Get it back to your sister, for safekeeping."

"Thank you," I said gratefully, and dropped it into her hand. She tucked it into her own pocket, and then pulled the drawstring on the plastic bag, sealing the rest of my possessions inside it. "Theoretically, you get all this back when I come to pick you up."

I nodded, trying to look unconcerned. The mention of her coming back to get me meant that she was, in fact, leaving me here, which of course I knew, but now that we were facing the moment itself, I wasn't sure I'd be able to keep my panic under control.

Catriona stepped forward. "Test that connection for a moment," she whispered. "Just to be sure."

I took a deep breath, and tugged slightly at the barrier within my own thoughts, teasing it open just a bit, so that I could feel some of Hannah and Milo's energy seep through.

"It's open," I told her with relief. "I can feel them."

Catriona gave one sharp nod of satisfaction. She fixed me with a very piercing look and murmured to me, "You can do this."

I couldn't answer her. I was too busy suppressing some kind of hysterical noise that was trying to escape me, something that was part scream, and part sob, and part maniacal laughter.

The sound of boots outside in the hallway descending the nearby staircase caused the two of us to jump apart. Catriona raised her voice, and began speaking to me as though we were already halfway through a heated conversation.

"It's not my bloody job to schedule hearings at the convenience of the accused," Catriona spat at me, just as the two Caomhnóir and Elin arrived back at the door of the cell. "It will be scheduled at the convenience and pleasure of the Traveler leadership, and not a moment before. If you're unhappy with these consequences, then you might next time consider not trifling with their laws."

I was not capable, while drowning in my current swamp of emotions, of manufacturing a retort. I simply shook my head, trying to look disgusted, and sank down upon the edge of the bed, dropping my head and looking down at my feet. Luckily, this response seemed adequate.

Catriona gave a convincingly exasperated sigh, and tossed the plastic bag with all of my clothes into the arms of the nearest Caomhnóir, who caught it deftly. "She's all yours, gentlemen," she said sardonically. "I don't think she'll give you too much trouble. She makes a show of being feisty, but there's not much fight in her. I expect she'll be out of here in a week or two. The Traveler Council wants this dealt with quickly."

"Very good," the taller of the Caomhnóir said. "Have you any other business to attend to while you're here? Will you be visiting your cousin?"

Catriona bristled at the mention of Lucida, as though the question were some kind of veiled insult. "No, I don't think I'll subject myself to that on this particular trip. Perhaps next time, when I'm feeling just a tad more masochistic. But by all means, pass along my well wishes to my darling traitor of a cousin. Give her a kiss for me."

The Caomhnóir looked at each other in slight confusion, and seemed to be silently asking each other whether that was a direct order, or sarcasm. Catriona did not bother to help them figure out which one it was.

"We'll be in touch with the hearing date," she said, tossing the comment over her shoulder at me casually, barely meeting my eye. "Until then, try to stay out of trouble, won't you?"

I did not reply, keeping my eyes fixed on my feet, feeling my heart thunder in my chest as I listened to her steps exit the cell along with the others. At the very last moment my head shot up. I was just in time to watch her disappear on the other side of the door. I caught her eye, and she gave me the shadow of a wink. It was all she could do in the moment, but I knew it was her way of wishing me good luck. And one thing was for sure, I thought, as I stared around the cell: I was going to need all the luck I could get.

16

WALKING

I T WAS HARD TO SAY what the worst part of that first day in the *príosún* was. It might've been the isolation. From the moment Catriona's face disappeared on the other side of the door until the time that the sun went down, I heard only ten words spoken to me. "Step away from your door!" was twice barked at me by a Caomhnóir whom I could not see, who then proceeded to shove a tray of food through the slot at the bottom of my door. It was possible the food itself was as bad, but I honestly couldn't say. I took barely three bites of the cold pile of mashed potatoes and gravy only when I started to feel a bit faint, but my mouth felt numb, and I tasted nothing.

It might have been the disorienting sense that I had absolutely no idea how much time had gone by. I had left my phone behind at Fairhaven, not that the guards would've let me keep it anyway. I had no watch, and could see no clock. My only points of reference were the shadows in the outer courtyard, which I could see from between the bars of my window. I watched them shorten until they all but disappeared around midday. It might've helped to watch them lengthen as well, but a deep gray bank of clouds rolled in from over the water, and all the shadows, and therefore all concept of time, faded away. At some point, when the darkness of clouds had turned to the darkness of evening, a deep voice shouted down the hallway, "Lights out!" And the single, flickering overhead light in my cell went out, along with what I could only assume was every other light on the cellblock, with the exception of a few bare bulbs that illuminated the corridor for the Caomhnóir who would be patrolling it on the night shift.

Then again, it may have been the noise. I'm not sure why I expected the *príosún* would be silent. Perhaps, because I was desperately trying to take in as many details of my surroundings as I could, I half-expected other prisoners to be doing the same. But instead, I was met with a constant and grating soundtrack of utter misery. All around me, close by and distant, from above and below me, was an endless symphony of sniffing, sobbing, shrieking, and moaning. I soon learned that the approach of the Caomhnóir making his rounds was accompanied by an upswing in volume and frequency of the sounds. All along my cellblock, I could hear voices pleading to be released, offering to trade favors, or else begging for sympathy. Others chose these moments to show their disdain and disgust for their captors by hurling insults and curses at the passing guards, banging on the doors, and chucking food trays against the walls, or else spitting through the tiny windows.

Throughout it all, I felt as though every cell in my body was tensed for some sign, some signal, that Finn was nearby. I knew that our encounter in the courtyard had shaken him even more badly than it had shaken me. And I knew, too, that he would find a way to get to me, even if it was only for a moment, and even just for a look, even if we could not exchange a single word. But I knew nothing about how this place worked. I did not know if he was free to come and go through the different parts of the *príosún*. I did not know if he would be allowed into the cellblock where I was being held, or at what time he might be able to slip away. Each time I heard a pair of boots in the hallway, I flew to the door. I watched figure after figure pass through the small sliver of the courtyard that I could view through my window, searching desperately for that familiar gait, the long hair, the proud bearing. But, he was nowhere to be seen, and the absence of him felt deeper, more gnawing than ever before, knowing that he must be very close by. I had not been so near to him since the wedding, and the thought that any moment might bring him into view made me feel like a walking bundle of exposed wiring. More than almost anything, the moment I could not stop reliving was the look upon his face. Such shock, such horror. And such agonizing worry. If absolutely nothing else, I needed to be able to tell him that I was okay, that I was not really in trouble, and that I was only here to help him. And even though I knew that he'd be angry that I had put myself in harm's way, at least he would be able to stop torturing himself over hypotheticals. But the hours ticked by, and there was not a trace of him.

We had all agreed that it would be best to keep the connection between Hannah and Milo and myself closed unless I really needed it. Catriona did not think that there would be any way for the Caomhnóir to discover and therefore stifle the connection, but it seemed best not to leave it open just in case. Once in a while, though, I could not resist opening that mental door just a crack, just to let some familiarity seep its way in. In these moments, I could feel Hannah and Milo reach through with unspoken questions, like tangled tentacles made of question marks. Each time, I simply sent a message back through to them. *Everything's fine. Just wanted to know that you were there.* Once it was nighttime, and it was truly safe to talk, I would pull the door wide, and filled them in on all of the details. But not yet.

As the hours ticked by, one of my fears was slowly dissipating. From the moment we had first formulated this plan, I had harbored a fear that the Caomhnóir would somehow know, somehow discover, that the charges against me and my subsequent arrest were all just a ruse, an act designed to get me inside the *príosún* walls. Even as we walked in, and my paperwork had been processed, and all had seemed to go as Catriona expected that it would, that creeping fear had continued, that perhaps the Caomhnóir were just playing along until Catriona had left. But as the hours passed, it became clear that I was being treated no differently than the rest of the prisoners in my cellblock. Indeed, the Caomhnóir seemed to be doing their best to ignore me as thoroughly as they were everyone else. This felt like a good sign. The longer I was treated like a normal prisoner, the more convinced I became that the Caomhnóir believed I really was one.

I waited for what was, in my best estimation, several hours after the lights in the cellblock went out. Over that time, the sounds around me lessened and quieted, until I was surrounded by a silence that was only occasionally punctuated by a moan or a cry. Somewhere very far off in the distance, on one of the floors below me, a woman was singing, though I could only catch snatches of the tune, and none of the words. The Caomhnóir who patrolled our cellblock seemed to do so with less frequency, and so I believed that perhaps the night shift had begun. It was, it seemed, as settled as a place like this was likely to become. Just as a sliver of moonlight worked its way down through the clouds, and across the wall of my cell, I opened the connection wide, and felt the warm embrace of familiar, welcoming energy.

"Oh, thank goodness," Hannah said, and her voice felt like the fiercest of hugs. "How are you holding up?"

"Honestly, I am more bored than anything else," I told her. "There's nothing to do, and no one to talk to. But I think, in this particular case, no news is very good news."

"I think you're right. Hang on," Milo said. "I'll be right back. I'm going to go get Catriona."

"What time is it?" I asked Hannah. "Apparently, no one uses clocks in prison."

"It's just after ten thirty," Hannah told me. "We've been waiting to hear from you for hours. I'm sure the waiting's been awful for you, but believe me, it was pretty terrible here, too. What's... what's it like?"

"Medieval. Isolating. Absolutely mind-numbingly dull," I told her honestly. "I can't imagine having to spend more than a few days here. I'm pretty sure I'd lose my grip on reality if I did. And a lot of people here have been here for years. That's probably why I keep hearing so much disjointed moaning and shouting."

"Did you... have you seen Finn?" Hannah asked, with the kind of hesitancy that suggested that she was afraid to know the answer to the question.

"Yes," I said, and braced myself mentally for her gasp of surprise. "I saw him almost right away, before we'd even come in from the courtyard. He was on his way out to do some kind of training exercise and he spotted me coming in with Catriona. But obviously, with the courtyard full of people, we haven't had a chance to speak yet."

Hannah groaned. "Oh, God. You know he's absolutely losing his mind right now."

"Yeah, I know," I said. "I've been trying not to think about that, actually. I'm sure he's trying to find a way to figure out where I am, and how to get to me. I just hope he doesn't get himself into trouble in the process."

"Oh, hang on," Hannah said, and I felt her pull away from me slightly before plunging back into the connection. "Okay, Catriona's here. I can relay everything that you're saying."

"Where are you right now?" I asked Hannah.

"In the Tracker office," Hannah said. "It seems like the most logical place to hang out and wait for you to get in touch with us. No one's going to be suspicious of Milo and me hanging around the Tracker office all day, not after your very public and very controversial arrest. We put out the story that we're here to figure out how to get you released."

"That was a good idea," I said. "How is everybody taking my dramatic exit?"

"As you would expect," Hannah said with a guilty sigh. "Karen is absolutely beside herself, even more so after we told her the real reason that you're at the *príosún*. When she promised to accept that being a Tracker was a dangerous job, I don't think she was anticipating anything like this. I'm pretty sure she's ready to go back on that promise right about now."

"Well, to be honest, I never anticipated anything like this either," I said. "She'll be okay, I'll talk to her when I... when I get back." My casual tone fooled neither of us.

"I promised her that I would update her every time I spoke to you," Hannah said. "She's been stalking me ever since."

"What about Savvy?" I asked.

"She's... well, she's pissed, actually."

"Pissed? Why would she be pissed?" I asked in surprise. "I mean, okay, yeah, it sucks a little bit that we didn't warn her ahead of time, but it was only so we wouldn't blow our cover. She's got to understand that, right?"

"Yeah, she understands that part, but that's not what she's pissed about," Hannah explained. "She's... well, she hasn't really articulated it, but it feels like she's angry that you didn't ask her to come along."

"Come along? This isn't a goddamn field trip! I don't want to put her in danger. Why the hell would I have asked her to come along?"

"That's just the thing," Hannah said. "I think she does want to put herself in danger. I think she's desperate to do something—anything, really—to avenge what happened to Bertie. I don't think it's going to be enough for her to sit around and wait for the feelings of grief to subside. I don't know, Jess. The hair, and now losing the access to her Gateway... she's not dealing with this very well. I'm afraid she's going to do something reckless."

I didn't know what to do with this new, unsettling piece of information. I had to put it aside for now, however. It was entirely too much to negotiate, and too much to think about without worrying about Savvy, too. I just had to trust that she would be okay until I got back.

Hannah interrupted my thoughts. "Okay, Catriona wants to know what you've noticed so far. Anything unusual?"

"Well, yeah, I mean, everything's unusual," I said impatiently. "This is my first time in the slammer, remember?"

"She says to curtail the attitude, and just tell her what you found out so far," Hannah said in a small, apologetic voice.

I sighed. "Okay, well, nothing too alarming, as far as I can tell. I don't have a watch, but the guards seem to be coming by at regular intervals. They've been practicing the same kinds of drills out in the courtyard that Catriona saw when we got here. I'm assuming those are routine, regardless of anything weird or underground or political that might be going on. All of the prisoners seem to be remaining prisoners, the meals are coming at regular times, and the guards seem to be completely ignoring my existence. Does that all seem like business as usual?"

"Yes," Hannah relayed to me. "Catriona says that all sounds as it should be. So, are you ready to go have a look around?"

"As ready as I'll ever be," I said, with more confidence than I felt. I knew it was useless trying to fake any kind of bravado for Hannah's sake. Every anxious feeling I had was playing across the threads of the connection like a bow on a fiddle. But I could at least make a show of bravery for Catriona.

"Here we go, then," Hannah said. "I'm just going to repeat all of Catriona's instructions verbatim from now on. Just pretend you're talking directly to her, okay?"

"Okay. So," I said. "Where am I going first?"

"I think the first crucial step," Hannah said, speaking for Catriona, "is to ensure that the Necromancers are still locked away as prisoners are supposed to be. It will give us a much better sense of how closely they and the Caomhnóir might be working together at this point. Remember, your drawing could have been showing us an eventuality that was a good long distance into the future. Understanding the role of the Necromancers at this point will give us an idea of just how far away that vision might be, or if we are dealing with an imminent danger."

"Okay, that makes sense," I said in a stoutly logical voice. "And then what?"

"If you don't notice anything strange going on with the Necromancers, then our next step is to spend some time following the Caomhnóir. See if you can determine who amongst them is shirking their responsibilities and slipping away when they're supposed to be on the clock, as Finn described. This will be a bit trickier, as there's no one specific place that I can send you to look for clues. You're just going to have to wander a bit, tail a few different Caomhnóir, and see if you can't smoke them out. I'll direct you to their barracks first, then maybe a few of the common areas."

The second, more nebulous part of the plan made me much more nervous. It left, in my opinion, far too much to chance and luck. Catriona could easily tell me the area of the *príosún* where the Necromancers were locked away, and it would be fairly straightforward to check that they were still in their cells. Simple enough. But the second objective? There seemed to be hundreds of Caomhnóir under this roof. Discovering which if any of them were bucking their usual duties, especially when I didn't know what those usual duties were, would be decidedly more difficult.

"Fine," I said, all the while wishing fervently that we had a more solid plan than just "float around and see what you find." From the jittery energy zipping around between Hannah, Milo, and me, I knew that I wasn't the only one.

"Why don't you move into your Walker state," Hannah told me, "and then Catriona can talk you through where to go once you leave the cell."

"Here goes everything," I muttered to myself, taking a deep breath to steel myself. "Hannah, do me a favor, okay?"

"Of course," Hannah said quickly. "Anything. What do you need?"

"Keep everyone quiet while I do this," I said. "It takes a lot of concentration. I can't have anyone else's feelings or thoughts running through my head while I'm attempting it, okay?"

"No problem," Hannah said. "Milo, did you get that?"

"I'll be quiet as a mouse in here," Milo said solemnly.

"Okay," I said again. "Here we go."

I pulled back from the connection—not closing it completely, but disengaging so that I could concentrate all my efforts on what I had to do. I crossed the cell and sat down on the edge of the metal-framed bed. I kicked off the odd, laceless shoes that were part of my uniform, and tucked them carefully under the bed. Then, I pulled back the scratchy wool blanket that comprised my only bedclothes, and slid myself underneath it, rolling my body toward the wall so that my face would not be visible to any Caomhnóir who were patrolling the hallway and might choose, for whatever reason, to peek into my cell. I curled myself into a ball, rested my cheek upon the thin, mildewed pillow, and reached around toward the nape of my neck, where my fingers found one of the braided soul catchers.

Squinting my eyes shut, and holding my breath, I took ahold of the braid tightly in my hand and gave it a sharp yank. I bit my tongue against the desire to cry out as I felt each hair part company with my scalp. I blinked rapidly to clear the tears from my streaming eyes and worked with fumbling fingers to tie the soul catcher around my wrist.

As I worked, I let my mind fall backward through my memories, landing gently upon the recollection of the first time I had ever Walked. I had had such doubts that I would be able to do it—sure that, if I left my body, I would never find my way back again. But Irina had looked into me and seen that I had the strength to do it.

"You are strong in soul," she had told me. "I can see it in the spaces behind your eyes, but you must choose. The choice is the hardest part."

It was true then, and it was true now. Even though I had Walked many times since Irina had spoken those words to me, I still feared the choice. But that was good, I argued to myself. Irina lost all fear of Walking, embraced her choice so fully that her body became akin to a torturous prison for her when she had to re-enter it. The fear kept me safe, I reasoned.

I closed my eyes and envisioned the two parts of myself, my body and my soul, my essence and the vessel that contained it. I focused on the ties that bound them together, imagined them as one with the fibers of the soul catcher now secured around my wrist. And then I whispered the Casting, being sure that I did so with both my lips and my heart, as Irina had directed me:

"*Sínim uaim thar dhoras mo choirp*
Ach an eochair coinním fós,
Bheith ag Siúl tráth i measc na marbh
Agus filleadh ansin athuair."[1]

Then I placed the soul catcher between my teeth and tore it

1. I reach beyond my body's door and yet retain the key, to Walk awhile amongst the dead and then return again.

apart between the third and fourth knots, where a bit of red thread peeked through the braided fibers.

The moment the hairs broke apart, my soul slipped its bonds as well. I hadn't Walked in a very long time, but the experience was like coming home. The weightlessness, the freedom, the utter lack of physical sensation. I felt buoyed up by the sheer purity of my own form and, for just a moment, I felt a thrill of the kind of joy that Irina must have felt when she Walked. Not because I now thought of my body as a prison, or because I never wanted to return to it, but because for the last twenty-four hours, my body had been a tense and tightly-knotted ball of stress and emotion and fear. And though I could still feel those emotions, I was deliciously free of the effects that they had had on my physical form. It was beyond relief; it was bliss. I enjoyed it for a brief moment, and then focused my energy on being able to take in the room around me.

I had been careful to keep the blanket pulled up to my chin when I was still inside my body, and I was glad to see as I glanced down at it that it seemed an absolute portrait of peaceful sleep. I did not think that anybody who passed by the cell would be able to tell that my soul had temporarily slipped its shell. If I'd still been in possession of lungs, I would've heaved a sigh of relief. Instead, my relief made me lighter, made my energy sparkle with a renewed lightness.

Relieved that I had managed to transition, I focused in now on the connection between Hannah and Milo and myself. Now that I was essentially made entirely of my own energy, finding the connection felt like plucking hundreds of strings upon a musical instrument to find the right note. After a few moments, however, fear began to creep in. No matter how many strings I plucked, no matter how many melodies I made, I could not seem to find the tune that would open the door between Hannah and Milo's thoughts, and my own.

Okay, I told myself. *Okay, don't panic. It probably works differently in this form. Maybe I don't have to open a door, or reach out to find them. Maybe, since I'm just pure thought and emotion and energy, they're already here with me and I just haven't noticed.* Praying that this was the case, I attempted to communicate.

"Is… is anyone there?" I released the thought and tried to feel where it might land, but it was like a puzzle piece without a matching hole.

"Hello?" I tried again. I felt my way out to the end of every single tentacle and tendril and wisp of my form, but I could find nothing but my own emotions singing back to me. Hannah and Milo were definitely not there.

I was seized with a terror so complete that it made me feel instantly like a ball of static, popping and zapping instead of floating free. I had to know if by Walking, I had somehow damaged the connection in some way. I turned back to face my body and focused upon it, trying to recall as precisely as possible the instructions that Irina had once given me. I had to visualize myself inside the space and that was how I moved to it. The moment that I pictured myself, wished myself to be connected again with the body that I had left down below me, I was there. The rejoining of my body and my soul was instantaneous and electric, and my body twitched and gasped with the force of it.

The moment that I was back inside my own head, I was bombarded by a chorus of frightened voices.

"Where did she go? Is it possible that... Oh, wait, no, she's here!" Hannah was saying.

"Oh, thank God! I thought... I mean, she was gone, right?" Milo cried.

"Jess! What happened? Where did you go?" Hannah demanded.

"The connection just completely severed. Not just as though the door was closed, but like there had never been any door at all!" Milo babbled hysterically.

"I know!" I told them. "Calm down, please. This is disorienting enough without the two of you flipping out in here!"

Hannah and Milo made fruitless attempts to calm themselves.

"It seems like the connection doesn't work when I'm in Walker form," I told them. "We've... we've never tried it before. It didn't occur to me that there would be any way—any form—that we couldn't communicate in."

"It doesn't make any sense," Milo said. "I mean, I'm already in spirit form. I don't have a body, and the connection always works for me."

"I don't understand it," Hannah chimed in. "We are all Bound together. There shouldn't be anything that can—"

She stopped mid-thought, and then I felt the truth hit her like the clanging of a gong. I put my hand to my forehead to stop the emotional ringing.

"It's our blood," Hannah said. "Our blood is where our gift lies. Our blood is what binds our Gateway together, and what binds us to each other."

The lightbulb went off over my own head as well. "Oh my God, you're right!" I told her. "When I'm separated from my body, that means I'm separated from my blood. And without the blood to bind us together, the connection doesn't work."

"Well that was... unexpected," Milo said. "And honestly, much more literal than I ever considered the whole 'blood' thing to be."

"No kidding," I agreed. "Then again, we are in completely uncharted territory here. I mean, has there ever been a Seer/ Walker/Muse who is bound through a Spirit Guide to the other half of her Gateway? My guess is probably not."

Milo snorted. "Our little Jess is such a unique little snowflake."

"Jokes aside," Hannah said, sounding frustrated, "what the hell do we do now? If you can't communicate with us when you're Walking, then how the hell is Catriona supposed to guide you through the *príosún*?"

"Yeah," I admitted. "This complicates an already complicated situation. Does Catriona have any insights?"

I felt Hannah pull out of the connection slightly to confer with Catriona. When she came back, I could practically feel her eyes rolling. "Catriona would like me to congratulate you on foiling her well-thought-out plan with your unnecessary complications."

"Tell her I'm sending her my deepest apologies and also a few well-chosen hand gestures," I snapped.

"So, what do we do now?" Milo asked.

"Well, it doesn't seem like we have any choice," I said resignedly. "I'm just going to have to go out there blind and see what I can find. Just ask Catriona for some general directions, and I'll try to do my best."

"General directions? Jess, you're not going out for a drive in an unknown area, you're sneaking through warded prison blocks crawling with enemies!" Hannah cried. "We've got to think of something else. Catriona telling you to turn right here and turn left there is just not going to cut it! We can't keep you safe like this, Jess, and if we can't keep you safe, then we need to abandon the plan and think of something else!"

"What kind of plan, Hannah?" I asked, my temper rising in my frustration. "You guys can't pull me out of here. Once I'm out, there's no way you're gonna be able to sneak me back in again. The Caomhnóir will get too suspicious! We're just going to have to—"

A sudden, sharp clanking sound made me jump, and I dropped the soul catcher onto the bed. I whipped around in alarm just in time to hear a familiar voice whisper my name.

"Jess! Jess, it's me!"

My heart leapt so high that I could scarcely breathe as I scrambled off the bed, dashed across the room, and dropped to a crouch by the tiny metal slot in the bottom of my door, which I could see now was propped open by a meager inch or two.

"Finn?" I asked, my voice so choked that I could barely get his name out.

"Yes, love. Yes, it's me. I'm here, I'm on my way to a shift change, so I don't have long," he replied, and though he was barely raising his voice above a whisper, I could hear the intensity of the emotion behind the words. I reached my fingers through the opening in the door and found his hands there waiting for me. He clutched at my fingers with a low cry and held them tightly, stroking the top of my hand with his thumb.

"What in blazes are you doing here?" he asked. "When I saw you in the courtyard, I very nearly lost control of myself. How in the world could they arrest you? What are the charges? I was only able to steal the briefest glance at your intake papers. I saw something about the Traveler Clans, but the clerk put the file away before I could get a good look at the details."

"Finn, calm down," I told him as soothingly as I could while my voice shook with tears. "I haven't really been arrested. There are no charges, not real ones anyway. Catriona manufactured them. She staged the entire arrest so that I would have a cover to get in here."

"Cover?" Finn repeated blankly. "I don't understand. A cover for what? Is this something to do with the Trackers?"

"Yes," I told him. "The Trackers are investigating what you told me last month, about what's happening with the Caomhnóir here."

"For Christ's sake, Jess!" Finn exclaimed, and his hands tightened around mine. "When I passed that information along to you, I didn't mean for you to come bursting into the place yourself! Damn it, it's too dangerous! All I meant for you to do was to pass my suspicions along to the Caomhnóir leadership. What in the world would possess you to come here?"

"I couldn't do what you asked me to do, Finn," I told him. "I couldn't just hand the information off to Seamus. Catriona and I both agreed that it was too dangerous. There's a very good chance that someone at Fairhaven is already aware of what's happening here, and we couldn't risk passing the information through the wrong person. We couldn't let them suspect that we knew what was going on."

"But that's just it, Jess," Finn replied. "I don't *know* what's going on. I still haven't managed to figure out—"

A sudden sound echoed from the cell across the hall. Finn froze, as did I. We spent a full minute in hushed anticipation to see if we had been discovered, but when no further sounds penetrated our self-imposed silence, we accepted that the sound was simply one of the prisoners talking in their sleep. Nevertheless, Finn was determined to be even quieter. He crouched so low to the doorway that he pressed his cheek to the stones of the floor. I lay flat on my stomach and did the same, so that only the width of the door separated his cheek from mine. He was poorly shaven, and his cheek looked more sunken than when last I'd seen him up close, but his eyes were bright and full of fire.

"You've got to get out of here," he repeated. "Please, Jess. Whatever this is, I can handle it, I can figure it out. There's no reason for you to—"

"Yes, there is," I told him. "There is a reason, Finn. It's not just what you told me, but since I saw you last, so much has happened that I... I don't even know where to begin. I don't know how much you know."

"How much I know about what?" Finn asked. "What's going on, Jess? What is it that I don't know about?"

My mind whirled. It was too much, too much to explain in this stolen moment that might be interrupted at any second.

"There's a Necromancer," I told him quickly. "His name is Charlie Wright."

"I know of him," Finn said, interrupting me. "They've got him locked up here."

"He's here? In the *priosún*?" My stomach turned over with fear. Why the hell hadn't I thought to ask about Charlie? Of course, he was here. This was where the Northern Clan housed all their most vile enemies. Where else would he be?

"Yes," Finn said. "I recognize the name. It's not every day we get a new Necromancer here—not anymore, anyway. It caused quite the flurry of excitement when they brought him."

I made a split-second decision not to get into the gory details of what had happened between Charlie Wright and myself. If I did that, I'd be lucky if I was able to stop Finn from charging off to the Necromancer cellblock right then and there, and murdering Charlie in his sleep. Not that I was against murdering Charlie on principle, but now was not the moment. No, I could save the whole story for when Finn and I were both safely out of the *príosún*. "I was part of the team of Trackers that brought him in," I told him, which wasn't technically a lie. "And before we did, he told me something that really disturbed me."

"And what was it?" Finn prompted me.

"He said something about our defenses. About how our defenses and allies had been breached, and that they would soon belong to the Necromancers."

"Your defenses and allies?" Finn asked.

"Those were the words he used," I said.

On the other side of the door, Finn shook his head in exasperation. "But that could mean any number of things. He's not necessarily referring to the *príosún*, or even the Caomhnóir. The Durupinen have centuries' worth of different kinds of defenses—Castings, fortresses, networks of hidden identities. How can you be sure this was what he meant?"

"I wasn't sure at the time," I told him. "But then... I had another vision."

Silence from the other side of the door met these words. I waited patiently for Finn to recover.

"A vision?" he repeated. "You mean... another prophetic drawing?"

"Yes," I admitted. "And I didn't only have it once. It has asserted itself over and over and over again. It shows no sign of changing, and no sign of relenting."

"What is it?" Finn asked. "What did you see in the vision?"

"The very same scene every time," I told him. "A view of this *príosún*, with Necromancers and Caomhnóir together swarming the castle walls as though prepared for battle. And a veritable army of spirits hovering in the sky above them."

Silence. Then...

"Dear God," Finn whispered.

"I know," I agreed, relieved that he finally seemed to grasp the gravity of the situation. "That's why I'm here. That's why I couldn't risk passing the information blindly along, or entrusting this mission to anyone else. I'm the one who had the vision. I'm the one who's meant to interpret it. It's supposed to be me, I just know it."

"Why is it always you?" Finn whispered, an edge of desperation in his voice.

"Just lucky, I guess," I replied.

"So, what are you supposed to do now that you've gotten inside the walls?" Finn asked. "What are you hoping to achieve?"

"That part is a little less clear," I admitted. "The first step was just to get inside the grounds, hence the false arrest. Now, I've got to try to explore the place, see if I can figure out if the Necromancers and the Caomhnóir are actually working together and, if so, what they're planning."

What little I could see of Finn's face looked incredulous. "How exactly do you propose to do that?" he asked. "I'm lucky I was able to find you at all, and even if I could just let you out of here, it would be minutes before you were discovered and locked back up again, this time with a twenty-four-hour guard for good measure. Not to mention what they'd do to me if I was caught releasing you."

"You don't have to let me out of here," I told him. "And absolutely no one is going to see me." I squeezed his hand. "I'm a Walker, remember?"

"Yes, but they will have prepared for such an eventuality," Finn said exasperatedly. "Each prospective prisoner that comes into the *príosún* is thoroughly profiled, and Castings are set up to counter all of their individual gifts. The Caomhnóir here will be fully informed of the fact that you are a Walker, and they will have made it impossible for you to take that form."

"But you're forgetting that Catriona is in on the plan," I reminded him. "She set up the paperwork. She's altered the Castings. I was attempting to Walk right before you showed up here, and it worked. Well, it mostly worked."

"What do you mean, mostly worked?" Finn asked. "How is it possible to *mostly* Walk?"

"Oh, the Walking part works just fine," I told him. "I had no problem leaving my body. It's my connection to Hannah and Milo, the one that was created through the Binding. It doesn't work when I'm in my Walker form. I've never tried to use it before while I was

Walking, so I didn't realize it would be affected. Hannah thinks it has something to do with the absence of my blood."

"Huh," Finn grunted, pondering this theory. "Interesting. No blood, no connection."

"Interesting, sure, but really inconvenient," I pointed out. "Catriona was supposed to guide me through the *príosún* while I was Walking. Now, without her instructions, I'm just going to be wandering aimlessly with no idea how to navigate the place. What started out as difficult is starting to feel impossible."

Footsteps echoed on a staircase nearby. Both of us jumped with fright.

"Not impossible," Finn said quickly. "Meet me at four o'clock on the second sub-level cell block. That's two floors down from the ground floor. Don't pass too closely to the cell doors on the first basement level: that's a spirit block, and they'll be able to see you. My shift will be ending then, and I'll be rotating to another floor. If you follow me, I'll take you right by the Caomhnóir sleeping quarters and common areas so you can check them out unseen. I'll point out a few of the Caomhnóir who have been acting suspiciously, so that you can tail them. But it will be up to you to make your way back up here and into your body, though, by the time they start the morning rotation at seven o'clock. That's when you'll be brought to the showers and outside for a walk, so you must be back in your body by then."

I squeezed his hand gratefully. "Thank you, Finn. Thank you for helping me with this."

"The sooner you find out what's going on, the sooner you'll be out of here safe and sound. That's all I care about," he replied, his voice gruff with emotion. "And this time, I'm going with you. I will not be parted from you again. Not for the Gateways. Not for anything. Code of Conduct be damned right to the depths of hell where it bloody well belongs." He pressed his lips to the top of my hand. A violent ache of longing shuddered through my body.

"I love you," he whispered. "Keep yourself safe."

"I love you, too," I managed to choke out over the tears now welling in my eyes and spilling over onto the floor. "We'll keep each other safe."

He pressed his lips to my hand one more time. "Four o'clock. Second basement level."

His face disappeared from the gap in the door. Out in the hallway,

I heard him jump to his feet and march away. I closed my eyes and did not move for a long time, trying to preserve the sensation of his hand upon mine.

17

BETRAYAL

H ANNAH, MILO, AND CATRIONA, who had been waiting in alarm and panic since I'd closed the connection, were relieved to hear that Finn had found me, and they all approved of Finn's suggested plan.

"It isn't ideal, of course. He can't risk communicating with you openly, and he can't deviate from his duties, or the leadership will get suspicious," Catriona complained via Hannah. "But it's a much better option than sending you out there on your own."

"Oh, my heart can't take it," Milo groaned.

"Can't take what?" I asked him.

"You and him! A stolen moment of holding hands through the gap in a prison door? That is some Russian tragedy shit right there. You two are a star-crossed love story of epic proportions, sweetness."

"Yeah well, if you ask me, epic love stories are great in theory, but they suck in reality," I said, unable to mask my bitterness in the raw emotional atmosphere of the connection. "Give me a boring old uninteresting love story any day."

"I'm not trying to minimize your pain, sweetness," Milo said, and his energy was tremulous and gentle. "I'm just expressing my prediction that you're due for a happy ending."

"I've never hoped more that you were right," I said to him. "Thanks, Milo."

I lay down and tried to close my eyes, but sleep was a possibility that was entirely out of my reach. I tossed and turned, watching the moonlight slip in and out from behind the clouds, and listening to the random restless sounds of the prisoners in the surrounding cells. I found myself wondering who they were, and what the hell they had done that was so terrible that they had landed themselves here. I also began to wonder, a bit uncomfortably, what it said about

233

the Durupinen that we maintained such a place. It didn't seem that any human being who had to stay here for any considerable length of time would be much of a human when they finally were free. And that was a crime of its own, wasn't it?

Hannah and Milo regularly updated me on the time, and when it finally drew close to three-thirty, we decided it was time for me to go. Better to be there early, and have to wait around for a bit, than to risk the possibility of missing Finn altogether. After all, he would not be able to see me in Walker form, and he would have to simply trust that I had arrived at the time and place that we had agreed to meet. If I showed myself to him, I risked showing myself to any other Caomhnóir who might be nearby, and that was a risk that I could not take.

I used the second of my stash of soul catchers to slip my physical bonds and Walk once more. It was even easier the second time than it had been the first—less disorientating, and even more blissful. Although I knew that Catriona had disabled the Castings, I still found myself trying to make my energy as small and unobtrusive as possible as I approached and attempted to pass through the cell door. But I needn't have worried. In this particular case, Catriona's smug confidence was completely warranted. I slipped through the door as though it were nothing and found myself on the other side in the long, dank corridor of the cellblock.

I drifted forward, envisioning myself occupying each new step along the path, so that I would not move too quickly and disorient myself. It was tricky at first, and I seemed to move in a jarring pattern of starts and stops, like someone attempting to drive a car for the first time by just slamming alternately on the gas and the brakes. I forced myself to slow down, and by the time I reached the staircase at the end of the cellblock, I was moving more smoothly and predictably.

Curious though I was, I had no intention of stopping along the way and sneaking a peek at who was being kept inside the other cells on my floor. Not only did I think it would be too disturbing to see them in various states of mental disarray, but I did not want to risk that one of them would be a Durupinen powerful enough to sense me, even as I did my best to keep my energy cloaked.

Just as I began to descend the staircase, I heard the boots behind me of the Caomhnóir making his rounds on our cellblock. I knew that he would not be able to see me, but nevertheless, I pressed my energy into as small and shadowy a space as I could manage as I waited for him to reverse direction and walk back to the other end of the block. He barely glanced into the cells as he passed them, his expression bored and sleepy. As he made his turn past the very last cell door, a voice cried out, and the sound of it sent a shard of ice cold fear right through my being.

"Back off, you useless bollard!" the voice shouted. "What's a woman got to do around here to get a clean glass of water? No one in their right mind would drink the filth that comes out of these taps. Are you listening to me? Dogs!"

I suddenly felt so full of tension, so full of shock, that my newly concentrated form might just explode with the force of it. I knew that voice. I knew that voice, and if I knew the woman it belonged to, then something was going to hit that door in three... two...

Bang.

Oh my God. Fiona.

I stayed obscured where I was until I was sure that the Caomhnóir on patrol was going to ignore the outburst. When his footsteps had died away in the opposite direction, I propelled myself forward until I was hovering just outside the window of Fiona's cell.

Fiona sat on the corner of the bed, massaging her knees with her hands and mumbling a steady stream of profanity under her breath. Her hair, unkempt on the best of days, hung lank and greasy against her head, and her eyes were heavily shadowed with exhaustion.

I willed myself into a visible form. It took several tries to remember how to communicate in my Walker form, but after a few failed attempts, I managed to whisper her name.

"Fiona!"

Fiona's head shot up and she stared wildly around for the source of the sound. When her eyes finally found my face in the window, her jaw dropped and she leapt to her feet.

"Christ on a bike!" she cried, and instantly slapped a hand over her own mouth, horrified at her outburst. She pulled it away again and said, in a barely audible whisper, "Jessica?! But... how... I don't..."

"It's okay, don't panic!" I told her, crossing the plane of her door and arriving inside her cell. "It's not what it looks like. I'm Walking."

A brief shadow of relief passed over Fiona's features, replaced almost immediately with renewed terror. "But I still don't understand how—"

"I'm here undercover. When you didn't come back, we knew something must be wrong. We knew the prophecy must be coming to a head faster than we imagined possible. So, the Trackers sent me in to try to unravel what's been happening."

"But, surely you didn't Walk all the way from Fairhaven!" Fiona gasped.

I shook my head. "No. That would have been impossible. I'm not experienced enough to Walk that far from my body, and anyway, the further a Walker travels, the thinner the bonds connecting her to her body are stretched. That was one of the many mistakes the Travelers made with Irina. She Walked too far for too long and forgot who she was. The distance was part of what drove her mad."

"So, your body is inside the *príosún*, then?" Fiona murmured. "But... how?"

"Catriona just whipped up a quick little false arrest scenario. It was pretty easy to convince people I'd done something that warranted jail time, seeing what a universal pain in the ass I am," I said with a shrug. "The plan is for me to assess the situation in here and get out again before things go too far south. But I'm starting to think it might be a bit late for that," I added, looking Fiona over once more. "What happened to you, Fiona? The *príosún* reported back that you'd gone home to take care of your mother, but we knew that couldn't be true."

Fiona snorted. "Well, they were looking in the wrong bloody place, weren't they? Dogs! I knew something was wrong the moment I arrived. The Caomhnóir leadership were... jumpy. Edgy, like. They all seemed real eager to get me out of here, and they weren't interested in even looking at the petition I'd brought on my mother's behalf. They brought me into a room—I'm not even sure what it was—a booking room, maybe? Then they started asking me all these strange questions about why I'd come and who I'd told about my trip. I asked them over and over again if I could see my mother, and they just kept giving me the runaround. Finally, I threatened to get the rest of the Council involved and they agreed to take me to where my mother was being held."

A muffled bang echoed through the hallway. Fiona shuffled over to the door and peered through her window for a sign of the

Caomhnóir, but the corridor was deserted. She turned back to me, her back pressed against the door, and continued in a hushed voice.

"They might have placated me with a quick visit and a promise for a hasty release, but then, on our way to my mother's cell block, I spotted that bastard, Charlie Wright."

"Charlie?!" I gasped, my entire form shuddering and blinking with fear. "Where did you... what was he..."

"A Caomhnóir was walking him across the courtyard, handcuffs in place," Fiona explained. "Most of the prisoners get time to walk around the courtyard, just for some fresh air and exercise, but not usually the high security ones. Necromancers, for instance, are not allowed such privileges. That pulled me up short. What was he doing outside of his cell, especially given the gravity of what he'd just been charged with? Still, I thought he might just be getting transferred to a different cell, or else being brought somewhere to face more interrogation. I might have let it go if it weren't for the branding."

"What branding?" I asked her. "What are you talking about?"

"This place is so full of old and new magic, of Castings upon Castings, that all of the Caomhnóir assigned here are branded with a protective rune when they arrive."

"But, when you say branded..." I began, a horror rising in me that even my lack of physical response couldn't weaken, "you don't actually mean..."

"I mean branded!" Fiona snapped. "Like goddamn highland cattle, with red hot iron on their flesh! It's one of the only ways to permanently protect them from the negative effects of so much protective magic in one place! They used to use tattoos, but even those lost efficacy over time. And who do you suppose had a freshly changed bandage in the very spot on the arm where the branding is applied?"

I felt a shudder of horror. "Charlie Wright."

"Absolutely," Fiona replied. "That was the moment I knew that your vision was unfolding right before my very eyes, and that we had not a moment to waste. But that realization came too late in the game for old Fiona, I'm afraid." Her lips pressed together in a rueful grimace. "The Caomhnóir escorting me noticed my preoccupation with Charlie. He must have realized that I'd caught on to something and so, instead of taking me to see my mum, they stashed me away here without so much as a pretext for doing it. Haven't spoken a word to me since."

"Didn't you hear us this morning when we came in? Catriona was right out in that hallway! Why didn't you say anything?" I asked.

Fiona shook her head. "I didn't hear her or anyone else, for that matter. The yellow bastards drugged my food. I was passed out cold until about an hour ago. I'm sure they did it just to ensure they could get Catriona in and out without raising her suspicions."

"And your mother?" I asked anxiously.

"I've got no idea," Fiona said, and her mask of disgust slipped just a bit to reveal true fear underneath. "Not sure if she's still here, or what kind of state she's in. She's been waiting for me for days now. She must be so confused."

"But your story makes it sound like all of the Caomhnóir are working with the Necromancers now," I said. "And that can't be true. Finn says he still doesn't know what's happening."

"Finn? You've spoken to Finn?" Fiona asked sharply.

"Yes," I said. "He saw me come in this morning with Catriona, and snuck up here on his way to his shift to see me."

"How much have you told him?" Fiona asked.

I frowned at the oddness of the question. "Everything. I told him everything."

Fiona groaned and dropped her face into her hands. "Foolish girl."

"What the hell is that supposed to mean?" I asked, bristling with an anger that made my form tingle with a crackling warmth.

"Jessica," Fiona said, and her voice was gentler than I expected. "You have to consider the possibility that Finn is subject to the same weaknesses as the others. How can you be sure that he hasn't been compromised?"

I laughed. "Finn? In league with Necromancers? Absolutely not."

"But how do you *know*?" Fiona repeated.

"Because I know him!" I cried, my voice rising above our carefully controlled volume for the first time. I took a moment to master myself before I continued. "I know him, Fiona."

"People change."

"Not him. Not like this."

"A place like this can do terrible things to a person," Fiona said, still pressing.

My frustration peaked, causing my form to flicker and fade as I fought to maintain it. "Fiona, if you think he's so untrustworthy, then why did you come all the way here just on his word? Why did you agree to try to find him and talk to him while you were here? That was mere days ago, and now all of a sudden, you think he's a traitor?"

"I don't know what to think anymore!" Fiona hissed.

"Well, lucky for the both of us, I do," I said bluntly. "I trust Finn Carey and I would stake my life on his honor."

"You'd better hope you're right, because you've just staked all our lives on it," Fiona said.

"I'll take that wager," I said coolly. "Gladly."

Fiona slumped and threw up her hands, resigning herself to my stubbornness. "Well, assuming your Mr. Carey is telling the truth, the coup has been gradual and all but silent. I don't know how it started, but it's infected the highest ranks of the Caomhnóir here. I was personally questioned by Eamon Gallows, the highest-ranking officer at the *príosún*. I've no doubt that it's on his orders that I've been locked up, which means he's certainly turned."

"But how can some of the Caomhnóir be working with the Necromancers while the others know nothing about it?"

"They'll have been careful about recruiting from within the ranks. They will have felt people out gradually and individually to ensure that they weren't discovered. I don't doubt they've been at it for months, maybe even years. There are plenty of Caomhnóir here who resent their lot in life and would jump at the opportunity to break free of this place. The hatred of the Durupinen runs deep with some of them. It's toxic, and the Necromancers have banked on that toxicity to garner support."

"Support for what?" I asked desperately. "What are they trying to do?"

"I wish I knew the answer to that," Fiona said, rubbing wearily at her temples. "It may be that they have no formal plan yet. But the endgame for Necromancers is always the same: overthrow Durupinen control of the Gateways. It's been their goal since time immemorial, and subverting the Caomhnóir is a damn brilliant way to go about it."

"Catriona is afraid that some of the Fairhaven Caomhnóir might be in on it, too," I said.

"Hmm." Fiona tapped at her chin thoughtfully. "It's possible, I suppose, but I doubt it. I was there when they drafted the communication to Seamus, claiming that I was back home in Scotland with my mother. If Seamus was part of the conspiracy, they surely would have told him where I was, wouldn't they?"

"I guess so." It was a relief to think that Seamus had not betrayed us all, but he was only one of dozens of Caomhnóir at Fairhaven. There were plenty of other places at which our ranks could have been infiltrated. "Look, Fiona, I've got to go. Finn is going meet me at the end of his shift and lead me to where the Caomhnóir common areas are, so that I can have a look around. With any luck, I'll get some answers about what's going on."

Fiona bit her lip, and I knew that she was barely restraining herself from expressing more doubts about Finn's reliability. "Be careful. Keep your eyes open and your guard up."

"I will," I promised her. "And I'll let you know what I find out just as soon as I can." I closed the distance between us, and though I couldn't hug her—I wasn't even sure I'd have dared to if I'd been in possession of arms—I tried to let my energy seep out toward her, tried to mentally wrap her in feelings of confidence and solidarity and hope. It seemed to work. She managed to give me a half-hearted smile, at any rate.

"Good luck, then, Jess," Fiona said. "I reckon you're going to need it."

I slipped down the hallway, now panicking slightly about the time. I hadn't counted on losing the time I spent in Fiona's cell, and I wasn't sure how long I had spent there, though I was sure it couldn't have been anywhere as long as half an hour. When I reached the ground level, however, I was relieved to see a clock on the wall near the doors to the courtyard. I still had twelve minutes before Finn and I were due to meet.

I approached the staircase to the lower levels with caution. It was a part of the *príosún* I had not yet seen, and I had no idea what to expect. It was clear as I descended, though, that these lower recesses were among the oldest parts of the castle. The stairs arced downward in a wide spiral. There were no railings or hand holds at all—the stairs simply dropped off into the darkness a few feet to my right. This wasn't a problem in my current state, but would have been terrifying had I been making this descent in my body. Rusty, empty brackets were spaced along the walls, the stones around them blackened with decades' worth of soot and smoke. In the earlier days of the castle, they must have held torches, but now, outdated electric light fixtures had been installed above them, suggesting the burning heads of the long-extinguished torches with naked, flickering bulbs. There had been a fire here decades and decades ago, Eleanora had once told me. The smell of it lingered behind, imbedded and baked into the surfaces that would not burn.

I arrived on the first landing and looked down the hallway as far as the meager lighting would penetrate. This was the uppermost basement level, the first of the maximum-security cellblocks. If the floor where I was being kept had seemed grim, it was nothing compared to these damp and miserable quarters, which Finn had said housed spirit prisoners. I did not stop to investigate, only sent a thankful prayer that there were no living people being held on this floor. The thought of a human being having to endure such a place with no light and no fresh air was too awful to contemplate. I descended one more flight of stairs and arrived in the second basement cellblock. All was still, except for a steady sound of dripping water, and the electrical hum of the old Edison bulbs above the torch brackets, which also ran the length of the hallway. Somewhere to my left, a scurrying sound of rodents. I was glad that I could not properly smell the place. I pressed my form against the wall between the staircase and the nearest cell door, exactly where Finn told me to wait for him. There was no sign of him as of yet, but this did not worry me. I was early, and I knew that it was his job to patrol the entire cellblock. He would come into view soon enough; he would have to ascend the staircase to make his way back to the Caomhnóir sleeping quarters, and so I knew that I could not miss him.

The minutes stretched on. I heard no echoing sound of boots, no coughs or sighs, no clanking of an ancient ring of skeleton keys. Someone was humming, a woman, but I could not tell if it was a spirit or a living voice. I only knew that it wasn't Finn's voice, and that was the only one I cared about hearing at the moment. The absence of it was beginning to feel like the absence of oxygen.

I started to grow antsy, impatient. I knew I hadn't been late for our scheduled meeting time, and yet I was sure that four o'clock had come and gone by now. What could be keeping him? Shift changes ought to run like clockwork, and Finn certainly wouldn't leave me waiting any longer than necessary, not when he knew how much I was counting on his guidance through the upper levels of the *príosún. Something is wrong,* I thought to myself. *Something is definitely wrong.*

I hung there indecisively for a moment. I wanted to search the cellblock, but I did not want to take the chance that Finn would somehow slip by me if I left the designated meeting place. I looked down the length of the corridor to where it disappeared around the corner. It was narrow, with cells lining just one side of the hallway. There were no additional hallways leading off this one down which he might be able to slip unnoticed. It was unlikely, I reasoned with myself, that we could pass each other in this hallway without seeing each other. Unless he were hiding inside one of the cells, which made absolutely no sense at all, he would have to walk past me in plain sight in order to reach the staircase. Reluctantly, I made the decision to traverse the hallway as far as I could and see if I could figure out why Finn had been held up.

Further and further into the subterranean passage I traveled, passing door after identical door, and light after identical light. It was disorienting; I felt like a subway train barreling down a deserted line after last call. As I rounded another corner, I saw a single wooden door off of the hallway to my left, across from the prisoner cells. Being careful to stay tuned to the corridor in case I missed him, I quickly pushed myself through the plane of the door and into the space behind it. It was a tiny, dingy bathroom, but also contained a small table, a folding chair, a mini fridge, and a pile of outdated magazines. It was also deserted, with no sign that Finn had been in it recently. Disappointed, I slipped back out into the hallway and continued to follow it around one last bend, until it ended in a blank expanse of stone wall.

My panic began to peak. Not only did it seem that Finn was not here to guard the cellblock, but no one else was here to guard it either, leaving whoever occupied the many cells on this floor to their own, unguarded devices.

Just calm down, I intoned to myself as I fruitlessly scanned the empty stone wall for some kind of explanation, half-hoping some Caomhnóir might've written on it with a piece of chalk, "Gone to the loo, back in five."

There could've been a change of plan, I reasoned. He could've arrived for his shift and then been told by a superior to report somewhere else. That kind of thing must happen all the time. It's not anything he would have any control over. It's not something that he could just pop back upstairs to inform me of, either. He would just have to trust that I would find my way around without his help, and without completely freaking out. So, that's what I was going to do, until I could figure things out. And then I'd kill him for making me panic like this, obviously.

I prepared myself to make the journey back down the long corridor when a thought suddenly occurred to me. Fiona had said that Charlie Wright had been let out of his cell, that he may possibly have been branded with protection—the same protection that the Caomhnóir all possessed. That meant that the Necromancers and the Caomhnóir must already be working together in some capacity. What if... what if this corridor was not being guarded because there was no one left here to guard?

What if the prisoners were no longer prisoners?

I looked along the seemingly endless wall of cell doors and found myself wondering: was it possible that each and every one of these cells was now empty? Somehow, that thought was even more terrifying than the possibility that each of the cells held a Necromancer bent on my destruction. At least in the second scenario, they were *in* the cells; they were contained. But if they'd been released... if they were roaming the castle unimpeded...

I approached the nearest door with extreme trepidation. And when I looked inside it, I was already prepared for what I would find.

Nothing. There was nothing. The cell was empty.

Quickly, I peered into the next cell, and then the next. I propelled myself past every cell in the entire ward one by one. Empty. All empty. Except...

The very first cell in the corridor—the one against whose wall I had pressed myself and waited those first few minutes for Finn to arrive, was the one cell that was occupied. Unlike the cells of the upper levels, which had been outfitted to make them fit for human habitation, this sewer hole of a space was barely fit for the rats that surely frequented it. Moisture glistened on the walls and iron chains and manacles hung from heavy iron pegs. A tattered bedroll occupied the back corner, along with a small collection of personal items—a hairbrush, a cup, a moldering magazine—hoarded by the occupant into a little pile the way a squirrel might hoard acorns.

And from the furthest corner of the room, the glint of a pair of eyes and a velvety chuckle penetrated the gloom...

"Well, well, well, it appears the rumors are true. Ms. Jessica Ballard has indeed penetrated the walls of Skye Príosún. Color me impressed," said a familiar, languid voice.

Lucida leaned forward, detaching herself from the shadows to get a better look at me. It was hard to believe, seeing her now, that she was the same flawlessly chic woman who had slipped through my open bedroom window in the dead of night barely five years previously. Her lustrous black hair, which she had always worn natural, was a tangled nest upon her head. Her face was all points and angles now, her cheekbones threatening to poke through her skin, which was tinged with a sallowness. The whites of her eyes had a yellowish quality to them as well, and the sharp, fierce light that used to shine from them had dulled, though not completely gone out. She wore a prison uniform identical to the one I had just left behind on my body upstairs, but hers had grown filthy and threadbare. One of her knees poked through the cotton of her pants, and she was barefoot.

The sight of her in this state was such a shock that I found it difficult to respond to her words. "Hello, Lucida," I said at last. "What rumors are you talking about?"

"Oh, poppet, haven't you heard? You're the talk of the town. The cat's meow. The girl of the moment."

"What are you on about, Lucida?" I snapped. "Just spit it out."

"I didn't believe them at first, oh no," Lucida said, biting her lip in a strange attempt at coyness. "I was sure they must have been mistaken. The Northern Clans would never use a powerful, precious little commodity such as yourself as simple bait. That would be ludicrous, I told myself. But it would appear that I was entirely mistaken. I've been forced to eat my words. Best tasting thing I've eaten in years, I reckon." She nudged a nearby food tray with her big toe. The contents of it appeared untouched.

Though it was more comfortable to have the solid steel door between us, I knew that Lucida couldn't hurt me while I was in this form, and so I broke the plane of the door and arrived on the other side, where I could see her better.

Her eyes widened as she watched me enter, and her face curved into a sardonic smile. "Impressive," she whispered. "Very impressive, indeed. I never had a chance to see this particular party trick of yours before they locked me up. I can see now why they made such a big fuss about it. You can just sail right in and out of these warded spaces, can't you? Highly useful."

"Who's been talking about my being here?" I asked her. "Who's been spreading rumors?"

"Oh, all the cool kids," Lucida insisted. "The Necromancers, the Caomhnóir... well, it's all really six of one, half a dozen of the other now, isn't it?"

"What do you mean?" I asked.

"All cozied up together, aren't they?" Lucida said in a stage whisper. "It's taken many years of planning and persuasion. They've been at it ever since we first arrived here, in the aftermath of the Prophecy. Nothing much came of it at first. It started out very subtle, like. A callous remark about the Durupinen here and there, thrown about in the presence of disgruntled Caomhnóir who were likely thinking very similar sentiments. I would see it once in a while: they would catch each other's eye, and an understanding would pass between them. And it just grew naturally out of a mutual hatred for the women who kept them stifled and under control. Full honor and duty are hard to maintain when you're treated like the help, rather than equals and distinguished warriors. One would think the Durupinen could figure that out, but then again, they always had a knack for abusing their own at their own expense. Just look at yours truly, for example." Her face broke into an angelic grin, which slipped off her features as quickly as it had appeared. "Just can't get out of their own bloody way," she added, shaking her head in disgust. "Goddamn fools."

"Well, what are you doing in here, then?" I spat at her. "Why aren't you out there, helping your Necromancer buddies take down the Durupinen, as usual?"

The smug light in Lucida's eyes flickered, and her face gave a twitch, like she might suddenly burst into tears. "The Necromancers and the Durupinen have one thing in common. They are both exceptionally good at casting aside those who they have deemed are no longer useful to them. I am no longer the invaluable key to the success of their plans. And so, I've been relegated to rot in this cell by Durupinen and Necromancers alike. Sweet, really, that they've been brought together in their mutual belief that I am now worthless."

I felt a great stab of pity for her, something I never thought I'd be able to muster. But she was such a pathetic sight, languishing there, still desperately cloaking herself in her signature bravado.

"So, you aren't working with them anymore?" I asked her dubiously.

"Alas, I am not," Lucida concurred. "Although, I very much doubt that you'll take me at my word on that."

"That's for damn sure," I muttered. "How long have they all been out of their cells?"

"Some Caomhnóir came through a few hours ago, and let them all out. I don't know where they've gone."

"And you don't know what they're planning?" I asked her, hardly expecting an answer.

Lucida cocked her head to one side, considering me. "It's like I just told you: I'm no longer their golden child. I'm not included in their plans."

"But you've been locked up down here with them," I pressed. "If they've abandoned you as completely as you say, and they probably don't pay much attention to you anymore, I bet you've overheard all kinds of things. I bet they've been careless."

Lucida smirked. "Who's a clever girl, then?" she whispered to me. "You're right, of course."

"And?"

Lucida paused again, and she seemed to be debating what to do. I'm not sure what convinced her to answer my question, but all of a sudden, her features crumpled, and her voice became small and hopeless. "They've turned all the Caomhnóir that they think will join them willingly. They decided the time has come to subdue the others, and claim dominion over the *príosún*."

"Subdue?" I asked, my energy beginning to crackle and pop with fear. "How? What are they planning to do to them?"

Lucida gave a shrug. "I don't know," she said. "But I do know that they've released all the spirit prisoners from their cells in order to do it."

"Have you seen Finn Carey?" I asked urgently. "My former Caomhnóir, Finn Carey. He was supposed to be down here, on this shift right now. Have you seen him?"

Lucida shook her head. "There's been no one on shift here for hours, not since they took the Necromancers out."

My mind was spinning. They must have intercepted Finn before he could make his way down here. But where had they brought him,

246

and what had they done with him? My fear was making me feel dizzy, and weak. Lucida's cell begin to swim in and out of focus.

"Something is wrong," I mumbled. "Something is wrong with me."

"That will be Castings, I expect," Lucida said quietly.

"Castings? What Castings?" She was nothing but a blur in front of me, now. A tingling sensation was spreading through my form.

"The ones they're surely putting on your body upstairs right now," Lucida said. She didn't sound smug at all. She sounded sad and resigned.

"On my body? But..."

"If Finn was supposed to meet you here, and he hasn't, that will mean they've captured him. And if they have, then they'll know by now that he's been working with you, and that you're Walking. My guess is that they'll find a way to trap you back in that body, so that you can't get away."

"But... they can't... I can't..." Everything was blinking and shuddering around me, going light and then dark. I couldn't see my own form any more, couldn't remember how to propel myself through space.

"I'm sorry, love," Lucida said. "The Necromancers are a force, and you can't stop them."

"Help me..." I whispered, and Lucida's eyes widened in shock. "It's not too late..."

She opened her mouth as though to answer me, but I never found out what it was she wanted to say. Suddenly, I felt myself being tugged and jerked, pulled and prodded, by invisible forces that I could neither resist nor fight against. I lost all my bearings, all of my ability to process my surroundings. All I knew was that I was being pulled against my will through space, and there was nothing that I could do to stop it. And then, as quickly as it had begun, it stopped, and I felt myself collide with my own body with the force of a car crash.

My eyes were streaming, and I was thrashing and kicking and shouting before I even knew that I had regained the physical form in which to do these things. A heavy weight was pressing down upon my torso, and I could feel hands holding my limbs down to the bed. My body was in a state of sheer animal panic, and now that my spirit had come back, the return of my sentience only intensified my instinct to fight myself free of whoever was attacking me.

Even as I struggled, I tried to blink the tears out of my eyes, and focus on how to control my sense of sight, so that I could see what was happening. But what I saw when I finally remembered how to use my eyes only made my panic peak.

Finn. Finn was holding my body down, and determinedly drawing runes onto my skin while muttering the words of a Casting.

"Finn!" I gasped at the sight of him. "Finn, what are you doing! What the hell are you doing!?"

He did not flinch, nor even seem to acknowledge the use of his name. He would not look at me, but kept his lips in a tight, thin line as he continued his work. Over his shoulder, I could see a second Caomhnóir, and his was also a face that I knew.

"Ambrose!" I cried out.

Ambrose did not ignore me, but looked up at the sound of his name, and his face split into a smug grin.

"It worked!" he said to Finn, who was still determinedly not looking at me. "The Castings worked, she's back in there."

Finn murmured a few last words, and then pushed himself up off the bed, removing his crushing weight from my body, so that I could finally take a proper breath. I looked down at myself. My arms were covered in an assortment of runes, as was my chest. My skin felt incredibly hot and tight, as though my insides were threatening to burst my seams. My head was throbbing, as were my feet, and I looked down to see that my ankles had been manacled to the end of the bed.

I looked up at Finn, who was placing his Casting materials back inside the Casting bag that was hanging from his belt. His face was utterly calm, unconcerned.

"Finn, what have they done to you?" I whispered. "This isn't you. What have they done?"

But when Finn raised his head, he did not answer me. He just stared straight ahead, oblivious to my struggles. Something was wrong with his eyes.

"There you are, then," Ambrose said, still grinning at me. "No more Walking for you. Took a thing or two out of the Traveler playbook and found some ways to keep you nice and safe in there. I wouldn't try Walking again if I were you, unless of course you prefer madness to sanity."

"You treacherous son of a bitch," I spat at him. "What have you done to Finn?"

"He's just another trusted foot soldier now," Ambrose said. "And now that you're safely contained, we've got more work to do." He pulled open my cell door, and Finn marched out of it without a single word, a single glance in my direction.

Ambrose made to follow him, but paused in the doorway, and turned back to face me. "The number of times I almost told you that your days of ordering me around were numbered," he said, so quietly it was almost as though he were speaking to himself. "We'll find a use for you soon, I expect. Until then, just sit tight. Like you have a choice."

He pulled the cell door closed with a resounding crash, and I heard him fasten all of the many locks and bolts before marching off down the hallway.

I had never felt so hopeless and so desperately trapped. Not only was I chained to a bed and locked in a cell, but they had managed to force my spirit back within the confines of my body and blocked all possibility of Walking out of it again. If ever there had been a moment that I understood exactly what it was like to be Irina, this was it. I had never thought of my body as a prison the way that she did, but now that I had been stuffed inside it, like a foot into a too-small shoe, I could feel every fiber, every cell of its restriction. It was as though my soul had expanded so much in my travels through the *príosún* that I now needed to find a new home, like a crab wandering the ocean floor for a larger shell. My pulse throbbed. My limbs shook and twitched. Every thought and feeling I had was screaming and pounding against its incarceration in my skin. Finally, a single thought fought its way clear of my tangled mess of emotions. As that single thought clarified itself inside my head, it became clear that it had bubbled up from my voice of reason, that single sane place within me that still had not given up, had refused to submit to the pain, and was still determined to see me safely out of this mess.

Open the connection. Tell the Council. Get help.

I repeated this thought slowly and methodically, like a mantra, until my soul and my body began to respond to it in unison. The two warring parts of myself realized that neither could win if we remained trapped here in the bonds of Necromancer magic. I just needed to pull myself together long enough to open the connection and get help—help that I knew was waiting for me to call upon it.

I tried to find that mental door that would connect me directly to Hannah and Milo, but with my body and my spirit desperate to disconnect from each other, it was not so easily found. Everything still felt very broken up, like a puzzle whose pieces had been left half-scattered across the table; the pieces all had a place that they fit, but everything was still too disorganized and confused to come together. Instead, I thought back to my attempts to find the connection while I was Walking. Then, it had felt more like plucking strings, rather than simply opening the door. Now, the inside of my head felt like something in between the two, no longer an exquisite harp of emotional strings, but a tangled jungle of them through which I would need to maneuver in order to find the connection.

It was such hard work, and I was tired, so very tired. The Walking, while exhilarating, had exhausted my mental resources. My spirit was still struggling against the binding feeling of being restrained against its will. It wasn't that I no longer wanted to be in my body, it was simply that I had not been allowed to enter it in a natural manner, but had been stuffed inside it haphazardly. I began, bit by bit, to untangle myself. I started with the very tips of my toes and worked my way up all the way to my head, unfurling my spirit into each corner and crevice. Slowly, very slowly, the desperate and constrained feelings began to subside. Finally, the tangled mass of feelings and thoughts in my head unraveled itself, and at last, I felt the mental light of Hannah and Milo peeking out through the crack of that familiar door. I had barely enough mental strength left to pull it open and...

"She's back!" I heard them cry. "Catriona, she's back!"

"Jess, how did you..." Milo began. Then he paused, as the tenor of my emotions washed over him. "What is it? What's wrong? Something's wrong!"

"Jess, what happened to you?" Hannah cried, as she, too, sensed that something was terribly wrong. "This connection feels strange."

"It's happening," I told them, and though I wanted to scream it at the top of my mental lungs, I felt as though I could barely produce a whisper.

"What's happening?" Hannah asked. "What are you talking about?"

"The Necromancers. The Caomhnóir. It's happening, whatever they're planning, it's already underway, and it's all my fault."

"Jess, I can barely hear you!" Hannah said.

"Just tell us what's happening," Milo said in a determinedly calm voice, as though to try to counteract Hannah's terrified energy, which was infecting all of us.

But I was so tired, I just didn't think that I could hold the door open by myself. Hannah and Milo seemed to realize this, and I could feel both of them straining to hold the connection open against my mind's desire to let it fall closed.

"I went Walking... found Fiona..."

"Fiona?" Hannah gasped. "She's there? But they said she went home!"

"They lied... they've got her... locked up..."

"Then what happened?" Milo prompted. "Come on Jess, stay with us."

"Tried to find Finn... but they got to him..."

"Got to him?" Milo asked. "What do you—"

"Saw Lucida... and she told me... the Necromancers... all freed..."

"Oh my God!" Hannah cried.

"And then they trapped me... performed some Castings, to pull me back inside my body, and trap me here... just like Irina..."

"You can't Walk anymore?" Milo asked.

"Trapped," I repeated. The door was just so heavy. I didn't know how much longer I could keep it open. "Finn did it... he is one of them... but he's not himself..."

"Finn?" Hannah cried. "Finn did that to you?"

"But it's not him," I tried to explain, but the words and thoughts were becoming so tangled and confused again. "They've done something to him... Finn would never..."

"But what's happening now?" Milo prompted. "Come on, Jess, stay with us, now."

"Don't know... Ambrose is here... he's part of it..."

"Ambrose?" Hannah and Milo shouted together.

"But he's here, isn't he?" Milo asked. "He's here at Fairhaven, isn't he?"

"Not anymore," I told them. "He was the leak from Fairhaven. It wasn't Seamus... but now they know. Somehow, they know that I'm not really a prisoner. They know that we're onto them, and they're moving to action..."

"What action?" Milo asked.

"They're going to try to take the *príosún*." The door slipped closed just a bit more. "All the Caomhnóir... subdued... they're going to fortify the place... take it for their own..."

I could feel Hannah pulling back from the connection to relay everything to Catriona, and when she did so, the door slipped even further closed. It was barely open now, just a tiny crack through which we could barely hear each other.

"You've got to send help," I cried out, with the last bit of mental energy that I had. "Tell everyone if you have to... tell them... the prophecy... the drawings. I don't care. Just get them here before it's too late..."

Hannah and Milo were shouting for me, but their voices seemed a million miles away as the door slipped closed at last. I felt them pounding against it, but I could not respond. All I could do was slide down into the quiet and the darkness of unconsciousness.

18

ALLIES

I HAD NO IDEA how much time had passed when I began to stir again. I only knew that there were strange sounds echoing around me, and I just wanted them to stop so that I could find the blissful nothingness of unconsciousness again.

The problem was, now that I'd heard the sounds, I couldn't ignore them. I also couldn't ignore the fact that my entire body was aching, and my head felt like somebody had removed my brains and replaced them with the stormy waves crashing outside on the cliffs.

The sound echoed again, a clanking and scraping and... someone cursing?

I peeled my eyes open. The room around me was blurry, but I remembered where I was. The walls and door of the cell came into focus just in time for me to realize that somebody was attempting to open it.

My whole body tensed into a fight or flight panic. Despite the pain and dizziness, I sat myself straight up in the bed, pulling myself as far back into the corner as I could with the manacles still attached to my ankles. I looked around me for something, anything, that I could use to defend myself, but there was nothing.

Whoever was trying to open the door was taking a very long time to do so, almost as though they didn't know which keys fit into which locks. I leaned forward to try to catch some of what the person was saying.

"No, you've already tried that one. Here, give it to me, you're useless."

A second voice answered, "This is the right key, it's just that the lock is rusted. Keep your hair on, woman, I've nearly got it."

I thought I recognized both of those voices, but it was impossible. There was no way...

There was a squeak, a grating screech, and then a metal clunk, and both voices cried out in victory. The door swung open on its hinges, and two figures stood in my doorway, two of the last people in the world that I would ever expect to see working together.

"See? I told you it was the right key," Fiona said, tossing a huge ring of keys back at Lucida as she walked across the room to where I still sat on the bed.

"What are you both doing out? What's going on?"

"We're springing you out of here," Fiona said.

"Unless of course you'd rather stay," Lucida added.

"Where did you get those keys?" I asked. "Where are all the guards?"

"Nearly every Caomhnóir and Necromancer in the place is gathering in the courtyard to prepare their defenses. Seems that they think a confrontation is imminent," Lucida explained. She examined the manacles around my ankles, and then began flipping through the giant ring of keys for the right tool to unlock them. "They left just one guard to patrol the cellblocks downstairs. He seemed to think it was the perfect opportunity to force himself upon the sole remaining prisoner. I thought it was the perfect opportunity to break his neck."

"You... you killed him?" I murmured.

"Thoroughly," Lucida replied without a trace of remorse. "He's lucky I didn't castrate him first for good measure. But there really wasn't time for those sorts of theatrics. Here we are." She separated a long brass key from the others on the ring and inserted it into the locks on the manacles. Within moments, my ankles were free.

"But... why are you up here? Why are you helping us?" I asked.

"That's exactly what I asked her when she showed up at my cell and let me out," Fiona said, crossing her arms and narrowing her eyes in Lucida's direction. "But she agreed that she would free my mother as well, so I could hardly say no to her. Still, I wouldn't mind knowing where this sudden outpouring of empathy is coming from."

"And I'll give her the same answer I gave you," said Lucida. "I don't know. I just am, all right?"

Fiona and I exchanged a long look, each of us silently asking the other the same question: How could we trust her? Neither of us had the answer.

"How do we know that you aren't just going to hand-deliver us straight to the Necromancers?" I asked Lucida.

"You don't," Lucida said, looking me dead in the eye. "I betrayed you before, and you would be a fool not to think that I would do it again. And I'm not going to sit here and tell you that I've had some kind of great bloody change of heart, all right? I still bear an awful lot of ill will toward the Durupinen, and that hasn't gone away. But the Necromancers have proved themselves to be fair weather friends. They care no more for me than the Durupinen ever did. If I stay here, they will use me any way they see fit, and then they'll discard me. I have no interest in being discarded again, and so I'm going to try to make a break for it. I don't know why I'm giving you both the opportunity to do the same, but I am. We don't have to like each other, or even be on the same team to get safely out of here. The choice is entirely yours."

I looked at Fiona again, who gave a helpless shrug. "She unlocked the doors and let us out," Fiona said, "which is a damn sight further than we would've gotten without her. If she turns on us, so be it, but I say we follow her. What choice have we got?"

"We might have another choice," I told her, as a memory struck me. "What time is it?"

"Just before midday," Fiona said. "Why?"

"Just before I passed out, I was able to get a message to Hannah and Milo at Fairhaven. They know what's happening, and I told them to send help. It's been hours now. It's possible that help could be here at any time."

Lucida snorted. "Maybe they've sent help, and maybe they haven't, but I have no illusions that that help is meant for me. I've got to find my way out of here regardless of who's on their way."

"That's your choice," I told her. I looked back at Fiona. "What do you think?"

"It seems foolhardy to wait for help that may or may not be on the way," Fiona said. "Can you open the connection and find out what's going on?"

I closed my eyes and tried to focus on finding and establishing the connection, but for some reason, whether it was the Castings that had forced me back inside my body, or just the spiritual exhaustion from Walking, I could not find it. With a cry of frustration I opened my eyes. "I can't," I told her. "These Castings have really messed with me. I'm still too weak."

"Look, even if the Durupinen are on their way," Lucida said, "even if they brought every bloody reinforcement that they have, they are still on the outside of these walls, and we are still on the inside. And that makes us hostages. And I've no interest in being a pawn in this game any longer. I've been sacrificed on both sides. There's no winning here for me."

I looked into Lucida's face, so vulnerable behind the mask of self-reliance. "I would tell them what you did for me," I told her quietly. "I would tell them how you helped us get out of here."

Lucida gave a bitter half smile. "Too little, too late, love, I reckon."

In that moment, I made the decision. I swung my legs over the side of the bed and slid them into my shoes. "Lucida is right. We're sitting ducks if we stay. And we're wasting time."

I looked to Fiona, and she gave a helpless sort of shrug. I turned back to Lucida. "All right, then. We are trusting that you want out of here badly enough to not betray us. We're with you. Let's get out of here."

"Brilliant," Lucida said, jumping to her feet. "Once more unto the breach, and all that."

I stood up. "Wait," I told her. "You should know that I'm not leaving here without Finn."

Lucida stared at me. "The Caomhnóir? He's a lost cause, Jess."

I crossed my arms. "I'm not leaving without him," I repeated.

Something shifted behind Lucida's eyes as understanding hit her. "Bloody hell," she groaned. "I'm not sacrificing myself for your goddamn love-life, Jessica!"

"I'm not asking you to," I said calmly. "If a moment comes when you need to choose between saving him, and saving yourself, I fully expect you to choose to save yourself. I won't fault you for that. But the Necromancers have done something to him—subdued him somehow. I think he's being controlled; that's the only explanation I can find for why he did this." And I held out my arms to show them the runes.

"There is another explanation," Lucida said bluntly. "But I doubt you're interested in hearing it."

Fiona made a sound through her nose, and I glanced at her. Her arms were crossed, and she was refusing to look at me. "Is that what you think, too?" I asked her. "You think he's really turned, and that he set me up?"

Fiona continued to look at her feet. She shrugged. "I don't know what to think," she muttered.

"Well, I do," I said, my teeth clenched against the inclination to shout. "When I saw him here, right before I discovered you in your cell, Fiona, he was himself. He was the Finn that I know and that I trust. The man who held me down and trapped me back inside my own body was not Finn. His eyes were empty. He did not know me. They've done something to him, and I need to find out what it is. If they've done it to him, they've probably done it to dozens of other Caomhnóir here."

Lucida let out a tiny gasp, and I snapped my gaze back onto her. "What?"

Lucida didn't answer at first. She seemed to be putting something together in her mind.

"What is it, Lucida? If you know something, or heard something, then you need to tell me!" I cried impatiently.

"The Blind Summoners," she whispered.

"What about them?" I asked eagerly.

"Wait a blooming minute," Fiona interjected. "What the hell are Blind Summoners?"

"It's the way they created their spirit army four years ago," Lucida said. "They used a Casting to separate the spirits from their essences. They trapped the essences in fire, which they carried on torches. Once their essences had been removed, the spirits were just empty vessels, waiting to be filled with instructions. They would do whatever the Necromancers asked."

"Christ on a bike," Fiona whispered.

"But what about the Blind Summoners?" I asked. "Why are you bringing them up now?"

"Because back when the Necromancers were experimenting with the concept of the Blind Summoners, they foresaw another use for them," Lucida said.

"Which was?" I asked impatiently.

"They had hoped that they may one day be able to use Blind Summoners as well to control living people. If they ordered the Blind Summoner to take over a living body—to Habitate with it by force—then, conceivably, they could control the living body in the same way that they had controlled the spirit force inside it."

"And do you think that's what they've done?" I asked her. "You think they've subdued the remaining Caomhnóir with Blind Summoners?"

Lucida shrugged. "I only know that it was something they once aspired to. I can't say for sure that that's what happened here. But if it truly is as you say, and your Caomhnóir has been taken over in some way..."

She didn't finish the sentence. She didn't have to. "And if we found them, you know the Castings to release the essences back into the spirits?"

"Yes, I do, but it wouldn't do any bloody good to perform it," Lucida said.

"Why not?" I cried.

"Because you can't put an essence back into a spirit while it's still inhabiting a body," Lucida said impatiently, as though this were supposed to be common knowledge as opposed to a completely uncharted territory of Durupinen magic. "The body acts as a barrier, and the essence can't find its way through the body to the spirit. It's not strong enough. The only way I can put the essences back into the spirits is if the spirits themselves are already outside of the Caomhnóir's bodies."

"But how do we do that?" I asked, feeling desperation creeping upon me. "How could we possibly get the spirits out of all of those bodies to put all of those Caomhnóir back in possession of themselves?"

"I can only think of one possibility," Lucida said, and her voice suddenly sounded small, and strangely hollow. "But I've no idea if I'm powerful enough to do it."

"Do what?" I asked her. "What would you have to do?"

She looked me in the eyes, her expression unreadable. "I'm a Caller, love. I have to Call them out."

§

Knowing how many Caomhnóir were stationed at the Skye Príosún, it was unnerving how deserted the halls of the fortress had become. I could not help but think, as we descended two flights of stairs to another prisoner cellblock, that it was all some sort of set-up. Surely, they were lulling us into a false sense of security, so that we would become careless and then they could pounce upon us unawares. I jumped at every tiny noise and looked over my shoulder so frequently that it was a miracle I didn't trip and fall flat on my face for lack of looking where I was going.

Fiona was able to direct us to the cell where her mother had last been kept. She peered into it, and her face went white. "She's not there," Fiona whispered, her breathing becoming more rapid. "I can't see her anywhere. What in the bollocking blazes have they done with her?"

But then all three of us heard a rapid scurrying sound and a strange, moaning cry. As we watched her, Fiona's face relaxed into a relieved smile. "No, it's all right," she told us over her shoulder. "She must've been sitting up against the inside of the door. She's there, I can see her now."

Lucida hurried forward with the set of keys, but Fiona held up a hand to stop her. "We've got to wait until she recognizes me," Fiona said. "Until she trusts me. Otherwise, when we open the door, she's likely to try to defend herself instead of coming with us willingly."

"You might've mentioned she was out of her bloody mind before you made me agree to help her out of here," Lucida spat at Fiona.

But Fiona ignored her completely. Her attention was entirely on her mother now, to whom she was speaking in the softest, most soothing voice that I had ever heard her use. If I'd closed my eyes, I never in a million years would've believed that it was Fiona speaking in such a way.

"Hello there, Mum," Fiona practically cooed. "That's right. No need to be afraid, now. It's Fiona, Mum. Can you see my face? I'm your family, remember? Look at my face, Mum. I'm not going to hurt you. It's your Fi, Mum. Look. Look, now."

Lucida and I held our breath, listening intently. We heard the shuffling of footsteps, and the soft murmuring of a voice, although it was impossible from where we were to make out what she was saying. Fiona, however, had no problem interpreting the sounds.

"That's right, Mum," she said in a voice that was practically a lullaby. "It is me. It's Fi. You know my face, don't you? You know my voice. I want to open your door, and get you out of here. Would you like that? Would you like to go home?"

I caught a snatch of singing from inside the cell, and realized with a start that it had been Fiona's mother who had been singing during those long hours when I was first locked inside my cell. The realization brought on an almost irresistible urge to cry.

It took several more minutes of coaxing, including Fiona singing along to whatever song her mother was soothing herself with inside the cell, before Fiona finally beckoned Lucida forward to open the door.

Lucida showed a surprising amount of restraint by keeping her mouth shut as she fumbled through the opening of the locks, and finally pushed the door open.

Fiona took a step cautiously into the cell, and emerged a moment later holding her mother's hand. I had met Fiona's mother exactly twice. The first time, she had attempted to murder me with a knife. The second time, she had appeared within the context of a drug-fueled vision in the Traveler camp and attempted to explain a prophetic vision that had been plaguing me. Both times, my interaction with her had been disturbing to say the least, and so I found myself stepping back cautiously as the old woman emerged from the cell.

A few moments of observing her, however, left me quite sure that there was nothing to fear from this woman. She was so much smaller, so much frailer than the last time that I had seen her in the flesh. Incarceration and mental deterioration had taken an obvious and very disturbing toll on her. Her palsied hands shook, and her eyes darted around the corridor, unable to focus on any one thing for more than a brief moment. She muttered constantly under her breath, and clung to Fiona as though she were the only thing keeping her from drifting away into nothingness.

"For Christ's sake, Fiona," Lucida whispered. "You'll never get her out of here if we are pursued."

"I assure you, you needn't wait for us," Fiona replied coolly. "You've already done what I've asked. You let her out of the cell. Leave the rest to me, and don't trouble yourself."

Lucida looked as though she had a few choice words for Fiona, but I placed a restraining hand upon her arm, and interjected quickly, "We can worry about that later. Let's keep going."

Lucida yanked her arm out of my grip, and gave me a sour look, but said nothing more about Fiona's mother. Instead, she pocketed the ring of keys, and jerked her head to indicate that we should follow her silently. Fiona took her mother's face in both hands, making sure that she focused upon her eyes before raising a finger to her lips. Fiona's mother's song died away, and she repeated the gesture, raising a violently trembling finger to her own lips and nodding solemnly.

The four of us slipped silently across the ground floor of the *príosún*. Only once did we have to pull ourselves back into a shadowy corner as a single Caomhnóir hurried past us. He was so

260

intent upon his destination, that he did not spare a single glance around him, which was lucky for us, but worrying when we considered what it was he must've been hurrying toward. We watched him disappear through a large set of wooden doors, pulling them closed behind him. I looked at Lucida, who was nodding in satisfaction.

"What did I tell you?" she said smugly. "That's the courtroom there, through those doors."

I, too, looked at the doors through which the Caomhnóir had disappeared, and felt the dread expanding deep in my stomach. To our other side, the doors to the outer courtyard stood, marking the exit that could possibly lead us to freedom. I ignored their lure, and turned back to Lucida again. "What's the plan, then?" I asked her.

"There is no plan, foolish child," she snapped at me. "The plan was to get out of here, but that's been blown to hell. Now, we wing it."

"But which way are we winging first?" I clarified.

Lucida slowly scanned the entire space, taking in the staircases both up and down, and all of the sets of doors. "That door there," she said pointing to a narrow and nondescript wooden door. "If we cut through there, it leads to a small chamber off of the main courtroom. There's a chance it may be empty, and it's a less exposed way of getting into the courtroom without being caught. I say we take it."

"I agree," I told her quickly. I looked over at Fiona, and she nodded in silent confirmation.

"Maybe Fiona and her mother ought to stay here," I suggested nervously. "If that place is going to be crawling with Caomhnóir, perhaps we should leave them somewhere that will provide them some cover."

Lucida shook her head. "That room *is* the best cover," she argued. "We are completely exposed out here. That room may provide us with a place to shelter while we assess the situation inside the courtroom. There's no telling when the Caomhnóir might discover that we've broken out, and when they do, they'll be swarming this bottom level. We can't stay out in the open like this."

She was right, of course. Lucida might've been a traitor, but she was still one of the best Trackers that the Durupinen had ever had. That expertise was still clearly visible as she prepared us to cross the room, and enter the chosen door. She kept to the shadows, skirting the perimeter of the room, keeping our backs up against the row of cells, and then the far wall. We moved only a few feet at a time, and when we finally reached the entrance she had pointed out, she insisted silently that we stay back while she tested the lock and slowly pushed the door inward. After looking around beyond it, she beckoned us forward, and we all crept through the door into the chamber beyond.

It was a small room, clearly used more for storage than for anything else. A few dozen wooden chairs were stacked along the back wall, along with several desks and a long wooden table. There were also several filing cabinets and a long row of hooks upon which a collection of dusty black robes was hanging. It was to these robes that Lucida gestured once she had had a look around the space. "You and your mother shelter back here," Lucida said, pointing to the robes. "Hide behind them, and cover yourselves completely. Don't argue," she growled, when Fiona looked obstinate and opened her mouth. "I'm not interested in your opinion. You asked me to get you out of here. This is the best way to achieve that goal. Now shut up and hide. And for God's sake, keep her quiet."

It was perhaps the first time I'd ever seen Fiona follow a direct order from anyone without raising hell first. Lucida stood with her arms crossed, overseeing the process until she was satisfied that Fiona and her mother were completely concealed. Then, she turned her attention to the opposite wall, where a closed door led to the courtroom beyond.

"All right then, Jess. You're a Tracker now. Let's see what you've learned." She crept forward toward the door, and I followed just behind her. She dropped to all fours, and I did the same, but I was not yet sure why she was doing so. Lucida lowered her face until it was level with the bottom edge of the door. Then she turned back to me, and I was surprised to see a satisfied smile upon her face.

"Now, you have a look just there," she said, "and tell me what you see."

Bemused, I dropped my face until my cheek was pressed to the cold stone of the floor. The gap between the door and the floor was so narrow, that I could not see anything of the room beyond but for a small sliver of light. I stared at it for a few moments, and then opened my mouth to tell her that I didn't understand what she was talking about. But then, the realization hit me. It was about the nature of the light itself that had seeped its way under the door. This castle was a cold, drafty place. The light was stark, and pale, and grim everywhere you looked. But the light bleeding out from the courtroom was... warm. It was not cold or white or flickering, like in every other part of the castle. It had a rosy glow, and as I moved my face still closer to the opening, I felt something else that was different, too: a gentle gust of warm, smoke-scented air.

"Fire," I whispered in wonder. "There's a fire in that room."

"And not just any fire, I reckon," Lucida said, nodding at me. "Can you feel it?"

But this time I did not need her to give me a hint. A creeping sensation had already begun along the back of my neck, raising the hairs there, and causing a sharp, rushing feeling within my veins. There was a very strong spirit presence on the other side of the wall, and it was not just from one spirit. The essences of dozens of souls were being housed within the room just on the other side of the door, and each of those essences was in dire distress.

"It's terrible," I whispered. "They're so confused, so scared."

Lucida's face gave a guilty twitch. "It's not natural, for them to be pulled apart in this way. It's a perversion."

"You helped to do that once," I reminded her. It wasn't meant to be an admonition. Just more of a realization.

"Once is not now," Lucida murmured.

I didn't really understand what she meant, but she had no intention of elaborating. She jumped to her feet, more catlike than I would've thought her capable, given how she had deteriorated behind bars, and put a hand to the handle of the door.

"Wait!" I hissed. "How do we know who is in there?"

"We don't," Lucida admitted. "So, we proceed with caution. At most, there are a few guards. But if you're determined to see this through, and reverse this Casting, then we've no choice but to take the chance, and deal with what we find. Understood?"

"Understood," I repeated. My heart was in my throat, but what else could we do? If we stood behind this closed door all day, we would be no closer to escaping, and no closer to rescuing Finn. Sooner or later, we would have to take the chance.

And later was no longer an option.

Lucida eased the door open just a crack, as slowly as she could, listening for any creak or screech of the old hinges. Luckily for us, they were blessedly quiet, and Lucida was able to open the door wide enough for us to slip through without making a single sound.

The interior of the room was lit with a golden dancing glow of a hundred torches placed in tall freestanding brackets all over the center of the room. They were not unguarded. A single Caomhnóir stood with his eyes trained on the main doors of the room, which meant that he stood with his back almost entirely turned toward us. Lucida slipped along the wall, to the first of a series of large Doric columns that lined the outer walls. She pressed herself up against the far side of it, and beckoned me to follow. I mimed the question of whether I should close the door behind me. Lucida nodded, but then raised a finger to her lips, imploring me to do so quietly. I eased the door shut without a problem, and then slipped along the wall to stand beside her, our shoulders pressed together in an attempt to disappear into the shadowy space beside the column.

It was hard for me to tear my eyes from the guard, but Lucida was taking in every solitary inch of the room. Her eyes darted from the ceiling, to the windows, to the rows of torches, as she silently counted each one. At last she nodded to herself, as though she had decided something, and pointed forcefully toward the very back of the room, which contained an elevated judge's seat, and a large rectangular corral full of chairs, that might have been a jurors' box. I watched as she crept forward, and then followed her along the wall, traveling the length of the room in just a few seconds. With a single silent bound, Lucida pulled herself away from the wall, and disappeared behind the jurors' box. Decidedly less gracefully, but thankfully equally silently, I did the same. We sat with both of our backs pressed against it, each of us panting as the rush of adrenaline took our breath away.

"What do we do now?" I whispered to her.

Lucida closed her eyes for a moment and shook her head. "There's so many of them," she replied nearly silently. "We can't get all of those torches safely out of here, and there's no way to protect them, even if I can Call all of the spirits out of the Caomhnóir who have been possessed."

"Do you think, if we were able to get past the guard..." I began, but Lucida rounded on me angrily.

"One guard is nothing," she hissed. "I can take care of him without breaking a sweat. The problem is the torches. It's good that we located them, that we know it really is Blind Summoners

264

that they're using, but how are we supposed to reverse this process when there are so many of them..."

There was a great, echoing sound of pounding upon the doors to the courtroom, and Lucida and I both froze. We heard the door creak open, and the set of footsteps enter the room.

"Your watch is done," a voice said. "Report to the courtyard for your new orders."

My heart exploded out of my chest. I knew that voice. I knew it as well as I knew my own name. I shifted onto my knees, and peered carefully around the side of the jury box. Lucida pulled me back, but not before I got a glimpse of the Caomhnóir who had arrived to relieve his brother.

It was Finn.

"What is wrong with you?" Lucida whispered. "Are you trying to get us killed?"

"It's him, Lucida," I whispered back. Her eyes widened, for the look on my face had left no doubt of who it was I was talking about.

"You're sure?"

"Of course I'm sure," I hissed back.

Under cover of our conversation, the first Caomhnóir had exited the room, and Finn was now standing sentinel in his place.

"What do we do?" I asked Lucida, pleading with her. "Please, we can't keep him here like this."

Lucida looked as though she were trying with all her might not to punch something, like me, for example. "I'm going to have to try to Call the spirit from him," she whispered, looking absolutely terrified at the very thought. She turned a desperate gaze upon me. "Can't you check your connection again? Can you see if help is on the way?"

I scoured through my own mental space, but I knew it was no good after only a few brief moments of trying. My mental and spiritual resources were completely exhausted. "I'm sorry, I can't find it. It's not opening. Maybe I should try to remove some of these runes," I added, looking down at my own forearms.

"No, don't waste your time with that," Lucida muttered through clenched teeth. "I've just got to try it, and hope for the best."

Lucida closed her eyes, and an unnatural stillness fell over her. Her hands, formerly clenched at her sides, relaxed into an open, welcoming gesture on either side of her legs. The moment I was sure that she had begun her attempt, I rose and peered cautiously around the jury box again, my eyes glued to Finn's form for any sign that the Calling was beginning to work. But I'd barely stared at him for more than a few seconds, before an echoing crash and a muffled cry made us jump.

I realized with a jolt of horror that the sound had come from the small ancillary chamber where we had left Fiona and her mother. Finn had sensed the direction that the sound had come from, too. Unsheathing a short, broad sword, he began to stalk slowly toward the door.

"Oh no!" I murmured. "We've got to do something! He's going to find them!" When Lucida did not respond, I turned toward her. She did not seem to have processed a single word I had uttered. Her eyes were still closed, and she was lost deep within the Calling.

I hesitated for just a moment more, desperate for someone to tell me what to do, but knowing that I had to make the decision myself. Out of options, and out of time, I did the only thing that I could do. I jumped to my feet and stepped out from behind the jury box.

"Finn."

19

HEART OF THE REBELLION

I CALLED HIS NAME GENTLY, the way I might've said it if the two of us were lying side by side, but he jumped as though I had screamed it at the top of my lungs. He turned the sword upon me, his eyes wide with shock.

"Finn, it's okay. You can put the sword down. It's me," I told him, and in spite of my fear, my face broke into a gentle, encouraging smile. "It's just me. You know me."

Finn cocked his head just slightly to one side, as though attempting to make sense of a language that he'd never heard before. Then he arranged his face back into a determined scowl and took a step toward me.

"Show yourself," he ordered.

Figuring that my best bet was to follow his orders, I stepped slowly out the rest of the way from behind the jury box, raising both of my hands so that he could see that I was unarmed.

"I know you're in there, Finn," I said. "I know you're in there, and that somewhere deep down, you know who I am."

But my words did not seem to penetrate his consciousness at all. He took two more steps toward me, raising the sword still higher. "Move slowly toward me," he barked. "Keep your hands where I can see them."

I did as I was told, shuffling slowly forward, keeping my hands by my ears. "Look at me, Finn," I urged him. "Don't I look even the least bit familiar to you?"

"That's it," Finn said, completely ignoring my words. "Just a few steps closer. There. Now stay where you are."

He closed the distance between us, and I was able to see his eyes up close. There was a strange cloudiness to them, as though I could see in their depths the parasitic creature that had taken hold of him. My fight or flight response was completely disabled. I at once feared him and was not capable of fearing him. The duality of my emotions incapacitated me as he drew ever closer.

Shifting the sword so that it rested comfortably in a single hand, Finn reached down to his belt, and pulled a pair of handcuffs from where they hung at his hip. "Turn around," he ordered, "and place your hands behind your back where I can see them, with your palms out."

I did as he asked me to do, and as I turned my back to him I threw a desperate glance toward the jury box. Was Lucida still trying? Was she making any progress? If she didn't succeed or give up soon, I would find myself right back in the cell where I started, or maybe worse.

As Finn stepped forward to put the handcuffs on my wrists, he seemed to become momentarily distracted. There was a torch just over my left shoulder, and the light of it seemed to dazzle him for a moment, even hypnotize him. There were dozens of torches in the room, and yet he could not seem to pull his eyes away from this one dancing flame. A strange thought struck me, and though it was simply a gut reaction, I knew somewhere deep down inside of me that it was right.

"You feel that, don't you?" I whispered to him. And now I was speaking not to Finn, but to the spirit that had taken hold of him. "You are not this body that you are controlling. The person you really were—really are—is right here," and I inclined my head slowly toward the torch.

Something shifted in his eyes, or perhaps it was a trick of the light? But I was sure for a moment that the spirit inside him had reacted to my words. Clutching this spark of reaction like a lifeline, I pressed on.

"If you listen, you're going to hear a familiar voice. That's *your* voice, your memories, your life. That's where you belong, not inside this man. Not as a slave to the monsters who tore you apart and trapped you inside there."

Finn was staring at the torch now, utterly mesmerized. The sword that he had been pointing so ferociously at my chest was now sinking, the point dropping toward the floor, as something within the flames took hold of him.

Ever so cautiously, I moved my foot just an inch across the floor toward him. He allowed the movement, seemed not even to notice it, and so I repeated it again, until I stood close enough to touch him. But I did not do so, not yet.

"Let him go," I implored the spirit. "He is the man I love, and neither of you deserve to be manipulated in this way. You have the strength to overcome this magic. Please let him go."

The sword clattered to the ground at his feet.

Something in his eyes shifted again. And suddenly, for just a moment, I was staring into the eyes that I knew, the eyes that saw into my soul, that sang to me in the deepest parts where I hungered. Without thinking, without waiting, I threw myself forward, and pressed my lips to his.

This was a mistake.

His body went rigid, and two strong hands clamped down firmly around my neck, pressing down on my windpipe, and pushing me back from him. My eyes flew open, and I stared back into the depths that were clouded once more. I couldn't breathe, couldn't think, couldn't fight back. My despair at seeing a stranger's eyes again left me feeling so broken that I almost wished the hands would hasten their job. Blackness began to gather at the edges of my vision, and my legs gave way underneath me, as I sank to my knees. I tried to say his name one last time, but there was no air left in me, and what was the point? I would simply be speaking to a man who wasn't there anymore.

At least I caught that last, fleeting glimpse of him.

Without warning, the hands slackened around my neck. The clouded eyes rolled up in his head, and Finn stumbled backward away from me. I collapsed onto my side, coughing and retching, but not daring to take my eyes off him, in case he attacked again. But he was not attacking. He was being attacked, or struggling against something that I could not see. I felt a tingling on the back of my neck and turned to look over my shoulder.

Lucida was standing up, and her face was alight with the power I'd only seen in one other person in my life. It radiated off her in waves, creating an irresistible pull for the spirit that was now fighting to keep possession of Finn's body. But it was powerless against her, unable to fight the command of a true Caller. I watched in amazement as a shadowy form shot straight up out of Finn's mouth, and rocketed toward the ceiling, before shooting like a comet toward the torch behind me. Instinctively, I crawled across the floor as far from the torch as I could get just as the spirit made contact with the flames. The orange glow exploded into a fiery, bright blue ball, sparking and popping like a tiny firework.

Lucida slumped to the side, catching herself on the edge of the jury box before her knees hit the ground. She steadied herself and looked determinedly at the torch, muttering a brief incantation. The words, whatever they may have been, caused the torch to expel the spirit upward, before calming into a gentle orange glow once more. I did not get a good look at the spirit, which did not linger, but shot straight for the roof of the courtroom, and made its escape out into the night.

A deep groan made me turn, in time to see Finn pulling himself groggily into a seated position. He ground a fist against the side of his head, as though he could punch the dizziness and disorientation out of it, and then blinked around the room, until his eyes fell on me.

"Jess!" he croaked.

And not giving a damn for the fact that we were supposed to be hiding from hundreds of Caomhnóir and Necromancers who wanted us dead, I let out a cry of joy that rang from my very toes, and threw myself forward. He caught me in his arms, and pulled me close to him, burying his face in the top of my head.

"What's happening?" he asked me. "They intercepted me before I could make my shift, and tied me up. I can't remember anything else."

"It doesn't matter," I told him. "You're okay now. Everything's okay."

Finn stared around the room at the forest of torches still burning. "What the hell is going on in here?"

"Blind Summoners," I told him, and he stared down at me in horror. "They're using them to subdue the Caomhnóir who refuse to join them. You were possessed by one, until a moment ago, when Lucida Called it out of you."

I turned over my shoulder and gave Lucida a grateful smile. She tried to return it, but the Calling had temporarily drained her, and it seemed all she could do to keep herself on her feet and catch her breath.

Finn, on the other hand, leapt to his feet, pulling me with him and then placing himself squarely between Lucida and myself. "What is she doing here?" he asked. "Who let her out of her cell?"

"It's okay," I told him. "You don't understand. She rescued me.

She rescued Fiona and her mother too. She's been helping us get out of here, and she's the one who just brought you back to me. She didn't have to do any of it, but she chose to. So, we're trusting her right now, okay?"

Finn looked at me as though I had temporarily lost my mind, and then looked back at Lucida, who managed a shrug.

"Don't look at me, mate," she said hoarsely. "I don't understand myself."

I placed a hand on Finn's face and forced him to look me in the eye. "Finn, you don't have to trust her. Just trust me, okay?"

His eyes softened. "I'll always trust you. Unfailingly."

"Good," I said. "Then trust me when I say that we need to find a way out of here, and fast. Help may be on the way, but we can't be sure of that."

"Help? What kind of help?" Finn asked.

"All the help that Fairhaven can send us, but I can't confirm it, because I can't get through my connection to Hannah and Milo because of these," I told him, raising my arms and showing him all of the runes.

"What is all of that?" he asked me. "Who—"

"Never mind that now," I said firmly. "Definitely not important. We've got to get out of this castle before they realize that we're gone from our cells. Do you know any way out of here that won't take us through the main courtyard? Because that's where they've gathered."

Finn pulled his eyebrows together in concentration. "We might be able to slip out by way of the catacomb archives," he murmured. "There's an entrance to them around the cliff side of the fortress. That'll take us clean around the other side from where the forces are gathering."

"I've heard of those archives," I said slowly. "Catriona mentioned them. She said that it was probably one of the resources in the castle that the Necromancers would most like to get their hands on. Do you think it's safe to go out that way?"

"If the Necromancers have taken the entire fortress, and are controlling all of the Caomhnóir, then those archives are as good as theirs," Finn said darkly. "Using them for an escape is not going to give them access to anything that they can't already get their hands on. But if we are able to quell this uprising before it gets out of hand, then we may be able to protect what's inside the archives before they have the opportunity to stake their claim on it."

I turned to Lucida. "What do you think?" I asked her.

"He knows the castle better than I do," she told me. "He's seen parts of it that I've never been permitted to see. If he says that's our best bet, then I say we take it."

I nodded and pointed to Finn's sword where it lay on the ground. "You're probably gonna want to take that," I told him.

He looked down at it in surprise, clearly wondering how it had gotten there, but picked it up and resheathed it without question. "Very well," he said stoutly. "Let's get out of here."

"Hang on," I told him. "We've got to get Fiona and her mother. They're hiding in the antechamber."

"The antechamber is our only chance of getting out of here unseen," Finn said. "We'll have to go through it anyway, if you want to avoid the security patrols. Both of you follow me, and keep close."

We crossed the courtroom at a run, dodging between the torches, and pulled open the door to the antechamber. I could hear Fiona making hushing sounds as her mother's voice rose in a whimper again.

"Fiona, it's okay, it's us," I said quietly. "You can come out now, we've got Finn, and he's going to help us out of here."

Fiona's frightened white face appeared between the folds of two black cloaks. "Oh, so you've got your Caomhnóir, then, eh? And how do we know he's not going to attack one of us next?"

"Attack?" Finn asked. "Why would I attack—"

"Because he's not possessed anymore," I told her. "Lucida called the Blind Summoner right out of him. She was right, it is how they're controlling the Caomhnóir. Well, at least some of them. Others, like Ambrose, are doing their bidding willingly."

Fiona stepped cautiously out from between the robes, pulling her mother along behind her by the hand. "Right, then," she said, still casting skeptical looks at Finn. "If you say so. Let's get the hell out of here."

But at that moment, Fiona's mother let out a gasp. She was staring, transfixed, at the many torches that lit the courtroom beyond the door, which Lucida had left ajar behind her. The flames danced in her mad old eyes, as a look of dawning comprehension broke over her face. She let out a keening cry, broke free of Fiona's restraining hand, and bolted for the door.

"Mum, no!" Fiona cried. "Mum, come back!"

All three of us flew after her, and found her darting back and forth between the torches, starting and crying out at each one as though it were a new monster in a house of horrors. Though she seemed able to comprehend little of what had been going on around her, she knew that there was something terribly wrong about each and every one of those flames. Whether it was simply a Durupinen instinct, or the confirmation of a half-forgotten glimpse of Seer vision, the sight sent her into an uncontrollable, animal panic. She began screaming, a guttural, grieving sound, and she flung herself toward the nearest torch, as though she meant to embrace it.

"Mum, no!" Fiona cried. She leapt forward, meaning to throw herself between the torch and her mother, but the old woman made an odd lurch to one side, and Fiona, trying to counter the movement, lost her balance. The two women and the torch toppled to the ground in a tangled heap, and Fiona began to scream.

It all happened so quickly that my mind barely had time to register the horror of what it was seeing. All I knew was that I could not see Fiona's face, because the licking flames had caught at her hair, and suddenly she was ablaze. Finn leapt into action, tearing the long vest that was a part of his uniform from his shoulders, and throwing himself down upon Fiona with it. Within seconds, he had managed to smother the flames, but I knew that Fiona was badly hurt.

Lucida, meanwhile, had tackled Fiona's mother to the ground and was lying on top of her, with one hand pressed over the old woman's mouth to muffle her continuing screams.

"We've got to get out of here," Lucida shouted. "The whole castle will have heard her caterwauling."

Finn clambered to his feet, wrapping his vest tenderly around Fiona's raw and reddened face. She continued to sob as he threw her over his shoulder in a fireman's carry. "This way," he ordered. "Now!"

I ran to Lucida, and the two of us yanked and tugged the old woman to her feet, and forced her to lumber along between us. We followed Finn back through into the antechamber just as the sounds of feet and shouts reached the main doors of the courtroom.

We flew down the hallway toward the sub-level stairs, abandoning any pretense of hiding or keeping quiet. We descended three flights, before we heard the first of the footsteps echoing on the stairs above us.

"Keep moving!" Finn shouted.

My breath seared my lungs, but I kept pushing forward, dragging the old woman mercilessly along with me. Ahead of us, Fiona bounced and whimpered on Finn's shoulder, still wrapped in his vest to protect her ravaged features.

Finally, we reached the sixth basement level, and the stairs disappeared from beneath our feet, to be replaced with an ancient, foul-smelling floor of mold and dust. Finn tore to his left where a narrow archway opened into a crumbling, dank tunnel.

"This way!" he cried.

We stumbled after him. The tunnel was narrow and low-ceilinged, and Lucida and I had to turn sideways so that we were running single file with Fiona's mother between us. Finn produced a flashlight from somewhere, and its dim, bouncing light was the only relief on an impossibly dark path as it twisted downward. More than once, my shoulders knocked into the wall, and I felt stones come loose and clatter to the ground on either side of me. A second's light from the flashlight beam revealed that it was not a stone I had knocked loose from the wall, but rather, a human skull.

"What the fuck?" I managed through my ragged, breathless gasps. "Was that what I think it was?"

"It's a catacomb," Lucida puffed from behind me. "Its walls are constructed almost entirely of bones. Don't think about it, just run, for God's sake."

But I did think about it, and my resulting horror provided me with a surge of adrenaline that powered me forward even though my legs and my lungs and every muscle in my body were screaming at me that I couldn't go any further. We plunged downward through the earth, tripping and stumbling and crying out with disgust as each new twist and turn brought another pile of bones within sight. Only one other time in my life had I been in such close proximity to human remains, in one of the mausoleums on the Fairhaven grounds. I'd been wholly unable to control my panic on that occasion, and so I did not try to control it now. I let it propel me forward, let my terror give me wings.

Footsteps and angry shouts echoed behind us, but it was

274

impossible to tell how close or far behind us they might be. The passage took a sharp turn to the right, and we suddenly found ourselves confronted with a door. Finn placed both hands upon it and murmured a brief Casting before wrenching it open, and we all tumbled through it. He slammed it shut behind us, and pulled a massive oaken plank across it, sealing our pursuers on the other side.

I had only a moment to stare around me, but the chamber in which we found ourselves was truly awe-inspiring. A cave deep within the earth, lined with shelf upon shelf upon shelf of scrolls and books, maps and globes. And all of it built upon centuries' worth of bones.

"This way, hurry!" Finn was calling to us before my eyes had even processed the complete insanity of our surroundings. Lucida and I pulled Fiona's mother up from where she had collapsed upon the floor and dragged her forward across the room, weaving our way between tables and cases and ancient throne-like chairs all stacked with books. Another door, identical to the first, stood at the far side of the archive, and we all ran through it, allowing Finn to seal it as he had done with the entrance.

The tunnel continued on the other side of the archives, but it was blessedly free of any visible human remains. Instead, it plunged sharply downward in a set of stone steps. We took them as quickly as we dared, digging our hands into the jagged walls of the tunnel to steady ourselves and prevent us from tumbling to the bottom in a broken heap.

At long last, after what felt like an eternity, the tunnel began to lighten, and the tang of salty sea spray reached my nose.

"Slow down and take the rest of this easy," Finn said. "Once we reach the entrance, the ledge is narrow, and it's likely to be slippery from the spray."

The tunnel opened onto one of the most magnificent sights I'd ever seen. We had emerged onto the very face of one of the great rocky cliffs that plunged down to the violent waters below. Sea spray lashed at our faces as we edged our way along the treacherous, narrow ledge carved into the rock. I did not dare look down, but kept my eyes fixed doggedly on the path just in front of my feet, placing each foot gingerly, testing the weight and the slickness of the rock before trusting each new step. Behind me,

Fiona's mother was babbling hysterically, but seemed too frightened that she might fall to put up any kind of struggle.

The ledge stepped down in a gradual descent to a narrow strip of sandy beach that had survived being swallowed by the ocean by virtue of a deep craggy inlet in the cliff face. When I felt the soft give of the sand beneath my feet, my legs completely collapsed out from under me, and I lay with my face pressed into the sand, struggling to get control over my breathing once again.

Whether out of pity, or because he, too, was too exhausted to keep going right away, Finn let us rest there in the sand for several minutes before he urged us back to our feet and onward. I turned and looked back up at the cliff face, but no one was pursuing us down the treacherous path. Whether they had not been able to penetrate through to the archives, or whether they had simply seen the danger of our escape route and decided not to pursue us, we never found out. Either way, it was a stroke of merciful luck for which I sent up a silent prayer of thanks.

The tiny beach wrapped around the base of the cliff for another quarter of a mile, and then ended in a steep and rocky set of steps that would lead us back up to the green grasses of the mainland. When we emerged above the edge of the cliff, I was astonished to see how far from the castle we had traveled. The five of us sank gratefully down into the camouflage of the tall grasses, and lay there silent for quite a long time.

It was Finn, again, who roused us from our exhaustion and urged us to move on. "We've got to go for help," he told me quietly. "Fiona is really badly injured. She needs medical attention."

Fiona lay where Finn had deposited her upon the ground. She was no longer whimpering, but her breathing was shallow and ragged. The majority of her head and face was still obscured inside Finn's vest. I did not think I could bear to look at what the fire had done to her.

Finn reached out a hand, and I took it, struggling to my feet. I turned to Lucida, intending to offer her the same help, but she was not looking at me. She was staring out over the water, and her eyes were wide.

"Lucida, what are you—"

But a distant sound of helicopter blades whipping through the air answered my question before I could finish asking it. Out over the water, a legion of helicopters, flying in formation like birds, was cutting through the afternoon sky toward us. We watched in amazement as they grew closer, feeling like castaways on a deserted island whose signal fire had been seen by a passing ship.

The helicopters soared over our heads, and off in the direction of the *príosún*, all except for one, which broke free of its formation, and circled back to land in the grass about a hundred yards from where we stood waving our arms and screaming ourselves hoarse in the attempt to signal them.

Several figures descended from the helicopter, and dropped down into the grass, running bent double until they were clear of the helicopter blades. The first to straighten up was the one to make my heart weak with happiness.

"Hannah!" I tried to cry out, but I had no voice left.

"Oh, thank goodness, thank goodness!" Hannah was sobbing, and she threw herself upon me in a hug so fierce that we both fell to the ground. "Oh, I'm sorry! I'm so sorry, I didn't mean to... Are you all right, did I hurt you?"

Hannah tried to pull away from me, but I pulled her back against me again for one last squeeze. "No, I'm fine," I told her. "I'm just exhausted and so damn happy to see you!"

The embrace suddenly became bitingly cold, as though someone had doused us both in an icy bucket of water from the sea behind us. But it was only Milo, babbling hysterically, and desperate to get in on the hugging. He was closely followed by Karen, whose words were likewise unintelligible through her tears.

"Okay, seriously can't breathe now," I gasped. And all three of them pulled themselves off me, leaving me to massage my ribs.

"What happened?" Hannah asked me. "We've been trying and trying to get through to you through the connection, but it was as though you had sealed it off."

"I didn't seal it off, I just couldn't access it," I explained. "They forced me back into my body, like the Travelers did to Irina, and something about the combination of Castings and the mental exhaustion from the Walking... I just couldn't do it."

But nobody was listening to my answer, for they had all suddenly realized who was there in the grass with me, and all of their expressions had turned wary. Several Caomhnóir, Elin, and Siobhán had all arrived now from the helicopter as well, all of them desperately trying to assess the situation in front of them.

"It's okay, everyone," I said to the group at large, and all eyes flicked toward me. "Everything's okay here. Finn wasn't part of the conspiracy, he was a victim. The Necromancers were using spirits to control the Caomhnóir who didn't want to join them. And Lucida was the one who got us all out of our cells, and helped us to escape. We would all be dead or captured if it weren't for her."

Lucida was barely daring to raise her eyes from the ground to meet the dubious and confrontational stares that had now been turned upon her. She did not speak to confirm what I had said, but merely sat quietly, waiting for judgments to fall upon her. There were more pressing matters, however.

"Fiona needs help," I told the Caomhnóir. "Do you have medical supplies on the helicopter? She's been badly burned."

The Caomhnóir leapt into action at once, approaching Fiona's prone figure on the ground and beginning to take her vital signs. A few moments of assessment later, they were lifting her gingerly between them and rushing her back to the helicopter.

"What's happening back at the *príosún*?" Hannah asked, turning all of our attention to the most pressing matter of all. "All we could gather from your message was that the Necromancers and the Caomhnóir had begun openly working together."

"They're preparing to make a stand, to claim the *príosún* for the Necromancers. They were planning to carry out the plan more quietly, and gradually, but we forced their hand," I said with a smile. "They figured out that I was there as a Tracker, not a prisoner, and so they knew that we were onto them. That set the wheels in motion, and then there was no stopping it."

"But what's happening now?" Milo asked. "How did you get out?"

But looking at him in his ghostly form, and Hannah beside him, had given me an idea. "The Necromancers have used Blind Summoners to turn all of the Caomhnóir into mindless foot soldiers," I told them. I ignored all of their gasps, and plunged on. "One of the chambers inside the castle is full of the torches containing all the spirits' essences. We were able to free Finn, but the rest of the Caomhnóir are still being controlled."

"How did you free him?" Hannah asked, her face pale with shock.

"I couldn't," I admitted. "It was Lucida. She was able to Call the spirit out of Finn's body and then used the Casting to reunite it with its essence again."

Again, everyone turned and stared at Lucida. Again, Lucida could only seem to stare at her own folded hands in her lap.

"Are you saying," Hannah whispered, "that the only way to rescue all these Caomhnóir is by Calling the spirits out of them?"

"Yes," I told her. "The Necromancers are only prepared to take the fortress with a full army under their control. But if all of the subjugated Caomhnóir were suddenly to come to their senses and turn on them..."

"Then their entire plot is foiled," Karen said quietly. "They can be taken down from within."

"Exactly," I told her. I took both of Hannah's hands in mine. "What do you think?" I asked her. "Do you think you can try it? I know it's a huge thing to ask of you, but it might be the key to everything."

I watched as resolve trumped the fear in Hannah's eyes. "I'll try," she said resolutely. "All I can do is try." She turned and looked at the distant shape of the castle. "Let's go, then," she said. "There's not a moment to lose."

Everyone started to turn and hurry back to the helicopter. Only Lucida remained sitting in the grass.

"Aren't you coming?" I asked her.

"Wouldn't that be a bit like crashing a party?" she muttered.

"Look, I don't know what's going to happen," I told her truthfully. "But I do know that you've had a hand in this already, and everyone needs to know it. And there may yet be something you can do to help stop all of this. If that still seems like something that you want to be a part of, then come with me." And I reached a hand out toward her.

Lucida stared at my hand for a moment as though she were half scared of it, and then reached out and took it.

We all crammed into the back of the helicopter, and it took off at once, buffeted back-and-forth by the strong ocean wind before it zoomed off in the direction of the *príosún*. We could see the place in front of the castle where all the other helicopters had landed, and touched down among them. Scores of Caomhnóir were scurrying around, consulting maps and making plans. Finn ran off to join them at once. Ahead, I could see a knot of Durupinen in their Council robes. Celeste was among them.

"Come on," I called to the others, plunging through the chaos toward the *príosún*.

I looked up at the castle just as I arrived by Celeste's side, and felt a thrill of fear and knowledge shoot through me like an electric current. The castle appeared exactly as I had seen it in my vision. If I had held the drawing up before me, it would be identical in every detail, from the placement of the flags, to the very figures that were gathering now upon the ramparts and battlements. The only element of the vision that was missing, was the spirits all hanging in the air above them.

And I suddenly understood why.

"This is it," I whispered. "This is the moment. We have to do it now."

Without uttering a word to Celeste, without telling anybody what we were planning to do, I reached back behind me and dragged Hannah forward by the hand. "Do you recognize this?" I asked her.

But she was already staring in awe at the sight before her, and I knew that she was sensing the same experience of déjà vu.

"All that's missing is the ghosts," she whispered.

"Only until you Call them out," I told her.

She looked at me, and her expression was full of wonder. "I always thought... I thought the spirits were part of the rebellion. I thought they were part of the attack."

I shook my head and smiled. "They're part of the rescue," I told her, and my face broke into a smile. "The vision wasn't of their victory. It was of how to defeat them."

Hannah returned my smile, and then turned to face the *príosún*. She closed her eyes, and began to concentrate.

An unnatural hush and stillness spread through the grounds. The shift in spirit energy was such that everyone knew instinctively that something was happening, and that Hannah was the source of it. All eyes turned to find her, and everyone seemed to hold their collective breath in anticipation of whatever it was that was building in the air around them.

Meanwhile, above on the battlements of the castle, the figures who had previously been milling about and organizing themselves had stopped. Some of the figures had gone completely motionless, while others circled around them in confusion.

"It's working," I whispered to Hannah. "Something is happening, keep at it."

The minutes stretched on, Hannah's concentration remained unbroken, but she was beginning to tremble. I looked at Milo and read the worry on his face. It had never taken her this long to Call spirits before. They had always responded so quickly, found her Call so irresistible. Why wasn't it working? What was I missing?"

Calling spirits who roamed free was one thing. Calling spirits out from living bodies was another. Perhaps it was too much for a single Caller to handle, however powerful she might be.

But we didn't have a single Caller. We had two.

I turned back over my shoulder, and scanned the crowd desperately for the face I needed to find. She was there, huddled beside a helicopter, still looking unsure if the people around her were going to ignore her, or arrest her. I ran to her and pulled her by the hand.

"Jess? What are you doing? Where are you—"

"Don't you understand? It's not just her. It's too much for one Caller," I panted as I pulled her forward through the crowd. "It's got to be both of you."

"Both of us what? What are you on about?" Lucida cried.

I pulled her to a stop right beside Hannah and pointed up at the *príosún*. "This is your chance, Lucida. This is your chance to help her now. You can't go back, but you can go forward. Help her. Help her do this."

And Lucida's bewilderment vanished as the truth hit her in the face. She hesitated one brief, tremulous moment more, and then she gave me a tiny nod, and closed her eyes.

The moment that the two Callers began working together, it was as though every particle of energy in the air were suddenly suspended. The wind dared not blow. Not a single person in the watchful crowd twitched even a muscle. And high above us, the figures upon the battlements became as still as statues. The earth itself seemed to hold its breath as the power between the two women built and rose, and at last, burst forth.

Like a tornado of spirit force, ghost after ghost twirled and soared and shot into the air high above the castle walls, and then hung suspended, perfectly still, like pale stars. We all gazed upon them, a magnificent constellation in the late afternoon sky, and then as one they rose up like a flock of birds and, allowing the wind and the salt air and our collective exhalation to rush back in and reclaim the stillness.

A storm of activity broke out all around us. Caomhnóir on the grounds, rushing to the gates of the *príosún* and trying to secure the perimeter. Up above our heads on the ramparts, Caomhnóir were coming to their senses and a mess of confused fighting broke out as they turned on the Necromancers and traitors amongst whom they now found themselves. Council members were running through the throngs on the ground, shouting in confusion and attempting to gain control of the situation, still unsure who was friend and who was foe in the battle now raging above.

Hannah and Lucida both seemed completely oblivious to the chaos as they opened their eyes, and the first thing that they gazed upon was each other. An ineffable something passed between them, an understanding that no one else standing upon the castle grounds that day could ever comprehend. Then they turned from each other without a word, unshakable in their understanding that the rebellion was over, and that something that had seemed irreparably damaged between then had begun, very slowly, to heal.

20

HORIZON

"S O... I WENT TO AN ACADEMIC conference in Paris for three days and you got arrested, staged a prison break, and thwarted a Necromancer coup that threatened the very existence of the Durupinen as we know it?" Tia's voice came through the phone in an almost unintelligible squeak.

"That about sums it up, yeah," I replied cheerfully. "Oh! And I rode in a helicopter, on purpose."

Tia sighed. "I clearly can't go anywhere ever again."

"Imagine what I could have gotten myself into if you'd been gone for a week?"

"I'd rather not, actually," Tia said dryly.

"So how was the conference? How did the presentation go? Did all the medical people love your paper? Did you do doctor things? Were you awarded a golden stethoscope?" I teased.

"You have no idea what people at medical conferences do, do you?"

"Not a clue. But please tell me. I want to hear all about it!"

"I can't believe you want to hear about a bunch of people reading research about meningitis and the surprising new benefits of gene therapy after the weekend you had. Everything must still be in shambles over there."

This was true enough. It had been only a day and a half since we had arrived back at Fairhaven, and the castle was in a general uproar dealing with the aftermath of the uprising at Skye Príosún. Though I knew that the challenges were far from over, it was hard to feel anything but hopeful that we would fight our way through the aftermath. The main source of that hopeful feeling was currently running his fingers through my hair and planting kisses on the top of my head.

"When will you be back?" Tia asked.

"I'm not sure," I admitted. "There's going to be a hell of a lot of Tracker paperwork on this one. Are you okay there at the flat without us?"

"I think I'm going to stay on campus for a bit, actually," Tia said. "The work will be a good distraction, and I met some great people at the conference."

"That's a great idea," I told her, glad that I didn't have to feel guilty for abandoning her, at least for the moment. "Call me later tonight, okay?"

"Yeah, I will," Tia said. "Think you can stay out of trouble until then?"

I looked up at Finn and grinned. "I make no promises."

I hung up the phone. "Sorry about that. Just had to check in with Tia."

"Apology not accepted. Your lips were otherwise occupied for entirely too long," Finn said, and leaned forward to kiss me.

My entire body seemed to transform into a sigh of contentment. I wasn't sure how long the euphoria of being together again would last, especially once the realities of the legality of our relationship set in, but for the moment, I could not bring myself to care. I would bask in this moment for as long as I damn well pleased.

I pulled away from him.

"I wasn't done kissing you," he complained.

"And I'm not done looking at you," I replied. "I can't shake the feeling that I'm going to open my eyes and you're going to be gone again."

"Not a chance," Finn said softly. "Never again."

There was a knock at the door, and then Hannah walked in, followed by Milo, who looked at the two of us like we were a viral YouTube video of puppies wearing sweaters.

"Are you going to gawk at us like that every time you see us together?" I asked him, amused. "Like, your face literally just morphed into a heart-eye emoji."

Milo shrugged, completely unabashed. "Stop being so cute and I'll stop gushing. Until then, I will haunt you with my heart-eyes."

Hannah was quick to close the door, however, and threw a nervous look out into the hallway as she did so. "Obviously, I'm thrilled that you're back, Finn, and nothing makes me happier than seeing the two of you together, but... aren't you nervous that you're going to get in trouble?"

"I don't think you're taking into account the theory of relativity," Finn said.

"Relativity?" Hannah repeated, looking confused. "You mean, like, Einstein?"

"In this case, I mean the severity of one crime as *relative* to another. When a considerable number of Caomhnóir have colluded in a plot to join forces with their most deadly enemies, it turns out that the Council doesn't pay much attention to the Caomhnóir snogging his Durupinen girlfriend," Finn said with a lopsided grin. "It's like being a jaywalker in a sea of shoplifters, really. It's all relative."

Hannah gave an anxious chuckle. "Well, yes, I know, but even so, someone is bound to complain."

I sighed. Despite the previous day's conversation with Celeste, Hannah could not shake her fears that Finn and I were going to be torn apart and locked away for the crime of daring to look at each other. I knew that, for the time being, at least, this would not be the case.

I did not realize that the day prior, when I had met with Celeste. On the contrary, I was absolute weak-kneed with fear about what would face me when I entered the High Priestess' office, Finn by my side.

"I did not summon Mr. Carey yet," Celeste said upon watching us enter.

"I realize that. But I need him here," I said, trying to keep the defiance in my voice to a bare minimum and failing spectacularly at doing so. "Anything you need to say to me, you can say to him."

Celeste's eyes lingered on our clasped hands, but she seemed to decide to ignore it, for the moment. She sat down behind her desk and clasped her hands pensively. "How are you both, then? It is my understanding that neither of you were injured in your escape?"

"We're fine, thank you," I said. Finn nodded once in agreement but did not speak. His fingers were like iron bands around my hand. I flexed my fingers gently and he took the hint, relaxing his grip.

"The first reason I wanted to ask you here, was to thank you, Jessica," Celeste said. "I will forever be grateful, as will the generations of Durupinen to come, for what you risked entering that *príosún*. I believe that you may have foiled the single most dangerous attack on the Durupinen since the Prophecy came to pass."

"You're welcome," I said stiffly.

Celeste shifted in her chair. "What I'm trying to understand is why you and Catriona neglected to tell me about the situation in the first place."

I did not answer right away, choosing instead to prolong the inevitable by asking a question in turn. "Does Catriona usually inform you before making decisions about the cases she handles as a Tracker."

"Generally, no," Celeste admitted. "But these were far from typical circumstances, and this was far from a standard case. I think you know that."

"We didn't want word to spread to the Caomhnóir of what our plan was," I said. "We didn't know how far or high the Necromancers had infiltrated into the ranks. We were scared of tipping them off before we could find out what was going on."

"I am not a Caomhnóir," Celeste said. "I am the High Priestess of the Northern Clans. Surely, you did not believe me incapable of keeping such information a secret."

"No, of course not," I said, a bit abashed.

"Then I can only assume that your real hesitation came from this," Celeste said, and she reached into her desk. She extracted a piece of paper and spread it across the desk between us.

My heart skipped a beat. It was my Seer drawing. Beside me, Finn seemed to have stopped breathing.

"Where did you get that?" I asked in a strangled whisper.

"Catriona gave it to me," she said. "She did not do so willingly, but as a last resort. She was asking me to mount an enormous attack upon the _príosún_. I would not do so without clear evidence that it was necessary. This was how she convinced me."

I closed my eyes and let out a breath I'd been holding since the drawing had appeared on the table. This was it, then. The secret was out. I felt an unexpected sense of relief. Whatever happened now, the crushing weight of this secret was gone from my shoulders. I almost didn't care what happened next.

"I need to know why you did not bring this to me right away," Celeste said, and her voice faltered on the line between trying to assert her authority and express her motherly tendencies. The result made her sound hurt and worried, rather than angry. It was this, perhaps, that made me answer the way that I did.

"Come on, Celeste," I said quietly. She perhaps should have

bristled at the informal use of her given name, but she did not. It seemed to soften her, to tear from her shoulders for just a moment a mantle that served only to separate two women who were trying to understand each other. "You know what my family has been through at the hands of Council members who let their fear guide their actions. What would the Council have made of this? What might they have done to me, in their desperation to get to the bottom of it? What are they likely to do now, when they realize what I can do?"

Celeste sighed. "I'm not sure I can answer the first two questions, except to say that your fears are not unfounded, and that it would have been quite easy, when faced with such a dire warning, to allow fear to overwhelm reason. We have done it before, and there can be no doubt that we will do it again. As to the third question, that I can answer with complete confidence. The Council will do nothing now, because I intend to tell them nothing."

I blinked. "I'm sorry, did you... did you just say that you intend to tell them..."

"Nothing," Celeste repeated firmly. "Not a word." And she took the drawing from the desktop and flung it onto the fire.

"I... that was a really nice gesture, but you know I made about a hundred of those, right?" I said breathlessly, watching the familiar image burn with a thrill of relief.

"Burn them," Celeste said. "Burn them all. No one else need ever know that they existed."

"But—"

Celeste put up a quelling hand. "There are days when I stare down the responsibilities of this job and despair, because I feel that I no better know how to handle them than a child. In those moments, I look to those around me for guidance, and I look to the past for wisdom. Sometimes, they yield little. Today, they yield me everything I could possibly need to know. We cannot move forward if we are stuck in the past. We cannot progress if the foundation upon which we stand is crumbling away, and we cannot allow fear to continue to mold and shape what we become in the future."

I watched her face, so tired and strained of late, transformed with a calm that can only come from absolute peace and confidence in her own decision. I could feel the calmness radiating from her, slowing my own pulse and relaxing the tenseness that had my body tied up in knots since the moment I'd entered her office.

Celeste went on, "Your gift as a Seer is useless to us if we abuse it. It is also useless to us if you are so terrified that you hide it from us. Therefore, I make one simple request of you."

"Which is?" I asked hesitantly.

"To use your discretion. When you feel that a vision places any of us in clear, imminent, or preventable danger, that you will bring it to me, and me alone," Celeste said. "Otherwise, I trust you to interpret and act upon your visions as you see fit."

"I... I can do that," I managed after stumbling and stuttering for several seconds.

"Thank you. I know that the trust between us has been broken as of late, and I know that it cannot be easy for you to put that trust in me now. And so, on that note, I would like to apologize to you," Celeste said, and then she looked directly at Finn. "To you both."

Finn and I glanced at each other, breath held, unsure of what was coming.

"Our laws, while well-intentioned, are tearing apart the very people they are trying to protect, and that has never been clearer to me than today. The laws have forced boys into roles for which they are ill-suited, broken hearts of those who would only seek to love one another, and driven a deep and damaging wedge between the Durupinen and Caomhnóir. It must change."

Finn's hand tightened around mine. I felt that I could have heard his heart pounding, if my own had not been making such a racket.

"Your sister is working on a piece of legislation that could change all of that," Celeste said. "And while I cannot single-handedly decree that it shall pass, I want you to know that I intend to throw my full weight behind it."

"Thank you," I told her. "Thank you so much."

"I am glad this new law could lift an undue burden from the two of you, but its effects will be much more far-reaching. It will mean a great upheaval to our system. It will be met with great resistance on all sides, but I believe, after the events of yesterday, we all must surely see that it is time for change. The Durupinen and the Caomhnóir cannot work together to protect the spirit world with such animosity bubbling between us. We must find a new way forward."

I looked at Finn, who smiled at me. "We agree," I said. "And we will help in the fight."

"I am glad to hear it," Celeste said. "And to that end, Mr. Carey, I would like to offer you a new posting."

Finn sat up straighter in his chair. "What's that, High Priestess?"

"I have asked Seamus to temporarily oversee the investigation at the *príosún*. It is an enormous job, and one that needs to be handled by our most trustworthy leaders. He has graciously accepted, and that leaves us with a gaping hole in our leadership here at Fairhaven. For that reason, I would like to ask you to oversee the training of our Novitiates."

Finn's jaw dropped. I had never seen him so lost for words. After a few stunned seconds, he shook his head and cleared his throat. "I would be honored, High Priestess, and will do my utmost to live up to the expectations of such a crucial role."

"I know you will," Celeste said, and she smiled at him. "Seamus saw great promise in you when you were in training, and I know he would approve. You have certainly proven your deep commitment to your duty, especially in light of your bravery yesterday. I know our Novitiates will be in capable hands."

"Thank you, ma'am," Finn muttered, inclining his head.

"Thank you both," Celeste said. "We've quite the challenge ahead of us, forging a new path. I am glad we shall be working together."

§

"Oi, you lot," Savvy cried out, busting into our room without knocking.

"Hey, Sav," I said. "I'd tell you to come in, but..."

"Oh," Savvy said sheepishly. "Right, yeah. Sorry. Got a little carried away. I was looking for Finn. Thought he might be in here."

Finn raised a hand in greeting. "And so, he is," he replied.

"Yeah, from now on I'm pretty sure you're just going to find him permanently glued to Jess at the mouth," Milo teased. I threw a pillow at him, which of course sailed right through him and onto the floor.

"Wondered if I might have a word with you, mate," Savvy said, looking uncharacteristically nervous. "In private, like."

Finn raised his eyebrows in surprise. "Of course," he said, looking puzzled, but jumping up from the bed anyway. "Let's talk in the hallway, shall we?"

"Yeah, cheers, mate," Savvy said, and gestured for him to follow her.

I watched the door close behind them, and turned to Hannah. "What's that about, I wonder?"

Hannah shrugged. "Who knows? I'm just glad to see her out and about. I feel like she's been doing nothing but moping in her room. Not that I blame her."

"No changes in Phoebe, then?" I asked.

Milo shook his head sadly. "I've been visiting every day, sometimes twice. No Gateway."

"I'll check on her again when I head down to see Fiona," I said.

"Have you been able to find out anything about her condition?" Hannah asked, her voice anxious. "Those burns... they looked so bad."

I shivered, the sounds of Fiona's screams echoing in my ears. "All I know is that she's stable. That's all Mrs. Mistlemoore would tell me."

"I have to admit that when we found out we were Durupinen, I didn't think we'd be spending quite so much time in hospital wards," Hannah said.

"Me, neither," I admitted. "Speaking of hospital wards, is... does anyone know if Lucida is still in there?"

Hannah shook her head. "No. They examined her but released her. She's in her old clan quarters here in the castle, with Catriona, at least, for now. They're monitoring her for malnourishment and a possible infection."

I watched Hannah for a moment, but she was determinedly keeping her face buried in a stack of papers. "How are you handling it?" I asked her.

"Handling what?" she asked stiffly.

"Come on, Hannah, you know what I mean," I said softly.

Hannah sighed and dropped her pen. "I don't know. I can't decide how I feel about it. I need more time."

"Fair enough," I said. "I don't know how much time you'll have, though. They're going to bring her appeal in front of the Council before long."

"I know," Hannah said. "I'll cross that bridge when I get to it, I guess."

The thought of Lucida back in the castle was a strange one. On the one hand, she had quite literally saved us all with her actions at the *príosún*. On the other hand... she was still Lucida. I wasn't sure if we'd ever be able to untangle the past from the present effectively enough to separate the two. Maybe I didn't even want to. The thought of it made my head ache and my mind flood with unpleasant memories.

Hannah was right. We needed more time.

Finn slipped back in through the door and closed it behind him. There was a curious expression on his face, rather like someone had just hit him over the head.

"What's up with Savvy," I asked him as he slid back onto the bed beside me.

"She... well, she just wanted to run an idea by me," Finn said cryptically.

"What idea?" I asked.

"I promised her I wouldn't tell anyone quite yet," Finn said, smiling ruefully at me.

"Not even me?" I asked.

"Not even you," Finn said. "I promised to let her tell you when she was ready. Let's just say that my job at Fairhaven just got quite a bit more interesting."

I pressed Finn for more hints, but he remained closed-lipped on the subject. Finally, I had to give up trying to wheedle the secret out of him so that I could get to the hospital ward for visiting hours.

§

Fiona was lying on her side in the far corner of the room, facing the wall. Her face was still heavily bandaged, and it was only the sound of my footsteps that alerted her to my presence.

"Hey there," I said by way of greeting. I pulled up a chair and sat beside her.

"Hey, yourself," Fiona said, not lifting her head from her pillow.

"How are you feeling?" I asked her.

"Bloody terrible," she said, her voice slurred with exhaustion and heavy sedatives. "That morphine, though. That's a bollocking miracle, isn't it?" She raised her arm an inch or so up off her bedclothes, so that I could see the IV that was keeping her well-supplied.

"What about your mother?" I asked her.

291

"They sent her home with my sister Nan," Fiona said. "They want her to... recover at home... where it's familiar, like..."

Her voice faded, and for a moment I thought she had fallen asleep, but then she grunted and went on, "You're alright, are you?" she murmured. "The drawing... what did the Council... how much trouble are we in...?"

"Don't worry about any of that right now," I told her. "It's still a secret. For now, at least."

Fiona breathed a sigh of relief. "Good. That's... that's good."

"I'm so sorry, Fiona," I whispered, emotion reaching its fingers up my throat, restricting my airway, choking me with tears. "This is all my fault. I never should have asked you to go there."

"Stop your bawling, girl," Fiona slurred impatiently. "I was goin' there anyway, whether you'd asked me or not. Had to... to get me mum out of there. That's all that matters. Got her out... and I'd do it again... only..."

"Only what?" I prompted.

"I... my eyes... I'm not sure if I..." Fiona mumbled, and her own voice broke. "What if I... what if I can't see? My work... my art..."

I swallowed back tears. "It'll be okay. Mrs. Mistlemoore is amazing... I'm sure she... that she can..."

"She's not a bloody miracle-worker," Fiona said. "Either I've damaged my sight or I haven't. Ain't no Casting that can turn back the clock."

"It'll be okay, Fiona," I whispered, knowing that the words were empty and that I had no power to make them true. "Somehow it will be okay."

Fiona gave a dry sob, but said nothing.

"Hey," I said, sharply enough that she shifted her weight on the bed to better hear me. "The first time I ever met you, you asked me if I wanted to do something real with my art. If I wanted to create something. And even though I was raw and undisciplined and untrained, you knew that I had the potential to do that. Because that's what an artist does. Now, I don't know what's going to happen with your eyes, but I know one thing about you for damn sure. You are an artist, and an artist always finds a way to create, no matter what. And if I have to make it my new full-time job to sit in your studio and throw paint cans at your head until you realize that, then that's what I'm damn well going to do!"

I was shouting now. I was shouting at her like she shouted at me the first time I'd ever met her, even though I had no intention of doing so. And just when I thought that she might break down and sob, or scream at me to leave, Fiona threw back her bandaged head and laughed so hard and so long that she gasped and coughed trying to control the peals of it. I gaped at her in shock, waiting for it to pass.

"Well, one thing is for certain" she said at last, still sputtering. Her fingers scrabbled around the bed until they found my fingers and squeezed them tight. "It was a lucky day for old Fiona when she let you through that door rather than closing it in your face."

§

I knew that Finn would be waiting for me outside the hospital ward doors. I did not realize that Catriona would be there, too.

"Hey, Catriona," I said. "If you're looking for someone to send to prison today, keep walking."

Catriona smirked at me. "Not to worry. I think the jail cells are going to be rather more occupied than usual as it is."

"It must be chaos over there," Finn said gravely.

"Too right it is," Catriona agreed. "It's going to be a bloody disaster trying to sort through which of the Caomhnóir were subjugated and which ones joined up willingly. Luckily, that's not my lookout. Here," she said, handing a folder to me.

"What's this?" I asked her, flipping it open.

"Your statement about the events at the *príosún*. I've taken the liberty of writing it for you," she said.

"You wrote my statement?" I repeated, looking it over. "Isn't that… illegal?"

Catriona waved an airy hand. "Legality is a relative term. Besides, you've spoken with Celeste, haven't you? We need to stick to a very specific version of events if we're going to keep your Seer abilities under wraps. This should do the trick. Read through it and commit it to memory. I've left the end of it blank, so that you can fill in the details of what happened once I left. Sign it and send it back over to me when you've finished."

"Okay," I said, tucking the folder under my arm. "Any word on the Necromancers that were involved?"

Catriona's face twisted. "It looks as though some of them managed to escape before we could secure the perimeter."

"Who?" I asked, my pulse beginning to race. "Do you know which ones?"

Catriona gave me a significant look that told me she knew exactly who I was thinking of. "Charlie Wright is among those still not accounted for."

"Shit," I muttered.

"So that means we may have more work to do," Catriona said, "Can I count on you?"

Beside me, Finn made a noise of dissent. The face I turned on him was so fierce that he actually let go of my hand and took a step back before pressing his lips together and nodding his head once. I turned back to Catriona. "Of course, you can," I told her. "If Charlie Wright is out there, I want in."

Catriona's face broke into a wide smile. "That's my girl."

I allowed myself a moment of surprise at being addressed thus by a woman who always seemed on the cusp of hating me, and then asked, "What about Lucida?"

"She's here... for now. That's all we know for the moment," she replied stiffly.

"Are you... how do you feel about that?" I asked, realizing that this question might be a bridge too far. "I mean, are you okay with it?"

A shiver of something dark passed over Catriona's features, a shadow there and gone in the space of a second. "I believe I told you once before, Jess. I'm always okay. And I don't much fancy repeating myself, that clear?"

"Sure, Catriona," I said softly. "Whatever you say."

"See to that statement," Catriona said, settling once again into her safe and distant official capacity of Tracker. "I want it by tomorrow." And then she turned and walked off down the hallway, the mantle of her golden mane wrapped protectively around her shoulders.

"Well," Finn said, turning to me with a sigh. "I'd like to think that things are going to calm down around here, but I'm not at all confident that's true."

"I think you're right," I said. "But I'm finding it difficult to be too worried about that right now."

He smiled. I slid my hand into his, entwining our fingers together, reveling in the sense of peace and contentment that filled me at the very reality of his nearness. Then we turned and walked together down the hall, unsure of what challenges might face us just over the line of the horizon, but confident that, whatever they may be, we would face them side by side.

And in the meantime, I thought to myself, it was one hell of a proverbial sunset.

About the Author

E.E. Holmes is a writer, teacher, and actor living in central Massachusetts with her husband, two children, and a small, but surprisingly loud dog. When not writing, she enjoys performing, watching unhealthy amounts of British television, and reading with her children. To learn more about E.E. Holmes and the World of the Gateway, please visit www.eeholmes.com

Made in the USA
Las Vegas, NV
03 February 2021